A TIME *for* HEROES

A TIME *for* HEROES

FRANK BARNARD

headline
review

First published in 2012 by HEADLINE REVIEW
An imprint of HEADLINE PUBLISHING GROUP

Cataloguing in Publication Data is available from the British Library

ISBN 9 780 7553 3893 1 (Hardback)
ISBN 9 780 7553 3894 8 (Trade paperback)

Typeset in Galliard by Palimpsest Book Production Limited,
Falkirk, Stirlingshire

Printed and bound in Great Britain by
Clays Ltd, St Ives plc

Headline's policy is to use papers that are natural, renewable and recyclable
products and made from wood grown in sustainable forests.
The logging and manufacturing processes are expected
to conform to the environmental
regulations of the country of origin.

HEADLINE PUBLISHING GROUP
An Hachette UK Company
338 Euston Road
London NW1 3BH

www.headline.co.uk
www.hachette.co.uk

To Helen and Kate,
daughters and mothers
of
sons and daughters

A time for heroes, a time for the brave,
A time for the craven, a time for the knave.

Anon, English (17th century)

Author's Note

Although my intention has been to make the background of this novel as authentic as possible it is entirely a work of fiction. Those who search for the great house High And Over near Rye will find only empty fields; similarly there is no garage on the Military Road and never has been. Near Alfriston there never was an Aelle Manor Farm, nor an RFC airfield at Chézy-au-Bois (no such place exists), nor a Bowman department store in Oxford Street. None of Guv Sutro's record attempts, successful or otherwise, ever took place and none of the air battles in either world war happened. Most importantly Guv Sutro himself, like all the other characters in this novel, is a product of the author's imagination and any resemblance to actual persons, living or dead, is coincidental.

Latimer was quickly in the cockpit of his Spitfire, talking to Control on the R/T. A raid was building up over the Pas de Calais and he was impatient to receive the order to take-off.

'What have you got for us, Control?'

'There's a plot on the table, Hannibal Red Leader, but hold your horses. We'll get you up soon enough.'

'Can't be soon enough. We need the height.'

Only twelve weeks ago, Will had not yet fired his guns in action. Since then he had engaged the enemy on fifteen occasions over France, the English Channel and the Southern Counties. He had four confirmed kills to his name, including a brace at Dunkirk, two probables and three damaged, placing him high on the list of the squadron's successful pilots.

In the eyes of the replacements posted to Hornchurch he was a man who had done what they had yet to do, and they regarded him with respect, wondering if they would measure up. They found out soon enough, discovering the difference between what they had been taught at flying school and what could never be taught but only learned in action: the difference between survival, if only for a short time, and the other thing – an end to it all, not necessarily quick; or being out of it in a hospital ward with nurses telling you not to be a silly boy, of course you'll fly again, and exchanging glances; or pretending you looked normal but not giving you a mirror; or being shut away behind barbed wire and wondering how the war would end.

That leave in Rye had been his last; the squadron no longer had pilots to spare. He had not given his father another thought. The only link with the life he had lived before was the photograph of Alice and her mother that Tim had given him at Glisy. He had cut off Lydia Sutro with scissors, leaving Alice on her own, then put her away in his bedside locker at Hornchurch, not on show, because she was not a girlfriend but a friend who was a girl. Another man had seen it once. He had only said, after a moment's deliberation: 'Oh yes, she looks very nice.' Which was not enough, so Will kept the picture to himself because it made him think of long summers, skies

41

unscarred by vapour trails, tanned limbs and hair bleached fair by sun and Alice always there, even when Tim was gone away to school. Not that he had much time for such reflections. His new existence was predictable and narrow: flying, fighting, snatching a sandwich and a mug of tea, an occasional beer but only if Jerry was lying low or the weather was bad and transport was on hand to the nearest pub where the pilots avoided serious talk and acted like insouciant schoolboys, and trying to sleep whenever he could, by day or night, unless that sleep was troubled by dreams that turned into nightmares and woke him; nightmares he never remembered on waking, left only with a sense that something horrible had passed.

There was nothing else, no room for anything else, but driving on, pushing, pushing, going up and going up and always coming back and hearing that Braddock or Hirst or Davis didn't make it, wouldn't be coming back, gone down a flamer or ditched in the Channel and broke into pieces or simply disappeared. It was like being in the grip of an obsession, focused on one objective: destroying those enemy machines conveniently marked with big black crosses and staying alive. Not that he really thought he would not survive. Nobody thought that. But somehow, infuriatingly, this belief could not still a touch of the shakes, a creeping anxiety that never went away, that grew into something close to dread before take-off but eased as soon as he was in the air. Like the others, it was something he never mentioned and hardly admitted to himself. It was just the way things were, to be put down to fatigue, a weakness to be pushed aside. It was ridiculous to be found wanting in this way because this was the life he had planned for himself as a very small boy, sitting in the aeroplanes in Guv Sutro's hangar at High And Over, imagining himself in the air searching the sky for Fokker Triplanes, fearless just like Guv. Except he realised he wasn't fearless. He could manage it all right and never let it show, but the fear was there and he felt that he wasn't matching up to the man who had shaped his life.

Now, like Latimer already strapped into his cockpit, he waited for the order to move into take-off positions with the others. Below him, an airman stood by the heavy battery on its trolley, its thick lead plugged into the recess in the starboard cowling, ready to provide electric power to start the engine. He had not fixed the straps of his four-point Sutton Harness in their tightest position because, at cockpit readiness, he liked to move around a little and keep the circulation going in his shoulders and upper back. When they were fixed as tight as they needed to be in combat, he was secured to his seat as firmly as if he was bolted in and part of the machine, with all the controls to hand and nothing to stretch out for. The discomfort was always outweighed by the adrenaline that built up rapidly once in the air. He never noticed it until he was back on the ground and able to inspect his bruises in the washroom mirror and soothe his cramps with a hot shower.

'Hannibal Red Leader to Control,' said Latimer. 'Come on, Control. How much longer before we get unstuck?'

'I can't stand the suspense,' someone said. 'If we don't get off soon I'm going home.'

The calm voice of Control crackled in their ears. 'Control to Hannibal Red Leader, don't fret, gentlemen. We'll have plenty of trade for you soon enough. Stand by.'

A fitter was on the wing root by Will's open cockpit. He handed him a beef sandwich and a glass of water. Will rinsed the water round his mouth. He didn't like to drink before a sortie, preferred to fly with an empty bladder. In the heat of action it was not unknown for a pilot to wet himself – attributed to g-forces naturally, never to nerves. He wanted to spit the water out but the only place was down the cockpit sides or in his lap so reluctantly he swallowed it instead. The meat in the sandwich was stringy and hard to get down and he handed it back. 'Eat it yourself, Corporal.' The man took a large bite, chewing with his mouth open, grinning encouragingly as though they were going to face the enemy together. Which, Will supposed, in a way they did.

Control came on. 'Hannibal Red Leader, there's a plot of seventy-plus mid-Channel.'

'That's more like it,' Latimer said. He looked from left to right at the pilots of A Flight, hunched in their cockpits, anonymous in their

43

flying gear and nodded slowly; soon, very soon. Somewhere above them, high and distant, they could hear air-firing. For someone, somewhere, the business had begun.

Then Control again. 'Hannibal Red Leader, two groups, one forty-plus south-west of the Thames Estuary. They don't appear to be coming in. The other, thirty-plus, heading your way.'

'Start up,' said Latimer. 'Take-off positions.'

With the control column hard against his chest, Will flicked the magneto switches and pressed the starter button. Fuel was pulsing through the lines. He raised a thumb to the man on the trolley-acc to turn on the power. The three blades of the propeller twitched and twitched again, the starter-motor whining under the cowling. Along the line engines began to fire, blue smoke and flame shooting back from the stub-exhausts, all the propellors moving now, kicking, stopping, catching, dissolving into blurs. The fitter slipped down off Will's wing as he waved the chocks away. Two men were at his wing-tips as he swung out to follow Latimer who led the six Spitfires of A Flight towards the perimeter road. Behind them, B Flight had also begun to move. The ground crew watched them go, some clapping, others clenching fists above their heads like boxers or standing with arms up straight, thumbs jerking in the air. The twelve machines gathered together at the threshold of the runway, the wind from their propellers flattening the grass, the thunder of their engines rolling across the surrounding farmland. Will saw a ploughman with a team of horses pull them to a halt and climb onto a fence to watch. Each flight of six arranged itself into vic-formation, three to a vic; the routine take-off pattern. Will was on Latimer's right, in the leading vic, Pat Holland on the other flank. He looked across but Latimer was on the R/T.

'Hannibal Leader to Control. We are ready. Leader calling sections, prepare for take-off.'

'Control to Hannibal Leader, scramble, scramble. Forty-plus bandits at twenty-thousand feet, heading towards Dungeness.'

A green flare curled up from the control tower. Before it hit the ground, bouncing through the turf like a glowing ball, the Spitfires began to roll. Will's body went light in the familiar way as his machine began to lift, the Spitfire rising, falling, rocking a little from side to side, caught by his quick, instinctive corrections on the controls. The ground was passing below his wings in a blur of speed but then began to slow and finally recede as he climbed away, the undercarriage thumping home.

'Hannibal Leader to Control,' said Latimer. 'Am airborne.'

Will turned slightly to check his position in the vic and, as he turned, easily, without restriction, realised that he had forgotten to tighten his harness. The locking pin was in position on his chest but the shoulder straps were loose, two grommets showing in the webbing, a good six inches of adjustment short. Nothing to be done. The Sutton was quick-release. If he withdrew the locking pin, all four straps, over his shoulders and across his lap, would fall away, leaving him as unprotected as if he was astride a horse. He moved against the straps to gauge the gap. It was not good. He knew the tremendous forces of deceleration, or wild manoeuvre. Latimer noticed his machine jinking oddly in his peripheral vision. 'Okay, Red Two?'

'Sutton's loose,' Will said. He felt exposed, vulnerable and uncertain. Bad attitude for combat.

'Christ, William,' Latimer said. 'Do you want to abort?'

Very quickly, with the skill of much practice, the squadron had arranged itself in battle formation and moved onto its course, on boost override to gain quick altitude, throttles fully forward, black smoke trailing from exhausts. It was a brave sight, that seemed to Will a culminating point in everything he had strived for. To turn away, not to be part of this, was unthinkable. He had recovered himself, and felt no fear or apprehension. Instead he wanted to whoop for joy.

'I'll stick with the party, Red Leader,' he said. 'I'd hate to miss the fun.'

He went through his usual drill: gunsights on, gun-button set to fire, all instruments checked, and then began the methodical scan for threats from any quarter, high sun refracting on the Perspex canopy, now fully closed. At 20,000 feet they throttled back, looking for the target of thirty-plus. Good odds today; often it was three times that and more.

'Control to Hannibal Leader, any joy?'

'Drawn a blank so far.'

'You should see them any time. They're very close.'

'Got 'em, Red Leader.' Pat Holland was hoarse with tension. 'Dead ahead. Heinkels, Junkers 88s with fighter escort.'

'Hannibal Leader to Control,' said Latimer quietly. 'Thirty-plus bandits in sight at twelve o'clock heading north. Getting in position. B Flight, take the bombers. A Flight, take the 109s.' A moment for the pilots to catch their breath, panting behind their oxygen masks. Then Latimer again, his voice quite changed, and urgent now. 'A Flight, line astern. Echelon starboard.' The Spitfires spread out fanwise. 'Attacking . . . *now*!'

Latimer peeled off, dropping down towards the dozen Messerschmitt 109s guarding the enemy bomber fleet 1,000 feet below. The others followed in curving power dives, still unseen and approaching fast with the advantage of height, however slim, and the glare of the sun behind them. Will's windscreen was filled with the tail-plane of Latimer's machine thirty feet ahead, every detail sharp, the elevators and rudder moving mildly despite the speed and roar of the headlong rush. His thumb trembled on the gun-button in the centre of his spade-grip control column and he arched it back in case the force of the dive pressed it down and he put a burst into his flight commander.

He was moving in his seat in an unusual way, pivoting from the hips, his elbows striking the cockpit sides. It felt like falling. Then he was through the enemy formation. Latimer had gone. He seemed to be alone. Tracer was coming across from right to left, in line with his cockpit but just below. He saw the glass nose of a Dornier and took a snap shot, two seconds only. Pieces flew off and the front gunner fell back inside. He pulled back on the stick, dragging his machine into a steep climbing turn to the left but the slackness in his belts made it hard to keep his balance. A Messerschmitt came past him in a half-roll, lazily, almost floating. He kicked the rudder to the left, put him neatly at right angles and pressed the gun-button with full deflection as he came through his sights. The 109 staggered in the air, puffed black and orange smoke, reared up then fell away into a vertical dive. Somewhere an Englishman was screaming, his R/T fixed on send.

The sky was full of aeroplanes and death, the machines twisting and wheeling like leaves caught in a freak of wind. Will was death. He had that power, caught in a kind of ecstasy, man and machine as one. This was a special day. His destiny. All was noise, vibration, flecks of curving scarlet tracer, slow at first then whipping past. Above and to the right he saw a Heinkel in a shallow, diving turn. Its wheels were down, grey smoke streaming from both engines. He pulled back in a loop and half-rolled off the top in his normal fluid way, except the Sutton did not hold his upper body. It made him slow. The Heinkel's rear gunner opened fire, white tracer now from cannon shells. Holes appeared in Will's port wing. He gave the Heinkel a five-second burst and saw the smoke turn into flame, pouring back across the wings and driven along the fuselage towards the tail. He banked away to find another target but not fixed by his harness was forced against the cockpit side and, for a moment, clumsy on the controls. In those lost seconds the German gunner, still at his station in the burning mass, got off a few last rounds. Will heard three shattering bangs, metallic, sharp, like bricks hurled onto corrugated iron. Something struck him in the leg and the controls were snatched away with sudden force. The cockpit smelled of engine oil and glycol coolant and there was a noise of rushing air.

Out of his control, the Spitfire pulled into a tight loop, forcing him so hard against his seat that he blacked out for a moment. Conscious again, he reached for the control column and found a slight response. The cockpit canopy had been blown away and his flying helmet, complete with oxygen mask, R/T lead and goggles, had been ripped off in the slipstream. That moment of exaltation, that sense of power, his special day, his destiny – all that had gone. His lower left leg was numb, his ears were ringing from the detonation and he sensed damage to his elevator controls, as if they were hanging by a single wire.

In an instant he knew the truth. He was an ordinary man, no hero after all. He was afraid and about to die unless he could bale out or put down somewhere before that wire broke and spun him to oblivion. He thought of jumping but heroes didn't jump. Guv Sutro never jumped. No parachutes then, of course, too bulky for the old machines or sheer bad form. Anyway, he felt too weak to pull himself up and topple clear. His mind was wandering. *Concentrate on the task in hand.* Not dying – that was it. Put the kite down and walk away, if he could still walk. He felt his leg and his hand came up red with blood. A gyppy leg. A gyppy ruddy leg. He began to laugh. Him and his father hobbling round the town. Two of a kind, which maybe they always had been. Alice wouldn't want him now, not with a gyppy leg. Now why had he thought that? What was she doing at this moment, all those thousands of miles away – Rhode Island, was it? Where the hell was Rhode Island anyway?

Concentrate, you bloody fool. Put the kite down and walk away. He was losing height and flying as slowly as he dared without risking a stall, waiting for that wire to snap. Smoke was coming back from the engine, getting denser like the smoke that turned to flame on the Heinkel. He really needed to put the bugger down. Less than 1,000 feet and passing through wispy cloud. Then he was clear and in a pale sun and not above land but over the sea, grey with ranks of rolling white-capped waves and no coast in sight.

Two

1

Fraser Sutro

No one knew how Fraser Sutro came to be called Guv, not even Guv himself. At a certain age, when he was still very young and before he had been sent away to school, it seemed to have come about somehow and stuck, perhaps after an ironic remark made by one of the farm-hands when the child attempted to boss him in the manner of his father.

Aelle Manor Farm lay in a combe on the chalk grassland east of the Cuckmere Valley, sheltered from the prevailing westerlies by dense and ancient woodland. There was some oak and beech but most of the trees were elm, their trunks bent and branches contorted by centuries of gales that blew in from the coast two miles away. Along this tidal estuary in the dark time after the Romans left the warrior Aelle led his Saxon horde from the German northland to found the kingdom of Sussex and, somehow, some time, as obscurely as the child Sutro had come to be known as Guv, the farm had taken Aelle's name.

Now, along the flood plain, the Cuckmere River still turned and twisted towards the sea as it had 1,400 years before, in the time of King Aelle, serpentine and picturesque, its fresh water mingling with salt on the shingle strands. The setting drew the trippers, who would row downstream from Alfriston to the Golden Galleon inn in their hired skiffs and take refreshment as they contemplated the sheer cliffs of the Seven Sisters, rolling away fold on fold along the Channel, waves striking the rocks below and rising in towers of spray, working at the chalk face until it weakened and fell and was sucked away, turning the water milky green.

Those who worked on the Sutro estate had no interest in the picturesque. The workers had grown up with the landscape and hardly saw it any more. When about the farm they welcomed the protection of the trees and had no need to see what prospects lay beyond. They knew it well enough. Their days were long, up at four to feed the shires, tack-up and climb the rutted lanes with two-strong teams to tend the fields or haul a heavy cart bound for market, or walk the high country shepherding the flocks of Southdown sheep that grazed a thousand acres. The boy was often with them, launching himself down the flagstone steps of the old manor house before the sky was light. He was never welcome, only suffered, piping up on matters he had no knowledge of, quick to take offence, just as quick to threaten to tell his father of some imagined slight. Those men with children of their own itched to deal him a cuff or two, to put him straight, and those without were glad they were without.

They could not look to the Colonel for relief. The Colonel was no farmer. He had bought the land fifteen years before, with no great interest in agriculture, but looking for some enterprise in which to invest his money of which he had a great deal, returning from the initial, brief war against the Boers a far wealthier man than when he had first set foot in the Transvaal as a career soldier of modest means with an unfashionable regiment. He had, somehow, made a fortune. In the ale-houses around Alfriston, and in more select surroundings, there was talk of diamonds. There was even talk that he had not been a Colonel.

Whatever the truth, these days the Colonel was rarely seen, occasionally showing at a door or window of the manor, unsteady and red faced, more often passing, muffled, in a fast-driven carriage bound for unknown destinations, leaving his bailiff Kemp to manage the estate, allowing his son to run as free as any native child on the great expanses of the veldt. He showed no interest in the boy – no interest, in fact, that could be discerned in anything around him, moving through life with a grunt, a nod, a shrug and an occasional show of anger or frustration, but at what it was difficult to tell. It was always so with those concerned with liquor, as the greyheads who still held to the old way of speaking put it. It had been better, they agreed, when the Colonel's wife had been alive, though some said that he had selected her as coldly as one might choose a thoroughbred mare at Tattershalls, with an eye to her family's position in the county, which lent him a vestige of respectability; an eye as well to the grand house and parkland east of Petworth to be shared one day with a single brother.

She had been plain and shy and not expected to marry, and her family had been content with that, its aspirations focused on the male line only. But the Colonel had pursued her with zeal, his personal wealth suggesting he might be no fortune-hunter, and so he overcame to some extent their natural opposition. And the girl was happy, her pale cheeks flushed from his attentions. Married, it even seemed he might be influenced by her mild and kindly nature, until the brat was born that killed her. At that point, all connection with Petworth ceased, along with the Colonel's further expectations. He resumed his former habits, leaving all farming matters to Edward Kemp, seen only occasionally on the estate, and then addressing the workers in the roughest tones, a manner emulated by his son.

Now, at eight, the child resembled an instinctive savage, looked after but not cared for by a widow from Seaford retained as house-keeper who disliked him as much as he detested her. He did not attend the village school because the Colonel did not think it appropriate, and so he could barely read or write, only what little he had learned, grudgingly, from the widow or the bailiff's boy, with whom, when school was out or holidays had begun, he made mischief where and when he could. Informed of these various scrapes the Colonel only sniffed and said, 'High spirits merely. Give him a free run. Harrow will knock him into shape soon enough.' The bailiff's attitude was different. He took the boy aside. 'I hear you've been cheeking my men. You shall stop it, lad, or it will be the worse for you.'

The child had drawn himself up. 'They're not your men, they're mine, or will be. And don't call me lad. My father will hear of this and it'll be the worse for *you*.'

At that Ted Kemp had suppressed a grudging smile. The boy had spirit, that was never in doubt. He sought danger and challenge at every turn, riding his unsaddled pony with the wild skill of a Red Indian brave, or scaling chalk cliffs to steal eggs from the nests of gulls, or sauntering into Alfriston to pick a fight with the largest, hardest opponent he could find, often losing but winning respect though that was not his aim; or when the snows came, tobogganing down the steeps of High And Over on the far side of the valley, the stronghold from which Aella's Saxon army once controlled his kingdom.

Guv lived, it seemed to Kemp, through his body not his brain, certain that he could not be touched physically by his adventures, or mentally by the opinions of others. Much like the Colonel, Kemp thought. It seemed Guv cared for no one except perhaps for Kemp's son Stan, not lacking in courage himself but impressionable, drawn into Guv's rash escapades, half-reluctant, half-excited, and usually coming off the worse. Kemp judged Guv no fit companion for Stan, who had cracked his skull when they trampled a tree-house to pieces on a dare and, falling first, had cushioned young Sutro's fall. But he could see no way to prevent the friendship, if friendship it was. He thought of his wife Enid, level headed and practical, and wondered what she might have said. But she had been taken by tuberculosis a few years back. He had no one to turn to, least of all the Colonel, and so he simply maintained a wary eye and told Stan, without much hope, that he should not be so easily led.

Levett, the head gardener, had it right when he came across the Sutro child casually poking out the small diamond-shaped window-panes in the rustic summerhouse with the handle of a trowel. 'That's sprig's looking for a purpose, and if he don't light upon it, the world had better watch out.'

Then, on an August afternoon in Berlin, soon after Guv Sutro reached, to the surprise of some, his eighth birthday, a man fell from the sky at an altitude of little more than fifty feet, broke his spine and died from his injuries the following day. The newspapers called him Birdman, pioneer of flight.

In the yard, one of the labourers, munching bread and a lump of cheese, was reading the *Daily Mail*. 'Park yourself, young Guv,' he said, 'and I'll show you something horrible.' He tapped the grainy photograph of the Birdman leaping from the summit of a steep hill, hanging from a pair of moth-like wings, watched by gaping crowds. 'He killed himself, he did.'

'How?'

'Why, he dashed himself to pieces trying to fly.'

'Nobody can fly.'

'Well, he did, for a bit – much good did it do him, bloody Prooshun.'

'Nobody can fly,' Guv said again.

'Cop a look at that,' said the labourer, jabbing at the picture, 'and tell me he ain't, you ruddy little know-all.'

'Guv stepped back. 'Don't call me a ruddy know-all.'

The labourer had learned to deal with such displays. He held his head on one side and grinned. 'Know what he had to say about the matter before he croaked?'

The boy was curious, as expected. 'You said he was dashed to pieces.'

'And so he were, but the bits held together long enough for his famous last words. Which were . . .' He paused, tantalisingly and then continued, reading with great deliberation and his grin still broader: '*Kleine Opfer mussen gebracht werden*. There, what do you make of that?'

'Nothing. It makes no sense.'

'It do in German, and that's what that is, his native tongue. In proper English, the paper says, it means "Small sacrifices must be made". Plenty of pluck, I'll give him that, even for a Prooshun.' The labourer squinted at the close-packed print. 'It gives his name and all.' He pronounced it slowly. 'Otto – well, he would be called bloody Otto, wouldn't he?' He resumed. 'Otto Lilienthal. Yuh, that's it. Otto Lilienthal.'

'Otto Lilienthal.' Guv tried to shape his tongue around the tricky name. It was like a password to another world. He took the copy of the *Daily Mail*. Sure enough the man was floating in the air, suspended beneath his wings, a man who said small sacrifices must be made, more like an Englishman than a German. Although perhaps a Birdman was a kind of universal creature, not bound by any nation, although he did not think that then but later, when he too had leaped from the summit of a hill supported by a pair of wings. For now he noted the newspaper's date: 11 August 1896, the day his life began.

2

Eleven years after the Birdman Lilienthal broke his back launching himself from his test hill in the suburbs of Berlin, an insubstantial-looking creation of willow, bamboo and cotton cloth, very similar to his, stood on trestles in a barn at Aelle Manor Farm. Nothing more remained to be done except load it onto a wagon, transport it to the top of High And Over and see if it would achieve its purpose: to fly.

Its pilot, if he could be called that because he had never so far taken to the air, stood alone in the shadowy interior with its smell of beasts and hay and dung, old and unchanging smells redolent of the past, and considered what lay ahead. Mingled with the farmyard reek was a delicate trace of the cotton fabric stretched across the wings, a span of seventeen feet, the slight acridity of the padded leather harness that would support him in his flight, and the whiff of Virginia blend as he drew on his briar and studied the glider with narrowed eyes through a haze of pale smoke. He had taken to a pipe to make him seem more mature than his nineteen years and now it was habitual.

Pinpoints of brilliant sunlight shone through gaps and knot-holes in the weather-boarded walls and played on the machine, lending the scene a theatrical air. And certainly Guv Sutro knew himself to be the principal player in the drama that was to be played out soon, and that knowledge gave him satisfaction on several levels; that he was about to attempt what very few men would contemplate, that here and now was the culmination of an ambition he had held ever since that day he had learned of Otto Lilienthal's death, and that if he was successful and did not die himself, he might make his name and have some kind of career in a field of endeavour still in its infancy. *If* he was successful . . .

He understood the theory well enough, how to move his weight from side to side and back and forth once aloft, shifting his body from below the shoulders, supported by the frame, to change the centre of gravity and exercise some limited directional control, wary of the glider's tendency to pitch. He had even made himself familiar with the fundamentals by enlisting Stan Kemp and two farmhands to lift the glider off its trestles while he dangled, wriggling, in position until one labourer burst out laughing and almost loosed his hold. And was promptly dismissed by Guv, but reinstated later when Stan's father intervened. But it was clear to Guv that mastery of winged flight could only be acquired one way. As Lilienthal had written, this man who completed two thousand glides of several hundred feet before his luck ran out: 'One can get a proper insight into the practice of flying only by actual flying experiments.'

Now, resting his hand on the wing of the glider, feeling the coolness of the taut cotton under his palm, knowing the machine was complete and ready to fly, would fly perhaps tomorrow and take him across the threshold of an unknown future, Guv thought back to the time when, as a child, he had tried to understand how air, thin air, could support a man; back to the fat scrapbook that told the story of the pioneers who had been there first, reading with painful slowness about the flights they had made, men who had been heroes until they tumbled to their deaths through human error or a failure of the flying machine itself. Stan Kemp shared his enthusiasm and together they would bend their heads over the cuttings in the manor house snug, Stan reading with facility, fast and well, not having to trace the words with a finger, explaining the more difficult passages in a way that Guv found hard to accept although there was no condescension in his manner, only simple companionability.

One day, Stan came back from the village school with a new skill.

Without saying why, he asked Guv to fetch a sheet of paper from the Colonel's study and there, in the garden, his tongue in the corner of his mouth, he began to fold the paper with great care until it rested in his hand, transformed into a small, winged dart. He held it above his head, pinched between his thumb and forefinger, then flicked it free. It caught the breeze and floated quite high across the yew hedge and landed in the yard, skittering across the mud. Soon Guv was making paper aeroplanes himself, to designs of his own invention, launching them from High And Over where, afterwards, he would lie on the close-cropped turf and study the gulls as they pivoted on currents of rising air, making delicate adjustments to their wings, a raised tip even, prompted by some instinct in their tiny brains, understanding without conscious thought what men had dreamed of since Icarus flew too close to the sun and melted his wings of wax and feathers and plunged into the Cretan Sea.

Guv wanted to be up there with the gulls, balancing on the air above the Downs or swooping towards the distant coast along the river plain, then making height above the Seven Sisters and looking down on everything suddenly small: small fields with tiny beasts, small winding roads and lanes, small villages and clustered cottages, small people, mere moving dots. Somehow he knew that this was how it would be when he also flew, because that was how he had fixed things in his mind, that he would fly, above and apart from the earthly and mundane, transcendant – not that he knew the word either then or later, but only sensed its meaning – of being above human experience.

Then, prowling the study of his absent father as he often did when the Colonel was away, Guv made a discovery. He had come across many things of interest, particularly in the drawers of the partners desk: a Webley service revolver with a stock of brass bullets in a waxed box, photographs of naked black women stretched out in front of grass huts, a roll of paper money and some coins marked *Durban Bank*, elaborately designed certificates recording ownership of something called shares in a mine somewhere, numbers of letters written in tiny script that Guv could not make out apart from occasional words like *love* and *dearest*, another in a bolder hand demanding that money should be paid without delay, *or regrettably, sir, steps will be taken*. On this occasion his eye was caught by a periodical tossed into the wastepaper basket that, on its cover, showed a woodcut illustration of a flying machine in flight. He found it was the *Illustrated London News*, marking the anniversary of Lilienthal's death with reminiscences about the Birdman's exploits, some facts about the theory of flight and diagrams to scale of the German's standard glider in which he lost his life.

Guv smoothed out the crumpled pages on the Colonel's desk and settled himself to read. It was a revelation. Darts made from folded paper seemed a poor substitute for the intricate creation of curved spars and cotton cloth revealed by the illustration. Immediately he had an urge to build a replica, toy sized with one of his lead soldiers as a tiny pilot, to prove Lilienthal's theories. But how? He found himself baffled by the technical terms, and the numbers meant even less so he sought out Stan Kemp to tell him what he needed to know. But when he showed him the plans, the bailiff's son almost forgot he was there, nodding with satisfaction, seeing quickly how the glider was constructed, interpreting the process, knowing immediately what the notes and numbers meant, moving his tongue in the corner of his mouth in that infuriating way. 'Yes,' he said, 'nothing too difficult here, I reckon.' And he started to explain how it might be done and Guv, with a spark of anger, felt the project slipping from his hands. In that moment of frustration he realised that he was ignorant, as ignorant as any of the labourers in the yard. He did not like the thought that a bailiff's son was cleverer than him: well, not cleverer perhaps but possessing knowledge that he had not had the opportunity to acquire. He snatched back the magazine without explaining and did not talk of it again, but neither did he give up, working on his own. Soon, small broken models of flying machines, poorly constructed, could be found like crushed insects at the foot of any handy slope, trodden beneath the boots of their designer when they refused to fly.

When Stan Kemp first saw them, he collected the remains and made suggestions. 'See, what's wrong here—'

'I don't need you to tell me. I'm working things out for myself.'

'Don't look like it to me. I'm only trying to help.'

'Who asked you? Just bugger off.'

At last Guv sought out the Colonel in his study and said, in his Sussex burr because he only talked with others who spoke in the same fashion: 'Sir, I want some schooling.'

The Colonel had stared at him over his whisky glass. 'Schooling?'

'I want to read and write as good as Stan. No, better. And know my numbers too.'

'Damned odd ambition for a foolheaded young pup like you. Plenty of time for that, I should have thought, when you go away. You'll get a proper schooling then, as I did, not the learning-by-rote fiddle-faddle they'd pump you full of in these parts, only to be unlearned when I send you to a proper establishment.' The Colonel had refreshed his drink and crossed to the study window, staring across the garden to the yard. 'Look at those damned malingerers. Why doesn't Kemp make them put their backs into their work? He could benefit from the methods we used to keep the blacks up to the mark at Kimberley.' He moved the whisky round his mouth. 'Remind me, how old are you now?'

'Nine.'

'Nine, I see. And any particular reason for this sudden urge for knowledge?'

'I'm going to be an aviator.'

'Ah, still on that tack, are we? It'll come to nothing, boy, depend on it. Besides, brains aren't required for that particular fad. In fact, I'd say a distinct lack of them is a necessity. In which case you're perfectly qualified already.' The Colonel chuckled to himself. 'But I'll tell you where you should take yourself if you really wish to fly.' For a moment Guv was hopeful. 'Beachy Head,' said the Colonel. 'It's a short trip, I understand, but you'll get the devil of a thrill on the way down.'

He laughed again but stopped when he saw his son's expression. There was something dangerous there, like a cornered animal. He remembered a wild dog he had disturbed, hunting game in the foothills of the Lebombo Mountains just west of Big Bend. The eye was the same, primitive and hostile, the body stiff with hatred. He had shot the dog, an easy conclusion. This was more complicated. He did not wish to be regarded with such hostility. Wasn't his life difficult enough? For an instant he felt an unaccountable apprehension about this child he hardly knew, or cared to know. And anyway, what possible difference could it make to him to provide the shaver with a little learning? At least it might stop the Seaford widow's persistent nagging that the boy was running as wild as a savage and would come, in her slipshod parlance, 'to a sticky end'. Now that he had thought it through, it struck the Colonel as another easy conclusion. He wondered why he had been so ill-at-ease, even for a moment.

'Well,' he said, trying to inject a note of paternal feeling into his voice, 'I suppose as your father I should welcome your request. Perhaps a tutor, to see whether you have anything between your ears. Later, Harrow, to put a little gloss on you. But you may abandon your childish fancies of taking to the skies. Your future lies here, at Aelle. When you come of age you will assume the duties of Mr Kemp and run the estate – under my direction, naturally.'

It was the first time that the Colonel had laid out Guv's future so clearly. He was to become a bailiff and work for his father for as long as his father lived. Guv stared at him, wondering how old he was. His face was deeply lined, perhaps from long exposure to the African sun, his cheeks striated with broken veins, his nose veined too and reddish-purple. But his frame was sturdy, his manner alert and he gave no hint of weakness. Guv thought he might live for ever.

Over the next two years, three tutors appeared and disappeared at Aelle Manor Farm in swift succession. The first, a teacher of advanced years and long retired, known to the Seaford widow as a member of the congregation at the Methodist chapel, was discovered by her displaying part of his anatomy to a curious Guv during a spelling test and bundled away before the Colonel found out. Soon afterwards, Guv was interested to learn, the teacher took that short flight off Beachy Head.

He was replaced by Miss Tuck, a lively young woman of good family, selected by the Colonel himself from an agency in London. She was a proficient teacher, patient and thorough in all subjects. To Guv she was not pretty but he liked her brown, dark-lashed eyes that seemed to contain a secret amusement, and her brown hair, thick and silky, gathered back from a fine forehead brushed with a scatter of tiny freckles. She made herself most agreeable to her pupil and would lean close to him when studying primers together. She smelled sweet, like flowers in high summer, and side by side at the table in the snug Guv could feel her warmth. He also watched the way she breathed, her blouse rising and falling and whatever lay beneath pressing against the fabric with each breath. Sometimes she caught him in this and would run her slim fingers across his cheek and smile and shake her head, without explanation. He was eleven by now and experiencing certain precocious changes in his body. Coarse hair had appeared around his penis that grew large when near Miss Tuck, pushing at the rough material of his short trousers until he was sure she must notice. At night he dreamed of her, and when he woke the bed was wet. But he was not alarmed and took it all as natural, in the way of things, understood by those who grew up on a farm. Only in his height was he concerned. Once he spoke of it to Miss Tuck. 'You're still a boy,' she said. 'You'll shoot up in a year or two, you'll see.'

'Stan Kemp's taller by a head.'

'Oh, Stan Kemp, why concern yourself with him? He's yeoman stock, great lump. You'll overtake him soon enough. Besides . . .'

'What?' said Guv.

Miss Tuck lowered her head a little, looking at him in a way he hadn't seen before. 'Nothing,' she said. 'It's simply that you're catching up in so many ways.'

To Guv it was as if she knew what stirred between his thighs. In her presence the palms of his hands were damp with sweat. In his bedroom with the curtains closed, cloaked by the dark, he imagined how it might be along the landing, how it might be to watch her as she undressed, watching perhaps from a secret place, her knowing he was there. He analysed things she said and did that seemed to have some other significance. 'You're catching up in so many ways.' What did she mean? Then the movement of her breasts beneath her blouse, her fingers brushing against his cheek, her pauses as though she had said too much, like some hidden language he had yet to understand.

Above his bed, the models of flying machines rotated on their threads, survivors of successful flights, not ground beneath his boots. Lilienthal's glider was there, a perfect scaled-down replica; Guv's version of Hargraves's model aerial craft that flapped its wings, powered by a rubber band; and Pichancourt's small mechanical bird, also driven by rubber bands that, when launched from High And Over, had flown a distance of 70 feet at a height of 25; none feasible without the knowledge imparted to him by unfathomable Miss Tuck, who gave him so much yet held so much back.

He felt a need to talk of her to Stan, who grinned and blushed and said she weren't no spring chicken but pleasant enough to look at, he supposed, and let's get on with finishing the latest Pitchandcaught; Stan now properly in his place, understanding the way it was and the way it would always be since Guv had acquired some learning quite equal to his own, the bailiff's boy prepared to follow, knowing that here might be the key to a future beyond the confines of the farm, and seeing in Guv a strength and self-belief he lacked, could never imagine possessing. Often, he thought, Guv seemed less boy, more man, especially in the way he spoke of Miss Tuck, like any farmhand with rough designs upon a village girl, saying what he would do to her, not that he had done it to any woman yet.

Unknown to Guv, the Colonel had Miss Tuck's six-month report. *My pupil does not possess an academic nature. His English comprehension and written work is poor, his Latin worse. He shows a passing interest in history and geography but only when related to the more violent periods of this country's past. In arithmetic and matters scientific, it must be said, he displays some aptitude because these benefit directly his hobby of constructing toy flying machines, which is to be encouraged, being evidence of a practical mind despite its cerebral limitations. He has a strong personality, confident and forceful, in advance of his years and shows,*

in my opinion, clear qualities of leadership that, with further develop-
ment at a suitable public school, might well qualify him to follow his
father in a military career.

Miss Tuck's sojourn at Aelle Manor Farm came to an abrupt end,
however, on an August night of oppressive heat, unrelieved by the
slightest coastal breeze. Through his open window Guv could hear
the panting of the dogs in the yard below, the occasional shriek of a
barn owl hunting prey across the river meadows and, somewhere
within the house, the sound of movement, restless as though someone
else was finding it impossible to sleep. He knew it was not the Seaford
widow because she was in the eastern wing, as far from him as possible.
He lay for a moment on his bed, naked, rubbing a hand across his
chest that was slippery with perspiration and briefly held himself. Then
he went out onto the landing and, following the rustling sounds,
stopped outside the room that was Miss Tuck's.

Faint lamplight showed around the door. He was certain he knew
what was about to happen, that this was what he and Miss Tuck had
been working towards in their faltering, ambiguous way, how it was
meant to be, an end to all uncertainty, a chance at last to experience
sensations he had only heard of and now was about to discover. He
was very big and anxious that he might come just standing there,
knowing she was close.

Without knocking he turned the handle and pushed the door open.
Miss Tuck was lying on her front, the sheets thrown back, raised up
on her elbows and also naked. He took in the swoop of her back, her
plump buttocks, her slim legs slightly apart. She looked surprised,
her eyes fixed on his erection, her lips curved in a curious smile,
showing her small white teeth as though she was about to speak. He
started to smile as well, thinking that because she had not screamed,
his instinct had been right. Behind her, something moved. A head
raised up, sparse hair awry and damp with sweat, with mottled cheeks
and a purplish nose. It was the Colonel . . .

Back in his room, and very small again, Guv heard Miss Tuck's
smothered laughter but it had no humour in it, only a kind of
desperation.

The next morning, with no pause for breakfast, Miss Tuck was returned to London. And the Colonel made no reference to the matter, other than to observe that another tutor must be found.

3

With the entrance examination for Harrow six months away, Miss Tuck was replaced by a crammer, a Cambridge man recommended by a member of one of the Colonel's London clubs. Dr Wallbank-Smith made a comfortable living drumming routinised information into the brains of the slow-witted, the lackadaisical and the indifferent offspring of those who could afford his substantial fees, providing them with a grounding in examination skills that were usually sufficient to secure them a place at one of the better public schools. He did not choose to live at the manor house, but took rooms at the Star Inn in the village and walked in each morning. It was suggested that the brisk airing cleared his head after an evening in the saloon bar, but he was single minded in his work, impersonal and inclined to use the edge of a rule applied to knuckles when not receiving the response he expected.

Soon after his arrival he was shown Guv's models of flying machines and did not laugh or scoff when his pupil told him of his intention to be an aviator. Instead he said it was his opinion that aeronautics was a coming thing. For this, though not for this alone, Guv submitted to Dr Wallbank-Smith's stern regime, concluding that if he himself had been a crammer, laughable as the thought was, he would use the same methods, respecting if reluctantly the Doctor's cold dedication to doing what must be done to achieve results.

Guv passed into Harrow School by the slimmest of margins and was deposited in the third division of the Fourth Form, 'the bottom of the barrel' as the Colonel observed, acquiring quite quickly the Harrow accent that he found reassured or intimidated people depending on their social status and, more slowly over the next five years, an average grasp of subjects that interested him, like mathematics, technical drawing and working with wood and metal, but very little of those that did not. For a time his tutors were encouraged by his studies of lepidoptera, until they realised he was only concerned with discovering what made them fly.

On the sportsfield his energy, his incisiveness under pressure and his urge to win whatever the odds marked him as a natural leader. In Harrow football, that violent hybrid of soccer and rugby with fewer rules, he played at wing and, still diminutive, sent numbers of opponents to the sick-room and occasionally to hospital after unflinching tackles, breaking his own nose twice but also many school records. In cricket he topped the batting and bowling averages but was censured for aiming the ball at the batsman not the wicket. In the boxing final he floored his opponent in twenty seconds, hitting him twice on the way down, a misdemeanour overlooked in the excitement of the moment.

To some, particularly the younger boys, this prowess made him a popular figure, a model of Harrovian martial spirit; to others, notably his peers, a rival until they realised they could not match him and had to choose between being viewed as allies or enemies. There was no middle path. This led to a group of the unconvinced gathering round the House Monitor Latimer who told his followers he was weary of this puffed-up swaggerer with such a high opinion of himself and that it was time someone took him down a peg or two.

Soon afterwards, a letter arrived on the Colonel's desk bearing the Harrow School crest. It advised him that his son had been involved in an unfortunate incident concerning another boy, and that he should make an appointment with the headmaster as a matter of urgency, because it was sufficiently serious to warrant expulsion.

Shown into the headmaster's study a few days later, the Colonel was waved to a seat. 'Before I go any further,' the headmaster said, 'I wish you to understand that until this regrettable occurrence, your son has made a reasonable effort academically, given his intellectual limitations, and his exploits in the field of physical endeavour have been nothing short of remarkable.'

The Colonel grunted. 'Well, what's he supposed to have done?'

'I'm afraid he has attacked a fellow pupil and beaten him severely.'

'Is that all?' The Colonel was relieved.

'Colonel Sutro, that is hardly the reaction one expects in the circumstances. The poor fellow has suffered a broken jaw, two cracked ribs and is at present receiving treatment in the local infirmary.'

'Your letter was not explicit,' said the Colonel. 'You merely mentioned an incident concerning another boy. I feared it might be some other nonsense.'

The headmaster ignored the point. 'Your son's reprehensible behaviour was further compounded, Colonel Sutro, by a most serious breach of school rules that came to our notice when investigating the matter. For some time it appears he has been frequenting a public house in the high street, consuming strong liquor and mixing with a most undesirable element. To the publican he has been passing himself off as a common labourer, apparently with complete success. I'm told his accent was entirely authentic. He has also been in the habit of forming liaisons with some of the females there, I shall not call them ladies.'

'What has this to do with a spot of fisticuffs?' said the Colonel. 'It seems quite another matter to me.'

'By no means, Colonel Sutro, there is a direct connection and what occurred can hardly be termed mere fisticuffs. Young Latimer was subjected to a violent and sustained beating that continued well after the unfortunate youth had ceased to be capable of defending himself, and took place outside the Crown and Anchor Inn where your son had been drinking. The consumption of strong ale no doubt contributed to the unforgivable violence of his assault.'

'Unforgivable, you say?'

'Certainly, and when I furnish you with the fullest details I hope sincerely that you will agree that your son should no longer remain at this school.'

The Colonel learned that Latimer, with his adherents, discovered Guv's jaunts to the Crown and Anchor and followed him there. The monitor claimed, speaking with some difficulty apparently through swollen lips, that he had intended to confront Guv over his transgression, appeal to his sense of honour as a Harrovian and remind him of the school motto *Stet Fortuna Domus* – Fortune For Those Who Dwell Here. To which Guv apparently retorted: 'You mean the pub?' At this, the headmaster said, the monitor stepped forward in righteous indignation and Guv knocked him flat and three others too, who fled. Abandoned, Latimer attempted to rise but was punched and pummelled in a most ungentlemanly way and even feet were employed in rendering him unconscious.

'This Latimer sounds to me like the worst kind of prig and toady,' said the Colonel, 'not to mention lily livered.'

'He comes of good family,' the headmaster retorted stiffly.

The Colonel rose. 'So did Caligula, Headmaster. However, I will remove my son from your establishment straight away. Besides, I believe he has acquired enough education for my purpose. Be so good as to have him and his belongings deposited at the front of the school, where I have a carriage waiting.'

Not necessarily to his credit, once restored to Aelle, the Colonel seemed prepared to brush the affair aside. 'Now you can make yourself useful,' he told Guv, 'and help Kemp about the farm.'

'In what way?' Guv asked.

'In whatever way he chooses. Your duty is here and you must learn from him all you can. He will not be here for ever. How old are you now?'

'Eighteen.'

'At your age I was already a serving officer and understood my responsibilities. You must learn yours, sir, and quickly. After all, why should I employ a bailiff when I have bred one?'

Back in his room at the manor house Guv made no effort to consult Edward Kemp about making himself useful and the Colonel, similarly, made no effort to find out if he had. At first Kemp himself occasionally tried to catch one or other of them to clarify the situation, explained to him vaguely by the Colonel, who muttered: 'Nose to the grindstone, Kemp, keep him at it, you know the sort of thing, the rudiments, man, the rudiments.' And after his unexplained return from Harrow Guv was evasive and showed no interest of the management of the estate. 'Yes, yes, Kemp, I know what my father said. He says a great many things. All in good time, but for the present I have another matter on my mind.' This other matter was taking shape in the black weather-boarded tithe barn, where first he had chalked out a design on the cobbled floor at the further end, not seen directly through the great double doors; an outline that resembled a giant bird with outstretched wings, as ancient-looking as the Long Man on the green slopes above Wilmington four miles away. Clearly the ambition was to construct a full-scale flying machine and, in time, its frame began to take shape, constructed from lengths of willow and bamboo, appearing delicate as though it might break if bent, and hardly able to support a man.

By now Edward Kemp knew that his son, who had long since left school and joined him on the farm, was part of the project but he did not question him too closely because Stan performed his duties diligently and well, and anyway, these lads who had known each from childhood were almost men. Who was he to tell him how to spend his scarce spare time? He was not too concerned. He doubted the scheme, whatever it was, would come to much. Meanwhile, perhaps some of young Sutro's superficial polish might rub off on Stanley, smooth his rougher edges, make him seem less the farm boy and more the gent. He had been startled by the change in Guv after he had been sent to Harrow, returning for the holidays with grafted-on toff's voice and supercilious manner, born an insolent scapegrace like his father but given that lordly self-belief that others mistook for breeding, which opened doors and closed up mouths. He knew it was only humbug, concealed the inner man and should not count so much. But because it did, Ted Kemp felt there was no reason why Stan should not acquire a touch or two of gentlemanly airs to ease his path through life.

By now, the Colonel was rarely seen and when he was, appeared preoccupied, often asking if strangers had been enquiring after him in the village. Once, when he was in town, a party in shabby city clothes called at the farm gate and asked in a surly manner when the master might be expected back, to be sent on his way with the dogs snapping at his heels. About that time Edward Kemp found himself unable to pay the men's wages and could get no sense from the bank in Brighton where the estate account was held, until the Colonel intervened and somehow the funds were released.

Guv had no interest in such matters. The estate could look after itself. It always had. What was so different now? There were rich pickings in agriculture, everyone knew that. Cheap labour to do the work and money to burn. But his complacency was disturbed slightly by an interview with his father, who unaccountably summoned him to his study and told him that he was about to return to South Africa. 'The situation has changed since the end of the war and my interests in the Cape require my urgent personal attention. Until now, sir, I have not been in the habit of explaining my movements to you, and you have not been in the habit of enquiring about them. However, on this occasion my absence may well be prolonged as I have certain knotty matters to resolve. Nothing need change here. Kemp has things squarely in hand and you will continue to be responsible to him. I trust that you are acquiring a sufficiency of useful knowledge?'

'Oh, certainly.'

The Colonel left next morning. Guv took him at his word. He had been told that nothing need change and nothing did. The months passed. In the barn he continued to work on the glider, joined at the end of each day by Stan. As they worked they talked into the night and not always about flying.

'Have you had a woman yet, Stan?'

'No, have you?'

'Yes, several. I came across a place near my old school where it was easy. At least, the females were.'

'Get away. What's it like then?'

'Time you found out for yourself.'

'I wouldn't know where to start.'

'Well, not in Alfriston that's for sure, unless you want a pitchfork in your backside.'

'I want a decent girl.'

'There's a lot to be said for the indecent variety.'

'This place you found, is that why you got yourself expelled?'

'Who says I got expelled? Never you mind. Besides, I've learned as much as I need to. There's going to be a war soon, all the chaps said so, a lot of the masters too, and bookworms won't be needed.'

'A war against who?'

'The French, the Germans, take your pick; it's all brewing up.'

'What will it be about?'

'Nothing in particular, I shouldn't think. The Frogs and Huns have been getting pretty uppish lately. Time we showed them what's what, and anyone else who cares to stick their nose in.'

'Shouldn't war be about something more important than just showing them other nations what's what?'

Guv came close, his eyes hard. 'I take it you agree that England is the finest, grandest country in the world?' Stan thought he could smell a trace of alcohol on his breath. 'Well, do you?' persisted Guv.

'Yes.'

'There you are then. What could be more worth fighting for? You will fight if you're called upon, I suppose?'

'Yes, if I must.'

'If you must? Not after a white feather, are you?'

'Not after a sock aside your head, are you? All I know is a teacher told us about this Roman wiseacre who said it were glorious to die for your country, no matter what, but we was damned if we could see the glory in it. Tom Hockley, he reckons we're being prepared as cannon fodder at some future time.'

'That's Horace you were talking about,' said Guv.

'No, Tom it were, right enough,' said Stan. 'And like he said, there were precious little glory at Spion Kop. Now I ain't claiming we wouldn't fight under any circumstances, but not just for glory, and not just because some bigwigs in London decide it's time to teach them foreigners what's what. That's all I'm saying. If it's like that, if that's all it is, it's just a waste.'

'Well,' said Guv, with a twist of his mouth, 'it could be old Horace didn't get it entirely right. In my book it's better the enemy believes it's glorious to die for his country, and help him achieve that ambition. If there's any glory going I'd prefer to sample it first-hand, alive and kicking.' He gave Stan a shove. 'And sample the indecent females eh?'

He went outside into the yard. Clouds were moving fast across a full moon and he could smell the surf, pounding hard against the shingle ridge at Cuckmere Haven that shielded the salt marsh and wet meadows in the valley from the influx of the sea.

'I think we're ready,' he said. 'But this needs to pass first.'

Stan had joined him, staring at the sky, his face washed with pale light, then in shadow as the moon was momentarily obscured. 'It will,' he said.

4

Next day dawned still and cool, mist hanging over the downland and everything running with dew, the ground slippery underfoot, but soon a light breeze dispersed the haze. Guv, alone in the barn, knew this was the moment. The glider rested on its trestles like a squashed bat, to an untrained eye a befuddling assembly of wood and cotton, clumsy and unwieldy, a parody of nature, a presage that man was not meant to fly and those who tried were dreamers following a path that led nowhere, except perhaps to a violent and very public death. At this moment such considerations did not occur to Guv. To him this was a milestone in a journey that, far from leading nowhere, made him part of a new brotherhood, one of a handful prepared to prove the sceptics wrong; to prove that winged, controlled flight was not the prerogative of cranks and eccentrics, of addle-brained inventors destined to expire in the wreckage of their own, fanciful contraptions, but as Dr Wallbank-Smith had affirmed all those years ago, a coming thing.

He heard the grind of steel-capped boots crossing the yard, the murmur of several voices. It was Stan arriving with the labourers who had volunteered to load the glider onto the timber wagon, to transport it to High And Over, but only one man came into the barn. 'You're resolved to do this thing?' said Edward Kemp.

'Of course.'

'I suppose I'm wasting my breath if in your father's absence I forbid it absolutely?'

'You suppose correctly. Are you here to help or hinder?'

'Well, I see you are determined, which is no surprise to me.' Kemp moved forward to study the machine. 'So, it's finished. Will it fly?'

'I'll find out soon.'

'Your father believed it would come to nothing.'

'It still might, but not here.'

'You understand I cannot lend a hand.'

'I wouldn't expect it.'

'But I can offer you one.' Kemp's grasp was firm. To Guv it was a vindication, the first time the bailiff had treated him as a grown man.

The echoes of the bells of St Andrew's Church that marked the end of Sunday morning service had hardly died away when the timber wagon with its uncommon load started out along the rutted lane to Alfriston, the glider almost brushing the hedgerows on either side, over the river by the weathered brick span of Long Bridge where the waters of the Cuckmere ran swift and clean and tendrils of green weed quivered in the current. Then they turned coastward onto the winding chalk highway that led through the village towards High And Over.

Very soon a curious crowd, drawn by the thud of hooves and rumble of the wagon's iron-banded wheels, was following on, throwing questions at Guv as he looked down at them from the bench-seat next to the wagoner. Many he had crossed or treated with contempt; many half hoped that he might break his neck. Guv knew this, although he was not concerned by it, barely giving it a moment's thought, but still he was surprised to see in the eyes of the villagers something close to grudging respect.

'So you be going to jump off High And Over then?'

'I'm well avised you'll land agin in Eastbourne.'

'Garn, I were avised it were France.'

'Africa, I were told.'

A freckled girl with shining eyes and cheeks of reddish-brown, the colour of ripe pippins, called up: 'Hey, master, would your wings carry me?' Beneath her blouse her breasts swayed as she stepped out beside the wagon. Then, shy at her boldness she slowed her pace, her cheeks redder still.

Guv stared back, running his eyes across her. 'Who is she?'

'That's Mary Grey,' Stan said, 'the wheelwright's girl.' He was striding by the nearside horse, hand resting on the jangling harness. He also looked back and the girl smiled and gave him a small, hesitant wave.

'I recall her now,' Guv said. 'She'd be with her father sometimes at the farm.'

The shires had reached the last steep climb to High And Over, heads bent and breathing hard through flared velvet nostrils. Guv jumped down but to the horses neither he nor the wagoner nor the glider were any weight at all, their only real burden the timber wagon itself. Five hundred feet below, the river valley was gradually coming into view and beyond it the smooth downland stretching away towards Beachy Head, the landscape broadening out with every pace, the air sharp and clear and, overhead, skylarks giving their liquid song above the cropped turf. Their hovering flight made many people dizzy when they looked up; dizzier still when, looking down again, they took in how the hillside dropped away. The venture had been the object of much rumour, but now, confronted by the stark danger of it, they were quieter, more reflective as though they understood they might witness tragedy not triumph.

'But you can't gainsay the chuckle-head is manful.'

'I wouldn't leap into that abyss for love nor money.'

But not all were brought round. 'Chuckle-head you had him, chuckle-head he be. P'raps we'll see what brains he's got spread out across yonder pasture.'

The wagon drew up on the highway next to the various winding tracks that led away to High And Over's highest point. From there the vista extended from the eastern cliffs of Cuckmere Haven across the promontory of Seaford Head with, at its foot, Seaford town itself to the port of Newhaven where, beyond the harbour mouth, a steam ferry was ploughing in from France, leaving a creamy wake in the green-blue sea.

The labourers from the farm loosened the hemp ropes that secured the load. Guv noticed that they were not laughing now, as they had when he had dangled from the glider in the barn trying to understand the rudiments of control. And what had Lilienthal said? 'One can get a proper insight into the practice of flying only by actual flying experiments.' Well, the time was now.

When the men lifted the machine clear of the wagon it put the wooden frame under stress and the cotton cloth on the wings and tail-plane flexed like skin, giving a momentary impression of a living thing. Then, moving in slow, shuffling steps like pallbearers at a funeral they carried it on a roundabout course through a meadow that lay back a little from the hilltop, avoiding the hazards of the paths that led between the stunted thorn trees, clumps of gorse and bramble to where Guv was waiting at his chosen launching spot, ringed around by a silent crowd. He was also silent, filling his pipe and lighting it with particular care, his eyes fixed on the valley below. He had made no special effort to dress himself for the occasion; roll-neck woollen sweater, tweed breeches secured below the knee, scuffed walking boots. The people watched him, some as they might watch a condemned man on the gallows, with morbid curiosity, others eager to see a gallant deed attempted, others carried along by the thrill of it, not understanding why they were there, fearful of what might occur but at the same time reluctant to turn and walk away, not wanting to miss it either.

The glider rested on its trestles, prepared for flight. Stan was beside Guv now. He joined him in staring out across the valley, occasionally glancing sideways at him to read what might be in his face but seeing nothing, only blankness, and looking away again. Guv licked a forefinger, held it up and nodded. 'Slight updraught, that should help.' But still he made no move.

A portly man with a bicycle pushed his way through the crowd towards them, threw the machine down and wiped the sweat from his face with a soiled handkerchief. 'In time, sir, good. I've just cycled up from Seaford station.' He reached into his Norfolk jacket and handed Guv a card. 'Sutcliffe, *Evening Argus*.'

Guv noted the 'sir'. The reporter was ten years older. Like the handshake of Edward Kemp it was a sign, from this point on, that this was how he might be viewed, a man apart, a model of grit and fortitude; a hero. Heroes were scarce, particularly when there were no wars. He had not thought of it like this before, only of the flying, of testing himself in the air, a private challenge. But to be hailed a hero could bring its own rewards. Courage was the only quality required, that was all, the commodity in which a professional hero dealt. Much else would be allowed and much forgiven.

The *Argus* man was standing by the glider. 'So this is your machine. I've not seen one before. It seems a marvellous thing.' He touched the wing.

'Stand back,' Stan said. 'You ain't welcome here, not at this time.'

'We was asked, old chap.'

'By who?'

'By him, of course.' The reporter nodded at Guv.

'He's right,' said Guv, returning the card. 'I thought a telegram wouldn't go amiss.' He took a final draw on his pipe, handed it to Stan, the bowl still hot, and moved towards the glider. A murmur rose from the crowd. Somewhere a dog barked. One of the labourers cleared his throat and spat.

'Hold hard, sir,' said the *Argus* man. 'Aren't you going to address the crowd? They expect a few words on such an auspicious occasion.'

'I hadn't considered it,' said Guv.

'Oh, they deserve it, surely?'

'Deserve it?'

'Yes, sir, deserve it. After all, they've come to lend you their support. A few fine words from you will be remembered. Particularly when I put 'em in the *Argus*.'

'Hmm.' Guv rubbed his chin, pulled out one of the trestles supporting the glider and stepped up. 'Ladies and gentlemen,' he began. Somewhere a baby screamed. 'And children.' There was laughter. A dog yapped. 'And dogs.' The laughter grew. 'Whatever you may be told, aeronautics, flying, is a coming thing.' That phrase again. 'This great old country of ours is lagging behind in the science of mastering the air. My ambition is to put that right.' Was this too big a claim, too strong? But no, he saw only eager faces. Somewhere someone cheered and applause rippled through the crowd.

'This is only a beginning,' he went on, 'to achieve the miracle of flight in a machine built with my own hands.' He caught Stan's eye, saw next to him his father. Somehow he had not expected the bailiff to be there. 'With some help from others under my direction.' He paused. He had never spoken in public before and found it came easily to him. 'My intention is to conduct my glider to the foot of the valley under complete control and far more quickly than it took us all to get up here.' More laughter, more applause. 'For those of you who do not know me, my name is Fraser Sutro. It is a name I hope to write in the annals of aviation.' Again, too much surely? This was something like a joke. But no, once more only applause and cheers. 'I thank you all for your interest and attendance.' He hesitated. Could he? Dare he really? 'What I am doing today, in my own small way,' he concluded, 'I do for dear old England.'

A rough voice shouted: 'Three cheers for good old Guv.' He saw it was Hogbin, one of the labourers, who had always talked against him. The cheers burst out.

The *Argus* man was beaming. 'Inspiring, sir, appropriate, most.' He tapped his notebook with his pencil. 'I have it down, you may be sure I have it down.'

After a careful inspection to make sure no damage had been sustained in the course of its short journey, the glider was taken up by the men and Guv moved quickly underneath, pushing his arms through the padded cuffs on the bars attached to the frame, feeling the lower braces pressing firmly against his ribs. In his study of the terrain before the launch he had considered where he might come down, but the passage of the flight was so unpredictable that he had given up, trusting to his reflex actions and luck.

He stood for a moment, still supported, his head and shoulders projecting above the upper plane of the wings, breathing evenly and hard as he used to on the springboard at the end of Eastbourne pier, waiting for that unconscious impulse that would propel him into space. Then he cried out something, more a bellow than an order to loose hold and stumbled forward, feeling the passage of the wings through thin air, arching his back to counteract the tendency to pitch nose-down, and felt a sudden lift, his boot-tips skimming across the turf and then not touching, hanging free. He turned his head a little and saw the people fifty feet below. He could barely hear them any more.

He felt a sense of solitude and calm, with the creak and sigh of his machine in flight, the coolness of the headwind across his face, the cries of gulls above the murmur of the breaking surf. The right-hand wing-tip began to dip but by swinging his hips and legs he corrected it quite easily, bringing it back level, and even found by craning forward that he could increase his speed, swooping towards the river meadows in an exhilarating rush. He looked around him, taking in the landscape horizon to horizon, not seen like this by any man before, and south but quite discernible, the coast of France, a smudge of white and green.

At first he had seemed to hang motionless, the glider making only gentle movements with the fluctuations of the breeze, but with the gradual loss of height the sense of speed increased; he needed speed, otherwise he risked a stall. That was how Lilienthal had died, stalling and dropping from fifty feet. But too much speed was dangerous too, could make the difference between a landing and a crash. He had covered perhaps 200 feet and was close to the river now, the grassland passing in a blur, and still had height to reach the further bank. Instantly this became his boundary mark, the natural climax of his flight, but his approach disturbed a heron fishing in the shallows. With a few beats of its arched wings it rose up slowly with a single harsh call of alarm and banked directly across his course.

Instinctively, Guv lunged to the right and the glider fell into a fast, corkscrew dive.

In the seconds left to him, nothing he could do made any kind of difference; all control was gone and he span giddily down as if caught in a whirlwind, pulling up his legs and bracing himself for impact. But instead of striking hard ground he plunged deep into water, fast-flowing and cold, the spars of the machine snapping and cracking around him. Something, some flailing component, struck him a violent blow to his right temple. Unconscious for a moment, he was held below the surface by the tangle of wreckage as it was swept along the river but as his head cleared he kicked himself free and swam towards the bank. He crouched there in the shallows, watching the remains of his machine drifting downstream before it was lost to sight around a bend. He put his hand to his head, feeling dull pain, and it came away crimson with blood; there was much blood dripping from his face, staining his wet clothing and spreading like ink blots in the muddy pools.

Crowds were rushing down the slope from High And Over. He realised they probably thought him dead. He went back in the water, splashing it over his face to wash away the blood, and swam across to the other bank, waving as the people ran towards him. Stan was among the first to reach him, his eyes distended, fighting for breath and unable to form words. Guv saw to his surprise that tears were spilling down his cheeks.

'You see?' Guv said. 'You see?'

Stan halted and bent over, his hands on his knees, panting, then straightened up. 'I saw, I blooming well saw. Lord, what a spectacle, what a coming down.' He held out something in his hand. It was Guv's pipe, its bowl still warm. Guv clamped it between his teeth at a jaunty angle and they laughed together as the crowd pressed in around them, peering at Guv in wonder as a man returned from the grave. The blood from his wound was already drying but the gory mess just made it better.

The *Argus* man was quickly there, waving his notebook. 'Ain't I got a story? Ain't I just! What was it like, sir? What was it like to fly?'

'Just what I imagined,' Guv said.

'And what was that?'

'Beyond imagination.'

'What next then, do you think?' The *Argus* man jerked his head downstream. 'Will you rebuild it, sir, and have another go?'

Guv considered. 'I doubt it. Powered flight is the way ahead. Those damned Yankees got there first. Time we put them in the shade.'

'For good old England, eh?'

'That's right. For good old England.'

The freckle-faced girl reached up and touched Guv's head. 'Poor thing. 'Tis a blessing you be whole.'

Guv rested his fingers on hers. 'I'm whole all right, don't you fret.'

'That nasty gash needs tending to, I think.'

'I think you're right,' Guv said.

Later, much later, he was in a tap room dimly lit by gaslight and a few candles, heavy with the smell of ale, sweat and tobacco smoke and filled with a crush of people. He had place of honour in a high-backed oak armchair next to the bar, but could not hear what the villagers shouted at him over the general din so only nodded and sipped his beer. He had drunk a quantity by now and none of it paid for. He did not know which inn this was by name, but thought it might be the fourth. He took another gulp from his mug, spilling some down his front, and when he brushed at it saw he was still wearing the bloodied, mud-stained sweater from the morning. Oh yes, he remembered now, he had gone back briefly to the farm but refused to change; no time, no inclination and anyway, the filthy garments would go down well. The peasantry were keen to fete their dauntless Birdman. Well, he would look the part. Edward Kemp had been at Aelle, and the Seaford widow had tended to his wound by no means gently, calling him all kinds of fool. His fingers went to his temple where he felt a dressing held in place with sticking plaster. 'Leave it be,' a soft voice said. For a moment he thought he was back in the Crown and Anchor on Harrow Hill. 'Cora?'

'No, not Cora,' said the freckle-faced girl. ''Tis Mary.'

Somewhere a concertina began to wheeze out one of the old tunes and soon the room rang in harmony:

When I was a little'un, my father did say
When the sun shines, that's the time to make hay
And when hay's been carted, don't never you fail
To drink gaffer's health in a pint of good ale.

'When the sun shines, that's the time to make hay,' Guv murmured to Cora who was Mary. 'My philosophy . . . exactly.' He began to rise and the tap room started to rush round in circles like his machine, his wrecked machine, caught in a whirlwind, all control gone and nothing to be done except pull up his legs and brace himself for impact. He pulled up his legs.

The song was ending:

When men goes to Parliament their pledge for to keep,
They does nothing else but just sit there and sleep.
The next that I vote for will be a female,
If she'll keep me awake with a pot of good ale.

'I'll vote for you, Cora,' Guv said.

'Mary.'

'I'll vote for you too.' He rose suddenly, swaying. 'I need some air. I'm going outside.' He knew she would follow. He stood outside waiting for her, the yellow light from the inn windows spilling out across the cobbles, shiny in a fine, penetrating drizzle. But she did not come. Instead Stan Kemp was there.

'You can't do this, Guv.'

'What?' But he knew what very well.

'She's just a maid. Her head's full of foolishness.'

'Damn you, Stan, don't give me lip. Get back inside with your caterwauling yokels and send her out. Then drink your gaffer's health in a pint of ale, like your ditty said.' He moved forward. 'I am your gaffer, am I not?'

'You got tongues wagging already,' Stan said, 'and Mary's got a life to live.'

'Time she started living, I'd say.'

'She has to live it here.'

'Ah,' said Guv, pulling his head back to make his focus sharp. 'I see, I think I understand. Our little chat about how's your father. You want to get there first and break your duck.'

Stan took a breath. 'You been knocked about enough today so I don't aim to add to it now. Besides, you're in no fit state.'

Guv stared at him in the yellow light for a long time, considering, and Stan waited for him to decide. Then he yawned and shrugged. 'You might be right at that, old man, you might be right. In no fit state to fight or fuck.' He took a few unsteady paces down the street, before turning and calling back: 'I won't forget this, Stanley, you may depend on it.' His meaning was unclear.

Back in the tap room a new song had begun:

I am a brisk and bonny lad and free from care and strife
And sweetly as the hours pass I love a country life.
At wake or fair I'm often there for pleasures I can see,
Though poor, I am contented and happy as can be.

Stan went over to the freckle-faced girl. She had not moved from the bench beside the high-backed oak armchair. Her father sat there now.

'He saw sense, I takes it? I must stand you a pint. See what trouble you caused, girl, setting your cap at the quality?' The girl began to cry. The wheelwright spat onto the sawdust boards.

And in the time of harvest, how cheerfully we go
Some with hooks and some with crooks and some with scythes
    we mow,
And when our corn is free from harm we have not far to
    roam,
We'll all away to celebrate the welcome harvest home.

As the last echoes died away, the singers looked around for Guv but he had gone. Poor devils, Stan thought, not really understanding why; something about their faces, merry and flushed with ale, drinking the health of a man who most of them barely knew and others had disliked until that morning, until a feat of daring changed it all and raised their spirits, as though they had somehow joined him on his flight. '*Would your wings carry me?*' Most led desperate lives. *And in the time of harvest, how cheerfully we go*. How could they trot out such twaddle, knowing the truth of it? It was a delusion and a dream that he supposed eased their daily toil, explained their eagerness to celebrate an act of boldness and self-reliance.

Poor devils, he thought again. Then it came to him: perhaps he was the same, facing a future already fixed for him, knowing the truth of it, looking at life with a girl like Mary Grey, pretty enough at first but plumping up with children, in a damp cottage somewhere and never enough money coming in and the work hard, always hard even if he became, in time, a bailiff. Perhaps a drink or two like this, to blur the edges, to make it bearable. Was that all there was? Would he lean here on this bar with perhaps the wheelwright, an old man now, urging him to spin the well-worn yarn? 'This 'ere son-in-law of mine, he knew our famous Birdman well. Even helped to build his blessed machine. Brave weren't in it on that memorable o-ccasion. True son of Alfriston, young Sutro was. He were a proper hero and no mistake.' Then no doubt a twinkle. 'He took a shine to our Mary an' all, oh didn't he just? But she were a level-headed girl and settled for our Stan. 'Twere probably for the best.' The image was so vivid that Stan felt for a moment that his fate was already settled, unchangeable, that he was trapped.

Unless somehow he broke away.

The wheelwright's daughter had ceased to sob, sniffing and wiping her nose with the back of her hand. She looked up at Stan in a questioning way, her eyes red rimmed, but he had no interest in her, not like that. He knew her well from schooldays and she held no mystery for him, inclined to act about, filling the air with empty chat and using her looks to make up for her want of effort. But why blame her, really? Soon she would go down to some village boy or passing stranger; it was surprising that she had eluded them so long. Then the cycle would start again; the brief pleasure of the bed and then the nippers, the scrimping to make ends meet, the unrelenting grind. *And in the time of harvest, how cheerfully we go.* But he still had recollections of the girl when they had played as children, paddling in the Cuckmere or sitting on the backs of oxen as they ploughed or roaming across the Downs. For this he had involved himself tonight, for a memory of days that seemed to stretch as long as weeks under a constant sun when everything seemed fresh. Guv's words came back to him. 'You want to get there first and break your duck.' He burned with the injustice of it. What did Guv know or care of Mary Grey except her pretty face and figure? Typical that he should use a cricketing expression, as if it was some kind of game, building up a score regardless of the cost to someone else.

He took the wheelwright's offered pint. The girl was smiling now, and hopeful, thinking his action might mean more than it did. A bailiff's son? Well, it was still a goodly catch. Stan Kemp, though plain, had broadened out, picked up a bit of Sutro polish, could be a man of substance; she certainly could do worse. She noticed he was looking at her in the oddest way. Was it tenderness or something else, an emotion she could not place?

Stan was thinking that he might have sunk himself because of her. 'I won't forget this,' Guv had said, 'you may depend on it.' What did that mean? That everything was over? Anything challenging or unusual in his life had been to do with Guv and his obsession. In his imagination he had flown with Guv that morning and covered every giddy yard. They had shared so much, for years. Although perhaps that wasn't quite correct; more that Guv had shared with him. And Guv was like the keeper of a door that opened to a world of unknown possibilities. He could push it open and they could both pass through, or he could close it in Stan's face and he would find himself a bailiff, doing bailiff's work and hitched to little Mary here or someone very like her. That could be the price he paid for taking her part tonight; that door closed in his face. All that talk of aero-nautics as the coming thing; maybe for him the coming thing had gone.

5

With the Colonel in the Cape, Guv had taken to using his study. Now, he sat with his feet up on the big desk, pipe on the go, studying again the report in the *Evening Argus*. It was only days since the flight from High And Over but already his life seemed to lack purpose. The project that had occupied him for so long was over and the wreckage of the glider, retrieved from the river, was piled up in the barn like a bonfire built for Guy Fawkes Night, quite beyond saving. The consolation was that locally at least he was a figure of note.

A DASHING AERONAUT, the *Argus* headline ran. *Mr Sutro's Splendid Feat.* He read on:

Soaring from the heights of the well-known Alfriston beauty spot, High And Over, Mr Fraser Sutro of Aelle Manor Farm conducted a successful flight of his glider on Sunday morning last, covering a distance of more than two hundred feet. Conditions were very calm when he launched his machine from the precipitous escarp-ment, and it seemed at first that he would come to earth in a meadow on the far side of the Cuckmere River but an encounter with a flock of birds (a flock, Guv noted, excellent, far better than a single heron), *compelled him to execute a sudden turn to avoid disaster and he descended into the river itself. His glider was much damaged but Mr Sutro emerged from the water none the worse for his mishap, waving to the considerable crowd of excited villagers that had assembled to witness the intrepid aviator's skill and daring. After his successful flight Mr Sutro, though only in his twentieth year, advised your correspondent that it is his inten-tion to write his name in the annals of aviation 'for dear old England', a statement that drew enthusiastic applause from*

spectators and does him great credit. We watch the future endeav-
ours of our young Sussex Birdman with much interest.

What those future endeavours might be was open to doubt. The glider was matchwood, the Colonel permitted him only a notional wage for his informal role as an apprentice bailiff, which barely covered the costs of alcohol and tobacco, although in the Colonel's absence he had been helping himself judiciously from his reserves, and he possessed no qualifications of any kind other than a small reputation as a fledgling aviator. The idea of constructing another machine was unappealing; the enthusiasm that had carried him through that long and complicated process had diminished now that he had flown. That was what he wanted, to fly. Let someone else provide the means. He had proved himself and had an urge to move on, but to what and how?

For the moment his future seemed limited to pretending an interest in the estate while dodging any real responsibility, faced with a way of life ruled by the seasons, and hoping that somehow, something might turn up. As to writing his name in the annals of aviation, he was unable to write his name even on the smallest cheque to fund those future endeavours of such interest to the *Evening Argus*.

Meanwhile, Stan Kemp had been to see him, oddly changed; it seemed to have to do with a quarrel on the night of the celebrations but Guv had only a fuzzy recollection, little beyond some angry words exchanged about a girl who had seemed to promise some pleasure but had not appeared. He also recalled vaguely that he had realised he was close to that crucial point in a drunk, the point at which he ceased to make any sense at all, and had somehow found his way home to fix himself a nightcap from the Colonel's sideboard before sleeping on the settle fully clothed. He had still not washed or shaved or eaten when Stan had been shown in with a sniff by the Seaford widow.

'About last night.'

'Good binge, eh?'

'Yes, good enough.'

'Hair of the dog?'

'No, thanks.' Stan had chewed his lip. 'It was something you said.'

'Said? Said about what?'

'That you wouldn't forget what happened, that I could depend on it. It left me a bit flummoxed. I've been wondering about your meaning.'

'Good grief, old man,' Guv said, 'it's plain enough, surely? Can't keep saying thanks, you know.' He assumed that was what he had meant. What else could it have been? He had no recollection of the comment at all.

Stan's expression changed. He seemed relieved and almost smiled. 'I'm not sure you've said thanks once.'

Guv poured himself a whisky and added a dash of soda. 'Well, I meant to. All the excitement, I suppose. Sure you won't have a snifter?'

Stan shook his head. 'I want you to know, you can count on me.'

'Never entered my mind I couldn't,' Guv said. He threw across the copy of the *Evening Argus*. 'Take a gander at that. The dashing Sussex Birdman. We're on the way, my boy.' Later he wondered: on the way to where? But Stan had swallowed it easily enough.

Guv heard the slither of tyres on mud and the clatter of a bicycle being thrown against the garden wall. He swung his feet off the top of the desk, pushed himself round in the Colonel's swivel chair and saw a telegraph boy coming up the front path, fumbling in his leather message pouch. To Guv's surprise the telegram was addressed to him. He had never received one before and thought, on impulse, that it could only have some connection with his flight; yes, an offer from a national newspaper, perhaps the *Daily Mail* since they were so keen on aviation, much impressed by the *Argus* piece and offering to further his career 'for dear old England'. That would certainly be their style; promoting a young blade prepared to risk all for King and Country. Fanciful, of course, but such things happened. Or he supposed they did. And if they did, why not to him?

The Seaford widow gave him the envelope and waited by the study door while he read the message through.

'Good Lord,' he said, 'the old man's gone missing in Belgravia.'

The widow looked sceptical, even more than usual. 'Belgravia? How can one go missing in Belgravia?'

'Belgravia near Kimberley, the Northern Cape. It seems the Governor's been staying in a hotel there. Hasn't been seen for days.'

'Well, no doubt the Colonel has his reasons.'

'No doubt – not that he'd confide in anyone, of course. I know he'd got some knotty matters to sort out, but what they were he didn't say.'

Two days later, a second telegram arrived. The Colonel's corpse had been discovered tossed into the Big Hole at Kimberley, two miles from the Belgravia township. Guv summoned Edward Kemp.

'Where does this leave us, Mr Kemp? Any ideas?'

'My poor boy, what a dreadful business. You have my deepest sympathy.'

Guv did not like being referred to as anyone's 'poor boy' but realised that this was not the moment to object. 'Thanks, but where does this leave us?

'Could it have been an accident?'

'Doubtful. His head was found half a mile away. I had an inkling the old man kept rum company but I must say this is a pretty turn of events.'

'This Big Hole . . .'

'A diamond mine. I've looked it up. Six hundred feet deep spread over forty acres. I always thought it was on the cards the Governor would find himself in a hole, but not one this big.'

The bailiff flinched. 'I still can't take it in. He seemed so indestructible.'

'Well, apparently not,' said Guv. 'Obviously he was involved in some sort of business dealings out there and fell foul of someone. The question is, Mr Kemp, what's to be done?'

'I'm afraid I'm at a loss. Nothing like this has happened to me before. It seems you're the Master now. You must take advice, professional advice. All I can say is that you can count on me.'

'That's funny,' Guv said. 'Your son has said the self-same thing.'

'I'm glad of it. May I hope that it works both ways?'

'You may,' said Guv.

That evening he walked to the top of High And Over and looked across the valley towards the farm. Behind him the sun was lowering over Seaford Bay, not yet touching the horizon but throwing great shadows across the landscape that gradually crept forwards to consume the wash of golden light. He could see the prospect was quite beautiful but his senses were not touched. Aelle nestled in its combe, apparently unchanged, but to him it was greatly changed; a home no longer, instead a commodity that could prove far more valuable than any paltry offer from some populist rag. He watched the shadows swallow up the farm. At his feet, beyond the muddy track, High And Over fell away looking fiercely steep but it seemed also changed, its challenge gone, like a horse fresh broken-in, tamed, no longer daunting though he would not admit it ever had been, even to himself.

Within a fortnight, news came from Kimberley that an inquest had returned a verdict of Wilful Murder by Some Person or Persons Unknown, and the Colonel's remains were duly deposited in the Gladstone Cemetery after a sparsely attended service at St Cyprian's Cathedral. Those present, not counting the Colonel, numbered only five; the priest, two representatives of the Cape police scanning the pews for suspects, a young black woman who wept throughout the service, apparently a servant at the Diamant Lodge Hotel, and the proprietor of the Diamant Lodge who later sent Guv a letter of condolence together with a substantial bill for the Colonel's board and lodging. By separate post came an equally hefty charge for the funeral arrangements.

As the months went by, Guv found himself involved in a succession of laborious and baffling meetings with the Sutros' legal and financial advisers that, piece by piece, presented an increasingly alarming picture of the situation. Aelle Manor Farm had been, as the accountant Armitage put it, 'mortgaged to the gills' with much of the money transferred to a South African bank. Over the years it had been invested in numerous ventures connected with the mining of diamonds in the Kimberley area; some, the earliest, risky and unwise but by a narrow margin within the bounds of normal business practice; others, distinctly shady – but for those who had been duped, too borderline and costly to contest. The residue of the Colonel's funds had gone towards the purchase of 4,000 acres of veldt south-west of Kimberley, plausibly promoted as a new diamond field rich in minerals. There was no shortage of investors, issued with impressive-looking share certificates and promised monthly interest on the money they put in. For a sufficient time they received these sums, but then the rates went down until they ceased entirely and the company reported with regret that, despite the initial promise of their surveys they could not find the diamonds they had hoped for. The shareholders commissioned their own survey and it was soon revealed that the so-called diamond field was barren wasteland that, for the purposes of launching the fraud, had been salted with rough diamonds.

At this time, the Colonel went missing from the Diamant Lodge Hotel together with an associate named Van Nierkerk. At this time also, the entire funds of the enterprise were withdrawn from its business account in Kimberley. Much later it was reported that Van Nierkerk had been seen in California, although it was never proved or any of the funds recovered. The only certainty was that when the Colonel's body was found, murdered by person or persons unknown, he did not have on him a single penny or possess anything of value except 4,000 acres of almost worthless scrub in the Cape and what might remain of his mortgaged property in England, where a host of creditors were pursuing their claims.

It took some time for the extent of the Colonel's debts and obligations to be confirmed by Larkin & Boot, his solicitors in Brighton. Presciently, given what they knew of his activities in a foreign land, they had somehow prevailed on him to appoint them executors of his estate in the event of his death and, in addition, to confirm Fraser Sutro as his sole beneficiary.

Summoned to the offices of Larkin & Boot, Guv quickly learned the truth – that his inheritance amounted to perhaps one quarter of the value of Aelle Manor Farm. The partner Boot looked sympathetic. 'I realise this will come as a shock to you, Mr Sutro, but I'm afraid the property must be sold to realise the capital and settle your father's debts, many of which are pressing.'

Guv glanced out of the window at the passing traffic in North Street. 'Oh, yes?'

'Tell me, what is the situation at the farm?'

'It trundles on.'

'Far better it should be disposed of as a going concern,' said Boot. 'I suggest an auction for the entirety. We can put the wheels in motion straight away. If a satisfactory outcome is achieved, and I am confident it will be because land of this quality is much sought-after in the county, your portion will be held in trust until you attain your majority,' at this he scanned his papers, 'which I see is a mere eight months from now. By then I'm sure all matters will be resolved, and well before that point is reached, I have no doubt that your financial advisers will be more than happy to identify some suitable investments.'

'Not diamond mines, I hope,' said Guv.

Boot laughed distantly. 'I do counsel you to give these matters your serious consideration. For a young man it will still represent a very significant sum, and from what has gone before you hardly need me to tell you how quickly such capital can be dissipated by unwise speculation.'

'I won't be needing any advice,' said Guv. 'I already know where the boodle's going.'

'May one ask what you have in mind for the, uh, boodle?'

'One may,' said Guv. 'But one declines to say.'

In the hallway of the office Boot held out his hand. 'Naturally I am aware of your aeronautical achievements, Mr Sutro. I really must congratulate you on your pluck. It was a close shave, by all accounts.'

Guv crushed Boot's fingers until he winced. 'No, not at all. I came down precisely where I wished.'

Boot wedged his bruised hand under his left armpit. 'Ah, well, that is reassuring. However, it does raise a ticklish matter. May I suggest that if you continue with this pastime, you make your wishes known, in the event of an unfortunate occurrence.'

'You mean a will?'

'Indeed.'

'Simple enough. The whole lot will go to the local home for wayward girls, a cause I strongly support. I'll pop round some time to make it legal. And by the way,' Guv added, 'aeronautics is no mere pastime. Once human flight's been mastered, the world will change. One day, Mr Boot, man may fly to the moon. Who knows? If it's in my lifetime I might even get a chance to invest in a green-cheese mine.'

Closing the front door, Boot sought out his partner. 'That young Sutro, Larkin, is a distinctly unlikeable specimen, much like his unlamented father.'

'Is he not some kind of local hero?' Larkin said.

'He certainly plays the part, though where you draw the line between courage and foolhardiness, or plain showing-off eludes me. He strikes me as a mannerless ne'er-do-well who's destined for a sticky end.'

'That sounds familiar,' said Larkin. 'Meanwhile, Boot, his money's good enough, no doubt.'

'Oh yes, you may be sure of that. Now I must tend my hand. The bounder gripped it so hard my fingers almost bled. I fear I won't be able to hold a pen all afternoon.'

Returned from Brighton, Guv called the Seaford widow into the study.

'Some unwelcome news. It seems the old man's wiped us out. We're up to our necks in debt and everything's going under the hammer. The lawyers have instructed me to make savings with immediate effect, so there it is, you'll have to go.'

'Go? Go where?' The widow steadied herself on the desk. 'Why, I've served your family for twelve years.'

'Hardly a family,' Guv said. 'My father's barely shown his face here and most of the time I've been away at school. Meanwhile you've had free run of the place. I'd say you've had the best of the bargain by far.'

'When your poor mother passed away—'

'I suggest you leave my poor mother out of this. If you're about to suggest that you stepped into the breach, don't. You never cared much for me and I certainly cared less for you. You were retained to perform certain duties for which you were adequately paid, and now your services are no longer needed.'

'Surely you can show me more consideration?'

'I have considered it,' said Guv, 'and my decision's made. Blame my father. The situation's not of my choosing and entirely out of my hands. I'm simply required to make ends meet. However, I'm prepared to offer reasonable compensation on the strict understanding that there's no argument or difficulty about the matter.'

The Seaford widow's face was white. When she spoke she spat out the words. 'Have you any idea how much I do here, my fine young fellow? A house like this doesn't run itself. There's everything to do. How do you propose to cope, I'd like to know?'

Guv began to fill his pipe from the Colonel's buffalo-head tobacco jar.

'It's been made clear to me I barely own a door-knob. As far as I'm concerned, the house can go hang. And less of the "fine young fellow".'

The Seaford widow sat down heavily on the settle, staring straight ahead. 'Twelve years.'

'As to the notice period, shall we say a week from today? I leave it to you to make the necessary arrangements regarding your possessions. Meanwhile, not a word to Mr Kemp or you'll be out of here without a brass farthing.'

When he was told, the bailiff was more resigned. 'I've been expecting something of the sort. Such businesses as this can't run on expectations. The lads and me, we've done our best but it's been a struggle for a good while now. Your father was deuced tight with cash although I'll own he let us be, to make of it what we could.'

'It's to be auctioned up-and-running,' Guv said. 'There's every chance the new owner will keep you on.'

'Not when he sees how we've been cutting corners,' said Edward Kemp. 'This land does us no credit. If he knows his business he'll draw his own conclusions and bring in another man. I'd best have a look about to see what else might be on offer, though in these parts prospects are precious thin.'

'Well, of course that's up to you. Meanwhile I'd be obliged if you'd put Stanley in the picture. I'm meeting someone in the village and I'm pressed for time.'

'He'll be hit hard,' said Kemp. 'He only knows this place. A word from you would help, perhaps tomorrow, man-to-man. You owe him that, I think, for old time's sake.'

'Well,' said Guv, 'that's a debt that's easily paid.'

In the morning, Guv crossed the water meadows to the ten-acre wood that lay beside the lane to Litlington. Soon he heard the thwack of billhooks, men's voices calling back and forth and caught the whiff of penny cigarettes drifting on the crisp, frosty air. The workers fell silent when he came upon them coppicing the hazel shrub that spread across the woodland floor between the standing oaks. They straightened up, their billhooks balanced in their hands, faces set hard and showing they had heard the news.

Guv nodded to Stan. 'Take a break.'

Stan glanced at his companions, then laid down his billhook on a folded sack. They walked a distance beneath the angular branches of the oaks, well shaped to make the frames of ships, 'the wooden walls of England', until the ironclads took their place and woods like this became neglected, dead trees left where they fell and not replaced, not gone for men-of-war, and only the whippy hazel cut for baskets, bean poles, fences, hurdles. Above, the canopy of the wood closed in, filtering the light so all around them was dark and green.

'Dad's taken it bad,' Stan said at last.

'No option, I'm afraid. The plain fact is the business has gone bust. Turns out the Governor's been playing fast-and-loose for years. If someone hadn't got there first I might have done for the old devil myself.'

They walked on, the deep carpet of fallen leaves crackling underfoot.

'So what's to do?'

They had come to a shallow stream that passed between high grassy banks, the water rippling across a bed of smooth stones with a faint tinkling sound like far-off bells.

'Well, no more mud-larking for me,' said Guv, 'that's for sure. I'll still come into a tidy sum when everything's paid off, and I'm damned if I'll risk it on a calling that's at the mercy of the taxman and whatever the bloody seasons choose to throw its way. No future in it, old man, no future at all.'

'Some of us have no choice.'

'No choice? Drop round tonight to hear a proposition. I won't deny it's got its risks as well – risks enough to make your hair fall out. One thing I'll promise, life won't be dull. Unless of course you prefer to live out your days trudging behind the backside of a horse or cutting twigs for baskets.'

After work Stan cleaned himself off at the water tap by the barn and walked across the yard to the manor house, drying his hands on his neckerchief. He was halfway up the path when the front door opened and Mary Grey came out. Behind her in the shadows of the hallway he saw Guv turn away. The girl came towards him, walking daintily, a slight smile on her lips. She hesitated as she came close and he took her arm.

'What brings you here, Mary?'

'I'm sure it's no business of yours.' The smile had gone. She looked peevish and pulled her arm away. 'You've no claim on me.'

'That don't mean I'm ain't concerned. We've been good enough pals, you won't deny that, I suppose?'

She softened. 'No, I won't deny that. Don't fret yourself, Stan. Everything's above board and respectable. Young Mr Sutro has offered me employment and I'm agreeable.'

'What employment?'

'Appears that ancient article from Seaford has got her marching orders. I'm to give a hand from time to time when called upon.' She laughed. 'Don't act so doubtful. Pa's aware.' She reached out and touched his hand. 'There's precious little on offer in this dead-alive place and a girl must take what she can get.'

'If she knows what she's a-getting,' Stan said, before moving on up to the house.

In the study Guv waved him to a chair. 'Before I start, I want to make one thing plain.'

'About this 'ere proposition?'

'Here's how it rests. You'd work for me. Not with me, *for* me. With all that that implies.'

'I see.'

'I wonder if you do? You're an independent-minded cuss inclined to speak your mind.'

'The gaffer right or wrong, that it?'

'Loyalty, Stan. You and I, we've got different ways. If I'm the gaffer then my way counts. Unless you're going to turn me down.'

'Ain't heard the proposition yet.'

'I'll come to that. But I want it understood that if we shake on it, I'll brook no interference in anything I may say or do that doesn't fit with your own opinions.'

'We've always rubbed along.'

'I saw you talking to the girl. Anything to say to that? She's just a maid, perhaps?'

'You told me you'd forgotten.'

'Came back to me, old man. Wagging tongues and suchlike. Funny what you remember when the old head clears.' Guv paused. 'She's going to do some tasks about the house. Her father's quite au fait. I saw him at the Star last night and bought him a pint or two.'

'A pint or two, is that her price?'

'She'll be more than properly paid for what she does.' Abruptly, Guv brought his fist down hard on the desk. 'Dammit, Stan, I haven't laid a finger on the creature. She's just a pretty thing to have around. You can't dispute she's an improvement on the Seaford baggage. Say if you want her for yourself. If not, lay off. Whatever happens, happens. If it does, she won't be the first and certainly not the last. Besides, she's not entirely witless, she can make her choice as well. Not that it's your concern, unless you want to make something of it. If so, tell me now and I can save my breath. It's up to you.'

6

With towers of cumulus approaching from the west, pure white above and bluish-black at their flattened bases, Guv had lifted off from the Brooklands flying village watched by a sceptical band of fellow aviators whose lugubrious predictions about the conditions he had shrugged aside. Grounded by fog for two days, he had waited long enough and was impatient to embark on the challenge he had set himself. Besides, he had made sure the word was out. He had the beginning of a name, in England at least, and the public was expectant.

On take-off, crosswinds, albeit slight, had posed their usual problem, calling for full-forward elevator to lift the heavy tail, but finally the Blériot had left the ground, the note of its engine shrill as he turned eastward in a gentle bank before climbing to 800 feet on a course for Dover. The little monoplane rocked in the unstable air but he held the Gnome rotary at a constant 12,000 revs with a deft touch on stick and rudder, careful not to stress the wings, countering the violent up and down gusts with the skill that, at the flying school at Pau, had earned him his wings in eight days when the less gifted took six weeks.

His plan was simple enough: to start the attempt from the good, flat field on the cliffs above Dover Harbour close to where Blériot himself had landed more than a year before to claim his place in history; forty minutes across the Channel to landfall at Cap Gris Nez, then inland from Boulogne, passing over St Ingelvert before touching down after another forty minutes at the landing ground between the dunes and forest at Le Touquet Paris-Plage where great crowds were predicted. The Blériot's fuel tank held twelve gallons, enough for two hours in the air, so the venture was entirely possible as long as the machine performed as it should and the weather held.

He refused to contemplate failure. A second attempt might be too late. Already Chatto back at Brooklands had talked of having a go himself with his Dumont Demoiselle. And then there was the prize money put up by *La Tribune du Nord* – five thousand francs, equivalent to more than a thousand pounds. At present Guv doubted he had a thousand pence. The bulk of the proceeds from the sale of Aelle Manor Farm had been swallowed up by the Colonel's debts. The residue that came to Guv had gone on flying training at the Louis Blériot school in Pau, the purchase of a Blériot XI, the model already proven on cross-country flights, and the renting of a wooden shed at the Brooklands flying village that doubled as rudimentary living quarters for himself and Stan Kemp. Some little income had been earned from minor awards for flights between various English cities and occasional displays at county shows but, despite securing him a headline or two, this had barely covered the Blériot's running costs. His small reputation would be forgotten soon enough without sufficient funds. *La Tribune du Nord* could put things right.

It was a lengthy trip, Weybridge to Dover, further than Dover to Le Touquet but without the hazard of the Channel in between and so, at Headcorn, Stan Kemp was waiting at a suitable field with enough fresh fuel to top him up and take him on. He could have transported his machine to Dover by road but that was not his way, too much like those comic photos of horses towing broken-down cars. An aeroplane was designed to fly, and fly it must, from the very start.

But now, despite the light following wind, he was covering the ground at barely thirty miles an hour even though he held his body low in the exposed wicker seat to smooth the airflow. Behind him somewhere, above the engine roar, he heard the grumble of thunder. Glancing back across his shoulder he saw the towers of cumulus gradually merging into anvil-shaped cumulonimbus reaching to perhaps 30,000 feet, their tops drawn up like feathers by the strength of the upper winds. From the cloud base lightning flickered down and struck the ground. Soon the first drops of rain spattered against the back of his gabardine flying suit.

He had planned to pick up the South Eastern Railways main line at Tonbridge and follow it to the Headcorn rendezvous, but everything below had grown blurred and indistinct in a deepening orange haze, and even at low altitude landmarks were difficult to identify. He dragged his fogged-up goggles onto his chest and came down to 500 feet, the buffeting severe. Then, for an instant, he glimpsed a mud-coloured river, stone ramparts and an ancient gatehouse – Tonbridge, he assumed – but he had missed the railway line, the Blériot tossed about by gusts of rising air and demanding constant small corrections.

The rain had turned to hail, the ice stones drumming on the fuselage and wings, striking so hard it seemed holes must appear in the taut fabric, holes that might turn to rips until the canvas pulled apart and brought him down. Changes to his heading and track by input on the rudder had no effect, his speed too slow to create sufficient airflow. His sluggish progress posed another threat: in such conditions – low pressure combined with humid air – pilots and machines had been caught by violent updraughts, sucked aloft into cumulonimbus storms to die at unheard-of altitudes, frozen and deprived of oxygen, or struck by one of the myriad lightning bolts.

The straggle of dwellings to the east of the town finally gave way to open country. By now the hail had turned to pounding rain but still he managed to check his bearing on the compass watch strung round his neck on cord and confirm he was on course. But where exactly? Visibility had improved a little but did not help. A church on a hill slipped slowly by, the gravestones vivid in the bilious light, then a road – no, not a road, a lane that twisted between dark woodland and petered out at a cluster of cottages, barns and oast-houses; no sign of people, the farmland for miles bristling with hop-poles or dense with apple orchards or grazed by sheep and cattle or hedged enclosures too small to contemplate a landing and anyway peppered with lethal mole-hills. Somewhere down there Stan Kemp was waiting, on the landing ground he had safely cleared close to the railway line and marked with a white canvas cross. But was it still ahead or already miles behind?

The Blériot's normally heavy tail-plane had grown light, affecting the angle of the wings, forcing him to compensate swiftly on the stick and bring the machine back from an imminent stall. He knew what this change in weight meant; fuel was running low. He took an adjustable spanner strapped to the side of his seat and, leaning forward, struck the brass fuel tank once, twice. It rang hollow, confirming that all that remained of the original twelve gallons was little more than vapour. His instinct was to throttle back and improve consumption, but he knew that without the meagre airspeed it demanded, the Blériot was unforgiving; if he reduced the engine revs even slightly he would fall from the sky. He also knew that the fuel tank could run dry at any moment. The only course was to put down now and take his chance.

The eye of the storm had passed to the north and although curtains of rain still drifted across his path, visibility had improved. Sunshine broke through and everything below was gold and glistening wet. Slowly, as he reduced height, a moated building came into view, a single castellated tower, the shell of an old manor house and a jumble of fallen masonry, once fortifications, that ran around a formal garden in the modern style. He was low enough now to see swans thrusting their way between dense spreads of water lilies on the black waters of the moat. On a hill that rose up behind the ruin, protected by woodland on three sides, was a substantial mansion, the glass in its mullioned windows flashing silver against the wet-gold of its sandstone walls. Ahead, in the valley and beyond the moated tower, were stable buildings with a brick yard and horses and a single figure looking up as he passed across at tree-top height, the shadow of his machine and the racket of its engine making the animals rear and jink, the figure grasping at a bridle, pulled off its feet.

A broad, flat area of close-mowed turf, a cricket pitch, opened up in front of him. On its far side, but a good distance away, was a brick pavilion and, next to it, a weather-boarded scorer's hut. He pushed forward on the stick, careful not to ease the throttle even now; Blériot had done that, cutting his motor at the end of his flight from Calais and crashing from 60 feet. Almost there; a firm pull back, the stick in his lap, and the landing gear was skimming the ground, the tyres starting to spin and rumble, cushioning the slight bounce – and at last he shut down the Gnome. The propellor froze, and as he rolled to a halt, leaving furrows across the cricket square scored by the Blériot's wheels, he caught the scent of crushed grass on the humid air, blending with the fumes of petrol and hot oil.

There was a heavy silence, the engine ticking and creaking as it began to cool, his ears still ringing from its bellow, and then he heard birdsong and distant voices. Two men were approaching him from the stables. He jumped down from the cockpit, pulled off his leather helmet and wiped his face with a rag from his overalls pocket. Closer to, he saw that they were not two men; one was a woman, stocky and dressed in dung-stained breeches and a smock-frock, her hair gathered into a snood of knotted thread more often seen on the hunting-field. He looked her over, as he looked over any woman, but she held no interest for him.

The man, bandy-legged in gaiters, pointed at the ruts in the turf. 'The Master ain't going to be enamoured of that.'

Guv turned his back on him and began to walk round the Blériot, looking for damage. 'Where is this place anyway?'

The woman had followed him, hanging back a little. 'Saxonshore.'

'And where the deuce is Saxonshore?'

'Not far from Rye, above the Marsh.' She spoke quietly but he was surprised that her accent was not half-bad. Her face was scarlet and she could not meet his eye, but he sensed that she was drawn to him as people often were by meeting a man who did what he did, who possessed abilities beyond their comprehension, performed deeds they could only gape at; a hero, a fearless flier, regarded with something close to awe. Of course, this reaction could take another form; the man now, keen to show he was less impressed. 'Why,' he said, 'close up, these contraptions ain't much more than an infant's pram with wings. 'Tis a miracle they gets off the ground at all.' He jerked his chin at Guv. 'You a noted personage then, like that there froggy Bleary-oh?'

Guv ignored him and waved an arm towards the mansion on the hill. 'Quite a pile they've got here,' he said to the woman.

She nodded. 'I suppose it is.'

'Any chance they'd have some petrol? I've about run out.'

'I should think so, yes. There's none at the stables. We can ask the chauffeur up at the house. He keeps a supply in the garage block.' She turned to the man. 'Harris, you get back to your work. I'll take care of this.' There was something in her tone that made Guv study her more closely, a touch of authority, learned perhaps from a father who might be anything round here; head groom, gamekeeper, even bailiff of the estate. Not the chauffeur, for she had spoken of him too lightly. Perhaps the butler's daughter. That would explain her assuming airs yet not quite able to carry it off, found work as a stable-maid no doubt, the dumpling not decorative enough to have about the house.

They set off up a curving path between banks of rhododendron and azalea. Below them, the ruins of the moated castle had grown quite small. It was a steep climb but the woman walked on strongly; she was fit at least. He paused for breath and looked down at the castle, like most of them probably knocked about to make it more picturesque. The woman came back down the slope. 'Exquisite, isn't it?' Still she avoided his eye, shifting her gaze from the ruins to the toes of her rubber boots.

'I'm Fraser Sutro,' he said. 'People call me Guv.'

She regarded the view more intently than ever. 'I thought you might be. I believe I've read of you in the popular press.' She held out her hand. 'I'm Lydia, Lydia Bowman.' The hand, when he took it, was damp with sweat and trembled slightly. He held it for longer than was proper, amused to see the colour mount in her cheeks. He could not resist such games.

'You help out with the horses, then?'

Lydia Bowman had clasped her hands together, the fingers interlocked.

'If you ride, you must. It's all part of it if you care for horses, quite indivisible.'

'So you ride?'

'Of course, don't you?'

'A dangerous beast, the horse – too unpredictable.'

'I'm surprised they hold any fears for you.'

'An animal has a will of its own. An aeroplane, now – well, it can let you down but it's usually your own fault; something you've done wrong or forgotten. Not some quirk of mischief or downright bloody-mindedness outside your control.'

'You must be in control then?'

'Of course. Unless I'm in control I die.'

They continued across the broad gravel drive in front of the mansion. In the garage-block, a man in a button-over chauffeur's uniform was polishing the coachwork of a Rolls-Royce. When he heard them at the door he straightened up and, to Guv's surprise, knuckled his forehead.

The woman waved the courtesy aside. 'This gentleman requires some petrol for his flying machine, Chandler. He has landed on the cricket ground. Can you attend to it?'

'Certainly, Miss Lydia.'

'Five or so gallons should do,' Guv said. 'Don't touch the machine. I'll fill her up myself.'

'When you've done that, Chandler,' said the woman, 'you'll find us in the house.' She glanced at Guv, then looked away quickly. 'I think you should meet my father. He's up-to-the-minute in all the latest innovations. I know he'd be fascinated to talk to you.' She bit her lip. 'That is, if you can spare the time.'

'There's plenty of daylight left,' Guv said, 'and your chap will take a while to get down to the pitch.' He understood by now that she was unlikely to introduce him to the butler.

She led him back towards the house where they mounted half a dozen steps to the porch, the lintel decorated with a coat-of-arms and a family motto in Latin that was beyond him. She took off her boots without thinking and pushed her feet into comfortable shoes. Then she caught herself. 'Oh, awfully sorry. I'm always being scolded for treading in mud.'

'I'll remove mine too,' Guv said. 'They're just as bad.' He kicked them off and she passed him a pair of house shoes. They were too big and he waded about the porch like a paddler up to his knees in the sea. She laughed, holding her hand over her mouth. There was something intimate about this business of removing boots; something that disturbed her particularly.

They passed through a lofty panelled hall hung with family portraits; the furniture dark and old, rich carpets on the parquet floor, tapestries, blue china on display above the stone fireplace carved with the same motto.

'*Non sine dignitas*,' he said. 'What does that mean?'

'Not without merit.'

'That's modest.'

'It is isn't it? I suppose you think it hardly sits with all of this. But the family has always been conscious of its good fortune.'

'Your family?'

'My family, yes. It's a good motto, I believe. Wealth can breed arrogance, and that must be resisted.'

'Did you make that up yourself?'

'Here's another for you. There are more important things in life than money.'

'Easy to say when you have it.'

'Don't you have it? I thought aviation was a costly business.'

'It is. That's why I no longer have it. This flight is my last throw. If I fail, I'll be looking for employment elsewhere. Perhaps you have a vacancy for a stable-boy?'

'Not very likely, given your attitude to horses.'

He had to give her that. She was plain as a stick and shy to a fault but had a neat tongue. A door opened at the far end of the hall. 'Poppa,' she said, 'a visitor for you.' The old man shared her features, or rather she shared his; the same snub nose, small eyes not saved by their pleasing blue, fleshy cheeks and prominent jaw, his figure portly and run to fat. In forty years she would look much the same.

'I heard voices,' the old man said.

'This is Fraser Sutro, Poppa, the aviator. You've spoken of him.'

'I heard the noise of your motor, my boy, and saw your machine pass over. A singular event at Saxonshore. We lead a somewhat reclusive existence here, Lydia and I.'

'I haven't done your cricket ground much good,' Guv said.

'Please don't concern yourself. It's never been my game. That was my father's obsession. Bit of a duffer at sports, if truth be told. Nowadays we just let the locals use the pitch from time to time, nothing serious, but they're likely lads so they'll soon put things to rights.'

They followed Bowman into his study; brass-mounted desk with scattered papers, leather chairs, shelves of books, a terrestrial globe on a wooden stand by the tall window that gave onto the terrace with, beyond a stone balustrade, the wooded valley where the battlements of the castle stood out between the trees. On the wall opposite the desk was a portrait of a young woman in a gold frame. She stared out, haughty and questioning, as though impatient to end the sitting, her thick dark hair worn up, a velvet choker at her throat, dressed in a white silk dress and holding a single red rose. 'My wife,' said Bowman, 'by Singer Sargent at the time of our marriage.' He paused. 'She is no longer with us.'

'She's in Rhode Island,' Lydia Bowman said quickly, 'with her family.'

'Visiting,' Bowman murmured almost to himself.

Guv said nothing, struck by the quirk of Nature that arranged for the mother's looks to pass her daughter by and endow her with her father's.

'I have read of your exploits,' Bowman said. 'A man of our times, indeed.' There was envy in his eyes; Guv saw he was admired. 'Yours is a hazardous business.'

'It has its risks, but they're risks worth taking. How else can we advance our knowledge? Man's progress always comes at a cost.'

Bowman nodded. 'And yet I fear that flying, for all its promise of conquering the air for peaceful means, will very soon be corrupted and used for quite another purpose. I have in mind Lord Northcliffe's pronouncement when Monsieur Blériot crossed the Channel, that England was no longer an island. It has even been rumoured along this coast that the Germans have already used their airships to spy on our ports and strongholds.'

'If war comes,' Guv said, 'and most of the chaps I know believe it will, there's going to be a new kind of fighting, fighting in the air, machine against machine, and may the best man win.'

'You sound eager,' Lydia Bowman said. 'Do you treat your life so lightly? I should have thought there was quite enough danger to keep you satisfied as it is.'

'I don't court danger for danger's sake,' Guv said. 'Everything has a purpose.'

'And what is that purpose, would you say?'

'To fly.'

Later, when afternoon tea had been served on the terrace, Guv and Lydia Bowman took the same curving path that led down between the rhododendrons and azalea. Beside the Blériot, in its distant paddock, stood a small Vulcan truck laden with half a dozen cans of fuel.

'What next?' said Lydia.

'Take off, fly to Dover, cross the Channel, land at Le Touquet, surrender myself to the adoring hordes, pocket five thousand francs.'

'And then?'

'Something similar, I suppose.'

'My father much admires you.'

'Really?'

'He never had a son, just me. He's quite the reverse of you, of course, never a touch of devil-may-care. It would hardly have suited the business. But it's a quality he greatly respects.' She had stopped beside a tent-shaped hut thatched with heather. She had changed her clothes; black skirt, white blouse with balloon sleeves. She had tried to do something with her hair. 'This is our ice-house. We don't use it any more. In wintertime we'd take great lumps of ice from the moat and store them here for summer. I remember it vaguely, when I was a little girl.'

'It's hard to see you as a little girl.'

'Oh, I was much the same. I've always been an awkward pudding, keen on horses and not much else, a cruel disappointment to Mama. You saw her portrait. Don't tell me your opinion. I imagine like everyone else you thought how sad it was that I didn't take after her.'

Guv side-stepped the trap. 'Your mother, why Rhode Island?'

'She comes from there and now she's gone back. Not visiting, gone back. She married Poppa with delusions of olde England; ancient pile, banquets lit by flaming torches, rich velvet gowns, rushes under the dining table in the hall, dogs fighting for bones. Romanticism was rather fashionable at the time. She found the reality somewhat dull. As you've seen, my father's a dear, but certainly no Sir Lancelot. All ended acrimoniously, I'm afraid, with that most American fad, divorce.' She hesitated, suddenly hot with embarrassment. 'Will you visit us again, do you think?'

'Us?'

'Poppa enjoyed meeting you so much. He's hardly needed in London these days. He always says the business looks after itself. He's short of a manly chat.'

'What is the business?'

'He owns a shop.'

'Business must be good.'

She laughed gently. 'Well,' she said, attempting to be casual, 'can we expect to see you again?'

'Of course,' Guv said. 'I'll buy you a *petit cadeau* in France with my hard-gotten gains.'

'There's nothing I could possibly want,' Lydia said, 'just nothing at all.'

He touched her arm. 'There must be something, surely?'

Three

1

Tim Sutro

A few days after Will Kemp took off from Glisy in his Hurricane bound for Hornchurch, on that still May morning in 1940 when the weather had cleared and Tim's squadron had been able to resume operations, it was at first rumoured and then confirmed that the Germans had broken through the Stenay gap between La Ferte and Sedan, where the Maginot Line petered out, that they had brushed aside the French defenders who believed themselves secure behind the natural barrier of the River Meuse and the thickly forested Ardennes and were pushing north towards the Channel coast. The word from Group was that soon they would be threatening the ports of Dunkirk, Calais and Boulogne.

The Lysanders were ordered to carry out various sorties: low-level reconnaissance, the dropping of supplies to Allied positions and, fitted with bombs, strike the advancing enemy transport and armoured columns. The cost was high. Three, although outnumbered, attacked Dornier bombers over St Omer and were hit by return fire. Two came down, one in flames and another, holed in its petrol tank, force-landing at Douai, its crew unhurt but burning their machine to prevent its capture. Only one got back to base, its rudder half shot away by cannon fire. Soon two more failed to return from tactical reconnaissance and another, already damaged, was shot down on its final approach at Glisy by a free-hunt Messerschmitt 109. Worse, working with another Lysander squadron on a supply-drop for the besieged garrison at Calais, three more crews were lost to flak and ground-fire from German troops who had already overrun the outlying defensive positions they were supplying.

The Bessoneau hangars, obvious targets for German fighters strafing almost unopposed, had been dismantled, the surviving Lysanders dispersed around the perimeter of the airfield close to the partial cover of the nearby woodland. The bell tents that served as the Officers' Mess had also been taken down and the aircrew, officers and men together, ate and slept by their machines while the fitters and riggers worked through the night readying them for what the next day might bring. Mick Porter had vanished, along with his gunner Bolton, somewhere over Le Quesnoy, so Tim was not called Tim-Tim any more. He remembered saying to Will: 'Not long now and we'll all be gone. We're under no illusions.' At that time he had still retained a touch of hope that they might survive.

Now the phrase came back to taunt him. *Not long now*. It was difficult to eat, food sour in his mouth, and like the others he had lost his taste for alcohol, sipping hot tea to rinse around his cheeks and soothe his throat. And yet he and Fred Hirst had somehow come through, pure luck of course, nothing to do with flying skill – the Lizzie did not lend itself to evasive action; no illusions about this either, simply that no enemy in the sky or on the ground had so far fixed on them as a lion picks out a particular prey.

He was leaning back against his machine's wheel spat eating Spam and eggs in silence, breaking the yolks with his fork and watching the yellow stuff spread across his plate, when Farrell, the squadron leader, came over and squatted down beside him. 'All right, Tim?'

'All right.'

'I'm pinching Fred Hirst to take Crawley's place in my kite. I need a chap who knows the score.'

Returning from reconnaissance, Farrell had been shot at from the ground – it seemed by French *poilus* – his gunner Crawley struck in the neck by a bullet that passed out through his jaw. The LAC was dead in the cockpit when Farrell landed.

'Where does that leave me?' Tim said.

'Talk to the adj. A job's come up and you've been volunteered.'

'Can I tell Hirst?'

'Of course. Better that way. Then send him to me.'

Fred Hirst was playing pontoon for French francs. His winnings were gathered in front of him. 'It's my lucky day, sir.' Tim did not know what to reply to that. It disturbed him to think of Hirst climbing into a cockpit still stained with Crawley's blood.

'A word,' was all he said. They walked together towards the perimeter where the farmland fell away into a small valley thick with stunted trees and yellow gorse. 'Quite like my neck of the woods,' said Tim.

'Okay,' said Hirst. 'What's up?'

'The Skipper's chosen you to replace Crawley.'

'Oh, bloody hell. I've really had it now. The CO's half the pilot you are.'

'Rubbish, Fred. He knows the Lizzie inside out. He's flown them since before the war.'

'Not in anger, sir. He's slow on the controls. Old Creepy said it was just a matter of time. Can't you get him to change his mind? I thought we were a ruddy good team. Why break it up?'

'Decision's made, I'm afraid. I'm sure you'll come through in the Skipper's hands.'

'What did I just say?' said Hirst. 'This is my lucky day. My lucky blinking day.' He drummed his fist into the palm of his left hand once, twice. 'Bugger. Bugger it all.' He was staring at the ground. 'So what have they got lined up for you?'

'I'm off to see the adjutant now. You'd better beetle off and find the Skipper.' They stood together for a moment. Tim broke the silence.

'I wanted to give you the news myself.'

'Ta, that means a lot.'

'We've had some trips.'

'Yes, that's for sure.' Hirst tried a grin.

Tim shook Hirst's hand. 'Well, Fred – that's it, I suppose. Good luck.'

'And good luck to you and all, Mr Sutro. I don't aim to get soppy about this but it's been a privilege to fly with you.'

'That's not what you said when we were down on the deck and surprised those Panzers parked up in the forest at Berlaimont.'

'You got us out of it all right,' Hirst said. 'I just hope the Skipper's as quick on the draw.'

Tim watched him go, a small man who looked still smaller believing his luck had run out.

Squadron headquarters was still to be found in the dilapidated farm outbuildings on the far side of the airfield because, Farrell reasoned, no one, not even the Hun, would expect it. 'The wretched shacks look as though they've been bombed already,' he had told the staff, and work parties had carried out what they called 'improvements' to make them appear more decrepit than ever. The adjutant was at his desk in the cattle stall as usual, talking on the phone. It was a bad line and his face was red from shouting.

'*Quoi? Quoi? Je ne comprends pas.* Oh, for Christ's sake! *Quoi? Parlez plus lentement,* dammit. Here, Tim, you've got the lingo. See if you can get some sense out of this johnnie.'

A man speaking precise French was pleased to inform the Commander of the Royal Air Force squadron at Glisy that the car with its single passenger promised for *treize heures et demie* would now arrive one hour late. He was desolated by this delay but would like confirmation on this line that the car had arrived safely, and expressed the hope that its passenger would be embarking on his onward journey as a matter of the greatest urgency.

Tim translated this information for the adjutant, who gestured for the phone and snapped, 'Okay, *monsieur*, I've got the gen. *Au revoir.*' He banged the phone down on its receiver. 'Actually, I've picked up a fair bit of the old *français* while we've been over here. It's when they gabble that I lose track. I'm told my accent's not bad so they always assume I'm fluent.'

'Who is he?' Tim asked.

'Classified, old boy. Don't know myself. Just following orders from Group. But this is where you come in. There's a Frog cloak-and-dagger type wants ferrying to Paris.'

'Why am I nominated?'

'To the other chaps Gay Parée means a pub crawl in the red-light district and a bad head next morning or worse, but you've got the language and you know your way around. Things are pretty chaotic right now. Who knows what you'll find when you deliver Alphonse? Whatever it is, you're more likely to be able to grasp the situation and fix on the best course of action.'

'The best course is to fly straight back here, surely?'

'Not necessarily, given the way things are unfolding. The Boche are moving bloody fast. Between you and me, we may be withdrawn to Hawkinge while we've still got the chance.'

'How am I meant to know if that happens?'

'Well, by all means try giving me a tinkle, but if a Panzer's coming up the garden path I can't promise you an answer. Failing that, see if you can get some sense out of Group. Meanwhile you're to await further orders on the ground at Le Bourget. They may have further need of you there.'

'And what about you, Adj?' Tim said. 'How do you and the rest of the ground staff plan to get out of here if the situation's as bad as you say?'

The adjutant shrugged. 'Oh, transport's on hand. We'll make our way to the coast by road as best we can. Prefer that actually, what with all these 109s on the prowl. But it hasn't come to that yet. Who knows? Perhaps we'll throw the buggers back even now.'

The engine of Tim's Lysander had already been run-up ready for take-off when a black Traction Avant arrived at the airfield with its single passenger, a slight figure in a gabardine raincoat with a briefcase chained to his wrist. It caused some amusement among the pilots. 'Bloody line-shoot.' But Farrell was quick to set them right. 'Belt up, chaps. He's taking just as many risks as you so he's entitled to some respect.'

It was not possible to tell the man's nationality because during the brief introductions he said nothing. He showed no inclination to shake hands, simply impatience to continue his journey. Settled in the rear seat of the Lysander he stared straight ahead, raising his arms reluctantly for the rigger to tighten his safety harness and only nodding when Tim at the controls looked back over his shoulder and gave him an enquiring thumbs-up. On the ground in the shadow of the machine's gull wing a small group watched Tim throttle up and start to move away. Farrell was there, and the adjutant, and Fred Hirst. They looked as though they envied him, their smiles tight, not spreading to their eyes.

He lifted away in the usual shallow, accelerating climb on a course that took them across the vast flatlands of Picardie, well west of the Route Nationale that ran from the Belgian frontier through Arras to Paris, a likely objective for the Luftwaffe in search of easy targets as convoys moved north to reinforce the defenders of the Channel ports. They passed slowly over open fields at 1,500 feet, some tinged faint green with germinating crops, others grazed by beasts that scattered at the approaching growl of the Lysander's motor. The landscape was washed with sunlight and appeared at peace; occasional signs of habitation, a few red-roofed dwellings ranged alongside narrow highways or gathered round a spired church; sometimes a solitary vehicle raising dust. Improbable, it seemed, that great armies might soon come this way, advancing towards the heart of France.

The Lysander was effectively unarmed, the rear Vickers machine-gun removed for speed and lightness. Besides, the man in the gabardine raincoat, not trained as a gunner, would be more likely to shoot off the tail-plane than down an enemy aircraft, not that he showed any inclination to play an active part, strapped mute and apparently resigned into his seat, his briefcase resting flat on his knees. That left Tim with two forward-facing Brownings in the wheel fairings, of marginal use as the Lysander had the aerobatic potential of a brick. His principal defence was to stay alert, running through the old routine, the routine that had helped to keep him alive so far, scanning the sky, high and low, left and right, not fast, not slow, methodical, unblinking, zig-zag, zig-zag, looking for those black dots, those far-off specks that might be on him in moments and send him down with a four-second burst. The sun, hanging in a cloudless sky, did not help, refracting on every scratch, bug mark and smear of oil on the windscreen and canopy. Even so, what they told you at flying training still held true, that the good old Lizzie provided excellent visibility. Except, as the crews quickly realised when they became operational, this also gave them a first-class view of what was coming and rather fewer options for how to avoid it.

Today there were no black dots. They passed over Montdidier, St-Just-en-Chaussée and Clermont, warm in the cockpit, soothed by the constant note of the big Bristol radial. It was as if they had gone up for a flip before the war when flying was for pleasure, for fun or, if you were Guv Sutro, to gild a reputation as a national hero.

Tim thought about his father now, thought back to their last encounter at High And Over, Mother and Alice already in Rhode Island, the Guv alone and restless, moving about the study, lighting and re-lighting his pipe, telling him how lucky he was to find himself in a war. 'How many generations get to fight for their country? I'll be in it soon, when I make those damned Ministry wallahs see sense.' He had paused. 'I only hope that when you're finally in action, you'll find it in yourself to do your duty.'

Fresh from training at Old Sarum, Tim had worn his uniform to please him, his wings still pristine on his tunic. He had made some remark about flying the Lysander on Army cooperation exercises, mild enough, not making any great claims about his prowess as a pilot. His father had thrown down his pipe. 'You can hardly call yourself a pilot, lumbering about the countryside in a Flying Carrot. Little more than driving a bus. Why couldn't you get yourself into a proper kite? A fighter, say, like young Kemp?' They had not parted well, his father avoiding his eye, working his jaw as they waited on the porch for the taxi to take him to Rye station.

'The squadron's off to France at dawn,' Tim had said.

'Wish to God I was.'

'Any advice?'

'In your contraption you're not much more than a target, so aggression hardly comes into it. Given that, the usual warmed-up cabbage. Don't fly straight and level for more than thirty seconds. Beware the Hun in the sun. If you're attacked, turn and meet 'em head-on. And if you're on leave, keep your cock in your trousers unless it's a nice French virgin.'

'Did you?'

'We're not talking about me.'

'Anything else?'

'Yes. Don't let down the Sutro name.'

From the back seat of the Austin Tim had looked back at the big house as they passed down the drive and saw that the front door was already closed.

North of Chantilly the plains began to be replaced by hill country scored with deep valleys, thickly forested, and Tim began the descent to the airfield at Le Bourget, six miles north-east of Paris itself, established in the Great War to protect the city from Zeppelin raids and, later, where thousands mobbed Lindbergh after his trans-Atlantic flight.

On approach they passed over roads busy with traffic, a few family cars and commercial vehicles, but much of it in the drab military camouflage of the French army. He had landed at the airfield before the war but only as a passenger in his father's de Havilland Dragon Rapide, brought along to witness Guv receive a Louis Blériot medal from the Fédération Aéronautique Internationale for setting a new altitude record in a Schoenfelder monoplane. There had been eight of them in the little Rapide, his mother and sister, the mechanic Paget who prepared Guv's planes and cars, a journalist and a photographer from a London aviation magazine, Max Schoenfelder and a young woman pilot, a glider champion, the German said, with white-blond hair swept straight back and cropped short like a boy's, and chill-blue eyes that held some sort of challenge, often fixed unblinkingly on his father. During the visit, Tim remembered, the three of them, Guv, Schoenfelder and the white-blonde, often returned to the Crillon shortly before dawn but this was never explained and, as far as he knew, no explanation ever asked for.

On the ground he taxied the Lysander towards the central terminal building, quite newly built, five tiers of Art Deco glass and concrete rising like some confection in a patisserie window, topped with the control tower under a phallic dome and flanked by viewing platforms where Parisians had once gaped dry mouthed at air shows, seen courage and skill and fiery death, or gathered to celebrate famous arrivals and departures. Deserted now, the building struck Tim as frivolous and irrelevant, as likely to be knocked flat as a construction of child's bricks.

From the direction of the bow-roofed hangars to his left, a helmeted l'Armée de l'Air motor-cyclist came towards him fast, swept round in a smooth curve and beckoned him to follow. Sitting well up above the engine with a fine all-round view, Tim had no need to weave the nose from side to side like other tail-wheel types and tracked the rider straight to the furthest hangar where men were waiting. He throttled back slowly, allowing the engine to cool, idling for a minute or two and then shut it down. Another black Citroën appeared from the depths of the hangar. Tim came back from the forward seat and slid open the rear cockpit canopy, helping his passenger to climb down the steel ladder pushed against the fuselage.

On the ground, dwarfed by the Lysander, the small man in the gabardine raincoat with the briefcase chained to his wrist was escorted to the car by two civilians but then, as he ducked down to slip onto the rear seat, he changed his mind and crossed to where Tim was talking to the ground-crew. He rattled the chain of the briefcase.

'I cannot shake you by the hand, but thank you for the *petit voyage.*'

'You are French then.'

'In this work, the less known about one the better.'

'Well,' Tim said, 'good luck.'

'Perhaps I have brought you some.'

'How's that?'

'In the present situation, Le Bourget is an improvement on Glisy, I would say.'

They walked across to the car. The man was visibly relaxed now, his mission almost over. 'I understand you are to remain here in case you are needed again. A welcome sojourn, no doubt.'

'I feel I'm letting the other chaps down.'

'It is not a question of that.' The man tapped his briefcase. 'This contains more than bureaucratic memoranda and yesterday's croissant. It is possible you have completed the most important flight of your life.'

As the car pulled away, a l'Armée de l'Air captain offered Tim a cigarette but he shook his head. 'Sorry, don't smoke.'

The officer lit a Gitane. 'My name's Lucchetti,' he said in good English. 'I'm to look after you.' He shrugged apologetically. 'It doesn't extend, I'm afraid, to a jaunt into the city.'

'That's all right. I'm hardly in the mood.'

The captain nodded at the Lysander. 'A curious bird.'

'I'm quite fond of the old bus,' Tim said. 'It's brought me through so far, anyway.'

'We'll try and make your stay here as pleasant as possible,' said Lucchetti. 'You'll find we eat quite well in the Mess. An improvement, I imagine, on what you've been used to.'

'Not at all,' said Tim. 'Our squadron's based next to a farm.' He began a fanciful description of how they had been enjoying new-laid eggs, milk still warm from the cow, cheese, all kinds of meat. 'And every morning baguettes and croissants delivered by bicycle from the village,' he added, struggling to keep his voice even at the preposterous image.

Lucchetti's response was suitably grave. '*Un vrai paradis, evidemment.*'

Tim attempted to compose himself. 'Then there's Madame Mailfert, the farmer's wife, an artist in the kitchen. Nothing's too good for her boys.' He had to pause for breath as the image of the real Madame Mailfert came to him, exaggerated like a character in a cartoon, beetle-like in pinafore and ankle-socks, face fixed in a perpetual scowl, always complaining to Farrell about some liberty taken on the Mailfert property, oblivious to the strong possibility that the Mailfert property might soon be blown to smithereens.

The French captain, with a smile that raised the left side of his mouth where the Gitane rested, waved him to be silent. 'Enough. I see that your visit here may not be such a hardship after all. We are likely, as you say, to get on.'

They heard a sudden burst of noise, a distant crackle, to Tim like Jumping Jacks on Guy Fawkes Night, hard to locate, the echoes running across the airfield; then a metallic thump, a momentary silence, the fierce revving of an engine and the squeal of tyres.

Lucchetti threw down his cigarette. 'It's possible you may have had a wasted journey.'

Beyond the main entrance to the airport the traffic on the Route Nationale was stationary. In the centre of the road, the black Citroën was wedged nose-first between the front and rear wheels of a lorry carrying live pigs, their pink bodies rearing up and jostling together, shrieking like lost souls. Steam and smoke rose from the Citroën's bonnet and the road was stained with oil and petrol, spreading across the tarmac like an ink blot. It seemed the car had crossed the busy road without attempting to turn right towards Paris, the absence of tyre-marks suggesting that the driver had not braked. Close to, it was possible to understand why: he had been dead already. Bullets had punched through the coachwork, leaving holes edged with silver where the paint had flaked off exposing the bare steel. They ran the length of the monocoque on the driver's side, a little below window height, a thorough job. Next to the driver, one of the escorts had fallen forwards into the footwell. On the rear seat his companion and the small man in the gabardine raincoat lay sprawled back, their eyes staring at the roof of the car, their mouths open. There was a great deal of blood.

Tim saw that the small man no longer had the briefcase chained to his wrist because his right hand was missing. 'Christ, who'd do such a thing?'

'The Left, the Right – who knows?' said Lucchetti. 'Not everyone opposes the Boche.'

At the main gate to the airfield the sentries told them two men had pulled onto the grass verge in a nondescript saloon car they could not name, asked for directions to Goussainville and shared a smoke and a swig or two of red wine. No, there was nothing about them that remained in the memory. Young only, perhaps late twenties, pleasant enough but one a little nervous; they'd noticed that at least. They had been warned to expect the Traction Avant with its driver and three passengers. As it approached the gate, the young men had returned to their vehicle in some haste. One sat himself behind the wheel with the engine running, which looking back they supposed was odd. The other, the nervous one, stood next to it with the passenger door open. They remembered him stooping down and reaching inside for something, but by then the Traction was at the entrance and they flagged it down because a lorry, yes, the lorry with the pigs, was coming. When the firing started they thought the airfield was being attacked and took cover, only to realise that the nervous man had run over to the Citroën with a handgun in one hand and what looked like a blade in the other; the meat cleaver that lay there on the grass with the spent cartridges. Before they could react, the assassin was back in the waiting car and it had sped off in the direction of Senlis.

That evening, Tim sat outside the terminal building in a canvas chair and watched the sun go down in a dying burst of crimson and gold that illuminated the undersides of small, drifting clouds, but soon the clouds turned grey, dark grey and then black as the last sliver of light sank below the horizon and the further reaches of the airfield were obscured by deepening shadow. He was drinking Pernod with Lucchetti and two other French officers. All three had been test pilots before the war and knew the Sutro name.

'So you wish to emulate your father,' said one. Like the others he had been surprised that Tim spoke their language well, and talked quickly, as if to catch him out.

'Not really,' Tim said. 'If it had not been for the war . . .'

'Of course, your father is much admired in France.' The man glanced at Lucchetti and there was a hint of irony in his expression. 'A true Englishman.'

'I had the pleasure of meeting him once,' said Lucchetti quickly, 'at the Professional Aviators Club in the Avenue Kléber, a reception in his honour to mark a new altitude record.'

Tim poured a little more water into his glass. 'Well, there's a coincidence for you. I was there.'

Lucchetti narrowed his eyes, trying to remember. 'His family – yes, a wife and a girl, a girl rather pink and shy in the English style. And now I recall a nervous young man who said nothing and seemed to wish he was somewhere else. He bore little resemblance to his father, in looks or manner. And that was you.'

'Down to a tee,' said Tim in English.

'It must be difficult,' said the first officer, 'to tread in the footsteps of a man like that.'

Lucchetti held up a hand. 'Enough, Girardon. Perhaps our guest does not care for the subject.'

Tim shook his head. 'It's not a problem for me. People find it interesting, a son apparently trapped in his father's life. It follows me, as I appear to follow him.' He took up the Pernod. 'Except for the war, I would not fly. It's not a passion for me and I'm not particularly good at it, but it was the natural choice because I don't like to march and I dislike boats. So yes, it must look as if I am treading in my father's footsteps, trying to fill his boots as we English say. The truth is, I have smaller feet and when this nonsense is over they'll take me in a quite different direction.'

'Bravo,' said Girardon. 'But why wait? Perhaps, Lucchetti, our friend's smaller feet can lead us in the direction of the Pigalle. I think we can assume the blockheads will not stir again tonight.'

'It's unwise to assume anything about the Boche, Gigi,' said Lucchetti. 'We've assumed too much already and see where it's got us.'

The third officer, Artaud, who had listened without much interest to the conversation and concentrated instead on lighting cigarette after cigarette, cupping his hands to shield the matches from the slight stir of air, spat out fragments of tobacco. 'Perhaps not Pigalle, but why not Mémère's place? If the Boche come knocking we can be back here and in our machines before the old girl's had time to write out the bill.' He threw the dregs of his Pernod onto the grass. 'Enough of this poison. I have an appetite for one of her omelettes and a carafe of cold Sémillon.'

The café was a mile or two from the airfield. Lucchetti drove them there fast in his Delahaye. He had raced at Le Mans and was keen to show his skill but on a tight bend he slid wide on soft tar and almost lost control.

'*Merde*!' Girardon protested. 'I'm resigned to being snuffed out by the Luftwaffe but not by a Corsican bandit with a death-wish.'

'All Corsicans have a death-wish,' Lucchetti shouted back. 'That's why we choose to be bandits.' But he continued at a more modest pace.

The café was set back from the road. In peacetime the gravel parking area had been crowded with lorries at lunchtime and the vehicles of locals in the evening. Now only a dark-coloured Peugeot stood close to the lace-curtained front door. Its driver sat at the bar drinking coffee and reading *Le Populaire*. He did not glance up when they came in.

'Interesting?' said Girardon, pointing at the newspaper.

The man turned on his bar stool and took in their uniforms. 'Not particularly. It was on the bar. Someone must have left it.'

'Still preaching Socialist balls about the Boche joining a united Europe so we can all enjoy lasting peace?'

'I don't know, Captain,' (the man had recognised the rank), 'I was only leafing through it. I've hardly read a word.' He finished his coffee quickly, threw some francs into the saucer with the bill and moved towards the door.

'Hey,' said Girardon. 'You've forgotten your newspaper.'

'I keep telling you,' said the man. 'It was on the bar.' They heard the Peugeot start up and drive away. Girardon was at the window.

'Communist swine. I'd bet a month's money that rag was his.'

When the old woman came out from the kitchen, with many kisses for her favourite fighter boys and a few, more restrained pecks for the *aviateur Anglais*, they asked if she knew the man. She told them she had never seen him before that morning. How was it that he had found a copy of *Le Populaire* on the bar? Impossible, she said, such material only began arguments. Anything forgotten of that nature was immediately cleared away. He must have had it with him when he arrived. Tim remembered Lucchetti's remark at the scene of the assassination, when he wondered who could carry out such a thing. 'The Left, the Right – who knows? Not everyone opposes the Boche.' Tim thought he knew France and understood its people, but now there was a difference, an atmosphere of uncertainty and doubt, in which suspicions could be aroused by something as simple as a man reading a newspaper and not admitting it was his.

As if he had read his thoughts, Lucchetti looked at Tim. 'This is what happens, this is what we've been brought to – everyone suspected, even a miserable little Red too scared to take his newspaper with him.'

They sat in a cubicle close to the kitchen door where they could hear the rattle of pans on the ancient range. When the old woman presented them with a creased menu and placed carafes of water and wine on the table, Lucchetti asked: 'I suppose, Mémère, you've heard what happened at the airfield today?'

'I have,' she said. 'Terrible, terrible. Why shed the blood of France when we have need of every drop? It seems we are our own enemy.'

'Well said, Mémère. Join us in a toast.' She fetched a small glass and stood beside them, smelling of cooking, tobacco and mild sweat, as Lucchetti poured wine from the carafe. 'Confusion to our enemies,' he said, 'including those we have bred ourselves.'

While they waited for their omelettes Tim looked around him. On the walls were photographs, some signed and framed in prominent positions, others pinned up carelessly in haphazard groups, yellowing with age; pilots by their machines, grim or carefree, in flying kit of all designs, and aeroplanes of every type: bi-planes, monoplanes, fighter prototypes, commercial airliners, anything that could get off the ground or crash into it. Many of the fliers, as Lucchetti pointed out, were dead. He and Girardon ran through the litany of disaster with Artaud occasionally remarking, 'Yes, that was a bad one.' Or: 'Except for that spectator with the cigar, he'd have walked away.' But living or long gone, they had all, at some time, visited Mémère's little place on the route from Le Bourget, had thumped out cheap melodies on the wormy piano or tilted the pin-table with its broken glass, its last payout a distant memory, as distant as many of the names of the fliers who stared out from the prints. But others had achieved a degree of fame, such as Lindbergh, Saint-Exupéry, Alan Cobham, Roland Garros. And Sutro.

'Here,' said Girardon. He lifted the photograph off its hook. Guv Sutro sat in the cockpit of the Schoenfelder prototype that had earned him honours in France, his face framed by his flying helmet and fixed in a half-smile, hard to interpret, triumphant or condescending. *Beating gravity* said the inscription above the big black scrawl of his signature. Girardon passed the photo to Tim, who took it in both hands. He knew that expression well, always hard to read, triumphant, condescending, both. He looked across the table at Lucchetti, whose sallow face showed sympathy.

'No escape,' the Corsican said.

Tim nodded. 'No escape.'

2

It was an overheard conversation between his mother and Mrs Sleightholme, when he supposed he was eight or nine years old, that made Tim aware, never having thought of it before, that he might be trapped in some way. Until then he had led a happy enough existence at High And Over, in term-time at Priory Grange, the small pre-preparatory school at Appledore where he did not distinguish himself in any way but was well enough liked, and during the holidays amusing himself about the estate with no shortage of friends because (he was not aware of this) he lived in a big house and had a father everyone seemed to know or wanted to know.

Most often though he spent his time with Will Kemp, who walked up from his father's garage, so was constantly on hand to play their habitual well-worn games: gallant knights in the castle ruins, pirates aboard the dinghy the gardeners used to clear the moat of weeds, Lancers on hobby horses charging the rusty cannon on the battlements that doubled as Russian guns, damming the many small streams thick with nettles and mosquitoes, munching apples in the tree house in the orchard, or Will pestering Paget as he busied himself about the garage and hangars, asking questions he ignored about the machines they had been instructed never to touch. Visitors, Tim found, and particularly small boys, were always greatly excited by the motor cars and aeroplanes standing silent in their half-dark interiors, but he had grown up with them and did not regard them as anything special. Then, sometimes, he and Will would be joined by Alice who arranged tiny crockery on picnic tables underneath the cedars on the lawn, serving them make-believe cakes and cups of tea until they grew bored and wandered off before Mother drew them back and joined the party and made it fun. Guv was rarely there and when he was did not sit down but just looked at them in his frowning way, his big hands on his hips, saying nothing until after a very short time he would turn and stride away, leaving pipe-smoke where he had been, like a memory or, Tim sometimes thought obscurely, rather like a hanging threat.

On the hot, still August day that Tim heard his mother and Mrs Sleightholme in conversation, he and Will had been picking wild strawberries that lined both sides of the tradesmen's drive, their mouths wet and pink from the juice. Tim had collected a handful for Mother and Alice and led the way back up the slope towards the house, past the stone fountain spouting cool white water that pattered on the surface of the green pool where carp moved lazily in the heat, on up the broad sandstone steps to the terrace and past the windows of his father's study where bees were busy in the climbing roses. Here he always felt a moment of apprehension, anxiety that he might have disturbed Guv in some way, prompting one of those sudden bellows of annoyance that made his stomach shrink. He did not understand why this might be, only that in some way he was an irritation. But on this day his father was away, 'in town' as they used to say without explaining where that town might be, and he skipped past the study windows without a moment of concern, feeling the sun fierce on his neck and arms and back and legs, hot through the thin stuff of his light shirt and shorts, as if it was shining particularly bright and hard, as if a cloud had passed, releasing a sudden warmth. Will had lagged behind, poking an ants' nest with a stick, and as

Tim approached the south terrace with its view of the jumbled ruin of the old castle in its little valley, he heard Mrs Sleightholme say his name and paused.

'Poor Timothy, one feels such sympathy for him. The little chap will find it hard to go through life carrying such a burden of achievement. For an only son, the captain is a quite impossible act to follow.'

He heard his mother's quiet voice. 'Tim has great qualities of his own. Not everyone's cut out to be a man of action.'

'Oh, of course,' said Mrs Sleightholme. 'How boring life would be. But then, how boring it would be without our great men.'

'You consider my husband a great man?'

'Oh, undoubtedly.' Mrs Sleightholme sounded taken aback. 'Don't you?' She laughed. 'Oh, I see, you're teasing.'

'More tea, Mrs Sleightholme, before you go?'

'That would be delightful. I hope you didn't think . . .'

'I assure you, Mrs Sleightholme, thinking didn't come into it.'

Tim smiled, knowing that somehow his mother had come out of the exchange rather well; she often did, slipping in a final remark that when considered later seemed to settle the matter very neatly. But still, he wondered what a burden of achievement might be and why he had, in Mrs Sleightholme's view, to carry it through life.

'Ah, here is your boy,' Mrs Sleightholme said as he took a breath and walked forward onto the terrace with the wild strawberries in his hand.

'Hello, Mrs Sleightholme.' Behind him, Will Kemp slipped into view.

'Ah, the garage lad. How nice. Rough, boyish games, no doubt.' There was a trace of disapproval in the woman's tone.

Tim had no response to that but fixed his face in a meaningless smile, not unfriendly but remote, not readable by adults. He felt a wetness in his hand. The strawberries were crushed and seeping in his palm. He formed a knuckle and hid the mess behind his back. His mother was saying, 'No need for you to stay, you chaps. Mrs Sleightholme's going soon, after she's finished her cup of tea,'

Alice appeared from the darkness of the house, stepping neatly out through the open French windows, narrowing her eyes against the glare. A daisy-chain rested lightly on the fine gold of her hair.

'Alice,' said Mrs Sleightholme. 'A vision. Delightful.'

Alice looked at Will. 'Hello.'

'Hello, Alice.'

They looked at each other, unaware of anyone else, then Alice turned and went back inside the house.

'Well,' said Mrs Sleightholme, 'I must be—'

Tim's mother stood up quickly. 'I'll see you to your motor.'

'Be sure, my dear, to put my little proposition to the Captain. The Rye Recreationists would love to hear about his exploits at first-hand, if he would honour us with his presence.'

'I really can't promise, Mrs Sleightholme, he has so many calls on his time. But I will certainly ask.'

'Sweet of you, my dear. What lovely children.' She glanced at Tim. 'I hope you didn't mind . . .'

'Don't give it another thought.'

The two women moved along the terrace towards the driveway at the front of the house where a Daimler and its driver waited. The man was studying the sky, shielding his eyes with a gloved hand. He pointed up, tracing with his forefinger the progress of two biplanes against the clouds. They reduced height, their engines not so noisy now and soon they were so close Tim could hear the air whispering over their wings. For a moment they were lost to sight, then suddenly swooped up from behind the woodland, wing-to-wing, circled several times over the house so low it seemed they must touch the chimney-pots before landing on the meadow that served as an airfield beyond the hangars.

'I say!' cried Mrs Sleightholme. 'How frightfully exciting.'

When Tim and the others reached the landing place, the aeroplanes were still moving, their engines roaring in sudden bursts of power, their rudders flapping from side to side, slipping slowly across the close-cropped grass, making Tim think of the big carp that sidled through the green waters of the fountain pool. Close to the shade of the hangars, both machines spun around together and their engines stopped, freezing their propellers. The men at the controls waved briefly to each other, threw back the straps of their harness and jumped down. Tim recognised his father and thought he knew the other pilot too.

As he came towards them Guv seemed unsteady on his feet, as if he had been a long time in the air. When he pulled off his leather helmet, his hair was tangled and dark with sweat. 'What's all this? A welcoming committee?' He jerked a thumb at his companion. 'You'll remember Wilkie,' he said to nobody in particular. The man nodded and grinned, knuckling his eyes. He had been to High And Over before, but in a car. He had brought a lady with him that time, Tim recalled, who laughed a lot at very little and Mother did not like her. His real name was Wilkinson-Clark and he had been with Guv during the war.

Tim, his mother, Mrs Sleightholme and Will had gathered in an uncertain, awkward little group. Only Alice, who had run down from the house, went forward and took her father's hand and, craning up on tiptoe, kissed him on an oily cheek. Tim noticed that Mrs Sleightholme had said nothing for ages, her straight-across mouth slightly open, her eyes shining behind her spectacles and fixed on his father in a peculiar way, like one of those women in robes who crouched in the corners of the dusty paintings that hung about the house, adoring Jesus doing a miracle or stuck up on His cross. When his mother said to Guv: 'Mrs Sleightholme has come to ask a favour,' Tim noticed that their visitor went bright red as if she had been naughty and said in a funny, low voice, 'Oh, it doesn't matter, really. Oh, please I beg of you, don't trouble the Captain now.' She sounded like one of Alice's timid friends trying to be on their best behaviour.

Guv, however, paid no attention to what she was saying; in fact, showed no sign that he was even aware of her existence. Instead, he and Wilkie started to recount the story of how they had purchased their aeroplanes that morning, as casually, it seemed, as if you might buy a toy. Tim could see they were full of it. They had met up at the Royal Flying Corps Club. They had been in London for days; so

London was 'town'. 'Who should turn up but old Toddy?' Guv said. He kept shooting looks at Mother as if to see her reaction. 'And the old reprobate tells us they're selling off de Havilland DH4s at Hendon for five pounds apiece. DH4s! I ask you! One of the finest crates on the Western Front. So off we go. Well, we couldn't say no. Handed over our fivers and here we are, the jolly old GAF.'

'What's the GAF?' said Tim.

'Guv's Air Force, you silly blighter. Tell you what, let's Wilkie and me take you youngsters up for a flip. Show you what you've been missing.' Will moved forward promptly and the Guv said, 'Hah!' in an approving way, but Tim stayed where he was, beside his mother. Her hand was resting on his shoulder. She called across to the Guv: 'Are you in a fit state?'

'What are you getting at? Didn't you see that touch-down?' He began to mutter under his breath. Tim heard Jesus mentioned several times.

Will was already shaking hands with Wilkinson-Clark and climbing into the rear cockpit of his DH4 where the air-gunner used to sit. Tim pulled away from the gentle restraint of his mother's hand. 'I have to go.' He had flown with the Guv before, had experienced some of the basic moves: stall turns, dives and even a loop, but he sensed, in this war machine, that this time it was going to be different. There was something wild in his father's manner, almost gleeful but mixed with anger too.

The two light bombers climbed away from High And Over towards Rye Bay. They flew quite close together. Tim could see Will looking across at him, strange in goggles that were too big for him. Below, ranks of white-tipped waves were rolling into the shingle beaches that curved away to Dungeness; inland the Romney marshland looked as flat as the Channel itself. Over his shoulder, as he twisted against his harness, he could see Rye on its hill-top, the houses huddled round the church as if they still feared the French.

He began to relax a little, soothed by the vibration of the engine that ran through every part of the aeroplane and every part of him. Then the nose dropped away, the engine began to scream and he felt himself pressed into his seat, his chin forced onto his breastbone, hardly able to breathe. A shadow flashed across them. Wilkie's machine passed so close he could see the wrinkles on the canvas of its tail-plane and the blodges of paint where the squadron numbers had been brushed over. Now his head fell back as the aeroplane pulled up into a vertical climb, the sky revolving above his head. It hung for a moment, its propeller catching the sun in a silver whirl, then tilted over and dropped towards the sea. They chased each other round the sky, twisting and zooming, climbing, stalling, spinning out, trying every trick that Guv and Wilkie knew, tricks that had brought them through the war. Then, for the tiniest moment he saw the other DH4 directly ahead and heard the Guv shout out above the engine roar: 'Banga-banga-banga-bang! Got you, you bloody bastard. Down you bloody well go.'

They turned towards Pett Level, and Guv came low across the harbour mouth, so low Tim saw the faces of a trawler crew making for the open sea. Guv put on a display and, to Tim, the world went mad, a kaleidoscope of sea and sky and cliffs and beach, the colours all mixed up and blurred, like a painting left out in the rain. It seemed impossible that in the forward cockpit his father's hand was firmly on the joystick, his feet kicking on the pedals, that he had complete control, imposing his will like a cowboy breaking in a wild horse.

The violence of the aerobatics pounded Tim against the cockpit sides until he felt he could not stand it any more, until he felt his whole frame was about to break, as if his head, as heavy as a cannon-ball, might come right off. Several times the air was forced from his lungs, coming out in a kind of scream that he could not hold back, so loud his father looked back and shouted something he could not hear. Finally, as they levelled out and turned inland, Tim found he had been sick, his body and the cockpit sticky with the stuff, pink mush from wild strawberries and other things, more mush and undigested fragments from food he had eaten earlier in the day.

Back on the ground, his father pulled himself upright in his cockpit. He was triumphant. 'Now that's how we came through against the Boche – outflew the buggers plain and simple. By God, that was grand. Did you see me nail old Wilkie? Lucky for him I wasn't one of Richthofen's Fokker Tripehounds.' Tim did not say anything, just staring back at him miserably, and Guv frowned. 'What's up? Didn't enjoy it? I rather thought you must have, when I heard you hollering.' He saw the vomit. 'Oh, good grief, you useless little washout.' He jumped down from the wing, shaking his head, pulling off his gloves.

Wilkinson-Clark had hurried over, Will Kemp a few paces behind. 'This kid's a blessed natural,' he said to Guv. 'Wish I'd had him in the back seat in France. Talk about a cool head. He took to it like a duck to water. How about your boy?'

Guv barely interrupted his stride. 'Do you feel as dead as you should?'

'Do *you*?' said Wilkinson-Clark. 'We let you get on my tail so the youngster here could let you have it with the jolly old Lewis guns. Thought you might have remembered that. You were a goner, old chum, before you had time to squeeze the trigger.' He looked across to where the crown of Tim's still head projected above the cockpit rim of Guv's machine. 'I say, is your boy all right?'

'Leave him,' Guv said. 'He can sort himself out.' He hurried on, passed the others without a word and vanished inside the house. Wilkinson-Clark went over to the DH4 and looked into Tim's cockpit.

'Oh crikey, what bad luck. Well, don't feel too badly, old lad. Happens to us all at some time or another.'

'Did it happen to my father?' asked Tim.

'Must have, old lad, must have.'

Tim's mother was there, and Alice, but the Daimler of Mrs Sleightholme was moving down the drive. Will walked alongside them for a bit, as they made their way to the kitchen to wash Tim down. He looked very pleased with himself, Tim noticed, and he was pleased for him because he had done well. But he envied him the praise he had earned, instead of being called a washout. He supposed he must be and wondered if Will thought he was too. There was something in Will's faint smile that suggested he might. For the first time in their lives he felt there was a barrier between them, as though something had been revealed that could never be forgotten. Then he was in the kitchen and Alice had been told to go and his clothes were being unbuttoned and he felt the coldness of fresh water on his face and body. His mother was saying: 'I don't know what your father was thinking of.'

'I know what he thinks now,' Tim said. 'He thinks I'm a useless little washout.'

'Of course he doesn't.'

'He does. He said so.'

'He was angry.'

'He's always angry. I let him down. I'm always letting him down. Why can't I be like Will?'

'Don't be ridiculous,' said his mother, as though she was suddenly short of breath. 'Why should you want to be like Will? You're your father's son. He loves you.'

Tim doubted that. He also doubted whether he loved his father. He admired him, certainly, but he wasn't alone there; it seemed the whole world did. And he wanted to win his approval, without really understanding why. But love? Well, he knew that everyone was meant to love their fathers, but because he wasn't sure he did he locked away his misgivings in a small compartment in his mind, putting them down to the kind of shabby brooding no doubt typical of useless little washouts.

3

In the café of Mémère, sitting in its big empty car park on the route from Le Bourget, the old café-owner turned on the crackly wireless on a shelf behind the bar so Tim and the three French pilots could listen to music as they ate. But it did not last long because an announcer came on to report that the Allied campaign to halt the German advance was achieving great success thanks to the characteristic *élan vital* displayed by the French army, and that many casualties had been inflicted. His voice was shrill with patriotic fervour.

Arnaud snorted. 'Only days ago, a short-wave station in Paris told us twenty-five thousand Boche had been wiped out in a frontal attack on the Maginot Line, when everyone knows they outflanked it.'

The bulletin concluded with the 'Marseillaise'. Then a softer melody began, Rina Ketty and 'J'attendrai'. 'Now that,' said Arnaud, 'is closer to the truth. We wait.'

In the hangars at Le Bourget, Lucchetti showed Tim his Morane fighter, dumpier, less elegant than a Spitfire but still useful-looking in its camouflage of matt khaki, a vertical Tricolor on its rudder, large roundels on its fuselage and wings. Tim settled himself in the cockpit and Lucchetti climbed up and leaned in explaining the controls. After the Lysander it seemed compact and handy. 'As different from my Lizzie as chalk and cheese.'

'Don't be too envious,' said Lucchetti. 'In my brief acquaintance with air combat I've made an uncomfortable discovery, that the 406 can't touch a Messerschmitt. It's eighty kilometres an hour slower, has inferior weapons, and armour that would hardly protect you from a child's pea-shooter. It does have one advantage though: it can out-turn a 109, very useful when he's trying to get on your tail, but not quite what the designer had in mind.' He turned to slip down from the wing. 'Our task is to defend Paris. Déjà vu, eh? Twenty-five years ago, they established this place for just that purpose.' He made a puffing sound with his lips, derisive, very Gallic. 'So far, I must admit we've had it easy. The Boche are mostly busy elsewhere. But we've got no illusions about our prospects. We'll do our best. And if we don't come through, at least our snaps will be on show in Mémère's café, along with all the other heroes.' Tim was on the ground beside him now. Lucchetti patted his shoulder.

'Your picture should be there as well, *mon copain*. If you have one, I'll make sure the old girl pins it up.'

'Can't help you there,' Tim said. 'Anyway, I'm no hero.'

'Nonsense. I wouldn't take off in that flying greenhouse of yours for a bet. And I've flown most things that have sprouted wings.'

Tim remembered the photograph of the FB5s lined up at Chézy-au-Bois, his father bristling with aggression in the foreground. He felt in his tunic pocket for the torn photograph he had retrieved from the mud and glued back together. 'How about this?'

'Ah, your father. No good, I'm afraid. Only one picture each, strict rule, even for Lindbergh.' Lucchetti looked quizzical. 'You wish to escape, but you carry that.'

'Not for sentiment's sake,' Tim said. 'Pure curiosity. I grew up with this image. When I got posted to Glisy, down the road from Chézy-au-Bois, I borrowed the snap from my father's collection with the idea of seeing the place for myself. Now I suppose it's become a kind of talisman, like a favourite silk scarf or a St Christopher charm given you by a girl – stuff you think might give you some protection, the kind of superstitious nonsense that plagues us all.'

'And did you go to Chézy-au-Bois?'

'Oh, yes,' said Tim. 'Of course, it's just fields, no trace of anything at all. Why should there be? Even the locals seem to have forgotten, or wish to. Understandable I suppose, considering what your country's gone through. Odd though, finding myself standing where the old man stood. He always seemed such a giant to me when I was a kid, and there I was in the same place at pretty much the same age, and in a war and flying, and he didn't seem so big after all.'

'Fathers are not big,' said Lucchetti. 'For a while we're little, that's all. But because they preceded us, they expect us to look up to them, without question. They assume they've got the right to dictate that we behave in such and such a way while they behave as they like. Mine, for example, is a philandering swine who deserted us all when we were still in our prams and gambled away a fortune until the money ran out and he came back, begging my mother to forgive him which, like a fool, she did. Now he says he is proud of me, thinks we are *simpatico*, sees in me what he knows of himself.'

'Does he realise he's wrong?'

'He's not wrong. He's right. I share many of his traits. There lies my difficulty.'

'Mine is the reverse,' Tim said. 'When my old man looks at me, he sees absolutely nothing of himself. How could he? He's the man of action, universally admired, and I'm just an ordinary type trying to do his bit.'

'I regret I can't agree that your father's universally admired,' said Lucchetti.

'I know he's got his critics.'

'I don't deny his achievements in the air, but there are those in France who say he has not always behaved as an English gentleman should. He made some unfortunate references to our country when he was presented with the Blériot medal. His views caused great consternation, particularly as he had taken to keeping questionable company at the time. I have a cousin in the foreign ministry and we were aware of certain connections.'

'His views didn't go very deep,' said Tim. 'He tended to see things in black and white. It's different now.'

'May I suggest,' said Lucchetti, 'that we agree our fathers are beyond explanation? And so not worth another thought? To hell with them both. Wait here.' A few minutes later he was back with a small Leica. 'Against your machine is best, I think.'

'What's this in aid of?'

'Mémère's display, of course! You may think of yourself as an ordinary type but she considered you the epitome of the *aviateur Anglais* – gallant, modest, most charming and a number of other things I won't embarrass you with.'

'Good Lord.'

'Does that surprise you? Now, over by the prop, if you please. And for God's sake don't smile. It can be taken for idiocy or conceit.'

Next morning, a neat young military attaché drove out from the British Embassy in the rue du Faubourg St Honoré and found Tim with the Lysander carrying out a pre-flight check. 'Everything tickety-boo?'

'So far, thanks.'

'I'm Dixon,' said the attaché. 'I've got some orders for you.' He passed over a sealed envelope. 'You're to read them in my presence, confirm that you understand and make any observations you may have – as a pilot, that is.'

Tim scanned the few paragraphs quickly. 'Northolt? I don't want to go to Northolt.'

'Oh, well it's all off then. I'll simply tell the powers-that-be that Pilot Officer Sutro doesn't want to go to Northolt. Sorry to have bothered you.'

'Look, my squadron's in action and I'm kicking my heels here. It's a waste of a pilot and a machine, when we could be doing something useful.'

'You've already done something useful,' said the attaché, 'delivering a party to Le Bourget.'

'Hardly useful,' Tim said. 'The party, as you call him came to an untimely end before he'd gone a hundred yards.'

'Oh, we recovered the documents our friend was carrying soon enough. We rather suspected something of the sort might be on the cards. Bit late on the scene, unfortunately, slight mix-up back at base – lost in translation, as you might say. The main thing is the post was popped into the correct pigeon-hole.' The attaché became confidential. 'You'll understand it's jolly useful to have a gash aeroplane on hand, particularly as things are. There's always the need to convey certain people from A to B in reasonable security with the minimum of delay.'

Tim remembered Guv's comment when he completed training on Lysanders at Old Sarum. 'Little more than driving a bus.'

The attaché was regarding him with a trace of sympathy. 'We're not just fighting the enemy in the front line, you know, keen as you may be to get back to your chums.'

'So who's my fare this time? Another spy?'

'Agent, old boy. Not spy. Credit where credit's due. But no, a different sort of fish on this occasion.'

'I want an assurance that after this I'll be operational again.'

'No can do. Like the rest of us you'll follow orders. You're not a special case, I'm afraid, despite your name.'

A few hours later, Tim was advised by the military attaché that his passenger had arrived, no agent this time but a French officer whose sky-blue *képi* and badges of rank marked him as a colonel of light cavalry, immaculate in well-pressed breeches and leather boots that disappointingly lacked spurs. He carried a briefcase that Tim noted with some relief was not chained to his wrist, and a small valise as if he was bound for a weekend in the country; or another country.

Lucchetti and the others had come to watch the take-off. The cavalry colonel was already in the Lysander's rear seat, Tim helping him to pull his harness tight. His *képi* was still in place but he was finding it difficult to maintain his dignity, tilted backwards in this weird and unwarlike British machine with its extravagant gull-wings that loomed above his head and looked as if they might snap off at the roots.

'He's like grand-papa, waiting for a fairground ride to start,' said Girardon.

'Little wonder he's nervous,' said Arnaud. 'He's heard how these devices have been dealt with by the Boche.'

Tim climbed down from the cockpit and walked across to the l' Armée de l'Air pilots. Lucchetti handed him a photograph. 'A souvenir. I developed it last night. I've printed another for Mémère. Let me know when you're next this way. We'll share a *pression* and you can admire yourself up there in her hall of fame.'

For a moment Tim felt a touch of satisfaction, like being told he was in line for a gong. Then he visualised his picture pinned up at Mémère's in some obscure corner, yellowing and curled at the edges, soiled with fly-dirts and tobacco smoke, picked out by an occasional befuddled patron: 'And who the hell is that?' But it was nice of Lucchetti to think of it.

'It was nice of you to think of it,' he said to Lucchetti, and slipped the print into his tunic pocket along with the damaged snap of Guv at Chézy-au-Bois.

The military attaché had not joined the group. Now he walked forward and shook Tim's hand. 'Happy landings,' he said quietly, glancing over his shoulder at the nearby French pilots, 'and remember, keep well away from Dieppe.' Earlier he had studied Tim's flight-plan:

a route from Le Bourget via Beauvais to the Somme estuary near Abbeville, before picking up the English coast at Eastbourne and so on to Northolt. 'Abbeville won't do, I'm afraid.'

'Really? Why?'

'Why do you think?'

'Good grief, you mean the Jerries are already there?'

'Keep your voice down, old boy. Don't want to spread alarm and despondency before it's absolutely necessary.'

When the Lysander climbed away from Le Bourget and turned onto a heading for Rouen, much further west, Tim and the French colonel were given a final view of the French capital, its landmarks shimmering in a haze of heat but still distinct; the white outline of the Sacré-Coeur on the city's highest point, the Eiffel Tower rising from the Left Bank of the Seine, the Arc de Triomphe celebrating another war in another century. The colonel removed his *képi* and rubbed his face vigorously with a linen handkerchief, not looking at Tim but staring back as Paris fell behind them, apparently reluctant to turn away, as if storing the prospect for some future time; as if he was saying goodbye.

They passed over the French coast at St Valéry-en-Caux. From 15,000 feet they could see that far to the east the sky was black with smoke and even above the engine noise heard the thud of artillery. The tiny outlines of aircraft wheeled and dived like gnats on a summer afternoon but they stayed a long way off, too occupied to notice the single Lysander that seemed to hang motionless above the Channel despite its airspeed indicator showing 180 knots. Below, boats left creamy wakes against the deep blue swell as they passed between the Straits – but whether merchantmen or warships, it was impossible to tell.

Less than an hour after leaving the harbour of St Valéry, they picked up the cliffs at Beachy Head, the lighthouse ringed by its usual circle of breaking waves, and as they flew above the Downs, the Sussex countryside began to expand before them, green and quite unchanged. One of those red-tiled villages, Tim knew, was Alfriston where Guv had spent his boyhood, flying his first glider from the great hill High

And Over that had given its name to Saxonshore, altered on a whim when the estate came into this father's hands.

He reduced height, easing down to 5,000 feet, low enough to smell the earth baked in the heat of early summer. Outside Firle, cricketers paused in their match to watch him pass overhead and a steam engine pulling three small carriages trundled along the railway line between Polegate and Lewes. Everything was fixed and normal, as though what lay behind had been an illusion; as if he had woken from a disturbing dream, a bad one, the kind that left you disorientated and in a sweat, in which everything had been so real it took you time to regain your senses, that almost made you laugh out loud with relief except that a vestige of horror remained so you didn't laugh but just felt grateful that it hadn't been true after all. Except he was awake and it had been true; was all too true across that short expanse of water and soon, maybe very soon, it might be true of what was happening here.

At Northolt, the French colonel was met by a Humber staff car. He thanked Tim briefly for the flight. 'I was at Verdun,' he said. 'How could we ever forget the price?'

At his elbow, a Ministry man who did not introduce himself fidgeted impatiently. 'We must get on, sir.'

The Humber moved smoothly away towards the main gate and the trunk road to London, much as the Citroën had rolled towards the main gate at Le Bourget and the Route Nationale to Paris. For an instant Tim's ears seemed to ring with phantom gunshots, but then the moment was gone. Such things did not happen here.

In the adjutant's office he was told he was to fly on to Hawkinge, to rejoin his squadron. 'So they're there then?'

'We understand so. If not, they soon will be.' The flight lieutenant was in his forties, spectacled, with thinning hair grey at the temples; on his tunic below his pilot's wings was stitched the medal ribbon of the DSO. An old Royal Flying Corps hand then, returned to the service in time of war. He noticed Tim's interest. 'Grounded this time, I'm afraid.' He touched the spectacles. 'Damned shame. Still, got to let you young 'uns have a go.'

136

He studied Tim's movement order, frowning, before he handed it across his desk. 'Sutro, eh? Any relation?'

'Afraid not.'

'Unusual name. Might be some connection, back in the days of yore.'

'You never know.'

'Some chums of mine flew with the feller in France.'

'Well,' said Tim, 'I'd best press on.'

The adjutant was reluctant to end the conversation, bored behind his desk. 'I hear you chaps have had a rough time of it out there.'

'What else do you hear, sir?'

'Things look pretty sticky generally, but no doubt it'll turn out all right in the end. It always does.'

'Any idea who my passenger was? He seemed a bit keyed up.'

'I get the impression that the *entente cordiale* is less *cordiale* than it used to be. No doubt he's been summoned for a good old British kick up the backside by the PM, to take back to Paris with him.'

At Hawkinge there was no sign of the squadron. The order had gone out and been acknowledged some days before, but nothing had been heard since. The situation was confused. Many aircraft were landing from sorties across the Channel supporting an army rumoured to be retreating, forced back to the sea by the power of the German attack. They were Hurricanes mostly, quickly refuelled and returned to battle. Others were returning from airfields in France where, as part of the Advanced Striking Force, they ran the risk of being overrun; Blenheims, Battles and the occasional Lysanders of other squadrons, many dispersed to satellite airfields to be returned to full strength with replacement aircraft and crews.

Tim's machine was pushed into a hangar for a duty inspection, regarded by the ground crew as something of a phenomenon for coming through the Battle of France without a scratch. Tim shrugged. 'Luck of the draw. Just hope to heavens the others make it back.' Not that he imagined many of the chaps were left; perhaps now none at all.

That evening in the Mess he drank too much and talked very little, diffident in the presence of the fighterpilots who had been in action over France several times that day, re-enacting dogfights with their hands, telling tall tales and laughing, always laughing with more than a hint of desperation. It was much like a session in his own squadron; perhaps all squadrons were the same. But now he sat in a corner part-hidden by the piano, like an old man watching youngsters at play, nostalgic for his childhood days. As he turned the beer glass in his hands he also turned over in his mind many things that vanished as quickly as they occurred to him, as if his brain was overloaded. He put it down to fatigue.

Events took their usual course in a dense fug of cigarette smoke infused with the reek of beer and sweat; the bawled indecent songs, the jubilant hoots that marked the smash of glasses, the settling of rules or lack of them for an impromptu game of rugby with the squadron leader's service cap. Tim found himself detected. 'More hands to the pump, old boy. Don't sit there like a bloody wallflower. Get stuck in.' Reluctantly he got stuck in and quickly found himself pressed down under a scrum of struggling bodies, unable to move or breathe. When he finally squirmed free, gasping for air, his lungs empty, his right knee suddenly buckled under him and he almost fell. The room began to revolve and he reached for the piano for support, realising he was more than a little tight. He mumbled his excuses while he still had the power of speech and weaved his way through the velvety darkness thick with the scent of trodden grass to the billet where they had found him a bed.

He slept uneasily, seeing figures that moved towards him like strangers approaching in the street, distant at first, anonymous, then close enough to identify: Will Kemp, Fred Hirst, the passenger at Glisy, Captain Lucchetti, old Mémère, the cavalry colonel with his sky-blue *képi* still square on his head, the adjutant at Northolt. They passed without a hint of recognition although he tried to catch their eye.

Once, near dawn, he dreamed he was standing in the nacelle of a Vickers FB5, rocking to its motion, trying to stay balanced as behind him the pilot struggled with the controls. The sides of the forward cockpit came up to his knees. Only by grasping the Lewis gun on its swivelling mount could he stop himself from falling into space. He heard shouting, and when he turned he saw the pilot was Guv, his eyes bulging behind his goggles, his face contorted, jabbing a gauntleted finger upwards, pointing, pointing at something he could not see, something in a blaze of light that must be diving down on them. He tried to spin the Lewis gun round to meet the attack but swayed and almost toppled out of the nacelle. 'You useless little washout,' Guv was bellowing. 'You useless bloody washout.' His words were drowned by a burst of machine-gun fire, above and to the left, coming from the blaze of light. Tim wrenched at the Lewis gun but it jammed on its mount, its barrel pointing directly at the Guv. His finger trembled on the trigger. Then something struck him hard in the leg and he started to fall.

A voice was speaking quietly by his ear. 'I know you're not on ops, sir,' the orderly said, 'but the gentlemen in this hut are on Readiness so I've been detailed to rouse them from their pits. I doubted you'd sleep through the racket when they're up and about so I've brought you a morning cuppa.'

'That's very decent of you. What on earth's the time?'

'Three-thirty, sir.'

Tim took the mug and balanced it on his chest. His eyelids seemed stuck together. The orderly was moving along the line of beds to a chorus of abuse. Further down the billet some hearties were already on their feet, towels around their necks, heading for the washhouse; the heavier sleepers groaning and pulling blankets over their heads. But in less than twenty minutes they were all in their flying kit and gone.

Tim finished his tea, rinsing his mouth with the stuff to rid it of the sour taste of ale and tried to doze a little longer but when he tried to move into a more comfortable position he felt a sudden, fierce pain in his right knee; of course, the wound he received manning the Lewis gun in the FB5. Then his senses returned. That damned scrum.

Throwing back the thin blanket he saw the joint was swollen and blotched a bilious pink. When he pushed himself up and tried to stand the leg seemed about to collapse, as though a hinge had been fixed behind the knee, ready to fold at any moment.

At sick-quarters the medical officer manipulated the limb in all directions, Tim wincing on the couch. 'I don't think anything's broken, but you can't be sure without surgery. Most likely damage to a cartilage. What I can tell you with some certainty is that it's likely to get worse before it gets better. So no more flying for you for the time being. Keep the weight off it as much as possible and find yourself a stick.'

'How long will I be out?'

'No idea, old chap. But don't be like most of the boys and try to get back in the cockpit too soon. It's not just your own life that you put at risk, you know.'

Tim couldn't resist. 'I thought that was the general idea.'

'Off with you, you cheeky young pup,' said the medical officer. 'I'm marking you down for sick leave. Well earned, from what I gather, knee or no knee. You may not be aware of it, but you're pretty done up. Fourteen days should put you right, then I'll see you again. Meanwhile, we'll keep you in the picture about your squadron. You can catch up with it when you're fit.'

4

The journey to Rye was a slow business; first, a lift to Folkestone in one of the motor pool lorries, then on by rail to Ashford and finally a dawdle along the branch line to Rye with frequent, unexplained stops under bridges, between embankments and outside stations. The more exposed delays created some anxiety, passengers craning their necks through carriage windows listening for the shriek of Stukas.

Sharing his first-class compartment with an elderly, genteel couple and a sub-lieutenant in the Royal Navy Volunteer Reserve, who slumped in the far corner snoring, smelling of spirits, Tim sat quietly reading *Punch*, resigned to whatever Fate might choose to toss his way, even an ignoble demise on the 17.00 hours stopper. He turned the page: two cartoon golfers, one holding the flag by the distant hole, the other about to putt; next to him, a German paratrooper. Putter, peevishly: 'Will you stop rustling that parachute!' He managed a dry chuckle as the train drew into Hamstreet, still ten miles short of its destination.

A young woman looked in through the open window. 'Would you mind awfully?' she said. 'I know it's first class but it's only a short hop to Rye, and the other compartments are packed to the gunnels. Don't give me away, there's a pet.' She saw his right leg, stretched out and supported on the heel, and the walking stick with its rubber ferule. 'No, don't move. I can easily skip across.'

She looked familiar to him despite the uniform of the Women's Land Army: breeches with woollen socks and lace-up shoes, a gabardine raincoat unbuttoned revealing a lumpish green pullover, a mannish shirt and tie and something close to a pork-pie hat. She sat down opposite and studied him through narrowed eyes; rather pretty eyes. 'I say,' she said, 'it's Tim, isn't it? I'm Jennifer, Jennifer Sleightholme.'

'Good Lord, so you are.'

'Don't say it like that. I know this outfit's frightful, but at least it shows I'm doing my bit.'

'What is your bit?'

'Oh, you name it. General farmwork, you know – caring for livestock, ploughing with horses, picking fruit, digging up potatoes, killing rats. It's jolly hard work but rather fun once you get used to it.'

'How do you kill rats?'

'We feed them flour and sugar Tuesday to Thursday and Warfarin on Friday. Monday we collect the corpses.'

'Good Lord.'

'You keep saying that. I thought you fighter boys said "good show" and "wizard prang".'

The train was pulling very slowly away from the station. 'I'm not a fighter boy,' Tim said.

'You look like one,' said Jennifer Sleightholme, nodding at his leg.

'Not sustained in the line of duty, I'm afraid – an idiotic accident.'

'But Alice wrote to me that you were over in France.'

'I was.'

'Aren't things awfully bad out there? We hear such tales.'

'Rye doesn't change then, the same old chit-chat.'

'Oh, it's pretty general, you'll find. Everyone's expecting an invasion.'

'I don't think it's quite got to that.'

'I'm glad you think so. Mother's talking of moving us all to relatives in Caithness. And please, don't say "Good Lord" again.'

'Bad show.'

'That's better.'

The train was passing across the Walland Marsh. Inland, the evening sun caught the stagnant waters of the Royal Military Canal, dug out as a line of defence against the Napoleonic army that never came.

'It's rather odd,' said Tim. 'I was thinking about your mother only the other day.'

'How nice.'

'Yes,' he said. He recalled it had not been nice, not nice at all. 'How is she?'

'Making Daddy's life hell. She thinks he should be back in uniform.' She took a small packet of Woodbine out of her raincoat pocket and a box of matches. The elderly gentleman cleared his throat and tapped the *No Smoking* sign. 'Oh, sorry, awful habit. I'm afraid us Land Girls aren't permitted many vices.'

Leaning his head a little to one side, Tim could see Rye perched on its hilltop, occasionally obscured by the grey smoke streaming back from the engine. Something rose in his throat.

As the train began to lose speed, jolting over the Guldeford level crossing, the naval officer woke up. He stared across at Jennifer approvingly. 'Why, it's Farmer Giles's favourite daughter.' He didn't wait for a response but peered out of the window. 'Where on earth are we? Is this Brighton?'

'Rye,' Tim said.

The officer ignored him. 'I'm joining my ship,' he said to Jennifer.

'Really?'

He pointed at the undulant gold stripes on his cuff. 'I'm in the wavy navy, training to be a Guns – HO, of course.'

'HO?'

'Hostilities Only. Then back to insurance. Just hope this business doesn't go on too long. I'm prone to sea-sickness. Although I'll be all right on the good ship HMS *King Alfred*.'

'Why's that?'

'It's not a ship. Used to be the municipal baths and recreation centre on Hove seafront. The Navy took it over in thirty-nine and designated it a training vessel. It's even got a captian.' He sat up. 'I say, you wouldn't care to give me your phone number, would you?'

'No.'

'Thought not. Didn't mind my asking?'

'Not at all.'

'Never know, do you?'

'You don't, do you?'

The RNVR man tipped his cap over his eyes, snuggled back into his corner and pretended to go to sleep. The elderly gentleman regarded him reprovingly. 'Extraordinary behaviour,' he murmured, glancing at Tim.

'Extraordinary times, sir.'

'Aren't they just?' said Jennifer.

Outside Rye station they stood by the taxi rank. 'Well,' said Tim, 'I know you're only up by the church, but may I drop you off?'

'No, thanks. I'd rather walk than be rattled to death over those cobbles.'

Tim lost his balance slightly, adjusting the shoulder-strap of his haversack and awkward on his stick. Jennifer Sleightholme steadied him with a firm hand. 'Do *you* want my phone number?'

'Yes, please,' he said.

She wrote it out for him on a scrap torn from her Woodbine packet. 'Didn't mind my asking?'

'Not at all.'

They laughed easily together and she went up on her toes and kissed him lightly on one cheek. Then she hurried off without looking back until, crossing Cinque Ports Street into the steep incline of Market Road, she stopped, turned and gave him a joyous wave; the kind of wave that reminded him of days spent by the sea, when you were waiting on the sands for a particular chum to arrive and suddenly the chum appeared, there on top of the dunes and about to rush down to join you, with the whole summer ahead. He dropped his case and waved back. He had known her only slightly as Alice's friend. Now it was as if they had just found each other.

George Frith already had the door of the Austin taxi open for him.

'Copped one then, Mr Sutro?'

'Nothing like that, Mr Frith.'

'Spot of leave then?'

'That's it.'

'Just the ticket, eh?' Frith started the engine. 'The usual, Mr Sutro?'

'The usual, Mr Frith.'

Keeping the weight off his injured knee did not seem, to Tim, a practical proposition. What was he meant to do? Elevate the limb and pass the time reading the newspapers, like an old buffer in a Bath chair on the esplanade at Eastbourne? He had decided to ignore the medical officer's advice and carry on as close to normal as he could; to simply walk it off. After all, fourteen God-given days lay before him and he did not want to waste them marooned at High And Over. If his remedy failed he still had time to follow doctor's orders. So, at the entrance to the estate, he asked Frith to set him down.

'You sure, Mr Sutro? You don't look so chipper to me and it's quite a step to the big house.'

Tim watched the Austin turn round and start back to Rye, then set off up the drive that rose steeply between great banks of rhododendrons, the purple flowers nodding in full bloom, vivid against the dark green and glossy leaves, the dense mass pierced by the trunks of fragrant pines. Immediately he knew it had been a mistake. The leg seemed to favour one position, stiff and straight; to bend the knee sent fierce spasms through the joint. As he toiled up the incline, with frequent pauses to ease the pain and regain his breath, he heard the double crack of a twelve-bore shotgun, saw rooks rising and cawing above their roosting place in Deadman's Copse a mile away. One was hit, exploding in a spray of feathers, spinning slowly down much like a Heinkel he had seen struck by anti-aircraft fire outside Péronne. When, after fifteen minutes of stop-and-start, he reached the little sandstone bridge that spanned the neck of the moat he took a longer break, surveying the ruins of the old castle and its wavering reflection in the wind-skimmed water. The walls of High And Over rose up on the further hill.

At last, in some pain now, he reached the porch and pushed open the oak door. He knew immediately that his father was not there; an instinct he had always possessed, to what purpose he could not tell, only aware that he had a moment to gather himself, to be ready. He placed his haversack on the table by the dinner gong but kept his stick, moving along the corridor to the kitchens. Mrs Carr was there, chopping vegetables, watched by Griggs, his jacket on the back of his chair, sipping a mug of tea. 'Mind if I pinch a raw carrot?' Tim said from the door. The cook gave a small yelp of surprise, holding her hand to her chest. 'Why, bless my soul, look who it is.'

Griggs was on his feet, pulling on his jacket. 'You fair made us jump, Master Tim. We'd no idea you were going to be back.'

'Until yesterday neither had I,' said Tim. He took a carrot. 'Guv'nor about?'

Griggs shook his head. 'He's laying into that there rookery. He'll be back for his meal come sundown.' He adjusted his tie, formal now. 'You'll be on leave, I fancy.'

'Just a week or so. And before you ask about the stick, silly mishap, nothing more.' Tim took a bite of the carrot. 'Anyway, Griggs, I've dumped my haversack in the hall. I wonder if you'd be kind enough to take it up to my room? And meanwhile, Mrs Carr, perhaps you could rustle up something for me on the terrace while I wait for my father to stop tormenting the rooks.'

He went back into the hall, through the garden lobby and down the broad steps to the southern terrace. Soon Griggs brought him what he had asked for: a glass of cool fresh milk and some wholemeal biscuits. He waited for the manservant to set the snack down and leave him to savour the prospect of the formal gardens that merged into open lawn, then fell away into the ragged areas of shrubbery, ferns and specimen trees, neglected to a careless eye but artfully picturesque. On such a day he had stood in this very place, his hand crimson with crushed wild strawberries, and seen the two DH4s appear above the trees. Below him somewhere, the crack of shots rang out across the valley, seeming to reverberate against the ramparts of the old castle below, the castle that had never seen a battle. He thought back to the Military Canal, not tested either; or the string of Martello towers along the Kent and Sussex coast, none of them touched by war; or Camber Castle, Henry the Eighth's bastion against invasion that never saw a Frenchman. Now coastal batteries, gun emplacements and concrete pillboxes peppered the landscape like acne on a lovely face. Would it be the same this time, constructions that one day might be seen merely as curiosities, as relics of another war that never reached these shores?

He had finished his milk and biscuits when he heard the shattering noise of an open exhaust; Guv on the stripped-down motor-cycle he used to get about the estate. He hated horses, 'no brakes', quite as much as he disliked walking. Tim went to the front of the house, leaving the walking stick in the hall, and hobbled out in time to see the Norton burst through the opening that, years before, despite his mother's protests, his father had ordered to be hacked out of the old yew hedge that shielded the orchards from Channel gales. Guv's Gap, as the gardeners dubbed it, gave him easy access to the further reaches of the estate where he went in search of prey to be potted; if edible, also for the pot. Guv was standing upright on the Norton's foot-pegs, flexing his legs to absorb the bumps and bounces, his shotgun strapped to his back, its barrel projecting above his left shoulder. Two cock pheasants hung round his neck, blood staining his waxed waistcoat. Between the yew hedge and the drive lay a short flight of steps and he jolted down them with throttle closed before giving the engine a final burst of power and dismounting in a drift of gravel dust. He was unshaven, his eyes inflamed and, with the twelve-bore on his back and the dead birds swinging on his chest, he had a wild and brigandish look.

'And where the blue blazes have you sprung from?' He pulled the Norton onto its stand and held up the kill. 'Twenty years ago I was bagging ruddy Fokkers, now it's a brace of longtails.'

'Out of season, aren't they?'

'Edict from on high extended the season until March. Now that we're back to shooting Hun instead of game, the buggers have been running riot damaging crops.'

'It's May.'

'Is that why you're here, to tell me what month it is?' He strode up the porch steps and past Tim into the house. 'Need to get these beauties strung up in the pantry.' In the hall he paused. 'Whose ruddy stick is that?'

'Mine.'

'Why leave it there?'

Tim thought of saying: Because I detest this kind of relentless quizzing that always ends with you telling me to pull myself together, that I'm not really hurt, not on a scale that matters, that you and your flying pals have suffered far worse and never let on or raised a murmur; because it's too predictable to bother with. Because I don't care.

'Why have you got it anyway? You look all right to me.'

'Forget it, Guv'nor, it's nothing serious.'

'Well, either you need it or you don't.'

'You were going to hang those birds.'

'Yes, so I was. Don't forget to grab that stick if you're feeling feeble, will you? What's the problem anyway?'

'Stubbed toe.'

'I see, a joke. Decidedly unfunny, given what some of the other fellows are going through.'

'I know very well what the other fellows are going through, thanks. Incidentally, you're dripping blood on the parquet flooring.'

147

'You've not learned manners in France, I see.'

'I've learned a lot of other things though,' said Tim. Something passed through him, like a charge of electricity; something between shock and excitation. He half expected his father to move towards him as he used to when displeased, coming very close, so close he could smell his sour breath, the purple veins bulging on his forehead, his sudden fury usually held in check but sometimes leading to a stinging blow across the buttocks. Now, however, he turned away expressionless and went down the corridor to the kitchens.

Tim found his bedroom much unchanged though coated with dust and rank with damp. Opening the heavy metal window, it resisted slightly as though gummed up with detritus; dirt and particles of windblown sand and salt, gritty on his hands. In the wardrobe his clothes showed signs of moth and mould. But still, it was pleasurable to change his uniform for a light shirt, jacket and cotton trousers that felt loose and comfortable and did not carry the accumulated whiff of perspiration, aviation fuel and oil. He looked through some of his mildewed books, saw no great intellect on display: school stories and historical yarns, Baines Reed, Stevenson, Conan Doyle; the science fantasies of Verne and Wells; the usual fare to inculcate the necessary values in the boyhood breast. Values that might carry him into war, knowing that God and right was on his side.

At dinner he found it odd to sit across the table from the man who, though he had not seen him for many months, had somehow shadowed his every move in France, a constant presence, always cropping up in memory or conversation or linked to places and events. He studied the hooded eyes, the arched and prominent nose, the deep lines in the cheeks that led down to the thrust-out chin; a famous face recognised by millions across the globe from countless photographs in the press, from newsreels about his exploits, from advertisements in which he endorsed a thousand products from commercial airlines to motor oils to cigarettes to a bright new brand of cornflakes. Or used to. That line of work and useful income had dropped off in recent years and not just due to war.

They were eating stewed rabbit, mostly in silence. Tim had not spoken of his time in France and his father had not asked. Nor had Tim explained why he was back in England or the nature and duration of his leave. Already he planned to get away, saying he could only stay at High And Over for a couple of days. His father nodded absently, showing no regret.

Tim learned that his mother and Alice were still with cousins in New England, as far as his father knew, but only Alice had written and even her letters had petered out when they remained unanswered. 'After all, what was there to say?' demanded Guv between mouthfuls. 'I'm here, they're there. Their choice. End of subject.'

'What kind of life do they lead?'

'God knows, sounds gruesome to me. The social whirl, I suppose, those infernal cocktails the Yanks go in for, empty gossip, the usual twaddle. American society, you know, the worst sort of society. I spent enough time over there to know the form.' He picked a lead pellet from between his teeth. 'This beetling off across the Pond when the chips are down, it's in the family, at least on your mother's side. Your grandmother did the self-same thing, for different reasons.'

'What reasons?'

Guv ignored the question, placing the pellet on his plate. 'Talking of your mother, she started sending food parcels to what she and her Yankee brethren clearly consider our beleaguered island, confounded cheek: tinned vegetables, tinned fruit, tinned sausages, tinned salmon, tinned butter, everything ruddy tinned. She even sent one to me, as though we're on the breadline here. I jolly soon put her right on that. But I understand some of her cronies in Rye are not too proud to reach for the can-opener.'

Before the meal Guv had, with some urgency, downed two brandies and ginger ale, Tim content with a Fremlins stout despite his father's scorn. But now they were halfway through their second bottle of claret. At first Tim drank easily, savouring the wine's quality, hoping it would have a mellow and soothing effect, help him through this ritual that neither of them wanted and neither could escape. And at first it seemed to work. He regarded his father forking the food into his mouth with quick, economic movements as though the plate might be removed at any moment. He felt . . . what did he feel? No warmth towards him, no affection, instead a kind of pity that he had come to this, alone in this great house, dining with a son he did not care for, abandoned by his wife and daughter, abandoned by his country. Boozy ramblings perhaps but undoubtedly a sorry case, tragic even, the tarnished hero with great deeds behind him and an uncertain future. But he had brought it on himself. Lucchetti's words came back to him, that time in Mémère's café: 'Your father has not always behaved as an English gentleman should. He took to keeping questionable company.'

Perhaps in this serene mood, in which he seemed to understand everything, he would question the old man on the matter, get to the truth at last. But then the illusion of insight passed, replaced by numb fatigue. No longer did he feel pity, only vexation, fixed at the table by a shred or two of filial duty. All he wanted now was darkness – darkness and the silence of his room, to stretch out on the dank bed still in his clothes and sleep; sleep an undreaming sleep without an orderly on hand to wake him at three thirty in the morning with a cup of tea.

Guv scraped his plate clean, wiping his mouth with the back of his hand.

'Well,' he said, 'are you going to fill me in or what?'

'Fill you in?'

'I assume you've been making yourself useful one way or another. I should think it's appropriate to give your father the bare bones of what you've been up to, without labouring the point.'

'I wasn't sure you'd be that interested, Guv'nor. You've made your opinion of Lysanders and the chaps who fly them pretty plain.'

'Don't be wet. No doubt they've got their uses. I've heard occasional mentions on the wireless. This is your chance to put me right.'

Tim gave a brief account of his squadron's time at Glisy, making little of its successes, failures and losses. He had no wish to confront the truth when the memory was so raw, to talk of it with anyone, least of all to this man who fixed him with his habitual, disparaging eye and demanded to be put right; had no wish, either, to search for suitable words that might convey the hatefulness of it all, the way those heady, early days had met with a brutal dawn when any illusions vanished as quickly as the crews who did not make it back. To talk of this, he felt, was pointless, a waste of breath. And so he mumbled through a quick and shallow summary of life and death at Glisy, not mentioning his own experiences or why he was back in England, allowing his father to assume the squadron had been withdrawn.

Griggs came in to clear the plates. 'Enjoy your supper, gents?'

'Dinner, man, dinner. And don't call us gents. What's for pudding?'

'Mrs Carr's junket.'

'The cat's in luck. We'll take coffee in the library and bring the port.'

'Righty-ho.'

'Christ Almighty,' Guv said when Griggs had gone. 'But what can you do? He's all that's left. And even he's answered the call and enrolled in the LDV.'

'LDV?'

'Local Defence Volunteers, some sort of old crocks' army cobbled together by the War House to repel invasion. Popularly known as Look Duck Vanish. Close to the mark, I shouldn't wonder. Griggs has been made a corporal, running about the countryside playing soldiers, and neglecting his duties here. And Paget is worse than useless after his involvement with the Mosley gang. Keeping his head down, I suppose, in case they string him up. It won't take long for my collection to go to rack and ruin. The hangar roof's already in a parlous state. And you can't find labour for love nor money.'

In the library, its shelves tight with handsomely bound volumes not read since the Bowman days and not much then, Griggs set down the coffee.

'Instant rubbish,' Guv said. 'But the port's real enough.' He leaned forward challengingly. 'I assume you will indulge?'

Tim sipped from the crystal glass, feeling the sweet, heavy liquid flow down his throat and into his stomach where it spread like treacle, mixing with the ersatz coffee and the undigested rabbit.

'Of course,' his father was saying, reaching for the bottle of port, 'this whole damned business will come to nothing.'

'If you're referring to the war, I'd say it's come to quite a lot already.'

'We'll iron out our differences, you mark my words.'

'You mean appeasement.'

'I'm no bloody pacifist, dammit. But I am talking about common-sense. No one can afford a protracted conflict on this scale, particularly if it's to be fought on two fronts.'

'Two fronts?'

'The way I see it, the Hun alliance with the Reds won't last; their ideologies are diametrically opposed. Eventually the Ruskies will have to be dealt with.'

At this point, increasingly befuddled as he was but hearing such phrases as 'protracted conflict' and 'ideologies diametrically opposed', it occurred to Tim that his father's words were not his own. He found he was hardly listening any more. 'Possible road to peace . . . heritage in danger of being thrown away . . . must mind Britain's business . . . question of economics . . . focus on the British Empire . . . must not be dragged into a Jewish quarrel . . . France will negotiate terms and so will we . . . simple choice . . . fight to no great purpose or join the victors . . . prospect of a united Europe.'

Tim stood up. He was not, for the moment, wondering what his father might say next; he was wondering where he might be sick. Then the nausea passed and he sat down again. 'You seem to have got it all worked out. Or someone has. What if you're wrong? Those swine are knocking seven bells out of us in France. They've taken most of the Channel ports. Do you honestly believe they'll be content to stand on the cliffs and watch us through binoculars?' Suddenly he was uncertain of himself. He seemed to be on the edge of saying something important but bleary with wine it wouldn't come. Finally: 'Where are you in all of this, Guv'nor? As far as I can see, you're restricted to ops against the local wildlife.'

To his surprise his father laughed. 'Didn't I say the same thing myself, swapping Fokkers for wildfowl?' He took up the bottle of port and filled his own glass but did not offer it to Tim. 'Don't bother yourself about me. It's just a matter of time. I'm ready.'

'Ready? Ready for what?'

'What indeed? That's the nub of it. As I say, it's just a matter of time and time will provide the answer.'

The nausea returned. 'I'm going up.'

'Good idea.'

At the door Tim turned. 'I believe you're sailing very close to the wind, Guv'nor.'

'Really.'

'If you're wrong, if Germany does invade, I wonder what your position would be then?'

'Position?'

'Stance, reaction, attitude.'

'Ah, I see.' Guv was slicing the end off a Havana cigar with his silver cutter. 'So you're taking it upon yourself to question my patriotism.' He held the cigar between his teeth but continued to work the sharp blade of the cutter with his thumb. 'I'll tell you this much, though God knows why the matter should be in doubt. I'm the staunchest patriot you'll find in a day's march, and if any nation in the world sets foot across the frontier of the British Empire as an aggressor I will fight for my country. But Hitler is a pragmatist. He's got nothing to gain by expending his resources on attempting to bring down a potential ally. Western Europe is not the East. And that's where his destiny lies, the East.' He applied a match to the cigar, puffing at it energetically, his face obscured by a grey haze of tobacco smoke.

'I'll be leaving in the morning,' Tim said.

'Excellent idea. I don't think we have anything more to say to each other.'

That night Tim wanted to sleep deeply in his familiar room where, stretched out in the darkness on the same old lumpy bed, he might have been eighteen again or eight and everything happening now a waking dream. But sleep refused to come and every conscious effort to drift off only made him more alert and tense. He went to the open window and stood there naked, feeling the night air's coolness on his body, looking across the garden towards the valley, all washed with silver moonlight, sharp and clear as day, fixed in what seemed at first an unbroken, brooding silence. Then he heard the grumble of far-off thunder, perhaps an early summer storm moving up the Channel, except that no lightning lit the sky and he knew it for a man-made storm, heavy guns in France.

Below him, from his father's study, a splash of yellow light fell across the flagstones of the terrace. He looked at his watch, three forty-five. What was the old man doing? Still drinking probably, that steady routine of refilling his glass with any liquor that came to hand, spread across hours and sometimes days, not drunk to the casual eye but petulant and quick to anger; passing time that once he had spent on flying when he did not fog his brain with booze until after he had landed, carried from his aircraft on the shoulders of the cheering mob, tipping up the magnum of Pol Roger, a champagne-swilling god. But in recent years the record-breaking game had grown familiar and overcrowded; familiar with no new routes to pioneer, flight times rarely beaten, the glamour seeming tawdry, even trivial as nations began to shape for war; overcrowded with pilots whose ambition outweighed their flying hours and skill, often amateurs and sometimes women, after glory with the best machines and beautiful flying suits and dreams that went down without a trace in some cold ocean, prompting the usual question: what's the point? And so the backers could not be found, the public turned away and dust began to gather on the famous planes that stood silent in the hangars of High And Over.

At first, in this vacuum, it seemed his reputation might be enough, that he would be sustained by fame alone, but he had begun to miss the press of people that once swirled around him after a successful flight, the journalists with their microphones and cameras, politicos eager to shake his hand, the jubilant, cheering crowds. He looked for something else, another form of public life and, through people he knew with particular views in England and abroad, he was taken up and acquired firm opinions, opinions to be aired, believing the people, his people would wish to hear them. And in the beginning they came, but more curious to see the great man up close than hear his stumbling rhetoric in numerous halls around the country with dubious companions posted on the doors to deal with troublemakers. But very quickly the audiences dwindled, providing the roughs with few hecklers to throw out because nobody cared enough to heckle. It became a scandal, then even worse, a joke. Guv found himself abandoned without really understanding why, snubbed by society as a whole, abandoned by the faction that had used his name and found it a liability. Everywhere doors were closed. And so he waited for the world to turn, for his predictions to be proved correct, for those doors to open once again, so he could pass through, vindicated, his character restored; waited and nursed a topped-up glass and wondered how it had all gone wrong.

Tim, back on his bed, abandoned any hope of sleep and reached for a book, something familiar and undemanding because his thoughts kept straying. *Treasure Island* came to hand, a tale he almost knew by heart. But long before Jim Hawkins heard Blind Pew's stick tap-tapping up the lane towards the Admiral Benbow Inn Tim drifted off at last, lying outside the blankets, the volume open on his chest.

He was woken by a distant racket he could not place at first, then recognised it as an aero engine being throttled up as though a pilot was taxiing out for take-off. At the window, looking towards the air strip by the hangars, he saw the outline of the De Havilland DH4 moving erratically through the early morning mist, its wheels bouncing over the dew-damp turf, vapour curling behind its wings. He looked at his watch: five fifteen. Already a pink dawn was rising to the east and clouds of agitated birds were wheeling in the sky. He dressed quickly; at the front door he met Griggs. 'What the hell's going on?'

The man shook his head. 'He will have it, Master Tim, when the mood's on him. Roots me out to swing the propeller and get him started. He won't go up. Fuel's rationed for estate purposes only. He's well aware of that. And he knows there's plenty of folk round here who'd like nothing better than make trouble for him. He just pootles about on the ground.'

The biplane had reached the furthest point of the air-strip where the windsock hung limp against its pole. It turned and halted, its propeller thrashing the air. When he drew closer, Tim could see his father's head sunk forward in the front cockpit, flying helmet in place, goggles on his forehead. His eyes were closed, his body rocking to the beat of the Rolls-Royce engine on tick-over. Tim pulled himself onto the wing and the change in weight made Guv Sutro open his eyes, puffy and red with burst veins. Squinting at Tim against the light he did not recognise his son. His head fell back, resting against the leather rim of the cockpit squab, nodding slightly to the revolutions of the propeller, his mouth fixed in a faint, distorted smile. When he spoke the words were slurred and indistinct. 'Dawn patrol, old man, bloody dawn patrol.' His head fell to one side and he began to snore. Tim reached for the instrument panel, flicked the various switches and levers to shut down the engine and jumped down from the wing. At the house he found Griggs.

'The Guv'nor's rather the worse for wear. When he's more himself, get him out of that damned aeroplane and back here. Then rustle up some of the men to push the machine back in the hangar – push, mind you. In future, Griggs, I want your promise that you won't agree to swing that ruddy prop. And pass the word to the others too. There's to be no more of this nonsense, understood?'

'Easier said than done, Master Tim. You know what he's like. Could cost me my job.'

'Well, I'm relying on you to do your best. You and I know he's in no fit state to be at the controls. If he wraps himself round a tree that could cost you your job as well.' Tim shivered in his light clothes. 'Now as we're up and about I'm going to take an early breakfast. And as soon as they open for business, order up a taxi to take me into Rye. I'm not staying on here.'

'That's a right pity,' Griggs said. 'We reckoned you might take the Captain out of himself.'

Tim took his breakfast in the small dining room – porridge, bacon and eggs, fresh toast and raspberry jam, a pot of strong Darjeeling tea – good enough to make him regret leaving except that the price of staying was impossibly high.

Mrs Carr came in to refresh the teapot with a jug of hot water. 'Your father,' she said. 'It's a terrible thing to see a great man brought so low.' She hesitated. 'Griggs tells me you won't be staying.' There was reproach in her voice.

'I'm afraid not.'

'He's so alone.'

'I appreciate your loyalty, Mrs Carr,' Tim said, 'but there it is. Give me a shout, please, when the taxi's here. My kit's already in the hall.'

Forty minutes later, he was in the back of George Frith's Austin as it descended the steep lane from High And Over to the Military Road that ran alongside the course of the River Rother as it flowed towards Rye Harbour and the open sea. He had not seen his father again but had caught a fleeting glimpse of Griggs advancing across the air-strip towards the silent DH4 that stood like a wraith from another age, enveloped in mist. A mile or two on they passed the Kemp garage with its shabby sign and broken clock. In the bungalow at the back a light showed in the front bedroom window. He thought he might call in before he reported back to Hawkinge, perhaps hear some news of Will.

He took a room in the George Hotel overlooking Rye High Street. At first it seemed much as usual, but then he noticed a change: more uniforms, less traffic, much of it military or official-looking, with labels on windscreens and drivers wearing armbands; the few townsfolk about not lingering to talk but hurrying by with faces fixed and sombre. There was a tension about the place, a sense of approaching menace, no doubt as there had been 600 years before when rumours spread around the town that French raiders had been sighted in Rye Bay.

Tim found the Sleightholmes' telephone number on the scrap of Woodbine packet in his wallet. Jennifer took the call. It was as though she had been expecting him to ring. 'But what are you doing in Rye? I thought . . . well, never mind that now. Afternoon tea at Fletchers House? I'd love to. But come here first, and wear your uniform. Mummy's always admired the Sutros so. I want to show you off.'

That morning he made himself climb the tower of St Mary's

Church, pushing down against his stick, pain shooting through his knee with every step but feeling that somehow he was achieving a small but satisfying victory. Beneath the Union flag cracking and flapping on its pole he looked across the Rother Estuary, as he had done so often before, this time aware how close the old port lay to the beaches to the south; the broad expanse of shingle where, if invasion came, the enemy would land. With gulls shrilling above the red-tiled rooftops, the sun breaking through a thin veil of cloud and warming his back, and the salty tang of a rising tide carried on the sea breeze, he could understand how, even now, such a thing might not seem possible to those who lived in this pleasant place. But he had been in France and knew it was.

Later, after a sandwich and glass of bitter in the hotel, he brushed his teeth, changed into his uniform and made his way, with frequent pauses, up Lion Street to the Sleightholmes'. His knee was swollen and the slightest pressure made him wince and curse.

The house overlooked the churchyard, timber-framed with leaded lights and a studded oak front door a step down from the cobbled street.

Jennifer's father peered out from the gloom. 'I'm Sleightholme,' he said unnecessarily. 'You're expected.'

Mrs Sleightholme was with her daughter in a low-ceilinged drawing room, another step down. She came towards him, took both his hands and kissed him warmly on both cheeks as though they were great friends. It was so easily done that Tim wondered if he had read too much into that light, single kiss he had received from Jennifer. Then Mrs Sleightholme stepped back and looked him up and down. Her dark eyes, quite like Jennifer's, took in the stick. 'Not sustained in action, I hear. But quite the dashing pilot. How proud your father must be, to see you follow in his footsteps.' She turned to her husband, who hung back in the doorway. 'Timothy was such a nervous child. Who would have imagined he'd be flying Spitfires?'

'Lysanders, actually.'

'Well, I'm sure that whatever it is, it's frightfully exciting. Have you shot down many Germans? Your father shot down masses.'

'I'd say he's rather brought himself down in recent years,' Sleightholme said sharply, then flushing, added: 'Anyway, how long's your leave?'

'Long enough. I'm feeling properly out of things, like playing truant from school.'

'Yes, I know just how you feel. In the trenches we used to dream of stuffing ourselves with smoked salmon and champers at the Savoy, taking in a show at the Gaiety across the road, generally acting the fool and leaving it all behind us for a bit. And yet after a day or two London seemed the loneliest place in the world and we couldn't wait to get back, among our own as it were.' Sleightholme moved forward a little, into the room. 'I'm told you're staying at the George.'

'More convenient as long as I've got this blasted stick. Somewhat marooned at High And Over.'

'You mean Saxonshore,' said Sleightholme. 'Never could fathom why your father thought fit to change the name of the place when he took over the estate.'

'You don't seem very keen on my father.'

'Doesn't matter much what I think. Like him I'm one of yesterday's men. Our opinions, whatever colour they may be, count for very little in a world that refuses to learn from its mistakes. Now it's up to you fellows to try and teach it sense. I certainly wish you luck.'

Mrs Sleightholme had been listening impatiently, her hands working. 'You're being tedious, Geoffrey.'

'My wife's quite right. Come on, you two, off you go. Despite the nation's privations, they say the folk at Fletchers House are managing to maintain their standards, for the time being at least.'

Returning slowly through the churchyard towards Lion Street Tim felt Jennifer take his arm and experienced a pleasant thrill.

'Sorry about Daddy,' she said. 'There's a certain atmosphere at the moment. He's signed up for the Local Defence Volunteers. He's insisted on being a private although he was a major on the Somme. Mummy's absolutely furious.'

'Why did he do that?' Tim said. They were walking slowly past the gravestones. He saw that many of the dead had reached a great age. He wondered what age he might reach.

'He doesn't want the responsibility. In the trenches he saw too many men die under his command. He says he just wants to be cannon-fodder this time round.'

As they neared the church the golden figures of the cherubic quarter boys in their niche above the clock-face began to strike their small bronze bells. Tim read out the verse that lay between them, lettered in gilt in a carved stone frame. '*For our time is a very shadow that passeth away.*'

Jennifer narrowed her eyes. 'I can hardly make that out. My eyes are next to useless.'

Tim read on. '*Wisdom of Solomon, chapter two, verse five.*'

'Now you're showing off.'

'It's not so much where it's from, it's what it says.'

'You're such fun.'

'Not much, am I?'

'A nice strong cuppa will perk you up.' She made a face. 'I know that sound flippant and uncaring. I don't mean to be. Of course what Daddy said is true, about you chaps feeling sort of lost and out of things back home. But as long as you're here you can't spend your time brooding, can you? Otherwise, what's the point?'

They found a corner table in the tea shop. The place was warm and poorly lit and smelled of pastries, jam and stewed tea. Only a few customers were there, leaning into quiet conversations while from the kitchen came the clash and clatter of cutlery and china and the occasional rush of water from a tap. Jennifer tipped a spoonful of sugar into her cup.

'I thought of us taking a trip to Pett Level to explore the rock pools. Pretend we were on our hols. But no can do for several reasons. No petrol for Daddy's car, you're in no fit state to ride a bike, and anyway, the place has been taken over by the Army – everyone turfed out of their homes, the beach lined with barbed wire and mined, and a huge artillery battery installed on the cliffs.'

'I was never much for paddling anyway.'

'Your sister was, she loved the sea.'

'Yes, she was always . . . full of energy.'

'She was my best friend. How is it I hardly got to know you then?'

'I don't know. I remember you.'

'Liar.'

'No, really. Buck teeth, boss eyed, hair scragged back. Who could resist?'

'You did, obviously. Shy, I suppose.' She imitated her mother's voice. 'Timothy was such a nervous child.'

Tim smiled. 'She's right. I was a dreadful little wet.'

'What happened?'

'Who's to say I've changed?'

'Me. I don't think you're wet in the slightest.' Jenny stirred her tea. 'Poor Alice. She was dreadfully smitten with that pal of yours, the garage-owner's son. Isn't he flying too?'

'Yes,' Tim said. 'Will Kemp. He's in fighters. It's not so long since he dropped in on me at my base near Amiens.' The waitress brought the bill and he stared at it absently. 'He asked for a photo I had of Alice. He was certainly sweet on her.'

Jennifer shook her head. 'So it was mutual then. She never let on – to him, I mean. I always told her she should confess all. But no, she wouldn't have it, stubborn to the end, as though there was something in the way that she couldn't even say to me. Perhaps she'd been told he was beneath her or some-such nonsense, as though that makes a shred of difference in this crackpot world.'

Tim placed some money in the saucer and signalled to the waitress.

'They had a lot in common, Will and my old man,' he said. 'But perhaps after all he'd achieved, the Guv'nor drew a line at Will being his son-in-law. Perhaps he reckoned his daughter could do better.'

Jennifer stood up. 'And so poor Alice went off to America without a word. What a stupid waste. Enjoy life's pleasures while you may, that's my motto. A month from now Fletchers might find itself packed with Gestapo hogging themselves on cream buns and beating up the waitress for spilling their tea in the saucer.'

*　　*　　*

Jennifer was owed a few days' leave so, while they could, they spent much time together keeping away from the house in Church Square and easy in each other's company. The sights of Rye were soon dispensed with, already so familiar that they hardly noticed them, absorbed with each other; but still, they made their way up the cobbled slope of West Street to Lamb House, in the steps of Kipling, Conrad and Stephen Crane, to pay brief homage to the memory of Henry James; sipped lemonade and took the sun on the sandy terrace below the fortifications of Ypres Tower where, for centuries, a light burned at night to guide vessels into the Rother estuary from the sea; and lunched in the Mermaid Inn, that favourite of the smuggling gangs who downed their ale with pistols ready cocked beside their tankards to dissuade a passing revenue man. They walked the streets with ghosts, the old town rich with history at every turn and poised on the brink of more.

A worldly friend of Jennifer's kept a flat in Watchbell Street, returning from her Whitehall job on occasional weekends. There, with the curtains drawn and breathing in another woman's scent, they touched each other's bodies in an intimate and affectionate way; discovered more than fleeting pleasure; the beginning of something deeper and more lasting. They both held back.

At first Tim had been clumsy and uncertain. He heard himself say, fatuously: 'Have you done this before?'

'Have you?' she said quickly.

He tried to recover himself. 'I asked first.'

'You beast. Well, no not really. This, I suppose, not more. Your turn.'

'Oh, much the same.' Not quite true; he had never gone this far. Somehow the pieces had never fallen into place.

'Well, that's all right then, isn't it?'

'Yes, I rather think it is.'

Rumours had begun to spread along the coast of some sort of reverse across the Channel. By the hour the stories grew more disturbing; the BEF pinned against the sea, its eastern flank exposed as the Belgian army, overwhelmed after stubborn resistance but low on ammunition and men, surrendered; for the first time mention of Dunkirk. Officially, news was scarce. But then, over the wireless set in the flat in Watchbell Street, scarcely listening at first because their thoughts were with each other, they heard a programme interrupted, an announcer calling for recruits. At first it seemed to make no sense: 'The Admiralty wants men experienced in marine internal combustion engines or service as engine men in yachts or motor boats. Others who have had charge of motor boats or have good knowledge of coastal navigation are needed as uncertified second hands.' Then details of where such volunteers should make their applications – the nearest registrar, the Royal Naval Reserve, the fishery officer – co-ordinated, then, and urgent, but still no hint in the announcer's voice that the appeal was in any way unusual; no suggestion of desperate measures.

An orchestra began to play Elgar and Jennifer turned off the wireless. 'What on earth does it mean?'

'It means it might be all up with us,' Tim said.

They sat together on the sofa near the French windows that opened onto the little first-floor balcony. Sunlight dappled the white-painted boards of the room, and over the crimson rooftops the gulls were twisting and crying. He held her close, trying to store the moment, their heads touching, her hand resting passively in his, small and fragile but calloused from her farmwork.

'I must go back.'

'But why? You can't fly. What can you do?'

'Not much, probably. But more than I can do here.'

They made no promises as he packed his kit-bag in his room at the George. 'It has been lovely,' she said. 'I'm sorry if that sounds vacuous, but it really has. But it doesn't seem to count for much with things as they are.'

'That crackpot world again.'

'Yes, it works both ways, doesn't it? You can say anything or nothing. In the long run it doesn't matter.'

'In the short run I suppose you might say life goes on.'

'But it doesn't, does it? It stops for lots of people, rather suddenly.

Touch wood,' she touched her head, 'you're going to come through all right but I don't want to be like some of the other girls, feeling sick with funk every time the postman calls.'

'So you'll try and forget all this?'

'No, I'll remember. It's the future I'll close my eyes to.'

'Shall I write?'

'I don't think so. We know how we feel at this moment. There's no need for words, now or later. And later we might feel very differently. Who knows what the Nazis have got lined up for us?'

'And if you find Fletchers crammed with Gestapo eating cream buns, what will you do then?'

'Shoot the buggers, I imagine. That's Daddy's view.'

'In that case our prospects don't sound particularly rosy, do they?'

'That's what I mean.'

She did not go to the station with him. On the train he realised he had not visited the garage to see Will's father; Will who had been sweet on Alice and Alice who had been sweet on Will and neither had said. But why waste time thinking about it? 'You can say anything or nothing. In the long run it doesn't matter.' He thought of Jennifer, with her eyes closed to the future. He thought he would write to her anyway, whatever she had said. He wanted to remain a part of her life, however small a part, however tenuous and fleeting that part might be. And there was no one else.

At Hawkinge, after a quick medical confirmed that he was still unfit for flying duties, they found a minor role for him in the operations room, seated on a balcony above the plotting table helping to oversee the WAAF operators moving counters to mark the developing squadron and enemy positions with their long-handled rakes. Over and behind Dunkirk the fighters were engaged in breaking up Luftwaffe formations bound for the beaches where thousands of Allied troops waited to be taken off. He was impatient to be part of it, back in the air. His knee was healing well but he still had to use the stick. He learned that the remnants of his squadron were somewhere in Hertfordshire, being equipped with fresh-trained aircrew and new Lysanders. As a pilot with recent battle experience there was talk of him being posted there as an instructor.

In the Mess a few days later the volume of the wireless was turned up so those aircrew not on operations could hear Anthony Eden, the Secretary of State for War, talk to the nation about the events unfolding in France; events, he disclosed, that could not be controlled. He called it 'the battle of the ports'. At Dunkirk, he said, the Germans claimed to have the British Expeditionary Force surrounded, but they had forgotten the sea. Thanks to the magnificent and untiring efforts of the Navy and Air Force, said Eden, it had been possible to embark more than four-fifths of the BEF; there was no braver epic in all the country's annals. The Army had gained immeasurably in experience of warfare and self-confidence. The vital weapon of an army, he went on, was its spirit. That spirit had been tried and tested in the furnace: it had not been found wanting. It was this refusal to accept defeat that was the guarantee of final victory. But brave hearts alone could not stand up against steel. The country needed more planes, more tanks, more guns. The British people must show the same discipline and the same self-sacrifice at home as the British Expeditionary Force had shown in the field. 'Their spirit must be our banner,' concluded Eden, 'their sacrifice our spur.'

When it was revealed that more than 300,000 men had been taken from the beaches while the Germans hung back for three days on the Führer's direct order, that they had nibbled at the edges of the fugitive Allied Army but failed to deliver the final, decisive blow, Tim learned later, much later, that his father had considered himself vindicated – had spoken of it to the few prepared to listen as proof that his beliefs about Germany's intentions towards Britain had been correct. He remembered him that night at High And Over, sucking at his cigar, his face obscured by grey tobacco smoke. 'Hitler is a pragmatist. He's got nothing to gain by expending his resources on attempting to bring down a potential ally.'

But very quickly the Germans had proved him wrong and made their objectives clear. And from his place on the balcony of the operations room, as Tim saw the great air battles begin to spread across the plotting table like an infestation, he recalled another of Guv's hot remarks. 'If any nation in the world sets foot across the frontier of the British Empire as an aggressor, I will fight for my country.' So far, the only enemy feet to touch British soil had been those of shot-down Luftwaffe crews. So where, he had wondered, did that leave his father?

His posting to Hatfield came through within a week. By then he had discarded the stick and learned to disguise the limp, eager to resume his flying duties. And when he did think back to his cut-short leave, it was not of High And Over but of rapt walks in the shadowed narrow streets of Rye and murmured conversations and times when there was no talk at all in the little flat in Watchbell Street where the sunlight fell across the white-painted boards from the open window and, outside, seabirds wheeled and called above the crooked roofs. But once, the day before he left Hawkinge, roused by the rising growl of Merlin engines, he stood by his billet and watched the fighters taking off for France, their sleek shapes black against the faint flush of the rising sun. And he thought of Will and felt regret that he had not made time to go to the garage on Military Road; the garage with its shabby sign and broken clock and dim light showing in the window of the bungalow at the back – the garage where another father waited, like so many thousands, for news about his son, news he might have shared.

Four

1

Stan Kemp

Although the days were warm it was cold in the bungalow; it was always cold in the bungalow. It stood in shadows to the north-east of the garage, quickly and carelessly constructed of concrete slabs soon after the business had been purchased, when at last the guns had fallen silent on the Western Front that bleak November when the Armistice had been signed. Then Rose had issued an ultimatum of her own, refusing to go on living in the small flat above the work-shops that reeked of what went on below – of petrol, oil and rubber tyres, of broken batteries, rusting steel and dirty leather. The stench of ailing motor cars was a rancid cocktail that seemed to permeate every crack and corner of their home. At first Guv had been sticky about the money for the new building. He talked of equal partners, of how equal partners put in money of their own, but Rose had gone to meet him in a pub in Rye, away from High And Over, and he had agreed to everything soon enough.

However, Rose was not content for long. The bungalow walls were thin and the metal windows rattled in the gales that roared across the Marsh, snatching off the roof-tiles and dashing sheets of rain against the panes. Inside, the windows ran with condensation, the beads of moisture trickling down the glass and gathering on sills in filmy pools. The furniture, cheap stuff from local auctions, felt clammy to the touch. The infant, barely two, would waken wailing in his cot, his blankets damp. Stan stood it better, coming through the war, surprised to be alive, damaged but alive – grateful, even. Life had been a mess, was still a mess. He had given up trying to make sense of it all. He accepted, that was it. He just accepted things as they were. He accepted Rose as she was. He had given up trying to make sense of her as well. The days, the cold days, went by. He assumed that this was how it would be, the cold days stretching away, far into the future or not so far perhaps. Who knew? No one knew. That was all that was certain.

And then she left. Not for good, she made that plain. She said she would come back from time to time, 'to see how you're getting on, you and the kiddie.' She rarely called the child by name, not William or Willy or Will but 'the kiddie', 'the nipper', 'the brat' or, fuddled with spirits and sentimental, 'the little 'un' or 'the tiny mite'. She promised she would bring some money, when she came, from a job she had in mind.

'What job?'

'Oh, just a job. You wouldn't understand. This place, it's not for me. Never has been, never will be. Better to admit it now. Better for all of us.'

'I don't see that.' He looked at her and thought her most beautiful and knew he would never be with another woman in any kind of significant way.

'You don't see nothing, Stanley. It's like you're blind. You got eyes but you don't use them. It's what I say, you don't understand.' Her hands were held out in front of her, small fists, her knuckles white. 'You don't . . . you don't get it. You don't get nothing. You're just . . . just carried along, like a bit of wood in a stream, going this way and that, spinning and getting caught up and being pulled free and carried along, just carried along.' Later, when she came out of the bedroom with her small suitcase, her hair fresh brushed and shiny, he stood between her and the door.

'You can't do this, Rose.'

'Can't I just.' Until this moment she had seemed rather sad, regretful at what she was somehow driven to do. Now her eyes were prominent, the lids clear of her pupils. 'Can't I bleeding just! Are you going to run me to the station, or do I have to walk? That'll get your precious neighbours yakking, I should think.' She shook her head. 'Christ, I hate this hole.'

'What about the business?'

'What bloody business? You know it's just that bastard's sop to try and shut us up.'

'What about the kid?'

'What about him? You're better at looking after the little bugger than I'll ever be. He won't even know I've gone.'

He did not see her again for six months. When she came she did not talk about her job or give him money; in fact, she asked for some. By then she had filled out a little, the dress the same but tighter across the chest and hips. He still thought her most beautiful, and despite everything that had gone before, he wished to be with her, even like this. From the very first he had always derived great satisfaction from taking her about with him, from being seen and envied by others, from picking up the glances of other men and sometimes women too, who never looked at him, of course, always at her. He knew jealousy, naturally, but was quite prepared to settle for that in return for being in her company in a way those others could never be. After all, he was still her husband and that meant something, surely? Even now, when she was leading some kind of life he knew nothing about.

That first time, when she came back without warning, she was affectionate enough, gave him a kiss that left lipstick on his cheeks and forehead that later he looked at in the mirror. She tickled the boy with every show of fondness and presented him with a tinplate aeroplane, rather old and showing signs of use, that he seized with a pudgy hand and zoomed about. She seemed as delighted as he was. 'Aren't you the bright one then? Bright as a bleeding button, you little piglet. That's what you are, a pink little piglet.' She thrust her fingers ferociously into the boy's ribs, making him writhe with pain and pleasure. Then, no more than three hours later, she got Stan to run her back to Rye in his Crossley van, in time for the three forty-five to Brighton. 'This smelly old thing,' she said. 'I'm sure a proper motor car would suit you just as well.' On the short journey she had bounced the boy on her knee. Now she passed him across to Stan and opened the passenger door. 'Well, cheery-bye for now, little piglet.' The child stared back at her in silence, his round face completely without expression. 'Suit yourself,' she said, easing her long legs out of the van and holding her handbag close. At the sight of her legs in silken stockings, remembering her smooth thighs and what lay above, Stan hoped for some sign of physical stimulation in his loins but as usual there was nothing there. She assumed he had been looking at her handbag. 'Real snakeskin,' she said, caressing it.

He nodded, not thinking of her legs now, or the bag really, just the purse inside that contained his two ten-bob notes. 'You must be doing well.'

'Oh, well enough.'

'When will we be seeing you again?'

She patted his cheek. 'We. That's sweet.' She patted his cheek again, a little harder, turned and went into the station booking office without a backward glance.

When they got back to the bungalow Stan sat next to the boy in his high-chair at the kitchen table watching him feed himself from a bowl of bread and milk, rejecting the spoon and grasping at the crusts with sticky pink fingers. The child had hardly spoken a word to Rose but seemed more talkative now. Stan listened to him prattle on, nodding absently. Pink little piglet, he was thinking, bright as a bleeding button. Poor little sod.

That was all twenty years ago. Rose had been right about one thing: the kid had turned out bright as a button. Why wouldn't he, in the circumstances? And now he was up there somewhere, maybe even at the controls of one of those distant machines he could hear patrolling the Channel coast. From the note of their engines it sounded as if they were climbing to make height before the Jerries swept in again from their airfields in the Pas de Calais. So much had changed for the boy but nothing had changed for Stan. He was sitting at that same table, where he had helped the child eat his bread and milk. His cracked and grease-black hands were wrapped around the mug of tea, the skin so tough he could not feel the heat. This was the time, at three, he made his pot of tea. At six, his supper. At ten his cocoa and so to bed. At dawn, whatever time that was, his bacon, eggs and toast. At twelve his midday meal. It was the pattern, day by day and month by month and year by year. Every day the same. There was a comfort to that sameness, knowing that life went on, dull maybe, oh deadly dull. But suiting him for as long as it might continue because it threw up no surprises, helped him to avoid those creeping doubts about what had happened once; might still occur. Such thoughts he found disturbing; he shunned such things.

This was his pattern, working on the cars and fending for himself, comfortable with the sameness, accustomed to the glacial workshop with its feeble stove, the concrete bungalow's biting chill. It was as if he had never been comfortable or warm, had quite forgotten the need if need it was because, alone, he could please himself. That suited him extremely well, to please himself after so much time spent pleasing others. Rose had been right about that as well. 'You're just carried along, like a bit of wood in a stream, going this way and that . . . just carried along.' Now he had things nicely under control. He told himself that often. Bloody dull all right, but nicely under control. He also told himself he was not lonely. He lived alone and that was different. Only sometimes did he have to struggle with himself, over-come with a vague sense of the futility of it all, the sadness, something beyond words that brought him to the brink of weeping, as when he had last seen Will around the time of the great balls-up at Dunkirk and he had felt great pride in the boy despite everything being such a rotten muddle, but somehow hadn't been able to tell him and had bitten it back, and only after he'd driven away had something started in his chest and gone up his throat and he'd found himself shaken by great sobs he couldn't explain or understand.

He heard car tyres crunch across the gravel by the petrol pumps, the distant ping of the office bell. George Frith was already unscrewing the fuel cap of his Austin. 'Fill her up, Stanley. I'm flush with coupons.'

'You'll find yourself in trouble one of these days, George.' The petrol began to splash into the tank.

The taxi driver lit a cigarette, cupping his hand to shield the match against the wind. 'I had young Sutro for a fare, a week or so back.'

'Oh, yes?'

'Bit of leave. Preferred to spend it with the Sleightholme girl. Stayed at the George instead of the big house. Word is, he's fallen out with his lordship. Thought he might call here, him and your William being so close.'

'No,' Stan said.

'Looked as if he'd been having a rough time of it. Wouldn't say why or how though. They never do, do they?' Frith took in Stan's awkward stance at the pump, the odd angle of his leg, and did not mention the nature of Tim's injury or his stick. 'I gather he's on them Lysanders. Bloody death-traps, by all accounts. Your boy's better off in the good old Spit. At least it gives him a sporting chance.'

'That's right.' Stan replaced the fuel cap and went into the office with Frith's money and coupons. Everything's nicely under control, he told himself urgently, unaware that he was speaking aloud. Everything's nicely under control.

In the bungalow he went into Will's room but it had the emptiness of a bird's nest when the fledglings have flown, its purpose gone. From the ceiling the aeroplane models revolved slowly on their lengths of thread, caught in the draught from the door. On the table by the window stood Will's collection of flying books. One had fallen flat. Guv's picture was on the back. As usual, his jaw stuck out, as usual his goggles were on his forehead, as usual his eyes were fixed on some distant point high above the clouds; his story written by a Fleet Street hack and published in his name. Stan had never read it. Someone in town had told him he was mentioned, but hadn't said how, and he hadn't cared to find out. But now he picked it up and opened it at the title page where Guv had scrawled 'To Will, affectionately, Guv. And below, in a slightly less expansive hand: *The Yankee ace Rickenbacker once told me that aviation proves we have the capacity to achieve the impossible. May you continue that tradition.* He felt an anger in his belly. What right had he? But then, of course, he had every right. He replaced it carefully, so he could not see the photograph of Guv.

Next to the books stood the tinplate toy that Rose had given to the boy all those years ago, lacking its propeller, lopsided on its damaged undercarriage with its single wheel. It had the look of a Vickers monoplane, the kind they used for training rich civilians at Brooklands before the war that failed to end all wars. He turned it curiously in his hand, then childlike held it above his head, swooping it into shallow turns and gentle dives, his eyes no longer good, his vision blurred so it gave the illusion of a real machine; much like those of the fledgling fliers who criss-crossed the skies at no real height above the Flying Village where Guv had rented that low-roofed wooden shed, just broad enough for a single machine, and made his mark as a coming man with Gustav Hamel, Sopwith, Hawker and the rest. Guv had been rarely on the ground, chasing money as much as records. His first success, from Dover to Le Touquet in the Blériot, had brought five thousand francs that helped him to outrun the constable, as he always put it. Next came the Brooklands to Brighton in less than an hour, triumphantly circling the Palace Pier; the Round Britain Race won by the French but with him well up at the end and introduced to the King; the altitude record of 11,000 feet, beaten by Hawker a month or so later; handicap races of every description, bringing in cash though never enough. Then came the project to fly the Atlantic for the *Daily Mail* prize of £10,000, with backing from Bowman, the department store chief, on whose great estate Guv had descended en route for Le Touquet Paris-Plage – a lucky connection he had maintained by various means, cannily making no mention of money until at last he had planted the seed of the trans-ocean attempt so subtly that Bowman came to believe the idea was his own. And soon, with preparations underway, it had become clear to Stan at least that as far as the Bowmans were concerned, Guv might have another scheme in mind.

Stan brought the tinplate monoplane in for a neat landing beside Will's books. He was no longer standing in the boy's bedroom. He was back at Brooklands with the splutter and roar of aero-engines ringing across the flying ground's flat expanse. Behind him, through the thrown-back doors of the wooden sheds with their white-lettered signs – *Avro, Bristol, Sopwith, Vickers* – he could hear the shouts of men at work, banging, sawing, scraping, something like chaotic music, fashioning machines for flight. A memory of the old excitement quickened his heart. It was very real to him at that moment, once more part of a brotherhood of high-born and low who shared a vision, pursued a common dream which proved that nothing was impossible, like Rickenbacker said, given man's capacity to achieve.

It was about this time he had first seen Rose, at the Bluebird Café next to the Flying Village where the pilots took refreshment and thrilled the swells with flying yarns, directing them to the tiny ticket office nearby where, for a fiver, they could be taken up for a flip themselves. There the girl had slipped between the tables set out in front of the café, serving trays of afternoon tea and clearing tables, her broad mouth fixed in a slight smile, as though diverted by what she saw and not at all brought down by her menial task. He remembered every detail of how she was dressed that day, a white lace cap, a long black dress of some satin stuff with broad lace collar and crisp white cuffs, buttoned from neck to waist, lace-trimmed apron reaching from waist to knees and small black boots buttoned from toe to ankle. Every part of that sombre uniform pointed to her physical form; her tiny feet, the roundness of her hips and narrow waist, the rise and fall of her breasts, the set of her shoulders and her long white neck. Under the little cap her hair was black and thick and blew about her cheeks; she spared a dainty hand from time to time to push the tendrils back.

The men studied her speculatively as she brushed against them. And as she moved among the tight-corseted ladies of quality perched at their tables correct and stiff, shielded from the sun by elaborate broad-brimmed hats and Japanese parasols, sipping from their china cups, she seemed to possess an air of dangerous liberation, her bright eyes, the clear blue of a summer sky, fixing on faces that caught her fancy and appearing to convey some wordless challenge or perhaps an invitation.

Watching her, caught breathless, Stan's eyes had somehow slowed down the way she moved until she appeared to drift, her body flexing beneath the dark material of her dress. He found he could not take a step, overcome by a strong, unknown desire; an impulse primitive and crude of which he felt ashamed but also relished. At that moment she had become aware of him and smiled directly at him in a way that went straight to his heart, as though they shared a secret, as though they both knew how it was with these people, as though they were conspirators somehow who could move as easily in this world as she moved between the tables, she in her menial costume, he in his oil-crusted overalls; as though this was a world that could not last.

He went back later that day, when they were closing the café. She was outside with another girl, wiping the wooden tables and propping the chairs against them. He had put on clean overalls and brushed his hair. The other girl nudged her when he tried to walk past casually. She laughed and called out to him, 'Hello, dear.' There was warmth in her voice and recognition, as though they knew each other already. He stopped and she came over to him, wiping her hands on a cloth. 'I saw you before, dear, didn't I? Are you a pilot?'

He was confused that she should think so. 'No, no, just a dogsbody.'

'Oh, pile it here, pile it there, eh?'

'Well, no, a bit more than that. I suppose you've heard of Guv Sutro?'

'Course I have. Everyone knows him, I shouldn't wonder. Me and Ivy have seen him about. Why, do you know him?'

'Yes, I work for him. With him. Preparing his planes.'

'Well, fancy that, dear. So you really are a chappie to be reckoned with.'

Was she joking? He looked for a sign but saw nothing. 'Hardly,' he said, staring at his boots, his face burning.

She looked across at the other girl waiting by the tables and gave her a wave. 'Well, better go.'

'What's your name, if you don't mind . . .'

'Why should I mind? Rose, dear, Rose Pringle.'

'Perhaps I'll see you again . . . Rose.'

'What's yours?'

'Stanley. Stan. Stan Kemp.'

'That'd be nice, Stan. Ta-ta then.'

He walked back to the Sutro shed feeling slightly faint, his legs spongy, running his tongue over his dry lips. That would be nice, she'd said. That would be nice. To see him again. To think she'd thought he was a pilot. He laughed to himself. But had she? Had she really? Was she just being – what? – kind, flirtatious, sarcastic? Maybe the other girl, that Ivy, had been smirking behind her hand. After all, how many pilots wore such filthy overalls? He was no longer laughing. He felt confused, as though something had happened in his life that was important, that had changed things. As though nothing would be the same again.

Now, standing in the boy's bedroom, alone in the silent bungalow, Stan wondered how different his life might have been if he had not felt compelled to take that carefully casual stroll to the Bluebird Café in the hope of seeing Rose again. He was nothing then and very little now. Why had she bothered? Amusement, diversion, habit? Later, much later, he was told that among the pilots she was regarded with amusement – pretty enough, but 'on the make' as they liked to put it around the sheds. They called her The Angler: once hooked she never threw you back. That always raised a great laugh but he did not understand why until, much later still, he discovered the truth and by then it had gone too far.

But back in that other existence before the war, before he had taken that casual stroll, before she had said 'that'd be nice' in that way of hers, before he had been hooked and landed, before the Germans started rattling their sabres, before the whole wide world became a madhouse, well, then, the only thing on his mind had been helping to plan the Atlantic flight, the venture to eclipse all ventures, when life for a lad from the depths of the country, still with Sussex mud on his boots, had seemed like a dream thanks to a pal who'd brought him along and given him chances and shown him a future beyond his imagining in this coming business if business it was, not just a pastime or sport, of conquering the air, of crossing the oceans, of circling the globe, even (like some writers predicted) of conquering space. And there he had been, in at the beginning with everything before him, his to grasp. Why, a few of the lads who worked on the planes had learned how to fly and even tested machines for the Brooklands designers. So why not him? But this was before he had taken that stroll and told her perhaps he'd see her again and she'd said, 'That'd be nice.' And he had believed her but then wasn't sure. Had never been sure since that long-ago day.

2

Stan had liked to get to the aeroplane shed early, as the sun was breaking over the rim of the great basin in which the Brooklands circuit and airfield lay. Its location was good for racing cars and aeroplanes because the banked track, rising to more than twenty feet above the central plateau and circling the perimeter for almost three miles, usually provided smooth conditions; calm air that meant drivers and pilots could concentrate on getting the most from their machines without being thrown off course by sudden gusts.

Stan cycled in from his lodgings in Byfleet a few minutes away. The street lay to the north of the track between the Railway Straight and the mainline from Weybridge to Woking. Many of the mechanics had digs along that stretch and in the evenings they would meet up in one or other of the local pubs and talk shop or exchange tall tales about their employers. They regarded themselves as the most modern of men, engaged in the most modern of occupations and nobody disagreed: it was as if they were followers of some black art beyond the comprehension of ordinary folk. The romance of aviation had rubbed off on them, set them apart even though they did not fly themselves. But they knew how it was done and, like Stan, saw no reason why, given luck and opportunity, they should not one day do so themselves: 'I mean, blimey, haven't some of the blokes done it already?' Others could see this too, those who did not work at Brooklands, and so they were regarded with a kind of awe, although they tried to hide it, this awareness that maybe this callow youth leaning against the bar with a tankard of beer, puffing at a cigarette to make himself appear more grown up, might have his foot on the first step of the ladder that led to a place with the elite, one of the chosen ones of whom they might say, one day: 'I knew him before he was famous, you know. Many's the time I've stood him a pint.'

Women were different, at least the women they met in the places they went to relax – the cafés and pubs and occasional fairgrounds. The men found they were sought out and popular. 'Had it easy,' as their rivals said. But Stan had grown wary. Girls like that cost time and money, expected you to take them for a bite to eat or buy them drinks. He failed to see the point of it all. What had he to gain? Trying to think of things to say, yet not wanting to take things any further (like some of the others claimed they had – oh, all the way, yes, all the way) because these girls were most particular kinds of girl. He'd seen it too many times, the kind who'd turn away when their plate was cleared or their glass was empty and just start eyeing up someone else, a better prospect leaving him a few quid down and knowing he'd been had.

It wasn't that he was uninterested in women, like some of the boys implied, just those sorts of women. And there had been little chance of meeting another sort as long as he worked at the Flying Village. Oh, no shortage of beauties there, of course, but the stuck-up Society type who looked straight through him as if he was invisible or disregarded him as some kind of lackey. This was why, the day before, it had seemed something like a miracle to attract the attention of that girl whose name was Rose (what a perfect name), so neat and demure in her costume and so at ease among the toffs, who'd told him it would be nice if they were to meet again.

He eased himself off the saddle of his bicycle, balancing on one pedal, and skidded to a stop outside the Sutro shed. His rear tyre raised a swirl of dust that caught the light of a radiant dawn emerging above the eastern banking, the tiny particles dancing in the golden beams, the shed's pine double doors washed with gold as well. At that moment everything seemed golden. He knew extreme happiness.

There was nowhere he would rather be than in this place and at this time; a theatre almost, a theatre of great deeds but real not imaginary – great deeds on the ground and in the air. And he was part of it, with a role to play, an important role relied on by one of the principal players. He even had a girl or, rather, had a girl in mind who he hoped – no, planned – to meet again and who had stirred in him disturbing fantasies. Probably it would go nowhere. But who could tell? He might be one of the chosen ones. In this place and at this time, anything seemed possible.

When he swung open the shed doors, the glittering light filled the interior, fixing every detail as clearly as a perfectly focused photograph. The Sopwith three-seater had the appearance of an immense toy, fragile and thrown together, quite incapable of flight. Yet only weeks before, Guv had taken it to 11,000 feet, a climb of more than forty minutes, to claim another record. Today it was expected to claim another prize.

After he had carried out the Sopwith's pre-flight checks, the shed clock showed it was still only six-thirty. He walked the 100 yards or so to the Bluebird Café, everything closed up, dew running wet on the big white sign: *Luncheons, teas, refreshments at popular prices*. It made him laugh: what price was popular? His heart was racing at the thought of her, the girl who worked here. Soon she would arrive. In an hour or two, perhaps he would take another stroll, just to nod and say hello. He laughed again. Everything this morning held a kind of magic for him.

He had not met the Bowmans before. When, at midday, they stepped down from the Rolls-Royce after a long drive from their big place near Rye, he was surprised how much alike were father and daughter. Guv had not spoken of them often, or at any length. But he knew there were certain expectations, on both sides, and somehow he had anticipated more; they looked so . . . ordinary, the pair of them and yet the old man was immensely rich, owned that great store in Oxford Street and more besides, even abroad so he'd heard. He watched the woman (for woman she was, hardly a girl) standing awkwardly to one side while Guv and her father talked, gazing at Guv with eyes

179

brimful of wonder, much as he must have gazed at Rose. She was richly but plainly dressed in the fashion but there was a heaviness about her that no fine clothes could hide. Her face had the weathered, brownish look of a countrywoman, her eyes small and round, pink rimmed from exposure to the elements; her jaw was her father's, long and prominent, and gave her a mannish look.

Guv had taken her hand briefly, something between a shake and a squeeze, smiled a tight smile and murmured some greeting, but that was all. Now his attention was all on the father. Guv did not introduce him, as he usually did, joshing slightly, 'This is Stan, the worst mechanic in the world but he's all I can afford,' or, more often, 'This is Stan, who keeps me in the air.' Instead he said: 'Everything all set, Kemp?' His voice was sharp and cold, as though Stan was any old hired hand, as though he'd just been taken on. A dogsbody. He felt suddenly sick, and all his imaginings about the future seemed to turn to nothing.

Guv took the Bowmans for a flight in the Sopwith before lunch. There was the predictable merriment as they were bundled into the cockpits in their unsuitable clothes, their borrowed goggles crooked on their anxious faces. Neither of them had been in the air before, and both were pop eyed with funk. Stan watched as the Sopwith flew round the circuit several times at 500 feet, performed a slight zoom that would have compressed them excitingly in their seats, lost height and came into land, gliding with engine shut down over the green-domed clubhouse of the automobile racing club and touching down without the slightest bounce.

As he helped the Bowmans struggle from the cockpits (once on the ground embracing each other with elation and relief), Guv said, in the same distant manner: 'There was a touch of wing-drop on landing. Check the ailerons, will you, while we have a bite to eat?' He looked at his watch. 'Captain Sutton should have been here by now. Send him on when he finally arrives.' Then he joined the Bowmans in the Daimler and the chauffeur drove them to the club restaurant on the crest of the members' hill where the menu and service, so Guv had once remarked to Stan, rivalled the West End.

Stan went over the Sopwith and, as he expected, found nothing wrong. He made a few minor adjustments to pass the time before settling himself in the warmth of the sun outside the shed to eat the sandwich made up for him by his landlady. Washing it down with a mug of tapwater, he heard the blare of a motor-cycle engine that cut out close by and then the crunch of boots on gravel. A shadow fell across him and he squinted up, the sunshine in his eyes. 'G'day, Kemp. The lion in his lair or is he already stalking his prey?'

Stan jumped up. 'He's with his guests, Captain Sutton.' He pointed at the members' hill. 'He said you should go on up.'

'Ah, bit peeved, eh?' Instead of concern, Sutton registered mild relief. 'Running somewhat late to join them now. Bit of trouble with the old Douglas. Ruddy oiled plugs. Reckon I'll give it a miss. Your skipper's far better at the blarney than me anyway. I'm just a cobber from Queensland. No doubt I'd put my foot in it and scupper our chances. I'll park myself here if I may. Care for a gasper?'

Stan fetched him a chair and they sat side by side, smoking companionably.

'The old bus behaving itself?' Sutton enquired.

'Just back from a flip,' Stan said. 'The Guv took them up to give them a thrill.'

'Let's hope it has the desired effect, makes Mr Moneybags reach for his chequebook.' The Australian stretched out his legs. He had made an effort to be smart: breeches, puttees, glossy brown boots. He wore the high-necked wrap-across 'maternity' tunic of the Royal Flying Corps with Sam Browne leather belt and pilot's wings, his forage cap tilted jauntily over his right ear. For a while they said nothing, Stan thinking that if the pilot had been punctual, he could have used this time to go down to the Bluebird Café. Then Sutton threw down the butt of his first smoke and opened his cigarette case.

'Help yourself.' He flicked his lighter and they both lit up. 'I suppose you think I'm a thoroughgoing gent.' Stan had no reply to that and stayed silent. 'Want to know how I got started? I fell in love with flying but there was nothing doing Down Under so I worked my passage to Europe on a grain ship. Wangled myself a job sweeping out hangars at the Blériot school in Pau, all the time learning about kites until they had to admit I might be a mechanic. That's where I met His Nibs. He was running through his inheritance at the time, we hit it off and I helped him dispense it among most of the whores in Aquitaine. We never got the clap but Christ knows why.' Sutton scratched his crutch reflectively. 'I was working for nothing at the time, just for the chance to go up occasionally, learn the ropes. But I had an ability that caught the eye of Blériot himself. Wound up as an instructor, flew machines for rich kids who wanted a share of the glory, broke a few records, got myself a reputation – bit rough at the edges but handy in the air, you know the score. But it's an over-crowded trade, the professional hero business, so when they formed the RFC I reckoned I'd turn respectable, become an officer and a gent, just as long as they'd grant me leave of absence if something big came along, something that might happen to reflect well on the Corps, something like this daring deed.' He looked across at Stan. 'Ever thought of signing on the dotted yourself?'

'What, join the RFC?'

'Come on, man. Surely you're not content to spend your life slaving away for old Sutro? You know all about aeroplanes, probably more than me. Wouldn't you'd like to learn how to fly one yourself, for free?'

'I suppose it's crossed my mind.'

'I could put a word in for you, if you like. You'd have to start at the bottom, of course, but we want blokes like you and you'd soon make your way. Give it a year or so and you might even find yourself decked out in this fancy dress as well, with a shiny new pilot's brevet on your left tit.'

'I don't know,' Stan said. 'There's a lot on at the moment. I couldn't let Guv down.'

'Your loyalty does you credit, Kemp, but have you wondered if it works the other way? If this trans-Atlantic wheeze comes off, a lot of people are going to be involved and you might just get lost in the crush. What price your loyalty then? But in the Corps such qualities are valued. And there's another consideration. I didn't just join up to improve my social status. Everyone knows we're going to be slugging it out with the Hun before too long. I want to be bloody sure I'm in a good position when the bell goes, so I've got some say about how we biff the bastards, a bit of control over my own destiny.'

'Why are you telling me all this?'

'Not quite sure. You've always struck me as a decent type, the type the service needs. And don't forget, I know your boss. Oh, he's something special all right, might even be a great man one day, but he's a selfish, ruthless, bullying bugger who'd sell his dear old grandma's false teeth to stay in the air.'

'And yet you'd share a cockpit with him, trying to cross the Atlantic?'

'In that situation nobody better.'

It started raining. They took their chairs inside the shed and watched it come down, drifts of grey drizzle sweeping across the plateau. The cars came in from the circuit, the few aeroplanes aloft touched down quickly and taxied in, hardly visible in clouds of opaque spray thrown up by their propellers. The bad weather was coming in from the west and seemed set for the rest of the day. When the Bowmans returned from lunch they said how lucky they had been to have good conditions for their flight.

Bowman seemed in good humour but Guv was sour, and short with Sutton. He took him aside. 'So you got here at last. Why in damnation didn't you join us? I needed support.'

'Why? Isn't the old man going to come across with the moolah?'

'I don't know. Something's on his mind.'

'He'll come round when he sees the designs.'

Soon Knighton-Cooper, the aeronautical engineer, was unrolling the blueprints in the small office at the back of the shed, tracing with his finger the huge machine with its 65 foot wingspan, its 200 horsepower motor and its fuel tank containing nearly 400 gallons, enough to take it from Newfoundland to any point in Britain or Ireland in 72 continuous hours, as required by Northcliffe to win the £10,000 prize. Guv had been scornful in briefing Knighton-Cooper. 'Seventy-two hours? Give me a plane that can cruise at a hundred miles an hour at ten thousand feet and I'll do it in twenty-five.'

Now, studying the plans, Bowman was reflective. 'It's a very great enterprise, gentlemen. Very great.'

'The only kind worth doing,' Guv said.

Bowman turned to Knighton-Cooper. 'Tell me, is your machine really capable of such a flight?'

'Not getting cold feet are you, sir?' There was a trace of concern in Guv's jocular tone.

'Well,' said Bowman, 'I must admit that when you're confronted with the reality, face to face with the magnitude of the task, it makes you question not only the possibility of success but also its ultimate value. Progress is one thing, but I have no wish to be responsible for the deaths of two fine men.' Stan noticed that at these words his daughter bit her lip.

Knighton-Cooper inclined his head slightly, suppressing a shrug. He had been in the aviation business long enough. 'I can give you no guarantee of that, sir, but I can certainly assure you that this aeroplane has been designed and will be constructed to the best of my company's ability. And that ability is considerable.'

Listening to this, Stan was not concerned with any great enterprise, or anxious in the slightest that Knighton-Cooper's design might not be capable of crossing an ocean. Guv did what Guv did and usually succeeded. For the moment he was thinking entirely about his own interests. Sutton could be right. What chance had he, a self-taught mechanic (hardly an engineer), against a team of expert ground crew, fully trained and no doubt poached from leading firms, all jockeying for the chance to build not just an aeroplane but also their careers? Even if he clung on somehow, probably in some inferior role, and Guv and Sutton returned triumphant, carried shoulder-high as national heroes, who would spare a thought for him? And if the worst happened and they and their blasted monster plane disappeared like so many before them, what would be left then? A rented shed, a secondhand Sopwith to be sold against Guv's debts and virtually nothing else, his only prospect to somehow start again, at Brooklands if he was lucky, if not (a prospect even worse) back on the land in Alfriston – a jumped-up lad cut down to size, good for a guffaw in the village pubs.

At this moment he wanted the whole daft scheme to fail, for daft he felt it was. He took some comfort from Bowman's obvious doubts. He wanted it so fervently that he imagined Bowman saying there and then: 'It's no good, gentlemen, my conscience compels me to withdraw. I could not live with the knowledge that I helped to send such gallant gentlemen to oblivion.' Yes, that was just the form of words that penny-dreadfuls would apply to such a situation. But Bowman said no such thing. Instead he mumbled: 'Well, we shall see, we shall see. Thank you for taking us up, my boy, a most memorable and exciting experience.' He shook hands with Knighton-Cooper and Captain Sutton, and nodded briefly at Stan before climbing into the Daimler that was to deliver him to a board meeting in Oxford Street where the matter was on the agenda. The rear window of the limousine was down and he noticed Guv's expression. 'Don't be glum, my boy. You must understand that what you require from us is a very considerable sum. It is not a decision to be made lightly, nor is it entirely down to me. But naturally I will do what I can.'

Guv roused himself. 'Of course, sir,' he said stiffly. 'Of course.'

As the car pulled away, the daughter fixed her eyes on Guv and pressed her gloved palm to the window, mouthing some words for him alone. Guv watched them go.

'I thought you said it was in the bag,' said Sutton.

Guv turned and went back into the shed. 'It'd better be,' he said over his shoulder, 'or the old bastard can wave goodbye to any ideas about having a son and heir.'

Stan realised then the significance of the daughter's hand pressed on the window glass and her silent message. As there was nothing he could do about the situation, he did his best to push it to the back of his mind. This was not difficult because his thoughts were almost entirely occupied with the girl at the Bluebird Café. He had seen her again, several times, and said hello before passing on hot and confused. He told himself the world was full of pretty women – not available

185

to him, of course, apart from admiring them at a distance – but lots of pretty women; hundreds, thousands. But this Rose, this particular miraculous girl, was not just pretty but what he supposed people called beautiful. He could not imagine there had ever been, was now or ever could be, another quite as beautiful.

Then, one April evening as he cycled away from the shed, he saw her walking slowly towards the circuit gates with a man, a young man. He felt sick until he noticed, with a leap of his heart, that they were not talking like lovers talked; not holding hands or arm-in-arm. He drew up boldly on his bike. 'Hello.'

'Oh, hello, Stan.' Good Lord, she remembered his name! 'This is my cousin, Harry Paget.' Cousin? Wonderful. 'He's looking for a job.'

'Know anything going, old man?' said Paget. Old man? What cheek.

Close to, he was not much more than a lad, seventeen or eighteen. But Stan's irritation was mixed with relief; relief that Paget was not only a cousin but also younger than Rose. He shook his head. 'No, sorry. I'm afraid you'll find they're looking for chaps with experience here.' Now why did he say that? Plain boasting, showing off, scoring a point? But Paget showed no sign of taking offence.

'Well, if you hear of anything, old man, perhaps you'd tip off Rose.' He gave her a grin. 'Cheerio, Cuz.'

Rose watched Paget hurry away. 'Your cousin,' said Stan.

'Don't you believe me?'

'Don't be silly. Course I do. I didn't mean . . .'

She started to walk. 'Well, what did you mean?'

'I don't know.' He fell in beside her, pushing his bicycle. 'Do you mind if . . . if I keep you company?'

'Do you mind, do you mind. You're always asking me if I mind.'

He had his face turned towards her as they approached the entrance gates, watching her profile against the blur of the distant banking. He could feel the muscles in his neck stretched tight, his throat constricted as if the effort of twisting his head was cutting off the blood supply to his brain; his senses were numbed and he felt dizzy

186

as she seemed to float along beside him. Still, he thought 'always' was a bit much. 'I don't think I am. Always asking if you mind, I mean.'

'Just teasing.' She laughed. 'Our first argument.'

'What sort of job's he's after, your cousin?'

'Oh, anything I shouldn't wonder. He's not in position to be choosy.'

She halted, turned and stared directly at him. 'You and your questions. He's lost his job because of me, if you must know. That's why I feel I ought to help him. An obligation, isn't that what they call it?'

Until quite recently, she told him, Rose had been in service in a grand house on a country estate near Weybridge. 'You wouldn't credit what they had us do. We was invisible, that's what we was. Never let your voice be heard by the ladies and gents unless they demanded it. Stand still when spoken to and look 'em in the eye. Never offer an opinion, though Gawd knows we was hard pressed enough at times. Always give room on the stairs. No visitors, friends or relatives. No "fraternising" as they called it unless you wanted to be kicked out without a hearing.' She paused to stamp her small, black-booted foot. 'They wouldn't even call you by your proper name. Couldn't be bothered to learn it. Called me Emma the whole time I was there. Who do they think they are, these people? One day, oh one day they'll get their comeuppance.' She had been a scullery maid, 'washing up pots and pans, sweeping the kitchen floor, trying to keep up with Monsieur's demands.'

'Monsieur?' said Stan.

'The French chef, and he didn't just use his hands for cooking.'

'Did your cousin work there too?'

'He did. Hallboy, they called him, cleaning boots, emptying chamber pots, chopping kindling, that kind of thing. Not that he complained. A job's a job these days and we had my Pa to thank for both of them.' Her father was the under-butler to the family, her mother a lady's maid. Both were still in place. Rose had been disowned. 'They accused me of leading on that fat old Frenchman, took his

187

word instead of mine. That kind of thing happens all the time to me. I can't help the way I look, Stan, can I? Sometimes I wish I was as plain as a pikestaff.'

'You mustn't say that. The way you look, it's a gift.'

'More like a bleeding liability, if you ask me. It got me kicked out, that's all I know. And poor Harry and all. Caught Monsieur trying to put his mitts up my skirt and dotted him one. Old frog-face rushed off to the Earl and got us both struck off the menu.'

'That's awful.'

'Ain't it the truth? Luckily, Ivy's a pal. She put in a word for me at the jolly old Bluebird so here I am.' She stopped, held out her hands and bobbed into a curtsy like a music-hall performer taking a bow.

Stan walked with her all the way back to the semi-detached villa where she had a room, a mile or so along the Byfleet road. It was a pleasant location, with pollarded beech trees lining the pavements, the properties three storeys tall and standing well back behind well-tended front gardens. He was surprised that she could afford to stay in such a place.

After that, she allowed him to walk her home occasionally, although she warned him not to make a habit of it because she did not like falling into habits. She remained a puzzle to him, sometimes almost fond, seeming to derive some pleasure from his company, taking his arm and calling him 'dear', listening to his attempts to entertain her with every sign of appreciation and making him feel quite witty and wise so a warmth ran through him, a delight; so he felt he might be one of the chosen ones, remembered what he had told himself not so long ago: 'At this time and at this place, anything is possible.' At other times though she was curt and cold, lost in her own thoughts, hardly acknowledging he was there and, when she did notice, seeming to find him a nuisance and irritation. 'I can't bear clinging, can't abide it. Makes me feel desperate, it does. I'll walk the rest on my own, if it's all the same to you.'

He often saw her talking to men, or more accurately men talking to her. They seemed drawn to her, as he was; pilots, mechanics, customers at the Bluebird Café. He hated them all but understood that jealousy was pointless, that he had no call on her, no call whatever; that he had to be content with what little she gave him. Of course, he could turn his back on her, try to forget her, but that was a prospect he could not bring himself to think about. Still, the acquaintanceship, for he could not claim it was any more than that, seemed to be going nowhere. Once he asked her: 'Do you like me, Rose?'

'Course I do. What a silly question. I wouldn't be here if I didn't like you, now would I?'

'But why do you like me? Is there any particular thing?'

'Well, I can't say there is, dear. 'Cos you're serious, I suppose, and don't try nothing on.'

It was as if he had walked into a brick wall. Although he had no idea how, he had been thinking of trying something on, some small thing like taking her hand or slipping his arm round her waist and leaning close to her and breathing in the perfume of her hair. Now it seemed that if he did any of these things, she would not like him any more.

The news from Bowman was that there was no news. The board's deliberations had been inconclusive. Further discussion was required. Meanwhile, Howard Pixton's Sopwith had won the Schneider Trophy for Britain, a speed event for seaplanes racing round the harbour at Monte Carlo. It was a blow to Guv who had turned down a chance to compete himself, caught up in the Atlantic bid. Worse still, the headlines were full of Gustav Hamel announcing his own Atlantic flight. Hamel, English-born despite his name, whose exploits outdid Guv's: dozens of distance records won, first airman to deliver aerial post, the pilot who in his Blériot looped the loop no fewer than fourteen times at Windsor, watched by the King and the Royal Family. Rumours came through that in the Martinsyde Works Hamel's machine, backed by a Scottish financier, was already taking shape. Perhaps the Sutro project would progress no further than the drawing board.

At this time, when everything was uncertain (the trans-Atlantic flight, not knowing where he was with Rose, if anywhere at all) Stan found a letter screwed up in the old oil drum they used to burn rubbish. He recognised the handwriting, had seen it many times at school, rather round and careful, as though the writer had leaned over the paper, tongue in the corner of the mouth, trying not to make mistakes or blot the ink. He read it through:

Dear Mr Sutro.

I hope this finds you well. We read lots about you in the Argus. *My pa says you have put Alfriston properly on the map. I often think back to those happy days together in the manor house. I hope you do as well. I am sorry to say my health or condition as you might say has not been very good of late. It has made it very difficult for me to keep on working so times are a bit hard for me. My pa does not know what ails me yet but soon I will have to decide what to do about it. Any help you might be able to give me would be most welcome and gratefully accepted. I hope that you do not mind me writing to you about this, but as I expect you can imagine I feel very alone at present. It would make all the difference in the world to know that I am in your thoughts for past friendship's sake.*

Looking forward to hearing from you.

Yours faithfully,

Mary (Grey)

Stan supposed she had added *(Grey)* in case she was confused with some other Mary. But he was sorry to learn that the girl was unwell and took the letter to Guv. 'I found this in the rubbish.'

'So?'

'I thought perhaps it got chucked out by mistake.'

'Now why did you think that? A long time ago I told you to lay off where this little floozie's concerned. That still stands, unless you've got designs in that direction. Otherwise, it's got bugger all to do with you.'

Next time he was in Weybridge Stan bought a postcard, a dull view of the high street but the best he could find, and wrote a brief reply in capital letters so his handwriting would not be recognised:

DEAR MISS GREY.

HOW NICE TO HEAR FROM YOU. I AM SORRY TO LEARN YOU ARE NOT TOO WELL. PERHAPS THIS CARD WILL HELP YOU KEEP YOUR PECKER UP,

YOURS SINCERELY.

FRASER SUTRO

He was working on the Sopwith a few days later when he heard the blare of Captain Sutton's Douglas. The Australian laid the machine on its side, not bothering to pull it onto its stand. 'Where is he? Is he here?'

'He's in the back.' Stan had moved away from the Sopwith, cleaning his hands on a rag.

Sutton pushed past him, shouting: 'Sutro, I want a word with you.'

Guv appeared, his face expressionless. 'Me, Sutton?'

'You swine, you bloody rotten swine! You've chucked me for some Brazilian bugger and you haven't got the decency to tell me to my face.'

'Who told you this?'

'Some little Fleet Street hack.'

Guv was unflustered. 'I don't know how the word got out but yes, he's right.'

'I know he's bloody right. I've talked to Bowman. He's brought me up to date.'

Guv frowned. 'You had no right to talk to Bowman.'

'I'd every right. My life was on the line, as well as yours.'

'Well, now it's not. No need for you to worry any more.'

'I wasn't worried, you pompous sod. But I want to hear the truth from you.'

'Steady on, Sutton. I've given you quite a lot of room. But I warn you, if you go on in this vein . . .'

'You'll what?'

'May I suggest you simmer down? Do you want an explanation or are you going to carry on making an idiotic fuss? Obviously I was going to put you in the picture. But someone's beaten me to it, that's all.'

'Hardly all,' said Sutton, his shoulders sinking a little. 'To hear this way that I've been replaced for no good reason . . .'

'With every good reason. Bowman won't fork out all the money, he must have told you that. The way he put it, they're unwilling to accept sole responsibility for such a hazardous enterprise. In other words, stand accused of sending us to a watery grave. They've agreed to chip in half. I don't know the state of your bank account, Sutton, but I'll bet you can't cough up the balance.'

'Don't be ridiculous.'

'Not ridiculous at all. Unless I can match the Bowman contribution, it's end of story.'

'So you went to Matos.'

'He's not just rich, Jean-Luc's stinking rich, heir to the biggest ruddy coffee plantation in Sau Paulo. And you know his record in the air, he's a pretty damned fine pilot. Obviously he jumped at the opportunity, and the money's already in place.'

'Go to blazes, Sutro. I'm a better flier than him any day of the week.'

'Maybe that's true. But let me be blunt. When it came down to it, it wasn't just ability in the air or even money, though there was no way round that particular difficulty. To be candid, Sutton, you've been a confounded liability, unreliable, late for meetings, sometimes not showing up at all, leaving all the chat to me, playing the role of the simple airman, not interested in how it's going to be done, just the doing of it. Well, that's no bloody good to me. But Jean-Luc's got a way with him, suitable for all occasions.'

'You mean he's a gentleman and I'm not?'

'I wouldn't put it that crudely myself.'

'You conveniently forget my responsibilities to the Corps, Sutro. My time's not necessarily my own.'

'Well, I hope you fulfil them better than you have your responsibilities to me.'

'Thanks for the lecture. I'll commit your comments to my diary when I get back to camp.'

Guv shook his head. 'Look, Sutton, it's just the way things have turned out. In my place you'd do the same.'

'Don't credit me with what you know of yourself. You've put me in bad with the RFC, made me look a bloody fool in public, and denied me the chance of a lifetime. You're an arrogant skunk, Sutro, an arrogant self-serving little skunk.'

Guv took a pace forward, his right arm drawn back, his fist quivering by his ear.

'Go on then,' Sutton said, 'and see what you get in return.' He stared at Guv for a long moment, then turned and walked slowly out of the shed. As he came close to Stan, he murmured, 'Remember Granny's false teeth.'

Guv followed him outside. 'One more thing, Sutton,' he called after him. 'If you choose to take this further and cause me trouble, I'll unleash the lawyers on you. Remember, I can afford it. You can't.' He stood with arms folded watching the Australian kick the Douglas into life and ride away. When he returned to the shed he came up to Stan so their faces were almost touching. 'What did Sutton say to you? Something about false teeth.'

'Nothing. A joke.'

'Damned odd,' Guv said. 'He didn't strike me as being in the mood to make jokes.' He prodded Stan's chest hard. 'Understand, a word of this to anyone and you're out too.'

Next morning, when Stan woke and went to the single window of his room and looked out, he saw that the small area of sky visible between the tiled roofs of the houses on the opposite side of the street was clear blue without a trace of cloud. Good flying weather, so lots of blokes up today, the air full of the racket of their motors, manoeuvring their machines above the circuit, always something new, making you feel there was no better place to be, up-to-the-minute, that was it, up-to-the-blinking-minute, pioneers of a science (for that's what it was, a science) that would change the world, the whole ruddy world. He heard, from downstairs, a rattle of pans, a kettle being filled; his landlady busy in the kitchen. The smell of toast and frying bacon drifted up the stairs. He had been lucky with his digs. The rent was fair and Mrs Templeton sent him off with a good breakfast in him, a packed lunch to take and, in the evening, set out for him and the other two lodgers, salesmen both, a plain and whole-some supper. Normally he would have felt that life was good. Instead he had a sick feeling in his stomach. So much had changed. What had seemed certain now seemed uncertain. Had Guv meant what he said, that his future hung on such a slender thread after so many years?

He went up to the shed early but Guv was not there. Outside, dusting off his boots with a handkerchief, was a youth he recognised as Rose's cousin.

'And what can we do for you?'

'Not so much of the "we", old man. I'm after your boss. I'm told there might be a job in the offing.'

'Who told you that?'

'The word's got about. Any objections?'

'To what?'

'Going after the job.'

'Why should I have? Anyway, what job is it?'

'Search me. Ain't it true there's something big on here? Maybe that's it, more hands to the pump. Whatever it is, I'll give it a go. I ain't too proud. Always ready to learn as long as there's room for promotion. Won't take too long, I reckon. I know my way around motor cars all right. Fettling one of these contraptions can't be that much different.'

'You'd be surprised.'

'I doubt it. When's the big cheese turn up?'

'Show him a bit of respect or you won't get past the door.'

'Likes a bit of kowtowing, does he? Thanks for the tip, old man.'

'Don't call me old man.'

'What shall I call you?'

'Nothing.'

'Righto, Nothing.'

'Less of your cheek. What's your name, anyway? I forget.'

'Paget, Harry Paget.'

Stan unlocked the shed. Paget followed him in. 'So this is where it all happens, eh?' He ran a hand over the taut canvas of the Sopwith's wing.

'Pack that in. Don't touch a blooming thing.'

'Keep your hair on, old man. What harm can it do? Got to learn, ain't I?'

'You're not hired yet.'

'Not yet.'

When Guv drove up in his Hispano-Suiza two-seater the youth went straight over to him. 'I'm on time, sir, as you can see.'

So Guv had been expecting him. 'Very well, then, follow me.'

Stan watched them go through to the office. They were there for ten minutes or more, the youth leaning forward all that time, turning his cap in his hands, grinning a lot and talking a lot, and Guv nodding as if he approved of what he heard. Several times he laughed out loud. When they came out, Guv smacked a hand on Paget's shoulder. 'This lad's going to join us. Starts tomorrow, seven sharp. Prompt mind, Paget, or Stan will have your guts for garters, never mind me.'

Later, Stan brewed the first tea of the day. 'So what's this Paget meant to do?'

'You tell me,' Guv said. 'It seemed to me you could do with an extra pair of hands.'

'How'd you get that idea?'

'I don't know. Just an impression, as if your mind's been elsewhere recently.' He took the offered mug. 'Look, Stanley, it's early days but I don't think you grasp the scale of this project. When they begin building the big kite over at the factory, this place is going to be up to its ears making components. Anything in that cockpit I want a personal hand in – and that's where you come in. But you're not going to be able to manage it on your own.'

'A kid like that's not going to be much good.'

'Train him up, for God's sake. Use your nous, and his. He's bright enough. But understand, he's only the first. It's not just you and me any more. That's something you've got to accept. If you don't, if you can't, well, let's hope it doesn't come to that.'

Stan recalled what Sutton had said. So it had begun. Sutton was right. 'So where did he come from?' he said. 'Did he just turn up out of the blue or what?'

'You played a part in that. That little floozie from the Bluebird put in a word for him when I was down there the other day. Her cousin, so she claimed. Said you'd tipped her off.'

'I never did.'

'She seemed to think so anyway. Not sweet on her, by any chance? I wouldn't blame you.'

'Course not.'

'I hope not, for your sake.'

'Why? What do you mean?'

'She's a bright little package but a lot of the fellows have spotted that already.'

'Including you?'

'Oh rot. She's of no interest to me. I'm just saying, it's obvious she knows a thing or two. Be careful, that's all. Besides . . .' Guv paused. 'Besides, I need to lay off bits of fluff for a while in case it gets back.'

'Gets back? Gets back to who?'

'To Bowman. I'm engaged to his daughter.'

The news of the engagement was soon in the papers. The press made much of it, the romance between the heiress to the Bowman empire and a hero of the air. It added spice to reports about the rivals, Hamel and Sutro, battling to win the prize to be first across the Atlantic.

Paget had proved proficient, with a quick mind and dexterous hands. Stan could see the way he cultivated Guv, edging close to impudence but acting in such a joshing way, plain sauce, that it made it hard to take offence. Occasionally he went too far. Then, at Guv's bark, he would flush and look extremely young again and bend quietly to a task, making it hard not to feel sorry for him. It was cleverly done.

To Stan he was dismissive, would always go to Guv if Guv was there. If not, he preferred to wait until he was, only taking Stan's directions with a great show of reluctance, questioning every order until the sense of it had been proved. He had a cleverness and cunning that filled Stan with suspicion and something close to fear. His only merit, to Stan, was the link to Rose. It gave him an excuse to talk about her in a roundabout fashion, eager to learn more about her. To learn everything really; where she had been and what she had done and if he might have a chance. A chance for what? For something, anything, whatever might come despite Guv's words of warning. As it was he learned very little. They seemed closed, these cousins, guarded and defensive. Paget shrugged off his clumsy probing. 'Ask her yourself, why don't you?' But he had an excuse to see her now, sharing (or so he pretended) an interest in the boy. It was not always easy. Quite early on, she told him: 'Harry says you were not at all nice to him when he turned up for his interview.'

'That's not true. I wasn't expecting it, that's all.'

'Don't your precious Guv tell you what's going on?'

'Why should he, I'd like to know? There's too much chit-chat as it is. We've got work to do.' He chewed his lip. 'Speaking of chit-chat, I gather I'm supposed to have tipped you off about the job.'

'Who told you that?'

'Who'd you think?'

'Well, you did, didn't you?'

'I did not.'

'Well, dear, it must have been somebody else then. I get into conversation with masses of boys here and it makes it hard to keep up.'

He looked at her, trying to see some flaw, some defect, something that would lessen her in his eyes, make her seem less than perfection so that she might appear more like other women, merely pretty, and so more bearable to him, no longer unique. But he found it impossible to believe there was another like her anywhere in the world. Only what she said, and the way she said it, was sometimes ugly.

Soon after Guv's engagement was announced, an envelope addressed to him in a familiar hand was delivered. It was partly obscured in a pile of mail. Paget took it through to the office before Stan could get to it. At lunch-break Guv called him through and handed him the letter. 'Know anything about this?'

Stan scanned it through:

Dear Mr Sutro,

Thanks ever so much for your card and kind thoughts. You don't know how much it means to me. Weybridge looks a very fine place indeed. You must be ever so busy with your flying machines and now getting wed to your grand lady. Things are much the same with me. Matters must take their course, I suppose. I have not told anyone about my situation. I'm feared I do not know which way to turn. But as you say, I must try to keep my pecker up. I understand how this places you but I am your friend and would do nothing to harm you, believe me. That is not to say that any help would not be most gratefully accepted.

Looking forward to hearing from you again,

Yours faithfully,

Mary

'The confounded woman mentions hearing from me again,' Guv said. 'What does it mean?'

Stan could not meet Guv's eye. 'I did send her a card.'

'The devil you did. From you or me?'

'From you. I didn't see the harm. I thought it would cheer her up.'

'You cheered her up, all right, you bloody fool.' Guv snatched back the letter, tore it carefully into pieces and dropped them in his wastepaper basket. 'And now she's into me. "I am your friend, I would do nothing to harm you." She makes her meaning clear as crystal. She believes her prospects have considerably improved.'

He stared out of the office window at the workshop where Paget was stretched out on a bench eating a sandwich and reading a penny-dreadful. 'If this gets out, Stanley, I'll destroy you. Your life . . .' he reconsidered, 'well, you won't have a life. Not a word, d'you hear? Least of all to that slippery little rat stuffing his face over there or that strumpet of a cousin of his at the Bluebird.'

Stan thought it most odd that, at the same time as appearing to have his life threatened in some way for a reason that was still not entirely clear, he should take a crumb of comfort from hearing Paget described as a slippery little rat. It was a small crumb, certainly, but it was still a crumb.

After that, no more letters came from Mary Grey, although Stan always looked for one in the post.

When, a few weeks later, Gustav Hamel went missing on a simple flight across the English Channel, it hit the Flying Village like a thunderbolt. If this could happen to Hamel, in such mundane circumstances, it could happen to any of them, not stunting or testing or otherwise tempting Fate but merely trundling from A to B. Imminent death was part of the game, always tugging at the sleeve, but never somehow your sleeve. There was always a reason for a pilot kicking the bucket (actual dying never mentioned) – some kind of failing, something that could have been avoided, a chain of mistakes that led, one by one, to disaster; mistakes you would never have made yourself. And if a failing of the machine, then somehow, you knew, you would have prevailed and got it down unlike poor old Max or Pip or Jumbo who always lacked that final touch of skill. But Hamel, among the best, the solid, thorough, experienced, gifted Hamel?

At first there was hope that he had put down somewhere, would telephone in. But gradually, as the few facts became known, it was clear that he was gone; vanished in his Morane Saulnier collected brand new from their Paris factory and en route for England and the Hendon Aerial Derby where he was billed to put on a display. As no trace of him was found, it was soon concluded that he had descended into the sea. Stan imagined the engine coughing, missing, stopping, the monoplane losing height, Hamel struggling in the cockpit doing what he could but knowing he was probably lost. Did he come down slowly, skimming the waves and settling like a wounded bird, Hamel intact and left with a shred of hope, or had it been fast and merciful, plunging hard and deep in a tangle of splintered frame and broken struts and wire and canvas? Whichever way, it seemed an obscure and squalid death, unwitnessed and inglorious. For Martinsyde it finished their trans-Atlantic plans, denied the star who was to have carried the project through.

That morning, when the few facts became known, Guv had come into the shed rubbing his hands together vigorously. 'Poor old Hamel. What a way to go. Just shows, don't it? Just shows.' He did not say what it showed. And he did not appear downcast. On the contrary he was quite chipper. He could not hold it in for long. He had anticipated Martinsyde's decision correctly. 'I'll wager a million dollars it's a one-horse race, my boys. Martinsyde won't go ahead without our Gus, their ace in the pack. Without him, the backers will fall away. We've got it to ourselves. If Knighton-Cooper's people come up with the goods, those ten thousand smackers are as good as ours.'

But Knighton-Cooper's people did not come up with the goods. Bowman's backing was withdrawn. Already nursing doubts, Hamel's disappearance was enough. In *The Times* Bowman gave his reasons. *If such a man can be lost over such a small stretch of water, how much greater the risks over the vast expanse of the Atlantic Ocean?* He repeated more firmly the assertion he had made to Guv and Sutton months earlier. *My company has no wish to be responsible for placing two gallant aviators in a position of the most extreme risk and peril.* He added, sentimentally, that he also had his daughter's happiness in mind, since soon she was to be married to Fraser Sutro. He had no doubts, he wrote, about the gallantry and resolve of his future son-in-law and his equally brave companion Jean-Luc Matos, but that on reflection perhaps the time for such a venture had not yet come. When it did, he was sure that Mr Sutro would be at the forefront of the adventurers ready to step forward. Perhaps by then the science of aeronautics would have advanced sufficiently to ensure success. As it was, though these were not his words, the deal was off.

After what he judged a decent interval (not so to them) Guv went round to Martinsyde to propose that he should take the place of Hamel. But the Martinsyde directors had read *The Times*, the Scottish financier had withdrawn, and even Matos was wavering now so Guv was unable to pledge his millions. Besides, as someone put it later, there was something uncomfortable and not quite British about this fellow Sutro's handling of the whole affair; an unseemly haste to step into a dead man's shoes.

Looking back, it seemed to Stan that Gustav Hamel's death was like a marker, an end and a beginning; an old order passing, predictable and secure, where the brave deeds of a few inspired the many, then everything turning dark, the whole world moving into shadow, where bravery was quickly commonplace and cheap as conflict spread across the map of Europe like a stain. No longer any squeamishness about a dead man's shoes. No time for that.

Once, towards the final days of peace, but learning that Germany had invaded France, Rose asked Stan, in a casual way, what it was all about.

He shrugged. 'I don't know, I'm sure. Everyone says we'll be in it soon.' He tried to look like a warrior should, stern and resolute. 'I suppose that must mean me.'

She considered his words for a moment. 'I read a paper the other day.'

'Oh yes?' He waited for her view of world events.

'It had the pictures of your boss's wedding. It must have been a lovely do.'

He felt a spurt of anger that she should utter such a triviality at that moment, with him about to go to war. He wanted her to worry for him, to be anxious, to express concern. But he was only one; he was well aware of that. One of a number of hopeful spooners eager for her favours. What number? A handful? A dozen? A hundred? All the blokes in the blinking Village and countless others beyond?

Rose did not catch his disappointment. 'She ain't no looker though is she, dear, that Lydia Bowman, despite them getting her up like a fourpenny handbag? Obviously her attraction lies elsewhere. Take that away and she'd be LOPH for certain.'

'LOPH?'

'Left On Papa's Hands.' She laughed. 'That Guv, he's a blinking chancer, he is. He'll come unstuck one day. That type always does.'

Stan made no comment. He wondered where she had obtained this knowledge, that Guv's type always came unstuck. But she had permitted him to hold her hand, her soft pink hand, and he did not want to spoil her mood. 'Would you say you're my girl, Rose?' he said suddenly. On impulse he had some idea of writing to her as his girl from foreign, warlike parts, perhaps crouching behind a parapet before an attack.

She thought about it for an unflattering length of time. 'I suppose you might say that, dear,' she said finally.

Once more that deadly, feeble question: 'You do . . . like me, don't you?'

'Course I do.' She assumed a dignified air. 'Otherwise I would not permit you to hold my hand.'

'But how much?' he persisted, yet fearful of the answer.

'Oh, I'm sure I don't know. What funny questions you ask.' Then she stopped and looked at him directly. 'Look, dear, you're a nice enough boy but nice ain't really enough, now is it, not for what you're asking? You're not well placed, are you, when it comes down to it? I don't object to walking out with you from time to time, but you're not in a position to take things any further. It's not your fault, it's just how things are. I'm not blaming you, understand, but we never go nowhere, not nowhere nice, and that's hardly enough for me.'

He wished she would stop saying 'nice'. 'If that's it, Rose, what about the flicks tomorrow and maybe after a bite to eat? Don't know why I didn't think of it before. It's just I like to walk with you, I suppose.'

'Flicks and a bite to eat,' she said. 'Yes, that sounds nice. But you really mustn't spend money you ain't got on me.'

Her apparent concern, if lightly expressed, touched him. 'Oh, I've got money,' he said. 'Course I have.' He squeezed her hand. 'Oh, Rose, I like you such an awful lot.' He hated himself for what he felt compelled to say and hated her for making him say it, but pulled back from the stronger declaration he ached to make.

She removed her hand to catch a loose curl that had escaped from under her small straw hat. 'That's nice, dear, really nice.'

At the same time, in London, a Foreign Office attaché was crossing the Mall and mounting the steps leading to the German Embassy in Carlton House. He carried an envelope that contained a document advising the German Ambassador that, with the delivery of this piece of paper, a state of war existed between Britain and Germany.

And as the greater tragedy took its course, a smaller one occurred that passed by all but a few. Stan read the letter from his father and the cutting from the *Argus*. The body of a woman had been recovered from the Cuckmere, identified as that of Mary Grey, floating among the hire skiffs at the Golden Galleon. Stan felt a fleeting sorrow; all so long ago, those days. So much had happened, so much was still to come. He found he could hardly recall the girl in any detail, a vague impression only of a pretty country face. He did not mention her passing to Guv. What was it to do with him? What would be the point?

3

Guv Sutro was quick to present himself for service with the military wing of the Royal Flying Corps; so quick that there was much droll speculation in Flying Village that 'married bliss' (laughter) was proving irksome. 'Rather him than me, old lad, despite her dowry.' Given Guv's own opinion of his abilities and record, it rankled that he was commissioned a second lieutenant and not a captain. And, despite his eagerness for action, his duties were at first minimal as the Corps dealt with the task of moving its headquarters and four operational squadrons from Farnborough to St Omer. Apart from a single flight that remained in Southern England to carry out coastal patrols, the sixty aircraft that landed in France represented the entire strength of British power in the air.

The War Office was also involved in a complex exercise, taking over Brooklands to develop and build military aircraft and operate a flying school. The martial ambitions of a single pilot would have to wait, so Guv's time was spent demonstrating, with suitable dash and vigour, various new prototypes to panels of high-ranking officers who marvelled that the wings did not come off. At last, with an overseas posting imminent, he was granted a week's leave and flew his Sopwith down to Saxonshore, the Bowman place near Rye, to await orders.

In all this time he did not explain to Stan or Paget whether they were still employed or not and, given his baleful mood, they did not ask. Each morning they reported to the shed as usual and invented work to pass the time. Once, Paget said: 'Any idea where all this kerfuffle leaves us?'

'You're very matey with the Guv,' Stan said. 'Why don't you ask him straight out?'

'I did. He said he'd got bigger things on his mind. Told me to bugger off.'

'Hardly surprising. Want to know what I think? He'll chuck us when it suits him. And really, it doesn't matter a fig because sooner or later blokes like you and me are going to find ourselves up to our necks in a stinking hole somewhere, fighting for King and Country whether we like it or not. I just hope it's a nice deep hole, that's all.'

'They can't make us go.'

'Can't they just? You'll see. They'll run through their volunteer army soon enough and then they'll come looking for us.'

'Well, I ain't going.'

'It won't be up to you. They call it conscription. Everyone will have to go, unless there's a ruddy good reason.'

'Such as?'

'I don't know – being in a special trade, I suppose, or bad health – that sort of thing.'

'If the time comes I reckon old Guv could pull a string or two in our favour, get us a nice cosy billet.'

'Why should he?'

'Oh, I can think of things.'

'Well, I can't think of any. And I wouldn't contemplate asking either.'

'Well, that's you ain't it?'

'Yes,' said Stan. 'I reckon it is.'

He was aware that he was not being entirely honest with Paget. He had no intention of seeking a cosy billet but he remembered what Captain Sutton had once said to him: 'I want to be bloody sure I'm in a good position when the bell goes, so I've got a bit of control over my destiny.' It seemed to him that to put himself forward now, while he stood at least some chance of being valued, might help him to achieve that bit of control over his own destiny and even, with a word or two from Sutton, to find his way into the RFC. Otherwise, if the war didn't finish by Christmas (no one said which Christmas), he had little doubt it would be the poor bloody infantry for him and that stinking hole somewhere, waiting to meet the unknown Hun who Fate had decreed would do for him. Did it mean string-pulling, if he somehow got in touch with Sutton? He supposed it did, but there was a difference surely between pulling them to get into something and pulling them to get out of it.

In all these deliberations he accepted that at some point he was bound to lose touch with Rose, not that she was really his to lose. Nothing ever advanced between them, there was nothing satisfactory about their times together; he simply felt trapped – trapped and helpless. What had she been nicknamed? The Angler, on the make. Of course, he was not alone – there were plenty more poor fish like him gasping on the bank. Knowing this did not make it easier to bear, but it did, finally, help him to come to a decision. He wrote a brief letter to Captain Sutton. He did not tell Rose of this, nor of his intention. If he received a positive response from Sutton he would tell her then, look for a hint of honest concern. Meanwhile, he tried to convince himself that she could not touch him so deeply any more, told himself that the war had jolted some sense into him.

It was a jolt, as well, for Stan and Paget to learn that Guv had given up the shed at Brooklands. 'I'm soon for France, thank God. There's nothing doing here, unless I want to risk my neck teaching schoolboys how to fly or testing buses for the chaps who are doing the actual fighting. I'm moving the Sopwith down to Rye. Close up this place and meet me there.' That was all; no mention of where this left them.

With the wooden doors of the shed at Brooklands closed and locked for the last time, Stan and Paget climbed into the rented Dennis motor lorry, down on its axles with equipment and spares, and set off on the long journey to Rye where a new hangar had been completed in the grounds of Saxonshore. The heat of an August day had lingered overnight, humid and oppressive, making it hard to sleep. In his airless room Stan, haunted by prospects of war, had woken in a sweat to find it was not a dream.

A grey, damp morning mist swirled behind the three-tonner as they passed through towns and villages decked with bunting; the national flag hanging limp from poles and windows and, in the larger places, floral arches stretched across the road with exhortations, *God Save the King, Answer the Call To Arms, Your King and Country Needs You.* Signs of much excitement, litter in the streets, discarded banners, coloured streamers, punctured drifting balloons, everywhere silent now, only a few inhabitants about, weary looking, like partygoers nursing bad heads after a spree.

It had gone ten when they reached Reigate but the sun had still not broken through, a vague nebula of yellow-gold in the eastern sky. Only when they crossed the Sussex border beyond Tunbridge Wells did the mist clear, leaving the countryside vivid green and washed with light, and everything grew warm again and dry. This was Stan's heritage, this landscape; he had forgotten. He passed the back of a gloved hand across his eyes and gripped the wheel more tightly. 'Dust,' he said.

At the wrought-iron gates to Saxonshore, Paget drummed his knuckles on the door of the lodge house. Behind him, the Dennis rocked and throbbed, blue fumes from its exhaust souring the fragrant summer air. At last an old man came out and swung back the gates, directing them up the curving drive that ran for a further quarter-mile flanked by great cedars, beech, oak and rhododendron before it dipped down to a stone bridge barely wide enough to take the lorry. To the left an unruffled lake and boathouse, to the right some kind of ruined castle surrounded by a moat; a corner tower with a fallen-in roof, broken ramparts dark with ivy, the moat's banks overhung by willows, lilies spread across the glasslike water that perfectly reflected the scene above.

A final, grinding first-gear climb between more banks of rhodo-dendrons and towering trees, and the sandstone bulk of Saxonshore came into view, its outline sharp against a mass of dense blue-green woodland that seemed to billow up like clouds, stretching away to the distant skyline. 'Bloody hell,' said Paget. 'What a pile.'

A man in mechanic's overalls approached them through an archway to the side of the house. 'You're late.'

Paget said quickly: 'Got lost coming up the blessed drive.'

'I'm Chandler,' the man said, without explaining. 'I'll show you where you're to dump the stuff.' He pulled himself onto the running board and they followed his directions. Around them the estate opened up. They could see now that Saxonshore sat on rising ground with a prospect of broad, open valleys to the east and south where horses and cattle moved slowly in the growing heat; close by the house, a pattern of extensive formal gardens gave way to parkland cropped by sheep and, far away, the untouched wild woods.

The hangar, on flat ground on the far side of a cricket ground, still smelled of fresh-sawn wood. It was bigger than expected, a larger version of the Brooklands shed, with space to house half a dozen machines. The Sopwith looked small against the further wall.

Chandler began to walk away. 'Hey,' Stan said. 'Aren't you going to help?'

Chandler spat. 'Not on your life. I'm the chauffeur here. This ain't my line of country.'

Paget watched him go and also spat. 'I'll bet that bugger was told to give us a hand. I'll queer his pitch if I get the chance.'

For two days they installed the equipment and stored the spares under Guv's occasional supervision. They were put up in a shared room over the kitchens behind the house. In the hangar they worked alone; Chandler did not appear again. Still Guv said nothing about their situation. Near the end, Paget finally came out with it. 'Look, Mr Sutro, we need to know where we stand. Are we employed or ain't we?'

Guv looked at Stan. 'There's certainly work here, but whether it's enough for two I couldn't say, with everything turned upside down.'

Stan heard his voice, like the voice of somebody else. 'You don't need to worry about me. I got plans of my own.' So it seemed he had burned his boats. He was quite surprised. Paget was saying: 'Well, that's all right then, ain't it? That clears the way. Unless that bloke Chandler's got something to say on the matter.'

Guv continued to stare at Stan. 'Chandler's the ancien regime, nothing to do with me.'

'Well, that's all right then, ain't it?' Paget said again. He glanced at Stan anxiously, as though fearing he might have made a mistake. Again, he looked a boy. 'You sure about this, old man?'

'Yes, I'm sure.'

Paget grinned at Guv. 'So I'll be staying on?'

Guv nodded. 'I suppose so, yes.' He still appeared uncertain. 'Make bloody sure you're up to the task or I'll have you out on your ear.' Before he returned to the house he took Stan aside and said quietly: 'I hope you know what you're doing, Stanley.'

'I think I do.'

'Only think? Sounds infernally woolly to me. Going to put me in the picture?'

'I'm not quite sure myself yet, but I've got a general idea.'

'I must say I'm surprised.'

'Well, I reckon there's going to be a lot of surprises over the next few years.'

Stan watched Guv pass out of sight down the path towards the house. In the hangar Paget had been listening. 'Touching scene, eh?'

'Make yourself useful, Paget. Put some petrol in the Dennis.'

That last evening he went alone down to the stone bridge between the lake and the moated castle. By the willows swans were dipping their heads and long necks beneath the water feeding on the vegetation, then moving to another spot, their white breasts dipping with each thrust of their legs. He heard someone coming along the path behind him, then a voice: 'I say, I know you, don't I?' The Bowman woman was standing a few paces away, bareheaded, her hair tied back with a twist of linen, an Indian shawl around her shoulders.

'Oh, hello, ma'am. I was just—'

She held up her hand, quite a large hand with a calloused palm. 'Please, don't ma'am me.' She looked across to the distant ruin. 'Quite perfect, isn't it? Everyone thinks it's a castle but it isn't really, you know; it's a fortified house. Five hundred years ago, the French were making a frightful nuisance of themselves in these parts. You never knew who might come calling.' She sighed. 'Now it's the Germans. It always seems to be the French or Germans, doesn't it?' She bent down, picked up a pebble and tossed it into the water. 'This ghastly war.' The ripples disturbed the water lilies, the blooms nodding a little as though they agreed with her about the ghastly war. 'I'm going down to the stables. You can keep me company, if you like.'

They went along together, down a stony path that wound between grassy banks past some kind of excavation overgrown with ferns. 'That's where they quarried the stone to build Saxonshore.'

'A long time ago, I expect.'

'Oh, not so long. About a hundred years. It's younger than it looks, a bit like me.' She walked quickly, long strides that made him stumble to keep up. As they drew near to the stable buildings she ducked under the broad branches of an immense beech, once four individual trees but now the trunks grown into one, ridged and gnarled, the lower branches reaching to the ground. She sat down on a cast-iron bench. 'I'm so glad to have this chance to talk. I intended to, before you left.' She signalled for him to sit beside her. 'It's Kemp, isn't it? I cannot call you Kemp.'

'Stanley, then.'

'I get the impression, Stanley, that as boys you and my husband were almost like brothers. Understand, my husband has talked very little of those times. I'm simply reading between the lines.'

Her husband? For a moment he had forgotten. She wasn't a Bowman any more, she was Mrs Sutro. 'Well, I wouldn't go that far,' Stan said. 'We were pals, that's all.'

'Still pals, would you say?'

Stan was uncomfortable with her questions. 'Well, things change don't they, and people? It's different now.'

'I never think people change, fundamentally,' Lydia Bowman said. She turned to face him more directly. 'This is most interesting to me, you see. I believe there is a quality in my husband that inspires others to follow – you most of all, perhaps. To support, to be swept along, to be part of whatever new project he may have in mind. We are drawn to him because he seems to be at the centre of things, and it places us at the centre of things as well. Perhaps that sounds too fanciful. I admire him greatly, you see, not merely as a husband but as a man. Do you, I wonder, knowing him better than most, recognise some truth in what I say?'

'He's firm in his opinions, I'll give you that,' said Stan. 'And when he wants a thing he'll go for it, come what may.' A distant voice muttered something about Granny's teeth. 'Other than that I wouldn't know.'

'But surely it's such qualities that have made you follow him so loyally all these years.'

'As young shavers all we thought about was flying. He was in a position to do something about it, that's all. For me, what better place to be?' Stan knew this was not enough, that she wanted him to go further, to confirm for her Guv's supposed virtues, to endorse her opinions of the man. But he felt he could not tell her what she wanted to hear so pulled back, hoping the subject would go away.

'I see I can't quite make you understand,' said Lydia Sutro. 'It was the same with Poppa. From the first moment I saw my husband I perceived in him this strength of purpose that singles him out from other men. And yet I fear Poppa still does not understand him as I do. Oh yes, he admires him as a bold spirit, but he views life in very different terms. He's such a gentle soul – a reluctant man of business, you might say. His ideal world is here, you see, at Saxonshore. He hates to spend a minute away and yet it seems he's been trapped in London for ages now, meeting after meeting, thanks to the men enlisting and leaving the store short staffed. They're employing women now, not just as shop assistants but in every kind of job – driving vans, cleaning windows, even stoking boilers. Poppa finds it most disturbing that women should be called on to perform such tasks.'

She smiled. 'Poor Poppa, such anxieties pressing upon him. His greatest, I must confess, was that I should choose to marry a pilot. Pilots, he said, have such short lives.' She leaned forward a little. 'You don't think my husband will have a short life, do you?' She did not wait for a reply. 'I'm positive he won't. There has always been some-thing about him that reassures me on that point. He is not the type. He is simply not the type. I made Poppa come round to that eventu-ally; I think so, anyway. He could see I was determined. He has always spoiled me, I'm afraid, his only child.' She pointed upwards. 'He had a tree-house made for me in this very beech. Such fun. I'd climb and climb while he sat right here, puffing at his pipe, his nose in some old book. From the top there's a marvellous view – of Saxonshore, of course, and the whole estate, and when it's clear Rye Bay.' She stood up. 'Now come and see my horses. Do you like horses, Stanley?'

'I know my way round horses, but I doubt they're the kind you've got.'

'My husband does not like me to maintain the deep interest in the stables that I used to. He is firm in his ways and his opinions, is he not? One can only comply. I'm sure he is right. We have people to do such work and to involve oneself to too great an extent denies them gainful employment.' A heartbeat's pause. 'But there used to be a pleasure in it.'

'What do you do instead?'

'Oh, wifely duties. You would not believe the social whirl when married to a popular hero.' She laughed to suggest it was said tongue-in-cheek, but Stan was not deceived. 'Yes, even in stuffy old Rye. And I still have Poppa to take care of. My life is exceedingly full.'

She led him to the stables where they inspected the hunters and the carriage horses. It was plain that the hands there liked her, chuckling and shaking their heads when she told Stan: 'These good fellows were glad to see the back of me, feeding, grooming, mucking out, generally in their way. Now I leave it all to them. I still ride out,' she added, 'but not so much.'

That night, in the small room over the kitchens, Paget said: 'I'll soon have this place to myself. No regrets, old man?'

'None at all.'

'I saw you gassing to the Missus over by the house. Go for a little promenade with her, did you?'

'She came across me.'

'Did she now? You want to watch out.' Paget guffawed at the thought. 'She's a caution and no mistake.'

'How do you mean?'

'Funny, like. Funny looking, funny acting. Course, I understand her attraction for old Guv, all right, I ain't that daft, but I don't envy him certain obligations. Still, like they say, you don't look at the mantelpiece . . .'

Stan reddened. 'You leave her alone. She's a decent sort. If you're to work here, you'll treat her with respect or I'll tip Guv the wink.'

'Will you now?'

'I will.'

'All right, old man. Keep your hair on. You must have had a nice promenade, that's all I can say.'

In the morning, ready for the long drive back to Brooklands in the Dennis, Stan reluctantly went to seek out Guv. He did not feel comfortable about simply driving away without another word. It seemed unsatisfactory, to place him in the wrong somehow, leaving on what amounted to his parting shot: 'There's going to be a lot of surprises over the next few years.' Looking back, it sounded resentful although he hadn't meant it like that at the time, just that with the world as it was, as it had suddenly become, nobody should be surprised by anything that happened any more, that nothing would be or could be the same as before. As for surprises, he was as surprised as anybody that it had come to this; but still, it wasn't a good way to leave things between him and Guv.

He parked the lorry on the further side of the drive in front of Saxonshore and walked across the gravel towards the porch. A plump man in formal dress, black jacket, black tie, stiff-collared white shirt, came out of the house and stood at the top of the steps with his arms folded. 'If you want attention, it's round the back.'

'I'm Kemp.'

'I know very well who you are. Round the back.'

Behind him appeared Lydia Sutro. 'It's all right, Lambert, you may return to your duties.'

The plump man gave Stan a long look, bowed his head briefly and left them. Lydia extended an arm and beckoned Stan towards her. 'You're after my husband, I imagine. You'll find him in the library.'

He followed her into the house, unwilling now, thinking it might have been better to drive away after all, avoid, forget, look to the future not the past. They moved from the hall and made their way through various rooms; tall ceilings with fancy plasterwork, great marble fireplaces, dark panelling, gold-framed paintings of people in old-fashioned outfits, blue china on little corner shelves, rich carpets spread across wide oak boards.

'I did enjoy our conversation,' Lydia was saying as she went ahead down a narrow corridor. 'I do hope we shall meet again.' She knocked on a heavy door, opened it and stood back to let Stan pass by into the library; shelves from floor to ceiling of leather-bound volumes, a confusion of heavy furniture, a large stone fireplace engraved with a motto – *Non sine dignitas* – that Stan supposed must be French. Why not in English so folk could understand it? But then, folk would not be admitted here unless they were in service. It came to him that he had been in service of a kind. He had a sudden sense of breaking free.

Guv was not reading a book but smoking his pipe by a bay window that gave onto the gardens and castle ruins. He looked like a weekend guest at a loose end, waiting for something to break the monotony. He turned slightly and drew on the pipe, his teeth clenched on the stem. 'Had second thoughts?'

Stan heard Lydia Bowman close the door behind him. 'By no means.'

'Then there's nothing more to be said. I was counting on you to watch my interests in this nest of vipers now I'm off to France. That bounder Paget doesn't fit the bill, but thanks to you he's my only choice. I call it damned disloyal.'

Stan remembered Captain Sutton's words: 'Your loyalty does you credit, Kemp, but have you wondered if it works the other way?' Now he had the answer. 'It's loyalty that's behind this,' he said. 'I'm volunteering, same as you.'

'Same as me? For what?'

'Somewhere I can use my skills.'

'You mean the RFC?'

'Don't see why not.'

'You're on a loser there. They've been swamped with applications from every flag-waving grease monkey in the business.'

'I'm better than most and I've worked for you. That must count for something.'

'Not without a reference, it don't. Why expect me to use my influence when you've left me in the lurch?'

'I don't expect you to do anything. I can make my own way.'

'You never have.'

'No, I suppose you're right. Well, it's different now.'

'Don't be so bloody naive, Stanley. You've left it too late. You'll find the RFC's got all the spannermen it needs. Volunteer and you'll be passed along to the foot-sloggers as cannon-fodder, instead of which you could have seen the war out here.'

'Come to that, so could you.'

'That's different.'

'Why?'

'Confound it, I'm a pilot. Pilots are in short supply. Ground wallahs aren't. You're a damned fool, Stanley.'

'Well, as this is the age of damned fools, I reckon I might fit in all right.'

Back at his lodgings in Byfleet Mrs Templeton had two envelopes for him. The first was from Captain Sutton, briefly back from France to collect a replacement Avro 504, who told him briskly that if he was still serious about enlisting in the RFC, he was quite prepared to recommend him. He would have to complete some military training first, naturally, pounding the square and all that rot. But all things being equal he would then have the choice of becoming an air mechanic or, if he wanted to get into the air himself, an observer. The Corps was still inventing itself, so opportunities were excellent for a keen young fellow who knew his stuff. The Captain had other matters to attend to while he was in Blighty so, for the next few days, he was to be found at the Flying Village, just taken over by the RFC. If Stan was interested, he should get his skates on and ask for him at the main gate as the circuit was now under military jurisdiction and barred to the public. Then he would see what might be done.

The second envelope, from his father, contained a brief covering note and a press cutting about an inquest into the death of Mary Amelia Grey of Alfriston whose corpse had been retrieved from the Cuckmere river. It seemed it was a mystery. On the evening of her disappearance, according to her father and other witnesses, she had shown no sign of anxiety or depression – quite the reverse, in fact, being more cheerful than of late and constantly asking what time it was as though she had an appointment to keep. The Coroner questioned what such an appointment might have been. She had not been seen in company that evening. Did the deceased have something else in mind? One could only speculate, lacking any pertinent statement made by the unfortunate woman to family or friends, and the absence of any explanatory note. What was certain, however, was that having somehow entered the water and subsequently drowned, her body had been swept downstream for several miles until it was discovered the following day among the hire skiffs at the Golden Galleon Inn, bruised and cut about certainly, but no more than was to be expected, tossed about as she must have been in the strong currents of the river. An autopsy revealed, to the distress of her family, that the deceased (a spinster) had been seven months' gone with child, a finding that might have some bearing on the tragedy although the Coroner was not prepared to comment further on that point. The verdict was Accidental Death.

That evening, Stan took his bike from the shed in Mrs Templeton's backyard and cycled to the various pubs favoured by Rose and the ever-changing circle of cronies she called her friends. He did not find her, but in the Plough was Ivy from the Bluebird Café. It was not late but she was already far gone, bleary on the edge of a chattering group that had lost interest in her. He bought her another whisky and soda.

'It's Stanley, ain't it?' she murmured. 'Thank you, Stanley. Here's mud in your eye.' She drained her glass and looked at him significantly but he wasn't ready to buy her another.

He took a mouthful of bitter. 'I was hoping to see Rose.'

She sat back heavily on the leather settle and raised an eyebrow. 'That's not very flattering, dear.' And sighed. 'You've heard about the poor old Bluebird, I suppose? Closed down thanks to the blooming war.'

'That's rotten luck. So you're looking for work?'

'Drowning my sorrows at present, ducks.' She pushed her glass towards him. He fetched her another whisky. 'Our Rose ran into a bit of trouble at the caff,' she said, 'just before we was told it was shutting up shop. A few days later and nobody would've cared.'

'What kind of trouble?'

'The usual kind. You know what blokes are like, always mistaking being friendly for something more. Some chinless toff claimed she'd led him on, touched him for some cash. His chums chipped in and said the same and Rose was out on her blinking ear.'

'Where is she now?'

'I don't know. Her digs, I suppose. She's lying low. There was talk of the law.'

It was still light when Stan leaned his bike against the gate of the villa where Rose had her room. It was a warm summer evening, the sun filtering down between the thick foliage of the beeches that lined the road, creating dancing shadows on the broad pavements. To his eyes there always seemed a magic about the place, simply because Rose chose to live there.

The front door was opened by a nervous maid. 'I'm looking for Miss Pringle,' Stanley said. The maid turned away, confused.

Behind her, a hoarse voice said from the darkness of the hallway: 'Who's looking for Miss Pringle? Join the club.' A man with dishevelled grey hair came forward unsteady on his feet, rank with spirits.

'But she lives here, doesn't she?'

'Did, certainly. Done a bunk. Not empty handed either. I gather I'm not the only dunderhead round here. Doesn't make it easier though. I say, are you the police?'

Stan backed away. 'Well, if she's not here no more . . .'

The man came out onto the top step. 'If and when you catch up with her, Constable, tell her this. She can keep my late wife's baubles and welcome to 'em. It's a price worth paying, to see the back of the little tramp.'

It occurred to Stan that he might never see Rose again and, for a moment, he felt the same sense of breaking free, of escaping that he had experienced with Guv. But this was different; this time his boats had been burned for him. And just as he had felt uncomfortable at the prospect of driving away from Saxonshore without another word, so this seemed a damp squib of an ending, leaving things unsaid, things that might have made a difference, things that might have changed the situation. Things that might have soothed his longing, this nagging need to see her, if only for one last time.

In the morning he cycled up to Brooklands, identified himself to the sentry of the Royal West Surreys guarding the main gate and showed him Captain Sutton's letter. He was collected by an RFC corporal. 'Thinking of joining the mob, are you?'

'Maybe.'

'We don't just take anybody, you know. You got to have relevant experience.'

217

'I see.' Stan realised they were following a familiar route. 'We heading for the old Bluebird then?'

'Officers Mess now. How d'you know it?'

'I was Guv Sutro's chief mechanic.'

'Blimey. Well, you'll be all right, I reckon.'

The weather was closing in, everything grounded, men and machines safely in the sheds as a great bank of stormcloud advanced towards the airfield, its upper rim lit by brilliant sun but deep black below where lightning forked towards the ground and thunder growled. Outside the Bluebird the tables were empty, no smart crowd at their leisure, no murmur of conversation, no sudden laughter – and still the storm moved closer, the thunder louder now, as startling as the heavy guns in France

On the way Stan had seen a few familiar faces, mechanics still in civilian jobs, but he learned that many had enlisted, mostly in the RFC. He worried that Guv was right. 'You've left it too late, they've got all the chaps they need.'

Lights were on in the café, bright against the darkness of the approaching storm. A roll of thunder sounded quite close by and Stan followed the corporal inside. At the tables, not so many of them now, a few red-eyed officers were talking shop over mugs of tea and eggs and bacon. Stan imagined Rose there in her black satin dress and white lace cap and apron; she'd liven them up.

The storm was directly overhead, rain drumming on the roof, the claps of thunder shivering the building. Captain Sutton was waiting for him in a corner away from the others. They shook hands. 'Thought we'd start with an informal chat, Kemp. You're lucky to catch me. If it wasn't for this filthy weather I'd have been on my way this morning. How's your gallant employer these days?'

'He's not my employer any more. I've quit to do this.'

'Gosh, that keen, are you? Well, it's a jolly good start. I wonder, did my sage advice have anything to do with it? Don't answer that. If you go west I don't want you on my conscience.' He ordered a pot of tea from the orderly. 'Now, if the brasshats were daft enough to consider taking you on, how would you answer this simple question? What's your preference, take to the air or stay on the ground?'

'I want to fly, I reckon. Otherwise I might as well be in any old outfit.'

'Not strictly true. Keeping our machines in the air is absolutely vital. No trade's more important than air mechanic. Chaps who really know their stuff are scarce. You fit the bill. And no one would think less of you if you'd rather keep your feet on the old terra firma.'

'Understood, sir, but your letter mentioned being an observer. That sounds the sort of thing, although I thought that kind of job was just for officers.'

'By no means, at least not at the moment. Understand, it's no picnic up there on reconnaissance or spotting for our artillery. Sitting duck's not in it once Archie's got your range. But anyone half-decent can put in for it, whatever their rank.' Sutton grinned. 'Not put off? Okay, so let me fire some more posers at you. Would you say you're a decent sailor?'

'Never tried.'

'Any good at sketching?'

'Not since school.'

'Map-reading up to scratch?'

'Never done none.'

'Oh dear. Well, at least I know the answer to the fourth one: aptitude for mechanics. Big tick there.'

'So it's no go then?'

'Oh, I wouldn't say that. I'll put you forward for an interview here at the end of this week, strongly recommended. That'll give you time to brush up on those other points. They may sound rum but they all have their place.'

'You have my assurance, sir,' Stan said, awkwardly formal, 'that I will do my utmost to justify your confidence in me.' He knew it was mawkish but it was how he felt.

'Don't thank me, old chap,' said Sutton. 'I may have done you the worst turn of your life. Ah, here's the tea. Sugar, I take it? One lump or two?'

Back at his lodgings, as he started up the stairs, Mrs Templeton came out of her room. 'A young woman's been asking after you.'

He gripped the banister hard. 'Oh yes? Did she give a name?'

'Ivy something. She scribbled her address. Wants you to go round as soon as you can.' Mrs Templeton passed him a scrap of paper, looking severe, making it plain she disapproved.

Stan thought suddenly: This must be to do with Rose. 'Suppose I'd better then.'

Ivy's place was a few streets away, closer to the railway line where the houses began to give way to factories and workshops, the area drab and dilapidated. He found the room, on the second floor at the back. Along the landing a man and woman were shouting at each other and a child was crying. He tapped lightly on Ivy's door. After a moment he heard a key being turned in the lock and it opened a little, secured on a chain.

'Why, hello, Stan,' Rose said. She undid the chain and stepped back to let him in. Behind her Ivy was sitting sideways on a bed smoking, tapping her ash onto the bare boards.

'Well, this is a surprise, Rose,' Stan said. It sounded mild compared to what he felt. He looked over her shoulder at Ivy. 'Why didn't you tell me she was here?'

Ivy removed the cigarette from her mouth and with an attempt at elegance held it somewhere near her right ear. 'How was I to know she'd want to see you, ducks?'

'You had me trailing right up Byfleet Road.'

The women laughed. 'Oh, blimey,' Rose said. 'You didn't knock up Champagne Charlie? How is the old codger?'

'He thought I was the police.' It made the women laugh all the more. 'He said you'd got some stuff of his wife's.'

Rose looked scornful. 'I like his cheek. They was gifts, whatever he says. It's just sour grapes because I wouldn't let him get his wicked way.' She was innocent now, fixing him with her dazzling eyes. 'They weren't worth nothing anyway, just paste.'

'How d'you know?'

'Been down the hockshop, if you must know. Needs must when

a girl's on her uppers.' She glanced at Ivy who had stretched out on the bed trying to blow smoke rings. 'Silly old masher, he wants to be careful, spreading fibs.'

'He won't be taking it any further,' said Stan, 'At least, that's what he told me.'

Ivy propped herself up on one elbow. 'I should think so and all. We reckon he was diddling his old woman, don't we, Rose? Sold the real stuff while she was busy kicking the bucket.'

'Too right, Ivy,' Rose said. 'And wants to keep it dark in case he's found out.'

Ivy fell back. 'He ain't got anything on us, the old bugger. We got something on him.'

Stan wondered what the chinless toff at the Bluebird might have to say about this, and those chums of his who claimed they had been similarly 'led on'. There was always an easy explanation. 'You know what blokes are like, mistaking being friendly for something else.' And now that woebegone gent in Byfleet Road was branded a downright crook who had duped his dying wife. What would Rose and Ivy have to say about him if he took them up on it and expressed his doubts? They'd throw him out and he did not want to be thrown out. He wanted Rose to himself for a bit, so he could tell her he was joining up – a warrior off to war saying farewell to a girl (his girl), who would not be seeing her again for a long, long time, maybe never. He wanted to see emotion ruffle that flawless face, some sign that she cared, that he mattered. He changed the subject before it spoiled the moment.

'How long you been here, Rose?'

'Oh, quite a few days now, ain't it, Ivy? Why?'

This was no better. He found himself looking around for another bed but there was only one in the single room, still rumpled from being slept in. Surely they couldn't share? Gross images came into his mind, as if from another person, a person he feared, shadowy but always there and more often these days, more often since he had known Rose, who roused in him feelings he never knew he had. 'Just wondered, that's all.'

'Ivy's off out, aren't you, Ivy?' Rose said abruptly.

Ivy sighed. 'I suppose I am.' She pushed herself off the bed and stubbed out her cigarette in a tin lid.

Stan pretended interest. 'Where you heading, Ivy?'

'Oh, the usual, I expect. Like to treat me to a snifter, ducks?'

He gave her two shillings and she pulled on a shabby coat. In the brief moment between her opening and closing the door they could hear the man and woman along the landing still shouting at each other, more loudly than before, and the child wailing. 'This is an awful place, Rose,' Stan said.

'Don't I know it, dear?' She went over to the bed and patted the muddle of bedclothes for him to sit beside her. She took his hand. 'That's why I'm slinging my hook.' He was sweating at her closeness, could smell her strong sweet perfume. 'I'll say this for you, Stanley,' she said, 'you've stuck with me, not like some. It's sweet, you tracking me down.' She leaned against him. 'Ivy won't be back for ages. What you feel like doing?'

He wasn't ready to answer that. What was she getting at? Suggesting a cup of tea, a bite to eat, a beer or two, or what? He thought he might understand her meaning but wasn't practised in these matters. If he got it wrong, bungled it, he'd just be another contemptuous rotter who tried to take advantage, who took being friendly for something else. Again he changed the subject.

'I've got some news,' he said lamely. No bombshell this, as intended. It trickled out.

'Have you, dear? What's that?'

'I'm enlisting in the RFC. I'm going to fly.'

'Well, ain't you the fine one? A regular hero. What made you want to do a thing like that?' Which seemed to suggest that while he might be a hero, he was also a fool.

'It seems the proper thing.'

'Oh, I wouldn't know about the proper thing, not if some's to be believed.' She ran her arm round his shoulder and stroked his neck. 'I suppose that bloody Guv put you up to it.'

'No, not at all. I've got the skills they want.'

'Flying, eh? Rather you than me. It's a long way down. You are a brave boy and no mistake.' She placed her other hand on his thigh. 'You like me, Stanley, don't you?'

'More than like.'

'Well, let's get cosy, shall we? Turn down the gas.' She slipped off the bed, undressed in a moment and stood before him on a scrap of grubby carpet, amused by his confusion. He had not seen a woman naked before. She pulled at his clothes.

'I love you, Rose,' he said.

'Course you do. And I love you.'

A thrill ran through him. 'Do you?'

'Course I do.'

He did not know what was expected of him. Her body was against his, smooth and cool and supple. So this was what folk made so much of, what all the fuss was about. She was panting, groaning, working him (it struck him even in the throes of pleasure) like some kind of apparatus with (it struck him also) practised hands. He finished rather soon. It had seemed a messy business but still she carried on, doing more for herself than him. At last she gave a long sigh, rested for a moment on his chest, then rolled aside and lay beside him spent, her body damp with effort, the narrow mattress wedging them together, the narrow mattress of the single bed. He thought about the bed, recalled the image it had summoned up and felt a pulse of fresh interest in his groin. He turned towards her, touched her breast. 'Now then,' she said. 'I think you've had your ration.' She did not say again that she loved him, either then or later.

She dressed quickly, taking no notice of him this time. 'You should get your things on too, dear. Ivy'll be back soon.' He wondered, had Ivy been told to give it an hour or so? Had this been planned and if so, why? She went over to a small mirror hanging on a nail and began to brush her hair.

He watched her, stirred by the intimacy of it. 'I didn't think I'd see you again, Rose.'

'Well, you've seen me good and proper now.'

'I didn't want to go without saying goodbye.'

'You're a dear, Stanley, a proper little gent.'

'I don't know what to say about all this, Rose. Where does it leave us?'

'Us? Oh, us. Well, I don't think it does to take things too serious in this horrible old world we live in. You just can't tell what's coming next. The way I look at it is, you've got to take your fun where you can find it. As long as it's with someone you're really fond of,' she added quickly.

'I hoped what's happened might change things.'

'Did you, dear?' she said casually. 'No, I don't think so, really.' She came over to him and ruffled his hair; he felt like a dog. 'You're sweet,' she said, and went back to the mirror. 'You'll soon forget me when you fall into the clutches of those naughty French mamzelles.'

'No,' he said. 'I won't.' He thought he heard Ivy on the landing. 'Look, Rose, will you let me write to you? You know, as my girl.'

'I can't stop you writing, can I?'

'But as my girl.'

'I don't know about that. I can't make no promises, see. It wouldn't be fair.'

'You said you loved me.'

'Well, that was in a manner of speaking.'

A door slammed somewhere; it wasn't Ivy. He had a little more time.

'All right then, not as my girl. As a friend, a good friend.'

'Yes, that's right,' she said. 'As a good friend, Stanley, a good friend. I've known that all along.'

He had no wish to be a friend, good or otherwise, but he understood it would have to do. He had intended a clean break; it was hopeless. He still lay gasping on the bank. 'You say you're moving on. So where do I send my letters?'

'Here, I suppose. Ivy ain't going nowhere. She can forward 'em on. Gawd knows where that might be. I do know I can't stay here a minute longer than I have to.' Did she glance at the bed? She looked wistful. 'I did have something in mind. Someone put me onto it, a real good position, but just my luck it ain't round here. They'd jump at me, he reckons.' That word 'he' struck hard. 'But it's no blooming good if you ain't got the wherewithal to go after it, is it?'

'Money, you mean?'

'That's it, dear, got it in one. Train fares, bus fares, bed and board, p'raps a few new clothes to look smart like. You know, impress 'em. But to be candid, Stan, I'm skint. I'll just have to see what I can pick up round here, but with things as they are . . .'

'I'll lend you some,' he heard himself say. 'Money, I mean. How much do you need?' He thought about his meagre savings and blanched.

'I couldn't let you do that.'

'How much do you need?'

'Are you serious, Stan?'

'Just tell me how much.'

'Twenty quid would tide me over.'

Tide her over! His scalp contracted. 'Yes, that's all right.' All right? Yet despite the enormity of it he felt a kind of gloating thrill that she would be indebted to him, that he would have some claim on her.

'You don't know how much this means to me,' she said. She put her arms round him and hugged him to her, entirely sexless. 'Never fear, I'll pay you back.'

He withdrew the twenty pounds next day. When he called at Ivy's place Rose was not there but Ivy promised she would give her the envelope when she returned. He asked if she was far. Ivy was sure she did not know. He was nervous about leaving the envelope with Ivy because he supposed she knew what it contained. Instead he said Rose could collect it at the branch office of his bank in Byfleet High Street. Ivy was insulted. He wondered why, given what he knew.

At the end of that week he was accepted by the Royal Flying Corps and began his training; a good recruit, as Sutton had expected. Within months the sleeves of his tunic bore the stripes of a lance corporal, the breast the single wing of an observer and he crossed to France to join his squadron. He did not see Rose again until she visited him in the military hospital in Folkestone almost a year later.

Five

1

Fraser Sutro

When the BE2 two-seater landed back at its base at St Omer after a reconnaissance flight east of Nieuport on the North Sea coast of Belgium photographing the German line, its pilot walked round the machine cursing and counting the bullet-holes. There were two in the fuselage, three in the wings and one in the tail-plane. All had been fired by British troops advancing through Flanders.

The sergeant observer pulled himself upright in the front cockpit, stepped out and shuffled back across the lower wing holding the bulky Graflex camera with one gauntleted hand, steadying himself on the wooden struts with the other. He joined his pilot and inspected the damage. 'Well, if Tommy Atkins reckons to beat the Hun he needs to brush up on his marksmanship.'

'I'm not laughing, Evans,' the pilot said. 'It's time Corps stopped sitting on its arse and did something to stop it. Next time it happens we'll bloody well shoot back. I'm going to tell Selby so, right now.'

Captain Selby was at his desk. The squadron commander looked up with his single eye, the other concealed behind a black patch. The injury, though recent, had not been sustained in battle. He had been struck in the face by a seagull, taking off from Swingate on the Dover cliffs. The sight in his damaged eye was expected to return but until it did he was restricted, as the Corps put it, to flying a desk. Meanwhile, he was callously known as Pew, after the blind beggar in *Treasure Island*. 'Get the pics all right, Sutro?' he said.

'No thanks to the idiots on the ground. At two thousand feet you can weave a bit and adjust your height when Archie gets your range. But come down and our damned squaddies poop off at anything that flies. My bus looks as if the moths have got at it, no matter there's a damned great Union Jack painted on the wings.'

'Your so-called idiots claim it looks like an Iron Cross,' said Selby, 'so they're not inclined to take chances. In their position you can hardly blame them. On top of that, they couldn't tell a BE2 from the Kaiser strapped to a Cody kite. However,' he held out a piece of paper, 'spare me your rant. Here's a late Christmas present from Corps. Spread the word to your B flight chaps.'

Guv read the order through. 'All aeroplanes of the RFC are to be marked on the underside and the rudder with concentric circles similar to those on French machines, the circles to be as large as possible.' He stared at Selby. 'Concentric circles? What the deuce are they?'

'Roundels, Sutro, like the Frogs use, except our bull's-eye's red, not blue. I've had this sketch done so the more artistic members of the flight can grab a brush and paint pot and get weaving straight away.'

'Christ Almighty,' Guv said. 'Bull's-eye's right. Now the sharp-shooters will really have something to aim at.'

'If that's all, Lieutenant,' said Selby, 'get those photographic plates off to Corps pronto and make out your report.'

In the Mess, Rupert Clements was looking sombre. 'What are you drinking, Guv?'

'Scotch – a large one. Those damned mudlarks have been up to their usual tricks, using us for target practice.'

'Yes, they loosed off at us as well – put a bullet through Sergeant Collins's sleeve. Still, things might be looking up. I imagine Pew's filled you in about the new markings? Could make a difference, don't you think?'

Guv raised his glass in an ironic toast. 'May we live to see it.'

The Mess was busier now with more pilots and officer observers returning from flights.

'You chaps ready for another, while I get one in?' said Max Porter. 'Silly question.' He signalled to the orderly for more whiskies. '*Vin blanc anglais* all round and make it sharpish.' He distributed cigarettes. 'Mick Mottram's gone west, along with Corporal Singer.'

Clements looked sick. 'Good God, are you sure?'

'How?' asked Guv.

'Albatros caught them napping. Not like Mick. Shakes you when an old hand cops it.'

Guv lit his pipe. 'Old hand, young hand, what's the difference? With our piddling rifles we don't stand an earthly against their infernal machine-guns. And it's not as if you can get yourself out of a scrape with fancy flying. If you want proof, check last month's casualty list. Attrition's the only reason I got B flight.' He grunted with satisfaction. 'That must have pained old Pew. Normally the one-eyed shyster would begrudge me a nail paring.'

'Change the record, Guv,' said Clements. 'The BE2's what we're stuck with, so we must just make the best of it.'

'It's a waste of good pilots. God knows, it takes long enough to train up chaps to be half capable. Then we send them off in a machine that couldn't pull the skin off a rice pudding, is about as manoeuvrable as a drunken elephant and has its seat positions all wrong.'

Porter groaned. 'Don't go on, there's a good chap. We're well aware of your theories.'

'It's more than theory, Max, it's commonsense. Look at the Hun – observer gunner at the back where he's got a good field of fire, pilot up front. Do the boffins at Farnborough take any notice? They do not. Instead they squeeze our observer up forrad between the wings, force him to lean out in the slipstream with his whacking great Box Brownie to get his snaps, and arm him with a .303 Lee Enfield in the hope that it might strike fear into the heart of the Hun. Under attack he stands more chance of getting his rifle tangled in the rigging and plugging his own pilot than hitting the enemy. Meanwhile we, the benighted chauffeurs, have to handle the bus and take an occasional potshot at the enemy with our toy pistols if and when he chooses to make a nuisance of himself. It's a bugger's muddle.'

Guv felt inside his tunic. 'If the backroom boys at Farnborough won't come up with the goods, we must do it ourselves. Take a dekko at this.' He smoothed out a sheet of graph paper that showed in profile a BE2. A childishly drawn figure faced backwards in the rear cockpit with a machine-gun on some sort of mount. The pilot was in the front cockpit and fixed above him, in the centre of the upper wing, was another machine-gun, facing forward. 'It is to scale,' Guv said encouragingly.

'That's about all it is,' said Porter. 'Are these Lewis guns, by any chance?'

'Probably, yes.'

'Do you know how much they weigh?'

'Not a clue.'

'Neither have I offhand, but it's a hell of a lot, not to mention the combined tonnage of the two porkers in the cockpits. You'd never get off the ground.'

'There are fellows I know back at Brooklands who could figure this out in a jiffy,' Guv said. 'Of course, this doodle is just to kick things off. Someone else can work on the details.'

Porter laughed. 'You'll be lucky. Pew won't help you kick it off, he'll kick it into touch. You know the official line, we're here to support the BEF; scout the terrain, plot targets for the gunners, liaise between HQ and the front line, avoid mixing it with the Hun unless he mixes it with us. Mostly their chaps are after the same kind of information as us. They've got their job to do, we've got ours. It's not often that they're troublesome.'

'It was once too often for Mottram,' said Guv. 'Besides, I may not bother Blind Pew. The chap's got enough on his plate. Far better to give it a try on the QT.' Guv began to fold the graph paper. 'I'll tell you frankly, I'm sick of playing second fiddle to that lot downstairs. We're little more than airborne spies. Not the idea at all, in my view.'

'And what is your view, Guv?' said Porter. 'As if we didn't know.'

'The Army's engaged on the ground, we should be engaged in the air. As it is, we're almost a sideshow. Everyone knows the top brass think we're a bunch of madmen, undisciplined, of limited value. I say we prove 'em wrong: take on the Hun man to man, machine to machine, knock 'em down and control the sky so their army would be fighting blind.'

'You say, you say,' said Porter. 'What's the good of you saying anything at all? Nobody listens to the great Sutro any more. Nobody cares. I'm afraid, old boy, that now you're just one of us.'

'An airborne spy, like it or not,' put in Clements. 'And didn't I detect a concession there about the importance of our humble trade – something about the desirability of rendering the enemy blind? That means you see the sense in it, however grudging.'

'Only if we poke the bastards' eyes out first. As it is, we spy on them, they spy on us so we cancel each other out.'

'Well, General Sutro,' said Porter, 'you may have made some telling points but after a couple of these tinctures I'm damned if I can recall 'em. What I do know is, you can't turn the BE2 into a silk purse. In peacetime it's a delight to fly. In wartime it's a sow's ear, however much you tinker with it. But this I will say in its favour: it's a stable old bus that almost flies itself and rarely kills the greenhorn. We leave that doubtful honour to the Hun.'

Clements nudged Porter. 'This is what it comes down to, Max. Our General here is ahead of his time. For heaven's sake, Guv, the war's only five months old. No one's worked out how to fight it yet, least of all in the air. It's no good, old man. You're stuck with the jolly old BE2 and the job they've given us to do. Resign yourself, make the best of it like the rest of us until they produce some decent designs.'

'Hah!' said Guv. 'Until hell freezes over, more likely. Well, unlike you fellows I've got connections and I believe the time has come to use them. If we think the strategy's wrong, it's up to us to say so. We're the chaps who've got to put it into practice. Oh, you can dismiss such things as nothing to do with you but, as someone once said, you may not be interested in strategy but strategy is interested in you.' He held up his glass to catch the orderly's eye. 'And my strategy? Make the commanders see some sense; go for the Hun like blazes, attack them with better machines and send 'em down in flamers. It's as simple as that.'

He lowered his voice, aware suddenly that others in the Mess were listening, and assumed a more reasonable tone. 'You may be content to quietly do your duty as sitting ducks,' he said, although his words by now were slurred, 'but that's not for me.'

Porter stretched back in his seat. 'The duck that squawked, eh? Well, with that attitude, old chum, you'll either end up court-martialled or winning a gong. It's a toss-up which.'

After Guv had left, Clements said, 'Don't put it about but I've got friends in high places as well.'

'Really?' said Porter.

'Yes. My uncle's best friend's a lighthouse-keeper.'

'I'll tell you something odd about Sutro,' said Porter. 'He once told me that before the war he never flew for amusement.'

'The deuce. Then what did he fly for?'

'Beats me. Orderly, *encore des drams de Scotch.*'

Back at his billet in the hamlet of Malhove, a short walk from the airfield, Guv was careful not to rattle his key in the door of his room in the Oboeuf farmhouse. Along the passage slumbered Paulette, Monsieur Oboeuf's sister-in-law who tended to the beasts; Paulette, thick set with huge breasts who called him her *chevalier anglais* and allowed him certain liberties – not notably pleasurable but for the time being it would have to do, cheaper and more convenient than the brothel in St Omer, with a few francs exchanged for friendship's sake. But not tonight. He had drunk too much and she was not required.

He lit the bedside candle with his cigarette-lighter and its yellow light seemed to warm the room. Lydia's letter lay folded where he had left it by the photograph of Saxonshore. He had noticed that the others had photographs as well, studio portraits mostly, wives, fiancées, sweethearts, pretty or made to look that way. He envied them that. He had a picture of a house. Oh, Lydia was there, a small and distant

231

figure in front of the great stone porch with, on its lintel, that coat-of-arms and motto: *non sine dignitas* – not without merit. No, she was not without merit, he reflected. It lay behind her.

He took up her letter, having nothing else to read. She called him dearest. Missed him most awfully, she said. But all was well. It was three months now. The child could be expected in June. The estate was somewhat rundown. More workers had enlisted and Lambert would soon be joining them despite his years – admirably patriotic, of course, but unsettling nonetheless, particularly for Poppa who had come to rely on him thoroughly. Still, she supposed that one must do without a butler in these straitened times, though Poppa was much cast down by it and by the effects of war generally, particularly the prospect of hostilities not ceasing by Christmas as everyone had hoped.

The new man, Paget, appeared capable though somewhat Bolshie in his manner and constantly at odds with the chauffeur Chandler. His cousin (*you will recall her, perhaps, a pretty little thing*) was no more than adequate as a lady's maid, inclined to spend her time in gossip and very thick with Paget – which was only to be expected perhaps, given their relationship – but a nuisance nonetheless. She wished him to tax her about it when next on leave as Poppa was disinclined to become involved and she found it too embarrassing herself. There was so much more to say, it seemed, but she did not have the words. She reminded him of his promise to come home safe. She knew his manly spirit and fearless nature, but he must not be rash and hazard his life unduly. He owed her that, and owed it to his future child. She said she loved him and sent him a dozen kisses.

He lay back on the odorous bed, a primitive farmyard smell. He felt less groggy now. He changed his mind about Paulette and slipped along the passage.

Guv did not reply to Lydia's letter, nor did he take further his design to improve the fighting capabilities of the BE2 because, next day, still happy from further liberal quantities of *vin blanc anglais*, Clements with his observer was also caught napping on reconnaissance over the Ypres sector and went the way of Mick Mottram. Like Mottram,

Clements had been in it from the beginning. He too had survived many close calls; attacks by enemy machines, engine failures, near collisions, adverse weather, the usual episodes in any pilot's life. But he had been popular, more popular than Mottram – a taciturn man – with an easy charm and gentle humour that somehow suggested he was secure from harm, and his death knocked back the flight; two gone in as many days. In Guv it aroused a burning rage, stirred not so much by the loss of Clements (Clements' charm had passed him by) but more because it endorsed his views, in the starkest and most timely way, about the bugger's muddle they were compelled to fly, the BE2. He craved to mix it with the Hun, on any terms, and listened with impatience to Captain Selby's briefing.

'It's the rottenest sort of luck, gentlemen, to lose such splendid types in a matter of days. It is also a hard lesson. When you're up, keep your wits about you every second of every minute. Never relax your vigilance. I need hardly remind you that Mottram and Clements were among the most experienced of us and yet, for a moment's inattention, they and their observers paid the ultimate price. We all know we're likely to encounter opposition from time to time. It follows that we must also expect losses. To a man we understand and accept that. However, when they occur, particularly in such a short space of time, it is hard to take. But we must not allow them to divert us from our course of action. Our duty is plain. We have been entrusted with the vital job of supporting our advancing forces on the ground, and I know I can depend on every one of you to pursue our objectives with the utmost resolve. Anything less would be to betray the memory and the sacrifice of those who are no longer with us. We must remain true to them as they would have remained true to us. That is all.'

'Sacrifice, eh?' said Max Porter as he and Guv walked towards the Bessoneau hangars to prepare their machines. 'If memory serves me right there are various definitions of that word: giving up something valuable for something more important, slaughtering a creature as an offering to a deity, incurring a loss to avoid a greater one. Take your pick. Personally, I don't like the sound of any of 'em. They all entail not being around to enjoy the glory. Your ravings of the other night are starting to sound less far-fetched. Still got your doodle of the BE2 decked out as a machine-gun platform, by any chance? Perhaps we should get the erks to give it a go and let the extra weight go hang.'

To Porter's amusement Guv appeared to take the suggestion seriously.

'I'll have to shelve that for the moment. Right now I've got something else in mind. I've had enough of the Hun sacrificing us. I'm going to have a shot at sacrificing him.'

'Don't tell me,' Porter said. 'You're going to ram the sods.'

The aircraft in reconnaissance flights took off individually and in their own time, no lifting away from the runway dashingly four abreast and gathering in formation. Guv let the others go, spreading out his flight-plan on the wing of his BE2, studying the flight's objectives with unusual care, objectives that took them deep into the Ypres sector.

The observer watched him curiously. 'Something up, Mr Sutro?'

'Change of plan, Sergeant.'

'Sir?'

'Look, Evans, the Hun's had it his own way long enough. I'm sick to death of playing goose to his fox. I'm sure you are as well. Well, it's time we showed we've got teeth of our own, even in a creaky old bus like this, and I've worked out how to do it. There'll be no damned snaps today, despite the orders. I take entire responsibility. If there's trouble when we return' (he did not say 'if' because it did not occur to him), 'you have my guarantee that you will be absolved from any blame, that you were simply obeying a direct order.' Guv slipped the flight-plan into the transparent map-holder that hung flat on his chest. 'Well, man, are you game?'

'Have I got any choice, sir?'

'Let me think about that,' Guv said. Then, 'I've thought. The answer's no. Now ferret out some warm togs, we're going to need them. And make sure your bladder's empty. We'll be climbing to ten thousand feet. Take a leak at that altitude and your pee will freeze. At best you'd get frostbite in your cock, at worst it'd snap off and you'd have to take it back to Blighty in your pocket as a souvenir for your wife.'

Soon, bulky in heavy sheepskin flying suits, as ponderous as deep-sea divers, they climbed into the BE2 and settled themselves in their cockpits. They did not speak, their breath showing white in the frigid air, hanging like ghosts of unsaid words. By the propeller a fitter was ready. Guv raised his thumb and began to bellow back the man's instructions.

'Switch off. Petrol on. Suck in.' The airman pulled down on the propeller, working against the resistance of the compression. 'Contact!'

'Contact!' The 90-horsepower engine caught, faltered, stopped. Once more then; and now it burst alive. Guv worked the throttle until the engine was properly warm, waved away the chocks, taxied out onto the level grassland of the St Omer airfield, turned into what little wind there was, gathered speed with a touch more power, bounced a little across the turf, once, twice, felt the tail-plane rise, eased back on the stick and lifted off with wheels still spinning, propeller a brownish blur, climbing up to 500 feet before banking north-east on a still-rising course for Ypres. To their right, the low winter sun hung above the horizon in a clear sky unmarked with cloud. Guv pulled back the cuff of his gauntlet and checked his Omega watch; a gift from Lydia when he left for France. 'When you look at this, my darling, think of me.' He did. He thought of how much it must have cost her, how easily she bought such things without a concern for price, without a word to him. In a shoulder-holster inside his flying suit he had another more deadly gift, also bought by her but chosen by himself: a Colt .45 automatic pistol from Aspreys in New Bond Street, less bulky than the Webley service revolver yet suitable for Government-issue cartridges.

They had been in the air for fifteen minutes, climbing in a shallow spiral, Guv careful not to overstress the engine. The altimeter showed 3,000 feet; 200 feet below, three tiny clouds appeared, followed by the crack of detonations. The smoke was white, British Archie then; the smoke from German anti-aircraft fire was black. More Archie,

235

rather closer. Guv weaved and climbed, lost height and climbed again and soon the gunners lost their range. Thirty minutes more to go. In their open cockpits the cold began to bite, the air grow thin. A mile above the earth and there to the east lay the front at Ypres where, a month before, the British and French had held the armies of von Falkenhayn and secured the Channel coast, digging in a defensive line of trenches matched by the Germans, close enough in places to hear their voices, smell their cooking.

Now, at 6,000 feet, Guv began to beat his thighs to get some feeling in his legs, Evans in the forward cockpit kneeling on his seat and facing to the rear, the barrel of his rifle wavering in the passing rush of air, his eyes raw-red behind his goggles and never still, alert for every trick of light or slightest movement in the huge bowl of sky in which they hung. The goggles gave him a fishlike, fearful look, like a bulge-eyed ocean-dweller alert for a hungry shark.

At 10,000 feet, the engine of the BE2 began to falter, struggling to maintain its beat. But Guv was unconcerned and still pulled back gently on the control column, curious to see how high the machine could go. Life seemed very good up here and he began to grin. To hell with the bloody Hun. He'd stay two miles above the earth, far from the squalid struggle going on below. He was above all that. Above all that: he found that thought extremely funny and began to laugh, but laughing found it hard to catch his breath. Evans was staring back at him, less nervous of the enemy (unlikely at this height) than of his pilot. He pointed down and opened his mouth, tongue extended, panting like a dog. Guv nodded, reluctant to concede but knowing he was right. The signs were there: euphoria, a dizziness, the onset of a thundering head, a misting of the eyes, numbness in the toes and fingers, the classic symptoms of a brain deprived of air. Worse, impairment of his judgement. He was not here to admire the scenery. He eased forward on the stick to shave off 1,500 feet and levelled out breathing more easily now, his eyesight cleared. On the ground, white ribbons of roads ran across a desert of mud to shells of towns and villages, past craters filled with water winking dully in the sun and stumps of trees like broken teeth. The trenches zigzagged southwards from the sea and in between ran no-man's land, a heel-scrape from a giant boot.

Banking to give himself a better view, Guv caught the faintest glint of something moving about 3,000 feet below, passing across the pale ruins of Ypres itself – another machine, but what? He thumped the cowling and pointed down and Evans raised a thumb. They dipped into a shallow dive, the needle of the altimeter inching lower, lower, the lateral distance perhaps ten miles, a difficult calculation this, to keep the sun behind and bring them to their quarry undetected, at the right height, the right moment to attack, ignoring the constant puffs of anti-aircraft fire that opened up around them like deadly blooms. For Guv there was no cool appraisal, instead obedience to an inner unacknowledged voice, an impulse deep within his brain that told him how to bring them neatly to the target, instinctive as an eagle spotting prey.

Now they were closer still, the sun fixed firm behind them, turning gold the surface of the wings; coming in a touch too fast, corrected with a tad less throttle, a raising of the nose, the engine idling in the dive, wind whistling through the struts, Evans crouching forward, his rifle hard against his shoulder. Not one aircraft below but two, a BE2 on a photo sortie unaware of the two-seater Albatros poised above, the newer type, torpedo shaped, the fuselage dull brown and bearing big black crosses edged with white, black crosses also on the pale grey wings.

Left hand steady on the stick, Guv removed his right gauntlet, reached inside his flying suit and withdrew the Colt automatic from its leather shoulder-holster, thumbed the safety catch to check it could not fire and pushed it barrel-first between his thighs. Still unseen, he slipped towards the Albatros, rocking in its turbulence, catching the pitch and toss, adjusting his airspeed to settle neatly in the blind spot below and behind the German's tail, the long smooth belly only yards above their heads. Once more he placed his left hand on the stick and seized the Colt, banging the butt on the cowling as a signal to Evans to open fire. Flicking off the safety catch, he squeezed off half a dozen shots, upwards and at an angle, startled by the noise, the pistol kicking in his hand, working the bullets along the plywood fuselage from back to front. A line of holes appeared like full stops on a sheet of paper. He heard the crash of Evans's rifle, saw more punctuation. The Albatros began to roll and pitch as if the pilot was struggling for control, then rose in a lazy climb. Guv had dived ahead, to deny the rear gunner an easy target, but not so steeply as to stress the wings; no liberties were to be taken with the BE2, not designed to cope with rough and sudden handling. He touched the rudder, banking left, still losing height. He could not see the Albatros. The sun had become his enemy now.

He raised a hand and saw a shadow flash above. It seemed he'd failed. In moments he'd be dead. A rapid burst of fire, and wood and canvas flew up from the centre of the BE2's upper wing. The bullets blew off part of Evans's head and he fell forward out of sight. Guv dropped a wing and half spun down, blood showering back from Evans's cockpit and covering his face and goggles. He dragged the goggles off, glaring up and waiting for the Hun; expecting the Albatros to dive down for the kill. But it was slipping, sliding 200 feet above, the engine roaring, shutting off, the pilot slumped, one moment head on chest, now fallen back. The observer in the rear cockpit was swinging the machine-gun round and down. Guv quarter rolled and fell away, the vibration so violent it blurred his vision. He had no choice. Why make it easy for the Hun? Better to go down in a cracked-up bus than hand the sod another scalp.

But the Albatros did not follow him down. Guv eased back gently on the stick and brought the machine into level flight. The Albatros had retained its height but was porpoising, yawing, crabbing as if in the hands of a novice. Guv throttled up and climbed; it took him time. The observer was no longer by his weapon but leaning forward, shaking his pilot's shoulder. Guv was alongside now, twenty yards away and holding station. The pilot's head fell round, his eyes were open, he tried to speak.

The observer looked across at Guv, a young man with a crimson flapping scarf. He pointed at the machine-gun on its mount, shook his head and shrugged; a jam. Guv nodded, reaching for his pistol. The observer had raised his arms above his head. Guv nodded again and moved a little closer, so the wing-tips almost touched. The pilot saw him, lifted his hand in a weak salute. Guv raised the Colt above the cockpit rim, placed six bullets through the fuselage where the pilot sat, and broke away. The Albatros lurched; it rose and fell, turned suddenly on its back and dropped into a savage spin. Artillery bursts still peppered the sky. No sign of the other BE2.

Over St Omer, Guv fired a red Very light to show he had an injured man on board. The damage from the German's fire had affected the angle of the wings so they did not pass cleanly through the air, compromising lift and making the controls stiff and heavy, the rigging wires flexing with a thwack, slack one moment, taut the next. A lapse of concentration, a clumsy touch and the machine could fold up like a piece of paper. Fish-tailing his rudder from side to side to scrub off speed, he floated in for a gentle landing and touched down nose-up without a bounce.

At the hangars he watched while they removed Evans from the front cockpit. It was a grisly business. Half his head had gone. The faces of the ground crew were grey with shock. Few of the pilots already down were there, preferring not to be reminded of the destructive power of Parabellum bullets.

On his way to the squadron office Guv met Max Porter.

'Christ, man, you're in a dreadful mess. Are you injured?'

'Not a scratch but Sergeant Evans caught a packet.'

'Has he had it?'

'I should say so. This is his blood, not mine.'

'That puts a downer on things.'

'What things?'

'Some fearless flier's brought down a ruddy Albatros stalking Freddie Craig. Nobody's claimed it yet. Crashed this side of our lines near Poperinge. The whole place has been buzzing with it. We had a bit of a drunk lined up.'

'That Hun was mine.'

'Good grief, old man, how did you pull that off?'

'As for the drunk,' Guv said, 'I should go ahead. It's what Evans would have wanted.'

In the office, Captain Selby was waiting for him. Guv gave him a casual salute. 'I watched you land,' said the squadron commander. 'I understand that Sergeant Evans is a casualty.'

'A goner, actually. Damned shame.'

'A shame, you say. Stand to attention, blast you, Sutro – I didn't say you could stand easy. Run me through the details of your trip, starting with the aerials you took.'

'No luck, the camera malfunctioned. Not one blessed plate exposed.'

'Convenient, wouldn't you say?'

'Not sure I understand.'

'You understand all right, you damned glory-seeker. I have it on good authority that you disobeyed orders, made no attempt to survey the sector you were designated and deliberately chose to engage an enemy aircraft in battle despite my repeated instructions to the contrary.'

'Where have you got all this?'

'Our battery commanders had a grandstand seat,' said Selby, adding reluctantly, 'Stand easy.' He was turning a fountain pen between his fingers. 'I assume you don't deny that it was you who tackled this Albatros that crashed near Poperinge. Well, I'm waiting. What's your explanation?'

'I've told you, the camera was u/s. It seemed to Evans and me—'

'Oh, you had a conflab about it, did you, at two thousand feet?'

'I didn't need to ask Evans the best course of action. We always saw eye to eye. As we were already up I simply thought we might as well make a nuisance of ourselves. When we came across the Albatros it suited us very well. May I suggest, Selby—'

'*Sir.*'

'May I suggest that you're going to look a fine fool if it comes out that you've told your pilots not to fight the enemy, that you had me arrested for shooting down a Hun.'

'Your soft soap doesn't wash with me, Lieutenant.' Selby placed an emphasis on the rank. 'Do you realise how many men's lives you've put in jeopardy by neglecting your duty and failing to return with vital intelligence about that sector of the front? A big push is imminent. Corps are livid.'

'Do they know the circumstances?'

'What circumstances?'

'The circumstances I've just described, dammit.'

'You don't expect me to believe that tosh, do you? I know you, Sutro.'

'And I know you, Selby. I think it's in the interest of your future career to make damned sure Corps understands and accepts the situation as I've explained it to you. After all, what's the alternative? Your flight failed to deliver the goods and you can't control your pilots? Hardly the stuff of Corps material, I'd say, if that's where your ambition lies.'

'I have one more piece of information for you,' said Selby quietly. 'We are getting reports, unconfirmed at the moment, that the crew of the Albatros had surrendered.'

'Really?'

'The observer was not quite dead when our people reached him. He claimed that with his pilot mortally wounded and his weapon ineffective they had cried quits. And yet their opponent shot them down in cold blood. I need hardly remind you that such an action is against the rules of war as set out in the Geneva Convention.'

'Are you going to take the word of a Hun against mine?'

'Is that all you have to say?'

'What should I say? Put it down to sour grapes. It was a fair fight. He lost. May I point out that this was probably the bastard who killed Mottram and Clements and God knows how many more of our chaps along the front. He certainly did for Sergeant Evans and he'd have done for me if he'd got the chance. But caught with his pants down he thought all he had to do was throw up his hands and we'd tuck him up in a nice cosy prison camp. Well, he's been tucked up all right, but nowhere cosy, instead some place he won't get up to any more mischief.' Guv said nothing for a moment and a silence hung between them. Then: 'I'd like to make an observation.'

'It'll be the first you've made today.'

'As a pilot yourself I should have thought congratulations might have been in order, instead of tearing me off a strip.'

'This is not a question of your ability in the air,' said Selby evenly, 'that's beyond doubt. It's a matter of discipline. It's my belief that you had no intention whatever of carrying out your reconnaissance sortie, that you were entirely occupied with the objective of tackling a Hun. You're not here to wage war as you think it should be waged. You're here to do what you're told, to obey orders. And if you can't do that, then you're no use to the RFC.'

'One fewer Albatros? I'd say that's quite useful.'

'Consider yourself grounded, Sutro,' said Selby, 'until further notice.'

Guv shook his head. 'It'll be interesting to hear what the other chaps have to say about that. They'll see things the way I do.' He turned at the door. 'It's no good, Selby. This is how it's going to be, knocking each other out of the sky, no holds barred. It's going to be a dirty business.'

'In that case, Lieutenant,' said Captain Selby, 'you're well suited to it. Dismissed.'

Guv went down to the hangar where the men were inspecting his BE2. Pinkish water was dripping from a rash of bullet-holes around the front cockpit where they had hosed it out. They assumed he was most concerned about the state of his machine. A rigger was pulling at the damage to the upper wings. 'Write-off, sir. Good for spares. Don't know how you got it down. One thing though.' The man jumped down and took Guv over to a work-bench. 'Look at that. Poor old Taffy gets it good and proper and yet his ruddy camera isn't touched.'

Guv turned the Graflex in his hands. 'You're wrong there, Corporal. This damned apparatus let us down. Leave it with me. I'll make sure it goes back to the photo section for repair.'

The men had gathered round. 'Have we got it right, sir? That it was you what downed the Hun?'

'Quite right.'

'Blimey, that'll do morale a bit of good. It's time we gave the buggers a taste of their own medicine.'

'My thoughts exactly,' Guv said, and added: 'This is only a beginning.'

Where had he said that before? Oh yes, at High And Over, before the Lilienthal flight all those years ago, the people pressing round and gazing at him in that particular way, with respect and something close to awe. He saw it now. Someone said hoarsely in his ear: 'Three cheers for Lieutenant Sutro.' The cheers rang round the hangar.

On his way to the Mess he ducked between two Nissen huts and bent back the shutter-lever of the Graflex so it jammed, as if Evans had been careless with it, climbing into his cockpit. He gave it to the first airman he saw, with instructions to take it to the photographic section as a matter of urgency.

A memorable drunk was held in the Mess that evening, to celebrate Guv's victory. His account of the incident was accepted without question. A toast was proposed to the memory of Sergeant Evans – 'Good old Evans,' was the general shout, though few of the officers had been particularly aware of him. More toasts followed, to Mick Mottram, Rupert Clements, their observers and anyone else they could recall who had failed to come back. The dead suitably honoured, various games were proposed. Much damage to furniture and fabric was caused, and many bottles and glasses smashed under the bemused gaze of the Mess staff who watched the proceedings like visitors to Regent's Park zoo.

A flush-faced pilot seized Guv's hand. 'I owe you my life, Sutro, picking off that Albatros on my tail.' He was swaying like a sailor in a storm. 'My mother . . .' he swallowed, '. . . my mother will be eternally indebted to you. I'm Craig, by the way, Freddie Craig. Not long arrived.'

Guv stared at him glassily, opened his mouth, closed it, looked away. 'Not long arrived?' he said finally. But when he looked back, Craig had gone.

At some point, Guv was hoisted shoulder-high and carried round the Mess until he struck his head on a low beam, rendering him unconscious for a minute or two until they emptied jugs of cold water over him. In the early hours a steward presented the senior officer present (Captain Selby apparently detained at Corps) with the Damage Book, which was promptly torn up and thrown into the air, its fragments fluttering down like confetti to an obscene version of 'Here Comes the Bride'. Selby's absence was commented upon unfavourably, and suggestions made that his visit to Corps was little more than a thin excuse. Perhaps, some murmured, as a professional military man with an eye to promotion (laughter), old Pew resented Guv's success. What other explanation could there be, to miss such a memorable drunk? Surely Corps could shelve a briefing until next morning, a matter of hours, if only they knew the reason? But still, it was as everyone agreed, a most successful evening; but for Freddie Craig and his observer, the last. The following day their names were added to the tally of those to be toasted on some future, similar occasion.

Without a machine or observer, Selby's order that Guv was grounded until the business of the Albatros had been properly investigated proved academic. The matter was taken no further after the captain's visit to Corps, an appointment made at his own request.

'You say, Captain Selby, that Lieutenant Sutro disobeyed your order and set out to deliberately engage the enemy.'

'That is correct.'

'His statement claims that as his camera was out of action he decided on his own initiative to stay in the air and do what he could to help his comrades.'

'That is what he claims.'

'You seem to imply a doubt. Is there any evidence that his statement is incorrect? For example, was the faulty camera inspected after his sortie?'

'It was, sir.'

'With what result?'

'The shutter-lever was damaged.'

'And that would make it inoperable?'

'It would, sir.'

'Therefore he was unable to secure the photographs of his section of the Ypres salient.'

'Correct.'

'And yet he chose to remain in the vicinity in case he could be of help to others in his flight?'

'He chose not to return to St Omer, certainly. Instead he was seen by battery commanders to embark immediately on a climb to extreme altitude.'

'What is extreme?'

'For the BE2, ten thousand feet. Such an ascent takes forty-five minutes and calls for far more preparation than a straightforward reconnaissance trip. For example, the ground crew confirm that Lieutenant Sutro's BE2 was carrying more fuel than is usual, and both he and his observer were kitted out in heavy gear, the kind that offers protection against the sub-zero temperatures to be encountered at that height. It indicated to me that he had something of this sort in mind all along.'

'But the camera, Captain, the camera. You are not suggesting that it was purposely damaged in some way? I should be very careful with your reply.' There was no reply. 'Now, Captain Selby, let us turn to this action in the air. Is it not true that the German Albatros is generally regarded to be a superior design to our British BE2?'

'Reluctantly I must agree.'

'Why superior, exactly?'

'It is faster, more manoeuvrable . . .'

'And equipped with a machine-gun, I understand.'

'That is so.'

'And yet you contend that Lieutenant Sutro, by pressing his attack upon this formidable machine despite the odds against him – a successful attack, mind you – was nonetheless at fault in disregarding your order not to engage and should therefore be subject to disciplinary action?'

'The fact remains that he disobeyed my direct orders and embarked on a hazardous venture that could have ended in disaster, with the loss of two machines and four valuable aircrew. It sets a bad example, sir, to the other men.'

'One might argue equally that it is a good example, a splendid example even, of taking the fight to the enemy though lightly armed and saving the lives of his fellow airmen, although at the cost of his gallant observer. Would you not agree that one might argue that?'

'It is an alternative view, certainly.'

'I would add that when it comes to the question of imposing discipline in your flight, I hope I do not have to remind you where that responsibility lies. But discipline, whatever the regulations may say, is not an exact science. It calls for sound judgement, a thorough understanding of the broader implications of the situation – pragmatism, if you like. The Royal Flying Corps is not the Brigade of Guards. As to Lieutenant Sutro, it seems clear that any question of disciplinary action would be quite inappropriate. We would, after all, be seen to be meting out punishment for a very spirited action that, after all, turned out rather well. I do not necessarily question your motives in this matter but pick your battles, Captain Selby, pick your battles. Now, be so good as to order Lieutenant Sutro to present himself before us without delay.'

Guv duly appeared in front of the same senior officers. 'Your reputation precedes you, Lieutenant Sutro,' said a major.

'Captain Selby is entitled to his own opinion.'

'I mean your reputation as an aviator before the war.' The major held up a typed report. 'You have been much praised in the popular press. Such attention might turn the head of any young man. It might even be that you believe the RFC is fortunate to have the benefit of your services.' The major looked again at the report. 'I see you have achieved many records. Do you, I wonder, wish to add one more? The first pilot to be dismissed from the Corps and despatched to the trenches for wilful disobedience?'

To the major's consternation, the lieutenant laughed. 'I think you'll find, sir, that the facts don't support such a serious charge.'

'It is hardly a matter for amusement, Lieutenant. However, proceed.'

Guv proceeded: the BE2 fuelled more heavily than usual? Can't be explained – a matter for the ground-crew chaps. High-altitude kit? It was December. The camera damaged? Well yes, perhaps by Sergeant Evans when boarding the BE2. A moment's carelessness and certainly regrettable; normally Evans was punctilious but these things happened to the best. Return to base? Weren't we here to fight? The tactics against the Hun? Improvisation, merely, no pre-planned ruse as some might claim; just climb and climb to gain the height advantage and come in from the sun, an untested theory yes, but possibly proven now. The enemy surrendered? Whose word to be believed, an English officer's or a dead German's? What had to be done was done, one fewer Hun to kill our pilots and observers and destroy our precious machines. Not following the flight commander's orders? All very well when safely on the ground, a different matter in the air where only the quick witted and decisive will survive; those pilots who can think for themselves and follow their own instincts.

Guv's attempt to elaborate on his opinions about the future of aerial warfare (the subservient role of the RFC as little more than airborne snoopers, the supply of faster, more agile, better armed fighting machines in the hands of single pilots not encumbered with observers, the need to rule the skies as Britain ruled the waves) was cut short and he was sent on his way.

The major blew out his cheeks. 'I prefer my courage in more modest packages. He has a swagger about him.'

'You cannot choose your heroes,' said the lieutenant colonel.

'An odd phrase. Where does choice come into it?'

'At this stage of the offensive, the Corps needs an example. We are not in the business, as the Germans are, of creating so-called aces with all the hoo-hah that such a policy entails, but nonetheless it's vital that our pilots are seen to be as proficient, as courageous and as successful as theirs. A little muted publicity would not, I think, be out of place. A gong might be in order, a nice citation in the *London Gazette*, "for conspicuous gallantry and skill et cetera", you know the sort of thing. That should oil the wheels with the War House.'

'Having seen this Sutro for myself,' said the major, 'I must admit a certain sympathy for Selby. I am not entirely sure that we have heard the unvarnished truth.'

'Oh, liberal coats of varnish certainly. But at this time a little gloss might not be misplaced, employed with discretion. As to Captain Selby, well, I admit it is not an ideal situation. Let us take pity on the fellow and sort out a posting for Sutro with the minimum of delay.'

'They've had some losses with the FB5s at Chézy-au-Bois.'

'Ideal. At least the Gunbus was designed as a destroyer and can look after itself in a fight, unlike the poor old BE2. That should satisfy our firebrand's aggressive tendencies for the time being. Put the wheels in motion straight away, and ditto for that gong. Let's hope it is not a posthumous award.'

'Naturally one must not hope for that.'

2

The leave boat did not sail from Boulogne for two hours. Guv stowed his kitbag on board and took a taxi into town. In a small almost empty bar in the old quarter in the shadow of the cathedral, he drank Pernod and talked about the war to the patron. He amused himself with ridiculous claims; he had shot down nine Boche, two this week. The patron treated him to a free Pernod. He was travelling to London to be presented with the Victoria Cross, the highest award for bravery, by the English King. The patron treated him to another free Pernod. The few customers had gathered round the bar. It was drinks on the house for all to celebrate *le pilote vaillant*. A woman came in, shabbily dressed but with a provocative eye. She was known to the clientèle. She sat down in a cubicle and looked around her speculatively. The patron knew her preference and went across with a brandy and soda. Guv said: 'Put that down to me.' He did not pay the patron the compliment of attempting French.

'*Merci, monsieur*,' said the woman. '*Très gentil.*'

Guv left the bar and sat down in the cubicle beside her. 'How much?' he said, again in English.

'*Comment?*'

'You know damned well.'

'Oh.' She affected disappointment, as though she had hoped he would not perceive her so quickly for what she was. 'Fifteen francs. I give you a very nice time.'

'My boat leaves soon. How much for not such a nice time?'

The woman wrinkled her nose, a not unattractive nose. 'My price is fifteen francs. What do you think I am?'

Guv did not bother to reply. His need was great. They left the bar to the usual shouts, *Vive* this, *Vive* that, and went to a small hotel that smelled of French cigarettes, burned garlic and drains. The proprietor showed no surprise at the woman appearing with an English airman and handed her a key. They went up narrow stairs to a sparsely furnished room: a bed, a bamboo table, two chairs, wash-basin with water jugs and towels, a print of the Virgin (perhaps a joke?) hanging crooked on a nail, a single dirty window overlooking a courtyard where cats squabbled over a scatter of discarded food.

'How are you called?' the woman said.

'Captain Selby.'

'*Non, non. Moi, je m'appelle Josette. Et vous?*'

'Captain Selby.'

She undressed but not entirely. He was naked and plainly ready, and waved for her to remove her thin petticoat.

'For fifteen francs you do not see all.'

Very quickly he did see all, and afterwards pulled on his uniform without washing and threw down fifteen francs on the bamboo table. The woman stared at him with hatred from the bed, rubbing her bruised arms. She spat and the blob of saliva landed on the bare boards, frothing slightly in the dust.

The leave boat was delayed, leaving after midnight escorted by three destroyers. The officers and men crowded the rails, eager to be the first to see the English coast. The sky was clear and moonlight flickered in the vessel's phosphorescent wake as it butted through the swell at twenty knots. Guv had gone below and slept.

At Folkestone a train was waiting by the quay, the locomotive with steam up ready for the onward journey to London, the men shuffling impatiently down the gangplank from the boat and gathering on the platform waiting for instructions. Soon carriage doors were slamming and banging like random cannon fire.

'Train leaves in four minutes, sir.'

'I've made my own arrangements.'

Near the harbour gates the Rolls was waiting, without its usual chauffeur. Harry Paget was at the wheel. He stepped down and took up Guv's kitbag. 'We got your telegram.'

'Obviously. Where's Chandler?'

'I'll tell you on the way,' said Paget, insouciant and unruffled, and swung the kitbag into the space beside the driver's seat, adding: 'Your boat was expected hours ago,' as though the wait had been a personal inconvenience.

Guv settled himself on the rear seat, closed the glass partition and lit his pipe. He had an itching in his crotch. Surely it was too soon to feel the effects of Mamzelle Fifteen Francs? He should have washed himself, except the water in the hotel jug had probably not been changed for weeks. A hot and careful bath at Saxonshore should do the trick.

They passed in silence along the sleeping streets of Hythe and Dymchurch, the murmur of slow-breaking waves on shingle in the half-light to their left. They had got as far as the stretch between Lydd and Camber, where the depths of the marsh fell away inland and dunes of stone not sand rose up between the winding road and the sea, before Paget slid back the partition and said over his shoulder conspiratorially: 'Want to hear about old Chandler now?'

'No,' Guv said, and banged the partition shut. At East Guldeford with its little church, the Rolls turned left and joined the military road that led to Rye, its huddle of buildings rising above a hanging mist. Paget did not speak again, his eyes fixed on the road ahead. At Saxonshore he opened the Rolls' rear door, followed Guv across the porch and dropped his kitbag in the hall, still without another word.

Lydia was coming slowly down the oak staircase, her hand gripping the balustrade. Behind her, at a turn of the stairs, hung a large portrait of her mother by Lavery. It was an awkward contrast, the painted image serene in a broad-brimmed straw hat and silken dress, posed against a spring landscape with the old castle snug in its fold of valley, and the heavy figure of her daughter (heavier still, by God) grunting down the staircase step by step, smiling that infuriating smile, that way she had, that blend of sweet pleasure, embarrassment for her lack of grace (worse than ever now), and tender love. Guv heard Paget close the hallway door, the motor of the Rolls start up, the tyres begin to graunch across the gravel towards the garage block.

Lydia was with him now, pressing close. He felt her distended belly hard against his pelvis. He did not care to see her face close to, so placed his arms around her and held her tight against his chest. She struggled for breath and, for a passing moment, he thought how simple it would be to fix her there, to hold her tighter still until she did not breathe at all.

She pulled back a little, gasping. 'My dear, you needn't crush me so. I'm here, I'm here. We've lots of time.'

He had to smile at that; that she mistook the firm embrace for fondness.

'Hardly,' he said. 'Only seven days. And I've not been granted leave to kick my heels. I've hush-hush business in Whitehall.'

'Well,' said Lydia, 'I've got you now. I suppose I must make the most of that.' She shivered. 'I've been at our bedroom window watching the drive since dawn. I thought you'd never come, perhaps that something . . . no, I will not express my fears. It's torture for those at home, you see, not knowing, never knowing. Oh, one has the wildest fancies. You hear such things, such awful things. So many families in the town – so many sons, so many brothers, husbands . . . why not your own, you think, why not your own?' She took his hand. 'Do forgive me, darling boy. I mustn't spoil things now you're here. You must be famished. Breakfast first, yes? Breakfast first.'

'No,' Guv said. 'First, a bath. I've been living in this damned uniform for months. I must stink to high heaven.'

'No, my dear, you don't,' said Lydia too quickly.

'I don't?'

Lydia was trapped. 'Oh, I don't know . . . I noticed a pleasant – a kind of, I don't know . . . perhaps . . . perhaps cologne.'

'I see,' Guv said. 'I understand. So I'm hardly through the door than I'm to be cross-questioned like some damned suburban clerk who's come home late from the office.'

'I didn't mean . . .' said Lydia. She looked forlorn; struck by a chance remark that betrayed a vague suspicion. Guv wondered, did she doubt him, really? It was not too late to pull back from a likely rift that might destroy her trust.

'Oh,' he said more reasonably, 'it was probably nurses on the leave boat. We were packed in like sardines.'

Lydia rallied a little. 'Nurses wearing perfume? That seems rather odd.'

'Odd? Why odd? They're on leave like the rest of us, after all. They're not all old dragons, you know.' He knew he was on dangerous ground but there was no reason for her not to understand that he found other women attractive. It put her a little off balance, as long as she did not conclude that he might take things further; suggested a touching loyalty even.

'You'll find some top-drawer girls working in the field hospitals and clearing stations,' he went on, 'girls who've been brought up to better things. You wouldn't deny them an opportunity to pamper themselves, I suppose, to let their hair down a little after what they've gone through?'

He realised he was talking too much, that there was a danger of finding himself at the bottom of a large pit, digging himself in deeper by the moment. How simple it would be to tell the truth. 'Well, actually there wasn't a single bloody nurse on board the boat. I shagged a cheap tart in Boulogne.'

'You seem to be an authority on nurses,' Lydia was saying with a lame attempt at playfulness.

Guv saw a chance to regain the initiative. 'I won't hear a word against them. They do a grand job.'

Lydia flushed. 'Oh dear, I can't seem to say anything right.'

He simulated rising anger. 'For what it's worth, some of our chaps had Blighty wounds. Naturally we'd find out where they were and pop along to help them keep their peckers up. A pretty ghastly experience, I can tell you. You can forget any foolish notions you may have about the ministering angel mopping a hero's fevered brow. They're angels all right, but they exist in hell. More likely they're carrying off the hero's severed leg. Hardly the stuff of romance. A dab of cologne?

Personally, Lydia,' (he used the name like a reproof), 'I'd let them bathe in the stuff if they cared to.' He paused, running the rather pleasing image through his mind. The difficult moments had passed.

A great deal of luggage was stacked up in the hall; travelling trunks, suitcases, valises, all freshly labelled. Lydia turned to it with relief.

'Poppa's leaving for Liverpool this afternoon.'

'A lot of stuff for a trip to Liverpool.'

'He's bound for New York on the *Lusitania*. He's staying with the Vanderbilts.'

'The Vanderbilts?' Guv had not been aware of the connection.

'They're friends of the family on Momma's side. These Rhode Island clans, they're very close.'

'I assumed the Old Man was persona non grata across the pond, your parents not seeing eye to eye.'

'Oh, by no means. These days, such things can be managed in a civilised fashion. Besides, he and Alfred Vanderbilt share a great enthusiasm for coaching in the old English style. They're planning a trip by coach from Newport to Mount Hope Bay. After that, they're sailing back to England together. Alfred wants to buy some heavy horses.'

'When does your father leave?'

'After lunch. He's sleeping now, preparing for the journey. But he'll be so happy that he's seen you before he goes to catch his train.' She took Guv's hand submissively now and he let her hold it briefly before he moved towards the stairs. 'Poppa's so tickled at the prospect of a grandchild. He had rather discounted the possibility.'

She began to move with him but he shook his head, as though repenting of what had gone before. 'No, dear,' (dear, a nice touch that), 'just give me a little time. It's quite a thing, being back with you, somewhat like a dream. I might wake up.' Inside his head he heard a hollow chuckle.

'Of course,' she said. 'Of course.' She kissed him gently on the cheek and watched him mount the stairs.

Soon, from the bedroom, as he stripped and found a dressing-gown, he heard water running in the master bathroom along the landing. When he pushed open the door he released great waves of steam that enveloped him like a warm and wet caress. He saw a slender figure by the bath in a long black dress and white apron, leaning over the steaming water and stirring it with her hand. She did not hear him until he was a pace or two away. Then she straightened up and smiled and swept back a curl of black hair from a forehead moist with sweat. 'Hello, you old devil, it's just how you like it. So hot I can hardly bear it.'

'Hello, Rose,' Guv said.

In the library at midday Alfred Bowman held the stem of the tiny sherry glass between his thumb and forefinger and held it to the light. 'I far prefer a Fino for its dryness and fragility. The others, Oloroso for example, or Amontillado, lie too heavily on my palate, particularly before a meal.' He noted Guv's expression, abstracted and somewhat flushed. 'But perhaps you don't agree?'

Agree? Agree to what? Guv came back with a jolt, his thoughts still in the stifling bathroom fug. Oh sherry, yes. A judgement called for on the sherry. Well, passable in a half-pint tankard, at the late stage of a damned good drunk when nothing mattered any more, except to see how plastered you might get and still stay on your feet. Otherwise, good for little more than washing out your mouth. 'No, no, sir,' he said to the expectant Bowman. 'It's certainly one to savour.'

'Yes, I thought so,' Bowman said and, pleased, began to roll the liquor round his cheeks, in mouthwash fashion.

In the dining room lunch was served by unfamiliar staff, Chandler's place taken by a homely specimen of considerable age with bad breath and a trembling hand, the female servants very young and made clumsy with nerves. They blushed when close to Guv.

'Thank you, Grimshaw,' Bowman said when plates of oxtail soup had been placed before them. 'You may withdraw.' Grimshaw bowed stiffly and emitted a faint fart.

'Poor Grimshaw,' said Bowman. 'Pressed into service, I'm afraid. Once butler to my father.'

'And Chandler?'

'A sorry tale. I do not wish to spoil our meal. Some little matter of petrol from the store that could not be accounted for. He had no explanation. The facts seemed plain enough when brought to my attention.'

'By whom?'

'Your fellow Paget, with great reluctance. Felt it was his duty. A most regrettable business. I did not pursue the affair in a legal sense, but took the more lenient course of dismissing Chandler on the spot without a reference. After all, he had been in our service for a considerable number of years. He took it badly, I'm afraid, made the most outrageous allegations.'

'Against Paget, I suppose.'

'Indeed. We parted on the poorest terms. The fellow enlisted straight away. I rather assumed his knowledge of automobiles would stand him in good stead but no, as is the way of these things the Army chose to ignore his skills and placed him in the infantry. I understand he was despatched to France. Nothing further has been heard.'

The soup was replaced with baked cod topped with a lumpen green-flecked sauce, and mashed potato. Lydia said: 'Poppa was remembering the first time we met you.'

'Oh yes?' Guv lowered the fork that was halfway to his mouth.

'We talked of flying, I recall,' said Bowman. 'Northcliffe was quite correct. Monsieur Blériot's Channel flight spelled the end of England as an island. It did not take long for the conquest of the air to be corrupted and used for war. And you were also right, my boy; that you foresaw a new kind of fighting – machine against machine and may the best man win.'

'It's not quite like that, sir, at least for the time being. We're mostly used in a reconnaissance role, photographing the enemy from the air, plotting targets for the gunners – aerial nosy-parkers. Pretty mundane stuff. Dicey enough, God knows, and calling for a special kind of guts, but hardly single-combat in the sky. Except . . .'

'Except?'

'I managed to down a Hun a week ago, strictly against orders, but it was worth a go. The whole thing's under wraps until they decide whether I'm a gold-plated hero or to be shot at dawn. That's why I'm here, to put my side of things.'

'This German . . .'

'Two Germans, actually.' Guv anticipated the next question. 'Yes, both gone west.'

'You speak so casually,' said Bowman. 'I suppose it must be done, but even so . . .'

'No point in brooding,' Guv told him breezily. 'Those Hun knew the score. It could just as easily have been me. As it was, they only did for my observer.'

Lydia pushed away her plate. 'I find I've quite lost my appetite.'

'Yes,' said Guv. 'Cod, wasn't it?'

Grimshaw supervised the clearing of the plates. 'Did you enjoy that, sir?'

'Local, was it?'

'Most certainly, sir.'

'How often do the catches come in these days?'

'Quite often, sir, but not as frequently as they used to.'

'The war, eh? We must all suffer, I suppose.'

'Indeed, sir.'

Steamed pudding and custard was presented. Bowman turned to safer topics. The business was bearing up, despite the country being on a wartime footing. After an initial lull customers had returned, although there were undeniably shortages of certain foodstuffs, clothing and, not least, of fuel (hence, the severe penalty he had been compelled to impose on Chandler). He supposed he must be thankful that the company was prevailing although he felt discomfort that this should be so while the nation's youth was suffering such privations with so many thousands laying down their lives. Yet the effects of war were not wholly detrimental; how ironic, for example, that labour shortages should be a thing of the past. Why, in London there was full employment with so many men away; the so-called unemployable suddenly required, the old, the sick, the destitute, even prisoners and children. And women in the most unsuitable of roles! On his last visit to the capital he had seen one driving an omnibus, another in police uniform and yet another, near St Pancras, unloading coal. In Regent's Street he had witnessed a young girl smoking a cigarette in public.

The world was topsy-turvy and, to his regret, he found himself out of step. The business was entrusted to more professional hands, he a mere figurehead; Saxonshore was large enough for other purposes, a school perhaps or a military hospital, but he could not bring himself to face up to such a painful decision. Even the estate was run by others, leaving him quite free to pass his days as he wished, to read a little and indulge himself with whims and fancies, his sojourn in America for example, amusing himself with idle pastimes with his wealthy friends, while all around were the manly virtues seen at times of war, such as selflessness and courage, love of country (not that he did not love his country), endurance and resolution. He felt himself of no significance, a shadow from another world.

Lydia took her father's hand. 'To listen to this dear man, you would not think he has given his life to the business. Or rather, his life was given to it; he had no choice. But he kept at it, although a career in the commercial world did not come naturally to him. Only recently has he been able to step back.' She kissed her father on the forehead. 'You have earned this time, Poppa. And may I urge you to make the most of your leisure? Because soon you will have new and pressing responsibilities, playing the doting grandfather.'

Bowman smiled. 'And I look forward to it with keen anticipation. But even you cannot deny that my life has been uneventful, perpetuating the family name in the minds of idle shoppers. Someone once said the function of a man is to live, not exist. Now I've no wish to emulate the deeds of your gallant husband. And this is no criticism of what he is compelled to do, although I cannot imagine living with the deaths of others on my conscience. But perhaps it is the Englishman in me that makes me hope, as I used to as a young boy, that I might be called upon one day to perform some small deed of note before I meet my maker.'

'And I hope just as fervently, Poppa,' said Lydia, 'that you are not.'

'Perhaps in my heart,' said Bowman, 'I wish so too. I suspect I might be found wanting.'

After brandies in the library with Guv, where little more was said, mere murmured pleasantries to occupy the awkward space that always hung between them when alone, Bowman's luggage was carried from the hall by Paget and deposited in the Rolls. As Guv and Lydia waved the old man off they saw him staring back at them through the car's rear window. It was positioned so high that he must have been half kneeling on the seat, and so small that it framed his eyes as they gazed intently at the great house and the two diminishing figures on the steps; gazed and gazed so long (until the motor reached the first sweep of drive) that Lydia understood with a pang of something close to grief that he was imprinting the image on his mind, in case he should not return.

In their bedroom that evening, with the house closed up, Guv was already in bed, turning the pages of the latest *Flight* magazine. Lydia sat at her dressing-table, straddling the small stool and brushing her hair. She turned awkwardly.

'It's wonderful to have you home,' she said, 'but I'm afraid we won't be able to be too . . . friendly tonight.'

'Oh? Why's that?'

'Womanly things, no need to go into details. The child, you know. I'm so sorry, my darling. I do understand how it must be for you. Are you too disappointed?'

'Your health comes first.'

'It's been such an anxiety,' said Lydia with relief, 'but I knew you'd understand. How wonderful you are.'

The next morning, back in uniform and arrived at St Pancras, he took a taxi to the War Office in Horse Guards Parade. He was escorted to a small windowless interview room at the back of the building and left alone. There was a hint of the police station about his surroundings, that contained only a plain, functional desk and three chairs. The buff-painted walls were bare of decoration and from the centre of the ceiling hung a single illuminated light bulb under a white enamel shade. It could have been any time of the day or night. A clerk looked in and asked him if he would like a cup of tea. Guv said he would but it did not arrive.

After fifteen minutes the door opened once more. Two men came in, one in the uniform of an Army captain, the other in civilian clothes. They did not speak immediately but sat down in the chairs and began to leaf through some papers, with an occasional glance at Guv. Finally, the captain said: 'So you're Sutro.'

'Yes. Who are you?'

'You don't need our names.'

'Prepared to tell me why I'm here?'

'Simple. We need to know whether you're just a vulgar adventurer or somebody we can work with.'

'Vulgar adventurer, yes it has a ring to it.'

'Have you heard of propaganda?' said the civilian.

'Publicity, you mean? Oh, certainly. Essential to any vulgar adventurer's bag of tricks.'

'We are in the business of promoting hatred,' said the captain. 'Hatred for the Hun. Atrocities, barbarism, general beastliness.'

The civilian leaned forward. 'Breaches of the conventions of war.'

'Yes,' said the captain. 'Anything along those lines. Naturally we do not permit such contraventions of decent behaviour ourselves. Otherwise we might compromise our reputation for playing the game with a straight bat. That goes without saying, does it not?'

'I see your point.'

'So,' said the civilian, 'we can safely assume that such matters concern the enemy alone?'

'Up to you, old man. I'm not quite sure I—'

The captain passed Guv a report that, given the number of rubber stamps it bore, had passed through several hands. In crisp prose Captain Selby gave a brief account of Guv's action against the Albatros. He threw doubt on his pilot's claim that the Graflex camera had malfunctioned, though that could not be proved as the observer responsible for the apparatus was dead. There was every indication that the subsequent flight had been preplanned (see appendix with ground crew affidavits). Engagement with the enemy aircraft ensued, following an admittedly skilful display of airmanship (see appendix where tactics noted). This engagement was successful, but at the cost of the BE2's observer. However, there was reason to believe that although the enemy surrendered Lieutenant Sutro pressed home his attack despite their inability to defend themselves, resulting in the destruction of the Albatros aircraft and its crew.

In summation, it was acknowledged that the incident could be considered a feat of arms. The officer concerned was a pilot second to none and his courage was beyond question. However, it was incontrovertible that he failed in his duty to secure reconnaissance photographs of a vital part of the Ypres salient on the eve of a major offensive. If his equipment failed (as he claimed), he was bound to return to base and report the situation. Instead of which he embarked on a reckless undertaking that could have ended in disaster. On the ground this officer was insubordinate and a bad influence on young and inexperienced pilots who might be tempted to follow his example. He was a threat to discipline in any squadron. As such, he (Captain Selby) recommended that Lieutenant Sutro should be transferred to another branch of the service where his qualities might be better recognised.

The captain took back the report. 'We are bound to show you this because it has gone through the usual obligatory channels. It is a matter of record, you understand, although clearly there remain doubts about matters of fact. In other words, Captain Selby's version of events and yours.'

Guv tilted back his chair. 'Who was flying my bus, I'd like to know? Who's in a better position to explain what happened – me or old Pew?'

'Pew?'

'Quite apart from beating the odds and bringing down an Albatros with a BE2, I see Selby fails to mention that I prevented the loss of another of our machines being stalked by that damned Hun.'

'No, he does not mention that. But it is a detail. As you've seen, he mentions a great deal else. So, what have you got to say on the matter?'

'Am I on the carpet?'

'For example, did the Graflex camera malfunction as you claim?'

'Of course.'

'Did you plan this sortie before leaving the ground?'

'Certainly not.'

'Did the Hun surrender to you as Captain Selby claims?'

'I made damned sure I shot him down before he had the chance.'

'Would you say you're a bad influence on your fellow pilots, as the major also suggests?'

'You should have been at the celebrations in the squadron Mess that evening. There you'd have had your answer. Not that Selby attended, of course. He was too busy bleating about me to Wing.'

'Enough of that, Lieutenant, unless you want to prejudice your case.'

'My case.'

'Oh, it could come to that. Whatever your opinion of Captain Selby, he is held in high regard in certain quarters. His opinions cannot be entirely discounted. However, it has to be said that you engendered some sympathy during your interview with Wing. Certainly they are reluctant to lose a good pilot at this stage of the war, so your account could stand as what we might call the official version if we judge it appropriate. That is why you are here today, instead of leading a platoon in Flanders. The matter is in your hands.'

'In what way?'

'Spreading the word about Hun beastliness is not the only objective in our remit,' said the civilian. 'We are also in the business of raising morale.'

The captain leaned forward on the desk. 'You have heard of the Frenchman Roland Garros, his exploits with his Morane?'

'Of course.'

'Already he has three enemy aircraft to his credit. An inspiration to his nation, you might say. From Germany, we are beginning to hear of other aviators, Max Immelmann, Oswald Boelcke, being raised up as heroes.'

'Ah, propaganda.'

'I see you grasp my meaning. Here it is not seen to be in our national character to beat the drum for the individual rather than the whole team. But that is not to say that certain discreet steps cannot be taken; a notice of an award for valour in the *London Gazette* in the most succinct and becomingly modest terms, perhaps a well-deserved promotion. In this way, no one could be accused of cheap theatrics. The facts alone would speak volumes about the kind of men the Germans must contend with.'

The captain rose to his feet and began to pace round the room. 'Of course, this is nothing new. We have had this idea in mind for some time now. Our problem has been, not to put too fine a point on it, identifying individuals who survive long enough for us to make such a proposal worthwhile. Of course, there have been numbers of possible candidates but either their gongs have come through post-humously, they've sustained injuries so terrible that we've been unable to expose them to the public because they'd damage morale, or they've been unsuitable for other reasons.'

'What other reasons?'

'Attitude, chiefly. A lot of you fellows are alike, splendidly spirited in the air but thoroughly indisciplined on the ground. You seem to assume that military codes of conduct don't apply, that you're quite at liberty to fashion your own rules as you go along.'

'Hardly surprising, is it? The Corps attracts a certain type – individualists who've had the means to learn to fly, or drive fast cars, or toboggan down the Cresta Run or put a hunter at a five-bar gate.'

'You may have noticed that such risk-takers are becoming in short supply. They're being replaced by a new breed – steadier chaps who've been trained as pilots in the service, still tigers when aloft, mind, but prepared to toe the line when not. Chaps who recognise the need for order.'

'Where's all this taking us?'

'To be blunt, we feel you might be our answer to Garros, Immelmann, Boelcke and the rest. With certain provisos.'

The civilian put his hands behind his head. 'You see, you strike us as someone who can look after himself, someone likely to survive somewhat longer than the others. Long enough for our purposes, at any rate.'

'And I've been called a callous swine,' said Guv. 'But please, go on. You mentioned provisos.'

'One, chiefly. You're a thorn in the side of any senior officer, particularly squadron commanders who, God knows, already have a difficult enough time of it without bumptious egotists throwing spanners in the works. You should be aware that you did not, by any means, win over everyone at Wing. Your account of events was not entirely accepted and some thought you swaggering and immodest, unlikeable qualities in an Englishman.'

'You require your protégés to be compliant and lovable?'

'Cut your cloth, Lieutenant Sutro, cut your cloth. Your past career suits you for an excellent future with the Corps, a good war, as you might say, that will stand you in good stead – assuming you live to return to your displays of skill and daring. Reassure us that everything said here has been understood, and will be complied with, and certain steps may be taken. That includes adherence to military discipline, a marked effort to control your natural braggadocio, and an undertaking that nothing will arise in future to contradict what may be described as the official version of your victory over the Albatros. It may be, for example, when our policy towards such things becomes a little more relaxed, as inevitably it will, that you'll find yourself meeting important personages or addressing a public meeting or being interviewed by the gentlemen of the press, and at such times the reputation and honour of the Corps will rest squarely in your hands. If, as I say, we have your reassurance on these points we can recommend that the wheels are put in motion.'

'Going back to that Albatros . . .' said Guv.

The captain sighed. 'Do I have your word?'

'Yes, all right, you have my word.'

'Very well. You will, of course, be posted to a new squadron. Meanwhile, enjoy the rest of your leave. I understand you married the Bowman girl.'

'That's right.'

'You are a lucky man.'

Guv frowned, searching the captain's pallid face for signs of irony.

'I was once a guest at their magical place near Rye,' said the captain. 'A delightful part of the world. The best of old England, eh? What we're all fighting for, in our different ways.'

Guv did not return to Saxonshore that night. He took a room at the Royal Aero Club in Piccadilly with a pleasant view of Green Park where, beyond the flow of traffic, the trees were in bud and couples moved along the walks arm-in-arm or held each other close on the scattered benches. In the bar there were rumours that he had done something of note in France.

'Come on, Sutro, let's hear the yarn from the horse's mouth.' He grinned enigmatically and shrugged it off, showing no trace of swagger, immodesty or braggadocio – to the surprise of his fellow members who often amused themselves by asking innocent questions about his latest exploits and standing well back, like a crowd on Bonfire Night watching the fuse of a penny rocket begin to fizz.

Later, he and Percy Fritchley, burned about the face and hands testing a two-seat Morane Parasol at Farnborough in which another man had died, cut through the park to St James's and along the Strand to the New Gaiety where they took seats in the front row of the stalls for Grossmith's musical farce *To-night's the Night*. Halfway through the first act, Grossmith himself, in his pleasant tenor, supported by a chorus of shapely dancers, launched into a ditty that caught Guv's mood:

> *If by some delightful chance, at a dinner or a dance*
> *Some delicious girl you meet, looking shy and soft and sweet*
> *Don't begin the usual thing, 'Does she tango, does she sing?'*
> *Just up and say 'How do? I'm in love with you.'*
> *It's the only, only way. Yes, the only, only way.*
> *She's the only girl, and it's only fair*
> *For she's only got half an hour to spare.*

Only kiss her on the spot with the only lips you've got
If she's only cute, she will only say 'That's the only kiss I've had
today!'
Then you only cough, But you don't leave off
It's the o-o-only!'

'That's a topping tune,' said Fritchley, the glare from the footlights playing cruelly on his face. He began to hum along as the girls went through their dance routine, their small feet drumming on the stage. A skittish brunette had picked out Guv but her interest turned to distaste when she saw his companion. Fritchley noticed. 'I'm afraid, old man, I'm rather cramping your style.'

'Don't give it another thought,' Guv said. He meant it, because he had not given it another thought himself. Such injuries were accepted as part of the game, and Fritchley's burns were by no means the worst he had seen. But for a moment he felt virtuous. It was what an English gentleman would say, a soft-spoken modest English gentleman without a hint of swagger who had barely heard of braggadocio; why, couldn't even spell it. He wondered, what would an English gentleman do next? He stood up and let the squab of his seat bang back. 'To hell with her. To hell with all of them. Let's pop across to Simpson's for a blow-out.' As they moved slowly towards the aisle he caught the eye of the little brunette. She winked; and with that wink he saw that dinner at Simpsons with a maimed chum was a poor substitute. So much for virtue . . .

Crossing the Strand, Fritchley began to reprise the tune sung by George Grossmith, then murmur, hesitantly, some verses of his own:

If by some delightful chance, when you're . . . uh . . . flying out
in France
Some old Boche machine you meet . . . yes . . . very slow and
obsolete

'That's damned good, Fritchley,' said Guv, at the door to Simpson's. 'Something like that could catch on with the chaps.'

'Stand me a snifter before grub,' said Fritchley, 'and we'll work something out.'

On the back of a menu, Guv writing with a borrowed pencil, Fritchley dictating because of the state of his hands, they devised more verses, sniggering over it like schoolboys in the back row of the class.

'Right, Sutro, where were we? Oh yes:

If some old Boche machine you meet, very slow and obsolete
Just put down your bally nose and say 'Chaps, here goes.'

Fritchley paused for inspiration. 'I know, I know:

Until his tail's damn near your prop, then shoot and do not stop,
So he crashes down in flames, and you can make another claim.
It's the o-o-only, o-o-only way . . .

A waiter in whites arrived at their table and with a flourish began to carve a joint of roast beef resting on the silver-topped trolley. Fritchley stared at it for a moment, gulping, then began to retch. 'Oh Christ, it reminds me . . .' He rose unsteadily to his feet and lurched towards the exit. Outside, he leaned against the wall, gasping for breath. 'Silly of me, but it looked like . . . looked like . . .' Guv found a taxi and directed the driver to take Fritchley back to the club. 'I'm terribly sorry about this, old man,' said Fritchley as Guv closed the door on him. 'Ashamed of myself, losing my grip like that. I can't seem to get poor old Venables out of my mind. These things catch you unawares.'

'Don't give it another thought,' said Guv for the second time that night.

As the taxi joined the flow of traffic going west, he checked his watch: enough time left to eat his meal and catch the last act of Grossmith's bit of nonsense. He had not forgotten that wink. The evening might not be such a washout, after all.

He stayed in London for two more days, spending each evening at the New Gaiety, collecting the skittish brunette at the stage door and going on to a discreet establishment in Bloomsbury where a small band played a repertoire of ragtime and sentimental ballads for officers who did not speak to each other but only to the girls they had brought with them or met there. After that, a brief interval passed in the little flat off Farringdon Road. Then back, alone, to Piccadilly.

By day he took a late breakfast, skipped through the newspapers in the club's reading room, played billiards, lunched heavily at the Criterion or the Ritz and slept it off in his room, preparing to watch yet another performance of *To-night's the Night*. He knew he could not postpone a return to Lydia much longer. It was not that he was having such a good time in Town, more that back at Saxonshore there was boredom but also great risk with Paget, the devious bastard, toadying up to the old man, bringing Chandler down on a trumped-up charge, installing his sluttish cousin.

He kicked himself for succumbing to the little tramp. Not that he thought she'd say a word. It wasn't in her interests. But he had to move her on, to somewhere handy and more discreet. She certainly was a stupendous fuck, up there with the best. He'd made it worth her while to keep her legs open and her trap shut. Paget he'd deal with somehow too.

Meanwhile, he needed to be back in France. This damned soft living didn't suit him; soft people, soft opinions, soft all round at a time that called for hardness. Bowman, for example, mewling on about his life of privilege and ease. 'Perhaps I might perform some small deed of note before I meet my maker.' What pompous rot. Guv hoped his father-in-law would meet his maker soon and clear the way for Lydia to land a useful legacy, although inevitably Saxonshore would pass into the hands of the mother. They had met, for the first and last time, at the wedding – a faded beauty, he supposed she would be called, but still striking with that gloss and assurance born of wealth, whose looks had passed her daughter by; wiry and full of vigour, from robust Puritan stock and likely to outlive them all. She had treated him with great suspicion. 'It may be that you are sincere. It may be that you are a scoundrel. I acknowledge that I have never seen my daughter happier. If that should change, if you treat her shabbily, treat her in any way that she, sweet creature, does not deserve, then all the influence that this family possesses will be brought to bear upon you. Of that make no mistake.' She had looked him up and down, not as a mother-in-law but as a natural woman regarding a natural man, their freshly forged relationship irrelevant, as though she understood the attraction he might hold for Lydia or any female, even her; as though she perceived in him what she knew of herself. He imagined she had conducted many affairs, despairing of her dry old English stick. At another time and another place he would have seen her as an opportunity and a challenge; age did not matter to him, only a well-set body and the ability to use it.

Rehearsing various pretexts to cut short his leave, the problem was solved for him by the delivery to the club of an order from the War Office directing him to report to his new squadron at Chézy-au-Bois near Amiens in four days' time, sooner than expected. Nothing else was mentioned; no medal, no promotion, no indication of wheels in motion, only that he had been despatched to France. No reason for complaint, of course. It was what he wanted. A brief return to Saxonshore to suffer no doubt tearful farewells, and then he could skedaddle with the perfect excuse.

At Rye station Paget met him with the Rolls. 'What ho, Guv. And how's The Smoke? Enjoy yourself, did you?'

Guv ignored him. When Paget held out his hand for the valise, he moved it out of reach. Paget narrowed his eyes. 'Summat up?'

'Only that I've got your number.'

'Don't follow.'

'I think you do.'

'Old Chandler, you mean? Well, I said I'd queer that bugger's pitch if I got the chance. He crossed me once too often.'

'I ought to fire you on the spot.'

'Oh, I don't think it'll come to that. I mean, I don't really work for you any more, do I? Not since Chandler got the boot.' Paget took out a packet of Woodbines, put one between his lips and patted his coat for matches. 'No point in asking you for a light, I suppose?' He found his matches and lit the cigarette. 'Things have changed a bit. You may have missed it. Me and old Bowman, we're pretty thick.

He's come to rely on me, and so's your missus. I reckon they'd be sorry to see me go. So I don't advise you to come the lord and master because you ain't exactly, are you?' He let tobacco smoke trickle down his nostrils. 'I reckon it's a downright shame what you put the good lady through, her expecting and all.' He threw down the half-smoked butt. 'Not that she knows the half of it yet.'

'I warn you, do anything in that direction and I'll see you dead.'

'The perfect solution, eh? Well, you'll not find me such an easy target as some.'

'What the blazes do you mean by that?'

'Why, the Germans of course,' said Paget. 'Ain't you fighting them in France? What else could I mean? No reason to get so blooming hoity-toity. I won't say nothing as long as you don't rock the boat. It's sailing along quite nicely at the moment. Be a pity to end up on the rocks.' He pulled on his driving gauntlets. 'We're all grown-ups, ain't we? You, me, your good lady wife, old Bowman,' he paused, 'Rose. My cuz is fond of Mrs S, you know. She'd be sorry to do anything to hurt her. As I say, no need to rock the boat.' He was leaning against the mudguard of the Rolls. 'Talking of boats, what about that *Lusitania* with all them swells on board? Lucky old bloke, your pa-in-law, hanging out with the nobs. That's what it's all about, ain't it? Sucking up, being agreeable to the right crowd, making your way. Be nice to see him back. He's quite a lonely old feller on the quiet. Many's the chat we've had, about this and that. I've got his ear, as you might say.'

Guv threw his valise into the back of the Rolls, climbed behind the wheel and started the engine. Paget watched him without moving. The car accelerated swiftly away. Paget, left standing on the station forecourt, watched it go. 'Hoity-toity, eh? Well, we shall see.'

3

The announcement in the supplement to the *London Gazette* was, as usual, brief. His Majesty the King was graciously pleased to award Lieutenant Fraser Sutro, Royal Flying Corps, the Military Cross for conspicuous gallantry and skill. He had engaged a German Albatros biplane, faster and equipped with a machine-gun, with great determination. Pressing home his attack despite his observer suffering mortal wounds and being unable to play any significant part in the action, he succeeded in bringing down the hostile aircraft single-handed though only lightly armed, thus saving another machine of his squadron from almost certain destruction and showing great nerve and courage, a fine example of fighting spirit.

The mention in the county press was just as concise, the barest details, in line with the Government's reluctance to identify individual pilots although, within the service, rather more was known. No one could argue with the facts. Like or loathe the chap, it had to be admitted that Guv Sutro had done damned well. In fact, there seemed to be less of the braggart about him these days. Perhaps he was learning some team spirit, after all. What other explanation could there be?

Soon afterwards his name was mentioned in *The Times* in a different context:

> *Sutro – on 24 April at Saxonshore, Rye, Sussex*
> *To Lydia (née Bowman), the wife of*
> *Lieutenant Fraser Sutro MC, Royal Flying Corps,*
> *a daughter.*

Guv, in France, had no plans to see the child immediately. He had expected a son. And anyway, he was busy familiarising himself with the Vickers FB5 at Chézy-au-Bois. As well, his new squadron was down in numbers for the usual reasons and he could hardly request leave after arriving as a pilot of note with something to prove. Besides, the rate of attrition suggested that soon he might at last secure promotion and find himself a flight commander, despite his lack of flying hours on the FB5, an opportunity he did not want to miss.

To the casual eye, the Gunbus appeared primitive and ungainly, a pusher with the rear-facing engine mounted behind the pilot, the crew contained in a blunt-nosed nacelle, the observer/gunner in the forward cockpit armed with a ring-mounted Lewis gun and, without an engine or propeller in the way, provided with a clear field of fire. The Gunbus did not have the clean lines of the BE2 or Morane Parasol; the forward section and the tail-plane appeared to be connected by a fragile arrangement of struts and wires that could hardly be described as a fuselage. But the FB5 was deceptively robust and, for Guv, held one significant attribute: it had been designed for what its makers described as 'offensive action in the air'. Already it had established its reputation as one of the best fighting machines in service, with numbers of victims to its name. And Guv was intent on adding to that reputation, and his.

Lydia's letter had assured him that the birth had been straightforward, that the child was healthy and so was she; she felt a little lonely without the two most important men in her life, she confessed, but hoped that she (and of course the baby, although its eyes weren't open yet) might see him soon. However, she realised she must not be selfish; it was the same for everyone in these awful times and she really must not think only of herself. Meanwhile, such welcome news, her father had sent a telegram confirming that he was about to sail from New York with Alfred Vanderbilt who was planning to purchase hounds and hunters in England. Not only that, but her mother had taken a cabin on the *Lusitania* as well, wishing to inspect her new granddaughter without delay. If only her darling boy could secure even a few days at home, wrote Lydia, her pleasure would be complete.

Her darling boy, meanwhile, was engaged on trench reconnaissance operations between Bapaume and Peronne, scorning flying at the usual height of 800 feet and tracking along the enemy lines at 300, scouting for troop movements, machine-gun nests and artillery positions. These he found and unaccountably survived, his gunner Hargreaves emptying many drums of ammunition and earning himself a mention in dispatches until a German shell exploded directly below his cockpit and he was disembowelled. Although on this occasion the machine was, as the other pilots predictably observed, shot to blazes with smashed instruments, splintered struts, canvas shredded from the upper and lower wings and flapping like loose skin, the engine streaming oil and fuel and even a landing wheel shot away, the new man Sutro somehow got it back to Chézy-au-Bois and suffered not a scratch. It was uncanny and inexplicable, particularly when Bentley-Pitt, the squadron commander who still flew on sorties (although the practice was discouraged), was sent down in flames by an Albatros over Bertincourt. Bentley-Pitt, noted for his prudence in the air, whose logbook contained 300 flying hours; Bentley-Pitt who, only the day before, had warned this fellow Sutro, within hearing in the Mess, that he was playing a dangerous game already dangerous enough, God knows, and that he should fly at a sensible height if he expected to see his newborn child. Now Bentley-Pitt had gone, leaving three children of his own. At Wing they scanned the roster for his replacement. 'Rotten luck, losing young Benson-Smith.'

'Bentley-Pitt, sir.'

'One of our steadier types. Put him in for an MC.'

'He had one already, sir.'

'Well, put him in for a posthumous bar. Any idea who'll plug the gap? What about this fellow Sutro we hear so much about? Seems to me he's setting a fine example and possesses the right amount of pluck. Perhaps we should promote him and put his leadership abilities to the test.'

'With respect, sir, we're looking for rather more than pluck. We need a level head. Sutro's not been long at Chézy and he may not be there much longer, if he carries on the way he's started. Should he survive, and come to understand we're looking for more than reckless courage, perhaps we might consider entrusting him with a flight. But first he's got to prove he possesses more than guts.'

'Nothing wrong with guts.'

'As long as you keep them inside your stomach, sir, unlike Flight Sergeant Hargreaves who had the dubious distinction of accompanying Lieutenant Sutro on his trips to pepper the Hun trenches until a burst of Archie did for him. It was a miracle the machine stayed in the air. As it was, it was a total write-off.'

'Such losses are regrettable, of course – a single man, a single machine – but remember, they should be balanced against the damage caused to enemy positions, the numbers killed, the fear instilled in the hearts of the survivors, the erosion of morale. That is, after all, why we're here. Multiply such effects a thousandfold and we might win the war. The bigger picture, my boy, the bigger picture.'

'That may be, sir, but you can also argue that Lieutenant Sutro has been directly responsible for the loss of two valuable aeroplanes and the deaths of his observers in a remarkably short space of time. Some may see him as an inspiration, hence the War House instructions that he should receive his gong, but others consider him an impetuous glory-seeker. Place him in charge of a flight or even a squadron and he could lead them to destruction, as surely as Lord Cardigan took the Light Brigade into the Valley of Death at Balaclava.'

'Oh, come now, you're over-dramatising, surely? However . . .'

'Sir?'

'It may be that you have a point. Let us bear Sutro in mind for future consideration, if he proves to have a future that can be counted in more than weeks. Perhaps he will learn to curb his wilder inclinations. If not, he may have a use in single-seater scouts where the only skin he has to look after is his own. Now, who else might suit?'

At Chézy-au-Bois Guv waited to be issued with a new machine and assigned a replacement observer/gunner, but he was to see his new daughter sooner than he expected. Shortly after Bentley-Pitt was killed, the rumour ran round the Mess.

'I say, rotten news about the *Lusitania*, eh?'

'What news?'

'Haven't you heard, Sutro? She's been torpedoed by a German U-boat.'

'Good God, I had people on board.'

'Oh, I shouldn't worry. The first reports say everyone's been saved.'

The first reports were wrong. The liner, ten miles short of the Irish coast with the Head of Kinsale in sight, had not been beached as first believed. She sank in eighteen minutes and over a thousand passengers and crew were drowned. The British press was quick to condemn this latest act of frightfulness: *the hideous policy of indiscriminate brutality* raged *The Times, which has placed the German race outside the pale.*

As more was known, accounts of tragedy and horror were tempered by tales of bravery and sacrifice. Guv began to read the news reports with rising hope. His eye was caught by the Vanderbilt name: the gallant millionaire who gave away his life-vest to the mother of a babe-in-arms, and also gave away his life. He was not alone; he and another member of the Vanderbilt party had been seen to help survivors into lifeboats. Another member of the Vanderbilt party? Could it be that old man Bowman had been granted his wish to perform some deed of note before he met his maker? Soon it was clear he had. Both men had been seen to wave the boats away, standing together at the rail as the liner began to dip and slide beneath the surface. Later, Guv ran his finger down the list of survivors, fewer than eight hundred, but the name of Mrs Alice Doty Bowman was not among them. Her loss was soon confirmed by a telegram from Lydia begging him to find some way of returning to Saxonshore, if only for a short while, as she doubted she could cope alone.

Guv had a strong urge to laugh, consumed by something close to joy, a sense that everything had come right. Composing himself to register appropriate shock and grief, he applied for compassionate leave and, still with no machine to fly, his application was treated with the greatest sympathy. Soon he was boarding the leave boat at Boulogne once again, without a diversion in the town, and bound for home. For home. For Saxonshore. He was overcome by euphoria. It was as if he was drunk.

He began to sing, bellowing the words into the darkness of the Channel surge, cold spray wet on his face, the salt-taste strong on his lips. He did not use the words composed by Fritchley at Simpson's. The original ones would do just fine:

> *You're the only man and it's only fair*
> *For you've only got half an hour to spare*
> *If you're only cute she'll only say,*
> *That's the only kiss that she's had today!*
> *It's the o-o-only, o-o-only way . . .*

The verses took him back to that show at the Gaiety and suggested many more such shows and entertainments to come, times when he would not have to justify himself to anyone about anything he might say or do because he did not have to be careful any more; because everything had come to him, thanks to one well-placed torpedo.

A naval officer went by on his way to the bridge. 'That's what I like to hear on board this ship, a happy man.'

'Oh yes,' said Guv. 'I'm happy all right. I've recently had some wonderful news.'

'What news?'

For a moment Guv was caught. 'My wife,' he said finally. 'She's had a child.'

'Congratulations. Boy or girl?'

'Girl,' said Guv. Ah yes, the child. He had quite forgotten.

4

A Crossley staff car was parked outside the Gare du Nord in the centre of Amiens to meet the express from Boulogne. The carriages had been packed with British and French troops, a dozen to every compartment whatever their rank, those standing supported by the man next to them, reaching out to seize the luggage rack as the train slowed suddenly or lurched across a set of points. In the corridors, others jostled for space, shoulder-to-shoulder, with many stretched out on the floors, heads resting on their packs, risking the tread of heavy boots in return for a little sleep. All were bound for Amiens, where transport was waiting to take them to their various sectors of the Front.

At Boulogne, Guv had left the other officers to fight for their rightful places in first class, using his seniority and elbows to secure himself a corner seat on a wooden bench in third. Now he stepped down onto the platform with his kitbag and valise with some reluctance, not because he did not want to rejoin his squadron but because the train was almost empty now and would have carried him, *première classe*, on to Paris.

On the forecourt the troops were beginning to form up, ready to be loaded into lorries like beasts bound for market. From among the ranks of the French, picturesque in their blue coats and red trousers, a *poilu* bleated like a lamb, raising a burst of laughter from his comrades and shouts of anger from their officers.

When Guv came out of the broad station entrance he recognised the corporal at the wheel of the Crossley who engaged gear and drew up slowly beside him. 'Hello, Mr Sutro. I'm here to collect the new CO.'

'Didn't know I'd been promoted,' Guv said. He tried to look amused but wondered, for a wild moment, if it could be true. Maybe not so wild; elevation to captain, entrusted abruptly with a squadron? In the unpredictability of war, such things happened. Then, behind him, he heard the nasal twang of a Queensland accent. 'Looking for me, Corporal? Hello, Sutro, I heard you were on my strength.' It was Sutton, no longer a captain but with major's crowns on his epaulettes.

Guv saluted in a perfunctory way. He nodded at the Australian's badges of rank. 'Congratulations, Sutton. I hadn't heard.'

'Means less flying, I'm afraid, dealing with all the bumph. Still, with firebrands like you on board I reckon the squadron's reputation in the air rests in safe enough hands.' Sutton had settled himself in the Crossley and was looking at Guv with a quizzical eye. The squadron's reputation in the air? What was he getting at? Was he making some petty distinction? 'Well,' said Sutton, 'do you want a lift or are you planning a little diversion en route?' He grinned knowingly as though recalling the times they had shared together, those times with the whores of Aquitaine all those years ago when they had been trainee pilots at Blériot's school at Pau.

Guv, conscious of the attentive corporal, did not grin back but stowed his luggage and took his place next to Sutton on the Crossley's rear seat. As they moved away from the station along the rue de Noyon, he occupied himself with filling his pipe from his tobacco pouch. They passed close to the cathedral, crossed the Somme by the Pont St Michel and, gathering speed, headed north along the Route de Doullens.

'So you married Miss Bowman,' Sutton said.

'That's right.'

'Rotten for your wife, that *Lusitania* business. But her father did wonderfully well – I imagine that's some comfort. No great surprise to me. I always thought he showed commendable nerve, pulling out of your Atlantic adventure.'

'Nerve, you call it?'

'Oh, yes. A pretty tough decision, I'd say, when things had gone so far. Of course, that was a time when lives didn't come so cheap.' Sutton leaned closer, so he could not be heard by the driver. 'I took it hard, you know, being kicked out in favour of your ruddy nut from Brazil. Still, no doubt we're both sufficiently grown up to start afresh, otherwise life might prove uncomfortable.'

'For me, you mean?' Guv removed his pipe. 'I won't give you cause for complaint.'

'So what are the other chaps at Chézy like?'

'Best make your own mind up on that.'

'Not very illuminating.'

'Very well. They're short on hours, most of them, and they lack the killer instinct. They don't hate, even when one of them goes west. They still treat the Hun as if he's a member of an opposing team, not a downright enemy.'

'A very English trait,' said the Australian. 'But I assume their pluck is not in doubt.'

'Oh, they'll do what's required of them all right, but they're disinclined to take more risks than they have to.'

'Unlike you, I hear. Well, as long as their instinct for self-preservation doesn't interfere with carrying out their responsibilities . . .'

'If your number's up, it's up. You and I know it's down to luck and there's damn-all you can do about it. Bullets aren't choosy. An inch either way makes the difference between another binge in the Mess and being shipped back in Blighty in a wooden box or, more likely, your corpse being churned to buggery by shells in no-man's land.'

Guv tamped and re-lit his pipe, and sparks flew in the slipstream of the Crossley. The road stretched ahead of them, almost straight, rising and falling with the gentle contours of the terrain. On either side flowed a monotony of level arable and pasture, relieved by clumps of dark woodland and the occasional distant spire that showed where a *hameau* lay, those straggles of mildewed dwellings lining a muddy street.

'We all have our way of dealing with these things,' said Sutton. 'A chap in my last outfit reckoned it was better to be killed quickly and get it over with. Couldn't stand the suspense.'

'What happened to him?'

'Oh, he's still on ops. Suffers agonies every time he goes up on a show. Ironically, he leads a charmed life. He may survive, he may not. Meanwhile, he spends whatever time he may have left in a total funk – that is, when he's sober.'

'If I see someone displaying signs of cracking up,' said Guv, 'I tell him he can make it easier on himself by considering himself already dead.'

'That must get them all crowding round for comfort,' said Sutton. He turned his head and stared out at the passing landscape. 'Good airfield country, by the way.'

'Where were you before?'

'Not far from St Pol, north-west of Arras. Blériots and BE2s. There from the start. Just a beetfield when we arrived. Took some tramping, I can tell you, and five hundred tons of cinders.'

They had passed through Villers Bocage, more than a *hameau*, not quite a town, and began to hear the blare of aero-engines being run up on the ground. An FB5 Gunbus passed overhead at 50 feet, coming in to land at Chézy-au-Bois a few miles down the road, as incongruous and graceless as a pterodactyl, its motor throttled back, its propeller thrashing slowly behind the nacelle. From their cockpits the pilot and observer waved. Sutton waved back and the pilot rocked his wings.

The squadron had been given notice of the arrival of its new commanding officer. All most of them knew was that he led from the front and now, to preserve his skills, had been put to the back. That did not sound much help. Good pilots were scarce.

Those machines not on operations had been arranged in line ready for inspection, close to the canvas hangars and bell tents where the men were billeted, pitched by the farm buildings in which the officers had their quarters. The inspection did not take long. Soon Sutton took up an FB5, put on a neat display that silenced any who might doubt his skill, and taxied in. He spoke briefly: 'That's probably the last time you fellows will see me in the air. It's not that I don't want to fly. My role as your squadron commander requires me not to. My task now is to make us one of the best darned operations on the Western Front. For that I require your full commitment and support. You will have mine in return. Carry on.'

That evening, he joined his officers in the Mess that had been established in a barn; a dining room with, in one corner, a stove that burned anything that came to hand and an anteroom that contained a bar and an assortment of battered but comfortable chairs. When he had downed a sufficient quantity of alcohol to show he was still one of the boys at heart, he made his excuses and left the others to conclude the evening as they wished, adding only that a briefing was to be held in his office at six ack emma sharp – 'sharp, mind you.' The point was taken.

'Sharp, eh?' said one of the flight commanders. 'What did I tell you, Rhodes? I said our Aussie's got a reputation as something of a stickler.'

'Bound to be,' said Rhodes. 'You don't build up a crack squadron with doses of sweetness and light. But I've been told he looks out for his chaps, as far as anyone can.'

'Let's hope you're right. A pal of mine got stuck with one of these Mad Majors, the kind of low-flying johnnie who knows no fear and can't understand it in anyone else; quite ready to sacrifice lives to his over-developed sense of duty. Earned paeans of praise from the high-ups, of course. That's why these types get away with it, despite the cost. At one point they suffered four casualities in a single day, fifteen in a week, delivering the goods. Naturally the sod survived it all and earned himself some kudos with Wing.'

'What happened to your pal?'

'He was lucky. Stopped a bullet from a Hun infantry column he was shooting up. Cost him a leg but now he's back in the Sceptred

Isle acting the wounded hero for bits of fluff. Otherwise that perishing fool would have done for him, as surely as if he pulled the trigger.'

'You're in that mould, aren't you, Sutro?' said Rhodes. 'God help us if you ever get a flight.'

Guv shrugged. 'So far, you lot have had it pretty easy. I know Sutton. He's tougher than a two-penny steak. You're going to find yourselves looking back on your time with Bentley-Pitt as a fond and distant memory.'

Davis ignored him. 'I suppose you've heard they given old Mentally Fit a bar to his MC?'

'A fat lot of good that'll do him,' said Rhodes. 'They should have made him a penguin like Sutton, while they had the chance.'

'Talking of bars,' said Davis, 'this is turning into a dry old do. Why don't we put a sock in this morbid gassing and rustle up another round, instead of giving ourselves the jitters?'

Rhodes snapped his fingers at the orderly for more whiskies. 'You flew with our shiny new CO before the war, didn't you, Sutro?'

'We came across each other.'

'More than that, surely?' said Davis. 'Weren't you going to fly the Atlantic together?'

'He let me down,' said Guv. 'Ancient history.' He looked at them hard. 'I don't expect that to go any further.'

There was an awkward pause, made more awkward by Davis. 'I say, aren't you just back from leave? Bag any bits of fluff?'

'You blithering idiot,' said Rhodes as the drinks arrived. 'Sutro's been on a compassionate.'

'Oh, crikey,' said Davis. 'Yes, I quite forgot. Apologies and all that. Rotten for you. Everything all right now?'

'Apart from my wife's parents going down in the *Lusitania*, you mean, while she was giving birth to their first grandchild?'

'Ah. Gosh. Oh dear. What can I say?'

'Nothing, I suggest,' said Rhodes. He filled their glasses. 'May I propose a toast to Major Bentley-Pitt? Here's to the dead already, hoorah for the next man who dies.'

Guv took his whisky in one gulp. 'I'm turning in. I'm trying out my replacement bus tomorrow, when my new observer reports for duty.'

'Old hand or new?'

'Don't know. He's been posted in from Merville. Should be here by morning.'

'Now isn't he a lucky lad?' said Rhodes.

Part of the officers' accommodation overlooked an iron-fenced yard, its cobbles thick with pungent dung from cows and pigs, picked at by a diminishing flock of chickens, most destined for the squadron pot despite stern warnings that pillagers of poultry would be dealt with severely (by senior ranks who did not seem to question where that particular evening's meal might have come from). When Guv entered his cell-like room he heard a rhythmic rubbing sound outside, like someone sawing wood. He opened the shuttered window. The smell of ordure was overpowering but like others quartered in this wing he had grown used to it. A sow was scratching her rump on the brick wall beside the sill. Holding onto the windowframe, he stuck out a leg and gave her a boot in the ribs. She moved slowly away, looking at him reproachfully. It was the kind of look that Lydia had given him when he touched on his (or as he put it, their) plans for Saxonshore; the resemblance was so close that he had to laugh out loud.

It had been a mixed leave. The matter of the estate was in the hands of lawyers, on both sides of the Atlantic. It seemed clear-cut enough. Lydia as the only child was the sole beneficiary. In Guv's terms, this meant he got the lot. He could see now that he had allowed himself to get carried away with the thought. Lydia, it seemed, did not necessarily share his view. What her view might be, he still did not know. He tried to discuss it with her but each time she reacted with convulsive sobs. Grief, he supposed. He would have to wait. How long? he wondered. He was impatient. He had various schemes in mind; to change the name of the place for a start. It meant nothing to him, Saxonshore. It was redolent of the Bowmans' wet nostalgia for the past, their preference for things old over things new. He had decided he would call it High And Over as a nod to the scene of his first success at Alfriston, solidly pegging the place to the here and now. What next? Post-war perhaps a flying school or a service offering flights to fashionable resorts in nearby France; Le Touquet, Montreuil, Dieppe. And what about that dank old relic of a castle in the valley, of interest only to a few musty academics and painters of bad water colours? Half jokingly (but was he joking?) he'd suggested it could be converted into a small hotel. Or perhaps the clubhouse of a golf course, the fairways, greens and hazards spread throughout the grounds.

He foresaw a restless generation emerging from the war, a generation eager to forget, seeking distraction, diversion, fun. Were these musings so much wild speculation or practical propositions worth serious consideration? Compared to farming, always vulnerable to the extremes of British weather, unpredictable prices and capricious politicians, such schemes looked like easy money. And still more could be made by giving the redundant farmworkers notice to quit their tenancies and putting the cottages up for rent at sensible prices or for freehold sale. It seemed to Guv that old Bowman, fixated on some golden age, a rural idyll that probably never was (no doubt a device to ease the pressures of his business life) had allowed the estate to sink into a state of creeping dereliction, employing a ramshackle band of time-serving clod-hoppers more usefully engaged at a factory bench and probably happier for it.

Well, when the time came these were matters that could be easily dealt with, providing a flow of income to finance his flying projects and keep him in the air. There was so much that might be achieved. Nothing was impossible for a determined and experienced pilot, as long as he had the best machines, the right team in support and sufficient funds from whatever source. The challenge of the Atlantic still remained. Why not the Pacific? Or England to Australia? Why not, in time, fly right round the world?

When his mind was brimming with such notions, Guv sometimes wondered what drove him. Destiny, he supposed, that useful word. It was something like a book already written, every word set down, he the central character turning it page by page, following a narrative planned for him all along. Even when Lydia had taken him into the nursery and he had stood by the cradle looking down at the pink scrap that was his daughter, the image had clicked in his mind somehow, as though he had seen her before, as though this was precisely how it was meant to be.

'You are not disappointed, my dear?' Lydia had asked. 'That I have not given you a son?'

He had not answered. A son would come, he was sure of that. Clearly, this was not the time. And timing was vital, if destiny was to be fulfilled. Why, if he himself had been born years too soon or years too late, he would have missed this war. No doubt for his unborn son, Fate had something else in store. No question of war, of course – no other war could follow this. But surely something that would make the world take notice, as the world had noticed him? Who could tell what possibilities might exist twenty, thirty years from now? If a flier like his father, well, who knew how aviation might have progressed by then, what opportunities might exist for a red-blooded lad with his father's stamp to enhance the Sutro name? And as for him, perhaps a broader stage, built on his achievements in the air, a magnet for those nonentities who had done nothing but regarded him in that special way he had long become used to because of what he had done, because up there (he always saw it in their eyes) it was as if he had been touched by God; hell, he almost believed it himself – that he had a power within him that could be used to shape the lives of men when, from the shambles left by war, a new order would emerge.

Lydia had taken the infant up and passed her to him. He rested her on his shoulder. She smelled as fresh as a new-picked apple. He felt in that moment that she was his, not Lydia's, that she would also be of importance to him, significant in his life. He could not imagine how, but then he did not have to. It was written; everything was written. But looking at the baby's unformed features he hoped to God that she did not inherit her mother's looks.

He had been surprised to discover that Rose Pringle was still tending to Lydia and the child. She did not perform her duties particularly well, although as far as he could tell there was a degree of affection between the women; natural, he supposed, given Lydia's reliance on the girl, throughout the pregnancy and birth. The thought of Rose's hands upon his child was abhorrent, but he had to admit she carried it off adequately; seeming respectful, attentive, kind. Outside the nursery, in an indulgent moment, he told her as much. She brushed his cheek with her fingers and her manner changed in an instant. 'Well, I'm a woman, aren't I, with woman's instincts? It all comes natural, don't it? I believe in doing what comes natural. Anyway, I know which side my bread's buttered, particularly now.'

'Now?'

'You know, what with things the way they are. You'll look out for me, Guv, I'm sure, now you're in a firm position.' She placed her hand on his crotch. 'You know I'm in favour of firm positions.'

He stepped back. 'You little trollop, I could dismiss you on the spot.'

She smiled. 'Oh, I believe Harry might have something to say about that.'

'Your damned cousin has a great deal to say about many things. Though less so now, I notice.'

'He's like me, dear. We both love buttered bread.'

Paget had certainly been quiet enough when he met Guv's train at Rye station. The contrast was comical; no more condescension, no transparent threats. There was deference in his manner. Guv could not resist baiting him. He leaned forward and slid open the glass window between driver and passenger. 'You're unusually tight lipped today, Paget.'

'Well, they're sorry times, ain't they?'

'Particularly sorry for you, no doubt. You must miss those cosy chats with my father-in-law – sucking up, to use your brutish lingo. So who do you reckon's your lord and master now? You seemed in doubt about it, last time we met.' Guv noticed that the back of Paget's neck turned red. 'You realise, I suppose, that I have the power to boot you straight into the PBI.'

'PBI? What's that when it's at home?'

284

'Poor bloody infantry – an apt acronym, I'd say.'

'I don't know nothing about no bloody acromins. You won't get no trouble from me. I know how the land lies. And I'm not just speaking for myself. Saxonshore suits me and Cuz fine. We'll do the decent thing by you. Our Rose is right fond of your missus and the babe.' Paget looked at Guv in the rear-view mirror. 'Fond of you and all.'

'Don't get sentimental on me, Paget, it won't wash.'

'You can please yourself.'

'Exactly right,' said Guv. 'You're a passable mechanic but that's hardly sufficient reason to save your skin. However, I've got plans for the estate and it suits me to have a devious little worm like you acting as my eyes and ears while I'm away, as long as you toe the line. Otherwise, that one-way ticket to the Somme.' He reached for the knob of the glass window to slide it shut. 'As you once told me, if you rock the boat it's likely to end up wrecked.' He thumped the window shut.

Guv breathed more easily after that. Rose and her detestable cousin were as good as gagged. And if it came to their word against his, who would be believed? He felt secure enough, in what remained of his leave, to visit Rose at various times of day and night and found it easier than he expected to overcome his initial distaste. She was like two different women, by turn the demure lady's maid and the stimulating slut; what an actress she would have made. He had abandoned, for the time being, the idea of installing her somewhere more discreet. As things were, it seemed to him the perfect arrangement: his wife and child cared for, his own needs looked after and readily on hand, and Paget brought to heel.

A memorial service for the Bowmans had been hastily arranged in Rye, to coincide with Lieutenant Sutro's compassionate leave, now nearly at an end. The pews of St Mary's Church were full. It was an odd affair; the trappings of a funeral without coffins. The bodies had not been recovered which, for a time, gave Lydia hope. Now there was numb acceptance. She could not bring herself to imagine her parents' final moments; she found some solace in her father's show of gallantry, but how had he and her mother died? She tried to shut out loathsome visions that came to her at night, their corpses caught by ocean currents, limbs twisting as if in some macabre dance, as though waving goodbye, goodbye, goodbye. She woke up suffused with horror, groaning: 'They've gone, they've gone. Their faces, oh their faces.' She clung to Guv, racked with anguish. But in the church she held herself in check, suppressing her emotions, fixing her eyes on the stained-glass images of Saviour and Saints in the great windows that filtered the warm sunlight into a wash of many colours that filled the nave. She found no reassurance in those noble, empty features; no reassurance either in the next inevitable hymn, sung so often in this little coastal town for those who lived and died by the sea that broke and hissed on the nearby pebble shore.

> *Eternal Father, strong to save,*
> *Whose arm hath bound the restless wave . . .*
> *Oh, hear us when we cry to Thee,*
> *For those in peril on the sea!*

For Lydia, the words were empty humbug. The Eternal Father's arm had not been strong; had not bounded the restless wave. The mourners, if mourners they were at a service not quite a funeral, droned on:

> *O Christ! Whose voice the waters heard*
> *And hushed their raging at Thy word . . .*
> *Oh, hear us when we cry to Thee,*
> *For those in peril on the sea!*

The waters had not heard Christ's voice. Nor had the commander of the U-boat who loosed death on a defenceless ship. Why plea for Him to hear cries for those in peril when it was too late? She thought she would never acknowledge God again or pray again or enter this church. The rector's address came as a distant murmur. 'This is not the place to dwell on the cruel circumstances that led to the loss of two such valued and respected members of our community . . . we stand together confronted with the reality of death and the hope of eternal life . . . no one will know how this devoted couple embarked on their final journey . . . what is certain is that a true son of Rye, christened and married in this very church, behaved as death was nearing him with a selfless courage that no words of mine can describe. I entrust that duty to another gallant gentleman who knew him far better than I.'

At the rector's signal Guv rose from his pew and stepped into the aisle, remembering the last time he had taken this same short walk. Then Lydia had been waiting for him at the altar, as meek and vulnerable as some creature in a jungle clearing stalked by a beast of prey. It had occurred to him a few paces away (as it must have done to many a Bengal tiger) that it might be a trap, but it had been too late to abandon the hunt.

He had not told Lydia of his arrangement with the rector and her hand clung to his for a moment, before it fell away. He did not speak from the pulpit but stood erect on the first step of the altar staring straight ahead, impeccable in his fresh-pressed uniform with the silver cross of his MC prominent under its white and purple ribbon. The congregation regarded him in that special way, with respect and admiration; yes, as if he had been touched by God, so high had he climbed above the world. To them he appeared serene, as though sustained by some inner strength.

His words were brief. 'Two people have passed from us who cannot be with us in body. But I am sure they are here in spirit. That they crossed over together, and were perhaps of some comfort to each other at the last, is of scant comfort to those they leave behind. But their names and their memory will live on. People will not speak of Alfred Bowman as a millionaire, as the owner of a great commercial enterprise, although that will remain his monument. They will talk of him as a hero and will salute his name.' He noticed that close to him, women had begun to weep; he had them in his hand. He raised his voice so his concluding words echoed round the white-washed walls, stuck about with memorials to the disregarded dead, just chiselled names on marble of fleeting interest to the aimless visitor before taking afternoon tea at the Mermaid Inn – though, when the Bowman tablet joined them, mention of the *Lusitania* might catch the eye.

'I hope,' he said, 'that the young men of Britain will act with the same cool bravery that this very perfect English gentleman displayed in assisting others until the end.' That was all. It had been well put; as well put as the tribute to Alfred Vanderbilt he had seen reprinted from the *New York Times*.

He walked back to his place and Lydia fell against him. She felt a rush of gratitude for him in her loss. She thanked God for him and had to smile a little, even in her misery, that her rejection of God should have lasted such a little moment. She held tightly to her husband's arm. He turned his head and, in that moment, he resembled one of the stained-glass saints, his face noble yet empty of expression. A shadow touched her soul. Odd, she thought, that in the closing hymn, shadows should feature in the final verse. She wondered if it had significance:

> *Hold Thou Thy cross before my closing eyes;*
> *Shine through the gloom and point me to the skies.*
> *Heaven's morning breaks, and earth's vain shadows flee;*
> *In life, in death, O Lord, abide with me.*

She prayed silently for her husband, that he might return to her from battle; that he should be safe and unharmed; that death would spare him to be her life-companion, to be a father to their child. Without him she felt she would be as nothing, without purpose. She entrusted his existence to heavenly powers that now she believed in once again.

Outside the church she was greeted by Dorothy Weaver. 'My dear, no words, no words . . .'

Guv recalled her from the wedding, one of Lydia's particular friends; at school together, somewhere where girls were told to run about like boys to deaden their senses, where vanity was a curse ('I'm glad I'm not pretty'), where everything was bottled up and sex was something beastly that lay in wait. Though somehow Dorothy had come out of it all right, no doubt (he reckoned) one of the gigglers in the dorm with midnight feasts smuggled in their knickers. The chaps with sisters had told him of such things. Now she was on the arm of a young lieutenant.

'Dotty,' Lydia said. 'Thank you so much for coming. You don't know what it means.'

The women embraced briefly. 'You haven't met my fiancé, Liddy. This is Geoffrey Sleightholme.'

'Awfully sad occasion,' said Sleightholme. 'The damnable Hun has put himself quite beyond the pale.'

Guv shook his hand. 'By disregarding the rules of war, you mean?'

'Of course. What else?'

'The rule may be that there are no rules, whatever they cook up in Geneva.'

'That's a pretty ghastly prospect.'

'Have you been across yet?'

'To France, you mean? No, not yet. But believe me, the fellows have really got their ginger up.'

'Ready to get at 'em, eh? I see you're with the Royal Sussex.'

'That's right, Sutro. Embarking for France next week. A pals battalion. The lads have known each other since they were knee-high to a grasshopper. A tip-top bunch. Can't wait to give the Jerries what-for.'

'So you're engaged,' Guv said. 'Plan on getting married before you sail?'

Sleightholme looked awkward. 'We've talked about it, old man. Dotty was all for it, weren't you, dear? But you don't know what your chances are, do you? Don't want to leave a merry widow behind, do we, Dotty?'

'Geoffrey, darling, please. This isn't the time.'

'No need to get upset, old girl. These things need to be said, not swept under the carpet. No illusions, eh? Might be a bit different for you, Sutro, being in the RFC?'

'Better odds, you mean?'

'Well, so I've heard.'

'You've heard quite wrong. It's called the Suicide Club. New pilots are lucky to last ten days.'

Sleightholme inclined his head stiffly. 'I see we've got off on the wrong foot.'

'No matter. Burned to a crisp in a flamer or blown to smithereens by an artillery shell, it comes to the same thing in the end. You're right, these things need to be said. No illusions, eh?'

In the car on the way back to Saxonshore, Guv said, 'Damned fool. He plays the hero to impress his girl. I'll wager he's using the perils of war to skip getting hitched. In reality he's as wet behind the ears as the rest of the schoolboys they're sending out these days; all that tosh about his tip-top bunch having their ginger up. He has no concept of what's coming their way. They'll all be dead inside a month.'

Lydia looked small in the rear seat of the Rolls. 'Dotty's a dear friend of mine. I wish you hadn't said what you said.'

'The chump said it himself – no illusions.'

'You didn't have to be so . . . blunt. We all know the realities of this horrible war, most of all now.'

'Do we? I doubt he does, not really. Come to that, do you?'

'Very well, I don't. I confess it. I only know I have lost two people dear to me. Those are my realities. I choose not to go further.' She fumbled in her handbag for a handkerchief. 'I don't think Geoffrey plays the hero. He knows the situation well enough. I believe he is quite sincere, but in the English way conceals it with bad jokes; that merry widow business. I believe he really cares for Dot and has no wish to spoil her life by giving her a dead husband to mourn. It is different, you know, mourning a good friend, a fiancé even, and a husband with whom you shared your vows.'

'From what you say, perhaps we should not have married.'

'No,' said Lydia, 'it is different for us. I have this conviction that you will always come back.'

'You cannot know that.'

Lydia tried to make light of it. She smiled. 'I do. You have told

me so yourself. You cannot die. You have so much more to do.'
She did not add that in the church she had prayed that death would
spare him and that, because she believed again, her prayer would be
answered.

On his last day at Saxonshore they had an inconclusive talk about
the estate; it could not be called a discussion. It was Lydia's position that what was hers was Guv's and she could not bring herself
to consider it further; perhaps in a month or two. She spent much
time with the baby, to be called Alice after her mother. There was
talk of a nanny being retained. It suited Guv. By now he had
discovered that the child did not always smell as fresh as a fresh-
picked apple, and had an inclination to yowl like a Hun whizz-bang
for no good reason. Also, he was resolved that Rose Pringle must
go, after all, and, at first, believed that a neat opportunity had
presented itself when she slipped into his study at gone midnight
on the day of his return to France. Lydia was safely asleep and he
had been down to the wine cellar that he still thought of as
Bowman's, and had worked his way through two bottles of 1875
Bordeaux, a finer vintage than anything he was likely to quaff in
the Chézy-au-Bois Mess.

Rose stood in front of him, perceiving instantly that he was heavy
with drink. 'I've missed,' she said.

'Missed?'

'My friends.'

'What the dickens are you getting at? What friends?'

'Them friends what come once a month.'

He understood. 'Impossible.'

'Why?'

'How can you be sure?'

'I'm sure all right.' Rose smiled. 'My question is, what are you
going to do about it?'

'Do?'

'Be careful how you answer, you old dog. I know your tricks.'

'What tricks?'

'Never you mind. The question is, what happens now?'

'Nothing, that's what happens. I'm going back to France. Say a word of this and—'

'Your secret's safe with me, dear; *our* secret, I should say. Don't leave it too long, that's all, or it'll start to show. Just don't do nothing sudden, either, like turning me into the street. You've had your fun but that's the thing about fun, I find; there's always a price to pay.'

On the long journey back to Amiens, Guv went over the situation many times. When he hailed the taxi at the Gare du Nord he was no closer to a solution than he had been at Waterloo. At Chézy-au-Bois he paid off the driver and went to see Sutton.

'Everything sorted, Sutro?'

'Well enough. Odd business, funeral sans coffins. Unfinished, as you might say. Half expected them to turn up saying it had all been a terrible mistake.'

'Oh, I think you can assume they're safely dead,' said Sutton.

'That's a bloody odd way of putting it.'

'No offence, I know how devoted you were to the old man. I've got some good news for you, by the way.' (There was a suggestion of *more* good news in Sutton's knowing tone.) 'Your new observer was posted in while you were away. Let's go over to the Sergeants Mess and winkle him out.'

The man was seated by a window reading the *Daily Mail*. 'Sergeant,' said Sutton. 'I want you to meet your pilot.'

The man lowered his newspaper and stood up slowly. It was Stan Kemp.

Six

1

Stan Kemp

The military hospital stood on The Leas with an easterly prospect of Folkestone harbour where convoys of boats set off for France, their rails crowded with men in khaki storing in their minds this last, receding image of their homeland, and where other boats returned with those not killed but shattered, stretchered by the bearers into fleets of ambulances and taken on to hospitals like the old manor house requisitioned on The Leas. This was where they had brought Stan Kemp.

He was in a ward of twenty-four beds, British, Belgian, Australian, Canadian, their nationalities set aside, a brotherhood of pain. He was a curiosity, not because of his wounds that, compared to some, were of lesser consequence (except to him), but because he was RFC; the only one. Even here the airman was seen as someone who stood apart, someone who fought a different, old-fashioned war; a war where individuals met in a trial of arms, who, if they fell, left a trail of fire to mark their passing and an identifiable corpse to bury with military honours, whose deaths were even noted by the victor, quick to salute a courageous foe; this at a time when most men's passing went unnoticed, their final moments unrecorded, their shredded carcasses hurriedly interred, often without a name, or never found and mingled forever with foreign soil. As well as a kind of grudging respect it was a perception that, among servicemen, could provoke envy and resentment . . .

293

Around the battles in the air, legends had also formed: of chivalrous acts, fliers who ceased to fire if an opponent ran out of ammunition, of downed pilots entertained in an enemy Mess before being delivered up as prisoners-of-war, of notes dropped on hostile airfields to confirm the death or capture of one of their number, or a wreath as a mark of respect if he had crashed on his own side of the lines. There was a mystique about such men, although only a few names were publicly known: Lanoe Hawker, Harvey-Kelly, Guynemer, Immelmann, Sutro.

When it became known that Stan had flown with Guv Sutro, it stirred some interest in his fellow patients. It took them out of themselves, away from the constant torment of their wounds and, in their imagination, carried aloft into the clouds. Stan told them what he could but it was not much that he could see. He did not subscribe to fables. He would tell them how it was, but nothing more. But gradually it came out. He had been with the squadron near Amiens for less than four months, Sutro's observer for all that time. They had flown Gunbuses, Vickers FB5s, on fighting duties, going up on two-hour patrols to attack targets identified by Wing or those they came across by themselves. There was little in the nature of reconnaissance about these trips, or Army cooperation. The squadron's brief was more offensive; they searched for Hun single-seaters, bombers, any machine snooping over the Allied lines, and made every effort to shoot them down. They also strafed the Hun on the ground: artillery positions, machine-gun nests, troop movements, concentrations of enemy infantry in their trenches – pretty well anything that showed signs of life on or near the enemy lines. There was no nonsense about giving the other bloke a chance. You set out to do for him before he did for you, or came back for another go.

What was it really like up there? Imagine yourself, Stan said, on the wrong side of a shooting gallery, stuff coming at you from every direction: bullets from other aircraft, artillery bursts ('Yes, they call it Archie, remind me to tell you why some time'), machine-gun and small-arms fire, the air humming like you'd poked a stick into a nest of wasps.

And what about this Sutro bloke? Oh yes, a proper hero but he'd cost the squadron plenty since being made up to flight commander. A first-class pilot, no doubt of that, but reckless with a total lack of fear. Fear wasn't in his nature. Those who did not fly with him would call him brave, and even some who did – until they learned the price. More often he was cursed by the blokes he led. Like when they went on strafing trips and he took them down to 100 feet, oblivious to bullets whistling round his ears, focused only on the target he had in mind. And every time the bugger came through it all without a scratch, unlike the poor sods who tried to follow his example and went west so fast you couldn't recall their faces.

For a time Stan said, the luck of the devil had rubbed off on him. Then, on patrol near Ypres, chasing an Aviatik reconnaissance machine across the German lines, a burst of Archie under the nacelle did for him good and proper and landed him here. He did not go into details but he knew them well enough. The shards of shrapnel had struck his left leg as he stood in the braced position at his Lewis gun in the forward cockpit of the FB5's nacelle, the largest portion passing through his thigh at an upward angle, cracking his femur, removing both testicles as neatly as if they had been snipped off with shears (leaving the penis quite untouched) and exiting within half an inch of his right hip. He would not only be a cripple, the surgeon had told him brusquely, but he would be an impotent cripple, and the sooner he came to terms with it the better he would feel. He had to remember, he was luckier than most.

He had been shown his X-rays. 'We've managed to dig out most of the ironmongery, Sergeant, but there are a few bits and pieces better left where they are. They shouldn't give you too much trouble, not for many years anyway. As for your other injuries, they're nice clean wounds and seem to be responding well. And your waterworks appear to be functioning reasonably normally, despite the trauma.'

His leg was encased in plaster, his toes protruding like small red plums. When he moved them, the pain shot through his body and froze his brain. The dressings in the area of his groin were changed twice a day by the young nurses, but he had gone beyond embarrassment. They had seen everything by now, after two years of war.

At first they had given him morphia but now he was left to cope by himself in case he became too dependent. Generally, they said, he was responding well and soon could be wheeled onto the terrace with its view of the Channel to take the sea-salt air away from the ward-smells of bedpans, seeping dressings and disinfectant.

At night, kept awake by the shouts and moans of the others, he looked for Nurse Park, the VAD. It was always better when she was on duty. She did not have the briskness and impatience of the professional nurses. She had become a nursing assistant when the boy she was to marry was killed at Mons. She was gentle and had a beautiful, sad smile. Her gentleness was like a balm; her beauty he tried to disregard. It did not matter that she was beautiful. He forced himself to confront the truth: that he was of no use to her or to any woman. But still, there was something between them, something he shared with her that the others did not; perhaps he reminded her of the boy who disappeared at Mons, perhaps she imagined he too had been bruised by the loss of someone held dear (and in way, he supposed, he had although death had not been involved), perhaps it was simple pity that of all the men in her ward, he was no longer a man. It did not matter. It was enough that an empathy existed, unexplained and never mentioned.

He had received no visitors. Shortly before his posting to Chézy-au-Bois, his father had died of an apoplexy bidding for a Sussex bull at Lewes cattle-market on behalf of his new employer. Living alone in a tithe cottage he had left only a few items of cheap furniture, a drawerful of family photos, some broken-backed volumes on animal husbandry and agricultural practice, newspaper cuttings of local events (the flight at High And Over all those years ago, a report on the auction of Aelle Manor Farm, its contents and land, news of notable hunts and shoots, the obituary of Colonel Sutro, the inquest on Mary Grey), a rack of pipes and sufficient savings to bury himself. Those others who might think of visiting him, and this included Guv, were drawn from the squadron and on their rare leaves they could hardly be expected to waste precious time visiting the mounting list of wounded dotted around the various military hospitals in the south.

They had better things to do. Which brought him full circle, imagining the better things they had to do.

And so he saw no one apart from the other patients and the staff, and did nothing; talked little except when spoken to, did not read, did not listen to the scratched records on the gramophone, only stared up at the ceiling above the bed where paint was peeling off like scorched skin (he had seen much scorched skin). In the ward, men would come and go. Those improved moved on to a cottage hospital closer to their homes, others succumbing to their injuries or infection. Meanwhile, among the stable still requiring constant care, he remained, sustained by the prospect of Nurse Park's beautiful, sad smile and occasional gentle conversations in the quiet times in the blue-lit ward at night. It was a surprise, then, when for a time she had been switched to day duty, that she told him he had a visitor.

'Who?'

'A Miss Pringle. She has come all the way from Hastings. She says you are firm friends. She will cheer you up no end. She's extremely pretty.'

When Nurse Park led Rose into the ward she looked, suddenly, quite ordinary by comparison. One of the men called out: 'Here, I say, good afternoon, young lady. Come to see me, have you?' Rose laughed in a warm and natural way. 'Perhaps later, my lad, if you behave yourself.' There was a sudden animation about the place.

Rose leaned over Stan's bed, careful not to place any pressure on his torso with her hands, and kissed him on the forehead. He was conscious of the others watching him being anointed by this scorcher, imagining their thoughts: *Blimey, what's he got we ain't?* He thought that very funny. Funny enough to make a cat laugh.

Rose took a pace back and held the palms of her hands flat against her cheeks. She looked like Mary Pickford in the moving pictures, theatrical but rather touching. 'Oh, my poor old Stan. What in the world have they done to you?'

'I stubbed my toe.'

'They ain't operated on your funny bone, I see.'

She sat down on the empty bed where Dassin, the little private from Antwerp, had died ten hours ago, calling for his mother. The fresh sheets were crisp and smooth and showed no sign of his struggle not to go.

Nurse Park came in. 'I'm terribly sorry Miss Pringle, but I'm afraid visitors aren't allowed to sit on the beds. May I ask you to use the chair?'

Rose made a face like an impudent child. When she moved to the chair, she scraped its legs on the parquet flooring. She watched the nurse move down the ward. 'Stuck-up cow, ain't she?' Before Stan could defend Nurse Park, she said, 'It's ever so good to see you, Stan, but I'm sorry to find you in the wars. You're quite the hero, so they say.'

'Who's they?'

'Common knowledge, dear.'

'How did you know I was here?'

'I got it from Guv Sutro. You must've heard. I worked for him and his missus for a bit. Our Harry fixed it up. Lady's maid to Mrs Sutro until she had her kid. Then they got some blinking nanny in and we didn't see eye to eye.'

'So you're still in touch with Guv.'

'Well, dear, you know how it is.'

He believed he did. He felt a familiar hollow sensation in his stomach that he had not experienced for a long, long time. He thought he had pushed the memory of her so far back in his mind that he could no longer be touched, so she was just a distant recollection like a character from a dream. Yet here she was, restored and quite unchanged, as if a day had not gone by since that time in Ivy's squalid room in Byfleet. How did it go? *Once hooked, she never throws you back.*

'You still ain't told me what's happened to you,' she said.

'Oh, it ain't much.'

'It don't look like it, neither. But I suppose I can't force you.'

'Why are you here?'

'Don't be daft. Soon as I heard, I had to come and see my Stan.'

My Stan? That bloody cat was laughing fit to bust. He doubted

298

she had given him a second's thought. He remembered the letters and cards he had sent but had never received one back. 'I wrote to you,' he said flatly.

'I know. Ivy passed them on all right.'

'You didn't reply.'

'I always meant to, dear. You know how it is.' She had said it again, assuming that somehow he knew how it was. He supposed he did. 'That reminds me.' She took up her handbag from the floor, opened it and took out a brown envelope. It contained a twenty-pound note. 'Remember, dear, how you got me out of a spot? I said I wouldn't forget.' He could see the others wondering why money was changing hands between a bloke like him and a girl like her. He tried to make her take it back but she refused. 'Don't be silly. It's yours, ain't it?' She glanced along the ward, raising her voice a little. 'Treat the boys to a little of what tickles their fancy.' It provoked a ripple of vulgar laughter, a croak of something close to mirth from O'Connor, the nearest man, who, on patrol in no-man's land, had stumbled across a tripwire and lost both legs to a German mine. She looked across at him and winked and Stan saw the poor devil, even in his ruined state, actually blush. She had them in that tiny hand of hers, she had them all. She began to murmur something to Stan that he could not catch but stopped and instead said brightly, 'I suppose you've heard Saxonshore ain't Saxonshore no more?'

'How's that?'

'Guv's rechristened it High And Over. It's all his now. He rules the roost. That silly bitch signed over the whole shebang.'

So, High And Over – an echo from so many years ago. The beginning and the end, after which nothing had been the same again.

Rose was telling him about her little place in Hastings near the castle, how she was looking for a new position but hadn't found one suitable yet. He wondered what she was doing for money, how she could afford a little place in Hastings, how she could hand over so easily a twenty-quid note. She was talking now about people he did not know and did not care to know, as though filling the time, bored with the prattle herself. Was it for this that she had travelled all the way from Hastings? He did not listen, devouring her with his eyes, as usual seeking some imperfection, some defect that would render her more ordinary, place her in his humdrum world, place her, even now, within his reach; that he might be worthy of this creature he knew to be unworthy.

Then she paused and took his hand, almost whispering, her words no longer empty but full of purpose. 'Stan, there's something I need to know.'

'Oh yes?'

Her voice was so low he could hardly hear her. 'You once said you wanted me to be your girl.'

'That's right.'

'I wouldn't promise, would I?'

'No, we settled for friends, as I recall. Good friends.'

'The question is . . .' he felt her grip tighten a little '. . . the thing is, are we still – good friends, I mean?'

'I suppose so, yes.' It seemed a joke. Good friends? He hadn't seen her for nearly a year. Had she even read his letters, or given him the slightest consideration? She withdrew her hand slowly, her expression wistful, another Pickford moment. He was not fooled exactly but part of him was quite prepared to be.

'I'm in need of a good friend now, Stan.'

'Are you?' he said stupidly. He did not feel in control of himself. It was as if he had been called up onto a music-hall stage by a magician in need of a stooge, wondering what was going to happen next, how much of an idiot he was going to be made to appear; a willing stooge.

'Yes,' she said, 'a good, good friend.' She sighed and touched his cheek. 'I just wanted to know if . . . if things were the same between us, if you'd still like me to . . . to be your girl.' It was said sweetly, tentatively, as though she was afraid he might refuse her.

'I don't think I understand.' He was thrilled yet stunned, acutely aware of O'Connor trying to eavesdrop on the other side of the ward.

'It's a simple enough question, dear.' She rose to her feet. 'I think perhaps it's time I went.'

'Wait,' he said. 'You can't.'

'Well, I ain't had an answer, have I?'

'Do you need to ask?'

'How can a girl be sure, dear, unless she asks? You blokes, you're fickle as the wind. All them French mamzelles.' She had not sat down again, shifting from foot to foot, fidgeting with her handbag.

He shook his head. 'Rose, I've not changed.'

She looked pleased, as if she had got what she came for. 'Well, now that's settled, there's things we need to talk about.' She glanced along the ward. 'But this ain't the time and place.'

She leaned over Stan again but this time kissed him on the mouth; his girl had kissed him on the mouth. He felt extreme joy in the softness of her lips and expected a sensation in his groin but nothing came; nothing would ever come. 'When will I see you again?'

'Soon, dear, very soon.' She went away from him, with her graceful walk, down the ward towards the double doors. She had a special smile for the handsome sergeant on crutches who shuffled back to let her pass. He said something to her and she laughed and looked back at Stan and there was something in that look that struck him like a blow, that shook his senses, that made him wonder if he had imagined the words that had passed between them. He had experienced such fantasies when floating in a sea of morphine. But then he had that kiss; the memory of that kiss to prove it had been no illusion.

She did not come to him again for more than two weeks. By then he was passing many hours outside, warmed by the sun. From the terrace the war-wounded could watch strollers on The Leas, the men in uniform or light civilian suits, the women in soft summer dresses, their faces shielded from the sun by broad-brimmed hats and parasols; nannies wheeling their charges in smart and well-sprung perambulators; children wheeling hoops or flying kites or throwing balls for bounding, barking dogs. It was a diverting parade but a reminder of the price they had been required to pay to safeguard this tranquil scene. And carried on the gentle summer breeze from beyond the flat horizon came the thud of distant guns to show the sacrifice went on.

Nurse Park was not on duty when Rose came the second time. Stan had propelled his wheelchair along a narrow gravel path to a small garden enclosed by clipped yew hedges with four square beds lined with neat box and densely planted with lavender. In the central space a fountain played. Afterwards, he would always associate the perfume of lavender and the gush of water on hot stone with this particular time and place. He was reading a comic novel about a bloke named Kipps, set in places along this coast, New Romney, Sandgate, Hythe, Folkestone; even The Leas was mentioned. It had been written by someone he had never heard of but that didn't mean anything; the weeks of doing nothing but convalesce, with little to sustain him but his thoughts, had revealed to him the depths of his ignorance. He had been raised to rely more on hands than brain, but now it seemed that might not be enough. He identified with Arthur Kipps, the little draper's assistant whose sudden acquisition of wealth, and a house on The Leas, projected him into a new social world mixing with the swells. But of course that was just fantasy. His own future was uncertain. In time he would find himself discharged from the hospital and the Flying Corps, 'no longer physically fit for service' was the phrase, with the prospect of a small pension and a chance to retrain. But retrain for what? Weaving baskets or making cheap furniture were poor substitutes for life in a fighter squadron. Well then, go it alone. But his only skill, aside from proficiency with a Lewis gun, was his knowledge of the aeroplane, and never again would he be capable of clambering about a machine in a Brooklands shed. Bench-work might be feasible, but what busy factory would employ a mechanic stuck at a bench?

Stan closed the book. He had read enough about Kipps's good fortune. The contrast to his own situation was disturbing. In the ward he had heard of blind and maimed ex-servicemen forming themselves into bands, displaying their medals and playing on street corners in the West End in return for a few coppers. Could it really come to that? Why not? What made *him* so special? O'Connor had tried to see the funny side. 'A ruddy band's no good to me, lads. I've got a tin ear. I stood up once for "O Come All Ye Faithful". Mistook it for the national anthem.' Everyone laughed until they remembered he had no legs and could no longer stand, for the anthem or anything else, and it spoiled the joke.

Over by the main building one of the nurses was saying, 'Sergeant Kemp? Yes, you'll find him in the knot garden.' He heard small shoes coming along the path, kicking up the gravel.

'Hello, Stan,' said Rose. 'You see, it's no good. You can't escape.' She kissed him briefly, not on the mouth this time but on the cheek. 'Blimey, ain't it hot? Let's get you into the shade. You'll burn up, stuck out here.' She pushed him into the shadow of the yew hedge and sat down on a slatted garden bench. 'What you reading then?'

'Nothing,' he said.

'Nothing worth discussing with me, eh?'

He did not want to hurt her and began to outline the story but soon saw she was not listening. She seemed to be abstracted, biting her lip and looking about her as though she feared that someone might appear. It was clear she had come to him with a purpose that she was not ready to disclose. Instead she talked again about her little place in Hastings, the jolly crowd at the Duke of Wellington, how she had been offered bar work there but had not thought it suitable. 'Particularly the way things are.' She looked at him meaningfully but he did not ask her to explain. He knew she would anyway. She snapped off a sprig of lavender and began to walk about, breathing in the scent. 'I am your girl, Stan, ain't I? That was the conclusion we come to last time I was here.' She made the arrangement sound as if it was legally binding. She threw down the lavender, knelt beside him and held his hand. 'Maybe you'll change your mind when you hear what I got to say. I don't mind telling you, dear, I'm nicely in the soup.'

'Are you?' he said stolidly. 'How?'

'I got no one else to turn to, Stan dear. I'm at my wits' end.' She drew in her breath. 'I'm in the family way.'

'Blimey,' he said. The passage of time meant nothing. He could only remember her standing before him in Ivy's room, naked on the grubby scrap of carpet, and then her body cool and supple, her quick hands guiding him in ways that pleased her. It had been his first experience of this strange act that people made so much of, and his last. Now he said: 'I never thought we done enough.'

Her expression changed. She began to laugh. 'Don't be daft. That was more than a year ago. What do you think I am, a bleeding elephant?' This levity was clearly not in her plan. She tried to compose herself. 'No, dear, it's not yours. We never done enough, even then.' She hid her face as though she was about to cry, or wanted to hide a smile. 'I know you love me, Stan. I reckon you're my only hope.'

'Whose is it, Rose?'

'You make it sound awful, as though there was lots of them. There wasn't, honest.'

'Whose is it?'

'Well, if you must know, it's your precious Guv's. I couldn't help myself. He was just too strong for me, in every blessed way.'

'And what's he got to say on the matter?'

'Not much. He wants it kept quiet.'

'I'll bet he does.' A great emotion washed over him. His thoughts were racing. If he understood her, it seemed he might have her, after all – not have her in any physical way that mattered, but be with her, share a life together, wake up every morning knowing she was there. It was enough. Surely it was enough? Surely he would take her on whatever terms? But could he, could he really? She had left him with no illusions. Once he had asked her about all those unknown men she mentioned so fleetingly, those other fish she had hooked. Her voice came to him now, teasing and dismissive. 'It's just how I am, dear. It's how a girl has to be in my line of work. No good being stand-offish, is it? And life would be horrible dull without a bit of fun, now wouldn't it?' She was not so casual now. And she had chosen him, from all the others.

'Are you saying,' he asked, 'that you want me to make an honest woman of you?' Even as he said it, the cliché had a hollow ring.

She raised her head, her eyes wide. 'Something like that, I suppose.'

He could not think what to say. 'I suppose Guv knows you're here.'

'He knows you've always been sweet on me.'

'That's not what I meant. Does he know you're here?'

'Not exactly, no. I told him I might talk to you about the . . . situation.'

'Anyone else?'

'How do you mean?'

'Plain enough, isn't it? Have you got anyone else lined up to get yourself out of this fix?'

'Course I ain't. That's a proper nasty thing to say. If that's your attitude . . .'

'Why me?' he said quickly. 'That's all I want to know.'

'Oh, Stan,' she said, 'do you really have to ask? I ain't always been decent to you, I must admit. But you've stuck with me through thick and thin. I'm a bit shop-soiled maybe, but I am fond of you in my way, very fond. So now, you see, you can have me if you like.'

Somewhere that cat began to chuckle. The matter could not be put off.

Stan fell into the jargon of the ward. 'Do you know the nature of my injuries?' It had been all round the squadron, of course; there was sympathy for him, naturally, but getting your balls shot off was the kind of thing that prompted much black humour, like being hit in the buttocks.

'Guv knows well enough,' he went on. 'Hasn't he put you in the picture?'

Rose shook her head. 'He never said.'

Perhaps it was true. After all, it would hardly suit Guv's purpose to put her off. So he told her, impersonally, how it was. He did not spare her. Her eyes began to dart from side to side, not fixing on his face. Her mouth was open slightly and she was breathing fast. Clearly she had not expected this. He imagined the countless calculations flitting through her brain, weighing up the odds. He was reminded of an old newsreel he had once seen of Leroy Jenkins, the doomed Birdman who jumped off the Eiffel Tower in 1912; balancing on the parapet with his useless wings, waiting for the right moment, screwing up his courage until that moment came and he launched himself into the void. In Rose's face he saw the same indecision. Should she jump or walk away? Her wings were stronger than poor old Leroy's. He had to ask himself the same question: was he prepared to jump as well? How strong were his wings? How strong was his belief?

'I can't pretend it ain't a shock, Stan,' she said finally.

'Changes things, I suppose?'

'I don't know. It needs thinking through, don't it?'

'Course it does. Particularly for a girl like you.'

'What you getting at exactly?'

'You know very well what I'm getting at. You once told me life would be dull without a little fun. I can't see life with a crock like me is a sunny prospect. I reckon you'd soon be looking for your fun elsewhere.'

'I could try turning over a new leaf,' she said. 'I don't deny I have my needs but there's more to life than that. Anyway, there's ways and means.'

'Oh yes?' he said, mystified.

'You're a decent man, Stanley, and decent men are in short supply. I ain't met one since my old grandpa used to dandle me on his knee.' She sighed. 'I was the apple of his eye.' Somehow, the mawkish sentiments coming from those over-reddened and generous lips created a distasteful image. She turned brisk. 'Look, I've lived a rackety old life, it's true, I ain't making no bones about that. But I want to start afresh. Is that so hard to believe? You've been straight with me. I'm being straight with you.' She knelt in front on him on the gravel radiating simple goodness, fixing him with unblinking eyes that held the fervour of a plaster saint.

'I'd be a good wife to you, Stanley, cross my heart.' He wanted to believe her but did not find it in him. 'I don't ask just for me,' she was saying. 'I ask for the kiddie's sake.'

It was all he could do to stop from laughing out loud, and yet he knew he was unable to resist. He suspected he might be about to make the worst mistake of his life. This creature that had consumed him for so long could actually be his at last. It was as miraculous as anything encountered by Arthur Kipps. But he felt compelled to be truly straight himself, as one of those decent men in short supply; to confront her with his fears about the future and give her the chance to walk away.

'You need to understand, Rose,' he said, 'that I'm on the scrap-heap now. They'll be chucking me out of the service soon. I'm a thoroughly rotten bet all round. You'd do much better to look elsewhere.'

To his surprise this did not set her back. 'That's not how I see it, Stan, and not how others see it neither.'

'What others?'

'You're reckoned to be one of the best mechanics going.'

'Who says?'

'All right, Guv says – but loads of others too, I bet. He ain't no fool when it comes to such matters, whatever else you might say about him.'

'It's no good, I've thought this through. They won't want cripples in the aeroplane sheds at Brooklands.'

'Why stick at blinking aeroplanes? What about motor cars? They've got engines ain't they, that need looking after just the same?'

'You don't understand. Those toffs who race at Brooklands want mechanics who ride along with them, leap about in the pits with the petrol cans, changing tyres and such.' Time for a touch of the old black humour to show a flash of spirit, balance his despair. 'Anyway, where would I put my walking stick?'

'Not them kind of motor cars. I'm talking about the ordinary sort. The roads will be full of 'em when this blooming war's over, and they'll all be going wrong at some time or another.'

'You seem to have got it all worked out,' said Stan.

'I see an opening, that's all, for both of us. A little garage, say, near a decent town looking after the local gentry and charging 'em through the nose. A set-up like that wouldn't call for no gymnastics and a chap like you could build it up. Who knows what it might lead to?'

'Did you dream this up on your own, or did you have some help?'

'I've got to admit it. There's an old forge just come up for sale near Rye, along the Military Road. There's talk of opening it up for motors. That's what put it in my head.'

'Businesses cost money, Rose. I haven't got a bean, and no prospects of accumulating none.'

'But we both know someone who's rolling in the stuff, don't we, someone we've both got a pull on? All those years you gave him. Why, he even put you here.'

'The Germans put me here.'

'Still loyal, after all he's done to you. For Gawd's sake, Stan, I'm carrying his kid. Can't you see? He owes us both.'

'They call this blackmail, don't they?'

'No, not at all. Partners, that'd be the footing and understood by all them gossipmongers in Rye; only natural for him to go halves with an old comrade he flew with in the war. Why, he'd be admired for it. And in time we'd buy him out. What's wrong with that as a proposition?'

'Halves, is it? Halves of what, I'd like to know.'

'That's what we'd put about. Equal partners. Kemp and Sutro over the door, in that order.'

'What happens if I say no?'

'You'd be a bleeding fool. This way you get a future: a wife, a kid, a job.'

'And you?'

'Security, you might call it, after all these years. It's time I settled down.'

'And Guv?'

'Security for him as well, as long as he toes the line.'

'Have you discussed this with him?'

'Not really, no. I've alluded to it, as you might say. You're the one it rests on.'

'When you alluded to it, what did he say?'

'What could he say? I got the impression he'd give it the nod.' Rose had been kneeling in front of him all this time. Now she stood up and brushed the dust from her long summer skirt. He noticed for the first time that her belly had grown. 'So, what do you think?'

He shook his head. 'I don't know. It'll take some working out.'

That night in the ward he turned the matter over in his mind until he was dizzy with it, but he always came to the same conclusion: that he would agree. He tried to redirect his thoughts, staring up at the ceiling with its curling paint. It did not look so much like scorched flesh now but, in the dim blue light, resembled more a tortured landscape, like no-man's land viewed from 1,000 feet and washed over by a hunter's moon. It made him think about Chézy-au-Bois and what had happened there: climbing into the front nacelle of the Gunbus with the world still dark and everything wet with dew, checking that the Lewis gun was secure in its ring-mounting so, in action, it would not spring loose on recoil, Guv settling himself at the controls, preparing to shout to the fitter to swing the prop; the rush of bone-numbing air with the old Beardmore hammering away behind them as they lifted off from the airfield where a low sun cast long shadows across the grass; then over enemy lines, raking the ground on strafing trips, moving with the twists and turns of the machine as Archie burst all round and bullets pinged and whined between the struts; or mix-ups at 10,000 feet, with aircraft wheeling, diving, falling, him yelling at Guv to close a gap or tighten a turn to bring an enemy's tail in range and loosing off half a drum; then drifting in with ammo gone and fuel running low, touching down at Jazzy-oh-Boy and rumbling back towards the hangars, looking for the others who made it back, counting those who had gone.

He could do whole flights in his imagination, from waking in his billet to preparing the machine (running methodically through every procedure) to re-enacting whatever sortie came to mind, seeing again a particular grey Fokker turn into his sights and shatter into flaming pieces or a horse-drawn gun-carriage bringing ammunition to Hun batteries go down in a tangle of animals, wagon and men as his bullets churned the supply route. These ghost-trips (not dreams but visions) were so vivid that he sweated with exhilaration and fear just as he had in action. Often they occupied the same space of time.

Other memories came to him: Sutton going up against orders and not coming back; Little Sister in her usual place over by the farm, watching for the flights to return and praying for their safety in Chézy's tiny church when she should have been praying for herself; lifts into

Amiens in the lorries, drinking too much in the *estaminets* but not going on to the brothels with the others because he wanted to be true to a girl who had no reason to be true to him. The other NCO observers had been scornful. 'Mr Sutro's already done for two poor fuckers. Get your end away while you can.' Instead he had saved himself for a time that never came, or had come in a different and unguessed form; as unexpected as his transfer from another Gunbus squadron at Villers-Bretonneux to Chézy-au-Bois.

2

Stan's posting to Chézy had been less of a coincidence than it might appear. Villers-Bretonneux lay less than 20 miles to the south and his transfer was logical when losses had to be replaced quickly to maintain a squadron's operational efficiency. Also, the Flying Corps' strength numbered not much more than 1,000 men, of whom observers formed a small proportion; and smaller still was that band of experienced hands good enough to be teamed with an expert pilot.

Certainly Guv had shown no particular sign of surprise when Major Sutton had taken him across to the Sergeants Mess to meet his new observer. Nor had Stan, throwing down the *Daily Mail* and coming to attention with a quick salute. Each had waited for the other to make the first move and neither did.

'Well,' said Sutton, 'you chaps are odd fish, I must say.'

Guv shrugged. 'It's a chance hardly worth remarking on. I don't give a fig for what's gone before. If we're to be thrown together like this, my principal concern is what the sergeant here can do for me now. Correct, Sergeant?'

Stan stiffened. 'Correct, sir.'

'Good. I'm glad that's clearly understood.'

'Stand easy, Kemp,' said Sutton. 'You're not in the Grenadiers. B Flight's due on offensive patrol in fifty minutes. Let's see how the old firm fares in action.'

On that first patrol, Guv chased down an LVG two-seater near

Albert. Stan identified it when it was four miles off and Guv worked his way towards it unnoticed until they had closed to within 50 yards. Hanging behind and slightly below the rocking fuselage as the LVG's observer took photographs of the Allied trenches Stan gave it twenty-six rounds without thinking of the men inside, only the need to destroy the machine. The LVG dived away steeply, trailing black smoke, and crashed behind British lines not far from Louvencourt, a few miles east of Chézy.

As soon as they landed back at the airfield, Guv found a pool car and drove them to the site, in search of a souvenir for the Officers Mess. The collection behind the bar did not include bits of an LVG. The German machine had scattered itself about a ploughed field but had not burned. Its Mercedes engine was being loaded onto a lorry by a work-party of engineers. 'So it was you fellows up there,' their officer said. 'Damned good show, we saw it all.'

The pilot was dead, a bullet in his stomach, a slow death, slow enough for him to retain a degree of control before they hit the ground. The observer, thrown clear with a deep wound to his head, was waiting to be collected by the Military Police. He was sitting against a hedge, the blood drying black on his pale face. When he was told who Guv was, he rose unsteadily to his feet and saluted. He noted Stan's rank and ignored him. He congratulated Guv on his victory and told him in faltering English that he was a *Leutnant* and seventeen years old. In the German way his pilot had been an *Unteroffizier*, an NCO. 'Well,' said Guv, 'your chauffeur did pretty well to get you down.' The *Leutnant* did not respond; he was expecting to be tortured and waiting for it to begin. His squadron had been told that such treatment was routine if taken alive.

'Sorry to disappoint you,' Guv said. 'If it was up to me, you might be dealt with differently. Instead you'll be carted off to Blighty to spend the rest of the war as a guest of His Majesty.'

The *Leutnant* was surprised. 'England, you mean? But how is that possible? Our navy controls the sea and England is entirely cut off.' Soon he was led away, concerned at the prospect of a hazardous Channel crossing.

Guv poked about the wreckage of the LVG and found a shred of canvas from the rudder bearing a portion of the German cross. In the car on the way back he said at last: 'You have to admit, this is a rum turn of affairs.'

'Sir?'

'You can cut out the sir when we're on our own. You and me, I mean. Seems as though we can't escape from each other.' They were descending a wooded hill with a valley below. On the other side of the valley the hills rose again; grey mist was hanging in the tops of the trees.

'You won't find me wanting,' Stan said.

'No,' said Guv. 'I don't expect to.' The car ploughed into a deep rut and threw up a shower of mud and stones that rattled against the windscreen like flak. 'Still, it's not been a bad beginning.'

'That lad was barely out of short trousers.'

'There is no little enemy, the saying goes.'

'He certainly had some childish ideas about how we behave.'

'You could call them childish but whatever their age there's an argument for shooting such fellows out of hand; one less risk of them escaping back to their lines to fight again, and one less to lock away in prison camp, taking food from British mouths.'

'Are you serious? That we should consider shooting prisoners out of hand?'

'You were trying to shoot the fellow, weren't you?'

'That's different.'

'Why? You killed his chum all right, as surely as if he'd been standing in the execution yard.'

'I don't think of it like that.'

'You should. You squeamish types always fall back on hot blood as an excuse, something done in the heat of action. Well, who cares what temperature your blood is when you kill? In my book, the last man standing wins. The Hun have shown they stand outside the normal bounds of behaviour. They should be dealt with in the same manner.' Guv was working fiercely at the wheel. 'I'd like to know what that pipsqueak thinks of his so-called invincible navy sending the *Lusitania* to the bottom of the ocean with a thousand innocent souls. There's cold blood for you. The line was drawn and we must repay them in kind.'

'I read of the sinking,' Stan said, 'and the part Mr Bowman played. He was brave all right but I was sorry to hear it.'

'Sorry, were you?' said Guv. They were emerging from the network of country lanes and turning onto the last, straight stretch of Route Nationale before the airfield. 'Well, it takes an atrocity or two to stiffen the sinews. How does it go? "When the blast of war blows in our ears, then imitate the action of the tiger." If I ever see your finger hesitate on that trigger, Stan, I'll have you court-martialled for dereliction of duty, my word against yours. No mercy to the Hun, do you hear, under any circumstances.' Guv thrust his right foot hard down on the throttle pedal. 'I'm sorry now I didn't have the chance to put a bullet in that puppet's Boche brain and stop his nonsense. Next time I will.' He brightened. 'But at least we have a trophy for our trouble.'

There were rumours of a ground offensive being mounted. The squadron spent less time patrolling the enemy lines in search of targets of opportunity on the ground and in the air, and more escorting reconnaissance and artillery observation flights. These were mostly BE2s and it was a frustrating business, circling above them as they went methodically about their work, watching black puffs of German artillery fire stain the air, hearing moments later the firework crack and shrill of hot shrapnel, unable to take much evasive action but compelled to hold position, scanning the sky for tell-tale specks of prowling foe, eyes dry with strain, neck muscles taut as wire. As the weeks passed it became, on paper, a dull routine: breakfast at five o'clock, a trip, sometimes a second breakfast at eight, another trip, a hurried lunch, a trip, some gulped-down tea and bread and jam, a final trip. But the operations still demanded much of body and mind. At 5,000 feet and 70 miles an hour, the air was thin, the temperature close to freezing. One of the pilots put it well. 'Wonderful view, damned cold.'

They carried sufficient fuel for a two-hour flight, fifteen minutes out to the lines, another fifteen back, the rest in limbo dodging Archie and waiting for the reconnaissance crews to finish their assignments. It tried the nerves and patience, particularly when they became aware of a new threat from the east. Often the enemy, faced with half a dozen machines, would veer away, preferring better odds. A single fighter would fancy his chances even less.

This changed with the death of Soapy Pears. C Flight's commander had no connection with the famous brand but his nickname was a natural fit; he was even, like the soap, mild and transparent. Despite his wartime occupation Captain Pears retained a scholarly air (he had been a Classics master), quite unaware of not-unkindly jokes behind his back. He never knew he had a nickname, nor of the new-fangled device that killed him.

On the day that Pears went down, C Flight's four circling crews watched the small dull-green monoplane approach from a little above their height with curiosity but no alarm. It resembled the doodle of a child, broad wings waist-high to the exposed pilot marked with black-on-white Teutonic crosses, a hooded metal engine cowl over a good-sized rotary engine, the tapered fuselage enclosed in canvas with, directly beneath the wings, large landing wheels on metal struts. They waited for it to turn away but instead it held its course, now close enough for them to see a machine-gun mounted fore-and-aft in front of the goggled figure in the single cockpit. They could not imagine what plan he had in mind, this gnome-like figure in his odd machine. A single fixed and forward-firing weapon would be of little use; the Hun's propeller was spinning at 1,000 revs a minute, his bullets would simply shoot it off. Perhaps this fellow was a madman, intent on a collision in the air.

Pears let the monoplane approach to within 400 yards, then banked away to meet it head-on, his observer swivelling his Lewis gun ready for an easy kill. The others heard a burst of fire. The Gunbus faltered, zoomed up slightly, then fell away in a shallow spin, throwing the observer into space, his outline (tiny, doll-like, with outstretched arms and legs) cartwheeling towards the ground. In thirty seconds he would be dead. Pears did not die so quickly, consumed by flames whipped fierce by the flat and lazy rotations of his machine. It struck a grove of shattered trees in a shower of fire and set the already blackened trunks alight. The monoplane banked away and climbed towards the sun.

Pears's number two, young Burslem, not long with the Flight, gave chase. The German's rate of climb was good; soon he had a useful height advantage. He turned with the sun behind him and dived down, meeting the Gunbus nose to nose. A burst and Burslem's observer fell back in his cockpit, the muzzle of his Lewis gun tilting upwards. Burslem dropped a wing, defenceless. The German had continued his dive below the Gunbus but now pulled up in a half-loop and rolled off the top, an Immelmann turn, so expertly performed that the watching crews guessed it might be Immelmann himself. Burslem had lost 1,000 feet, his zigzag course marked by a twisting trail of oil-black smoke, trying for Chézy. The monoplane half rolled, dropped its nose, plunged down and gave the Gunbus a second burst from 50 yards. It fell to pieces in the air.

The German pulled away and turned for home. He was not followed; there was no point, he was too fast. Soon it became known that some scoundrel of a neutral Dutchman had come up with the trick of firing a machine-gun through the arc of a spinning propeller without hitting the blades, and sold it to the Kaiser. It was rumoured that he had offered this synchronisation gear to the Allies, but had been turned down. As a bonus, he also designed the little monoplane armed with the device. It was the start of the Fokker Scourge.

Within a week the squadron lost two more machines, although from different flights. By then command of C Flight had passed to Captain Fraser Sutro, his promotion finally confirmed. Before their first patrol he gathered the pilots, observers and ground crew together and addressed them from the observer's cockpit of his FB5, 'Like some bible-thumper in his ruddy pulpit,' one observer murmured next to Stan. Guv stared down at his silent congregation. They stared back, their expressions almost sullen. Pears had been a popular flight commander; he had led them well and with as much regard for their welfare as any leader was permitted. This new man had a reputation they did not like; he got men killed. They did not bother to conceal their resentment. Most felt there was nothing to lose in this world as they were already half in the next.

Neither did Guv approve of what he saw. 'I get the distinct impression that the Hun's latest toy has got you fellows rattled. If so, you couldn't be more wrong. Let's consider what we're facing. Have we seen squadrons of the things? No, just a handful flown by chaps who appear to know their stuff. So obviously both the machines and the men to fly them are in short supply. By the time they've sorted themselves out we'll have got our hands on our own new types, the FE2 and DH2. I happen to know they're more than a match for any damned Fokker. And so is the old Gunbus, come to that, as long as it's handled right. In my book, and from now on that's your book too, these Fokkers', (he gave the word a twist and expected a murmur of amusement but none came), 'have had it cushy thanks to the element of surprise. Downright unsporting, I say, sneaking up on folk and pooping off through the prop.' (Once more, no reaction). 'Well, now we're wise to their little game and they're in for a shock. The Fokker is no more than a tarted-up Morane-Saulnier pre-war racer with a Parabellum MG14 stuck on its nose, a weapon as dangerous to its pilot as to us because it jams more often than traffic in Piccadilly and is apt to get out of sync and shoot his prop to bits.'

A voice sounded in the middle of the little group. 'Pity it didn't happen when Soapy and Dick Burslem went west.'

Guv was standing now with his hands on his hips, legs stretched apart, his chin stuck out, scanning the faces of the men below him. 'I don't know who said that and I don't want to know. It smacks of low morale. I'm no fool. I don't underrate the advantage this new device gives our opposite numbers, for the time being at least. After all, it means a pilot no longer has to aim a gun, he can aim his aeroplane. But now we know of this we can adopt tactics to counter it. Before, he had us cold. At home I hear the defeatists are already talking of a Fokker Scourge. Well, in my book that's just a fable dreamed up by the yellow press and we're going to prove to that gang of traitorous hacks, and the mugs who read their rags, that they couldn't be more wrong. A new pilot, not of this squadron, once asked me for tips on staying alive. I'll tell you what I told him. That's not our bloody business. Our business is making sure the other bugger doesn't stay alive. And the best way of doing that is to attack. And that's what C Flight is going to do – attack. No longer are we required to act as nursemaids to BE2s and their like; the other flights are going to take care of that. I have obtained Wing's blessing to go Fokker hunting. Naturally that means operating in Hunland because it's *verboten* for Fokkers to venture over our lines in case we knock one down and learn their secret. Now, I won't pull any punches. Taking the fight to the enemy means much greater risks for us all, but if you're averse to risk you wouldn't be here now; you'd be a conchie digging up potatoes in East Anglia. So, pilots to me while I explain the drill. And to all of you, as the Bard put it: "Screw your courage to the sticking-place. And we'll not fail." Good hunting.'

As the pilots began to collect by the Gunbus for their pre-flight briefing Stan heard one say: 'Something of a theatrical gesture, wouldn't you say?'

'Screwing your courage, you mean? *Henry The Fifth*, ain't it?'

'It's the Scottish play, you confounded philistine.'

'Oh yes, I have it now. Lady Macbeth. Not the most reliable of advisers, I'd have thought.'

That day, C Flight climbed to its ceiling of 7,000 feet and hung in the sun over enemy territory between Douai and Cambrai. No Fokkers rose to meet the challenge. But 30 miles away near Lille, a brace accounted for three reconnaissance BE2s with all crews lost. It was a bad beginning and a worse end. After a spell of stalking shadows, C Flight was returned to normal duties, its fruitless foray regarded in the squadron as something of a joke. Among the NCOs it was rumoured that Major Sutton was not pleased that Mr Sutro had gone behind his back to Wing to make the case for his flight's assignment. 'Old Nobby in the CO's office says the old man was fucking livid.'

The big push that had called for so much surveillance work had proved to be a small one. The Germans quickly pushed back and what little ground gained was lost. It was said that 10,000 men had died for every step of the advance. The squadron returned to strafing targets on the ground, as ordered by Wing, or attacking the few Hun machines (no Fokkers) that came its way. Guv took his crews down lower than any other flight and deeper into hostile territory. He had never seen enough or stayed long enough to be satisfied with the results. C Flight's patrols always lasted the longest of all, its Gunbuses returning to base with fuel tanks almost empty – 'running on mist,' the pilots said. One machine was lost like that, gliding down with a dead engine close to Allied lines and upending itself in no-man's land where it was shelled to bits. But its crew escaped, scrambling through shell-holes and human remains to the front-line trenches where they found a lorry to return them to Chézy-au-Bois and a storm of abuse from their flight commander for letting him down.

He always told his men he did not expect them to do anything he was not prepared to do himself; scant comfort. He invariably volunteered C Flight for the most hazardous missions and took them into the hottest situations, disregarding anti-aircraft fire entirely and instructing the others to do the same. When men did not come back it was because they had disregarded orders or were incompetent or careless; only occasionally would he concede bad luck as a contributory factor, 'but in my book' (that book again), 'you make your own luck'.

When the flights were stood down with their quota of patrols completed or adverse weather was beginning to lift or threatening to move in, he would take up his machine to see if the lines had altered, rushing along the trenches at 100 feet with Stan at the Lewis gun spraying the grey-clad figures that ran for cover or tried to fire back. Stan did not know how many men he killed. The whole business had begun to seem senseless, the wretched troops scattering like rats chased by a terrier, with Guv going round again so he could pick off more. By now Stan had grown numb, and was ready to die. It was simply a matter of time. He had even considered bringing that moment forward, by stepping out of the nacelle at 5,000 feet, taking that long, last look at the world as it came up towards him at 100 miles an hour; that final glimpse that so many others had known. It was not so much that he feared the impact that would turn him into a fleshy sack of broken bones, because that would be over in an instant, but the time left to him as he fell, the thoughts that might occupy his still lucid brain (men did not faint as the public was told; it was a lie concocted to comfort the bereaved). It was a prospect that, in the dark hours before dawn, woke him in a sweat consumed with dread. But it was a prospect he had learned to live with so he concluded that he would leave the matter to the Germans, or his pilot. He did not think he would have long to wait. Nor did his fellow observers. 'You're flying with a fanatic, you poor sod. He's not human.'

Stan did not reply. He never did. He supposed it was fear; fear of it getting back to Guv, although he did not know what more Guv could do to make his life intolerable. There was no friendship or even fellow feeling to be lost. They hardly spoke a word. It was as if nothing had gone before. Guv gave his orders; he obeyed, that was all. He was no more than an appendage to the Lewis gun, but if there was a shred of comfort, he was not a special case. He was treated as dispassionately as the rest, the flight formed into a single weapon with which Guv waged his personal war. Its effectiveness could not be denied; its pilots claimed more enemy planes shot down and ground targets destroyed than both the other flights. It also lost more men and machines, but this was accepted by Wing as the cost of success; such zeal was admired.

A general on a tour of inspection had remarked, within the hearing of those on parade, that young Sutro was an object lesson in uncompromising leadership; that he displayed an admirable sense of duty that his brother officers would do well to emulate. At this Major Sutton had cleared his throat, but it was difficult to deal with an officer who had influential friends (and had shown he was prepared to use them) and achieved results, at whatever price. Besides, Guv Sutro was made much of outside the squadron and outside the service; this pre-war record-breaker giving the Hun a bloody nose, owner of a great estate, a true son of Albion with an MC already to his name;

mentioned in the press; a man to watch. RFC recruiters reported that volunteers were up: the Sutro factor. In Whitehall there was an unofficial line: if the facts did not fit the growing legend, ignore the facts. Blemishes to his record were brushed away. No man could wage a faultless war, this was understood. At various times his actions had been questionable and doubts expressed, but nothing had been proved. Most recently, it could now be seen, his so-called Fokker hunt had been premature, denying the squadron a flight at a vital moment (costing perhaps how many lives?). His commanding officer had opposed the idea but the decision had been taken elsewhere. Well, it was murmured with a smile, what can you expect from these flying johnnies? They have a different view of discipline, and by Jove they get things done. Certainly, Captain Sutro had been instructed not to circumvent the normal chain of command again, but it was hardly his fault that the infernal Hun had chosen to move to another sector. Good grief, it could have worked and then imagine the fuss that would have been made. Anyway, no doubt the Fokkers would return and then hold on; Sutro's chaps would teach them a thing or two. These advocates did not add that half those chaps who had gathered round to hear Guv's sermon from his mount were dead, their Gunbuses piles of expensive scrap.

But then Guv Sutro claimed his Fokker and from that day on it was rare to hear a word against him, until the matter of the Little Sister.

Stan had felt the end of his bed kicked hard. Guv had come into the bell tent in his flying kit. Beyond him, glimpsed through the flap, a thin mist hung over the landing ground. 'Rouse yourself, Sergeant. Take-off in ten minutes.' Outside, pulling on his leather coat, clumsy in his heavy boots, Stan stumbled towards the lined-up FB5s, unshaven, with furred teeth but a hastily emptied bladder. Somewhere beyond the farm buildings a cockerel started up and dogs began to bark, woken by the cries of the ground crew and the clank and clatter of their work as they readied Guv's machine. The air was rich with the smell of petrol, grass and clinging damp. He did not know the time, only that it was barely light. The cloud base hung no more than 200 feet above the airfield; the kind of cloud in which pilots lost their bearings, flew unwittingly upside down and dived to their deaths when they believed that they were climbing; the kind in which whole flights could lose formation, collide or emerge in blazing sunlight completely lost and 50 miles from home. No risks of that kind today, the squadron grounded unless the cloud dispersed or thinned. Unless your name was Sutro.

Guv was already in his cockpit, bristling with impatience. 'Christ, man, pull your finger out. What do you think this is, a taxi rank?'

Ready at his gun position, Stan buckled his helmet tight but not too tight beneath his chin, and positioned his goggles ready on his forehead. He checked the Lewis quickly and showed Guv a circled thumb and forefinger.

'Balloon busting!' he heard yelled across the space between the cockpits. 'There's a sitter near Le Cateau.'

Guv pointed upwards with a gloved finger. 'They'll never expect an attack in conditions like this.' The fitter was behind them at the prop. 'Switch off. Petrol on. Suck in.' The engine coughed as the propeller was moved. 'Contact!'

The propeller was swung, the engine fired and the Gunbus came alive, its whole frame shaking with the Beardmore's power, bouncing slowly across the turf and turning into wind, then rushing, lifting and quickly lost to view in the low, dense mass of cloud. They rose up through it, looking for the first pale sign of light, like some mammal of the deep seeking the surface of the sea and air to fill its lungs. They came out at 2,000 feet, into the usual brilliant world of far horizons, huge cloud formations creating mighty peaks and valleys, the eastern ranges touched gold by a veiled sun, the western tinted silver from a full moon yet to set. They did not relish the beauty of this magical land; they knew that in every fold, in every shadow, in every play of light, death might lie concealed. They climbed to 6,000 feet and flew due east for thirty minutes until breaks in the cloud base began to show and they were able to identify a little to the north the dark mass of Cambrai, twenty miles behind the German front. Directly ahead lay Le Cateau; they would go beyond it, turn back and come on it from the east, the ground defences less likely to expect an attack from that direction.

The cloud was thinner now and near Avesnes Guv shed some height and put the machine in a shallow turn. A mile to their right the roads were thick with marching men, convoys of supplies, light artillery pieces pulled by teams of horses, bigger guns towed by heavy lorries. Stan looked back at Guv and slapped the barrel of the Vickers, but his pilot shook his head and pointed firmly forwards. If they were to bust a balloon they needed the element of surprise. Strafing these tempting targets, and provoking the inevitable storm of fire, would warn the Le Cateau defences that some kind of action, sudden and unexplained, was happening towards Avesnes. They would be ready at their gunsights when the Gunbus appeared, if it appeared at all.

Only a few shots were aimed their way as those on the ground caught brief glimpses of an unknown aircraft moving to their south through broken cloud. It was hard to be sure of markings at that distance; only those with the keenest eyes or the most hot-headed ignored the rule: if in doubt, don't fire. For mistakes like that, the penalties were severe.

At Le Cateau the observation balloon hung almost motionless at half their height, a large Teutonic cross emblazoned on its bulging flank. In his wicker basket the observer was studying artillery strikes on Allied positions through his field glasses, his back towards them. Directly below at the motorised winch, a crew was waiting to reel the balloon back down when the reconnaissance was finished or at the first sign of danger. More men were at their posts inside a sand-bagged anti-aircraft battery of three truck-mounted guns.

It had started to rain, driving against Stan's face, blurring his vision through his goggles, stinging his nose and cheeks and making the cockpit floor slippery underfoot. Again, he looked back at Guv who made a swooping movement with his right hand and nodded vigorously. Stan felt his body go light as the Gunbus dipped towards its target. Still they had not been seen. He knew he must hold his fire. Squeeze the trigger too soon and his bullets would pass harmlessly through the balloon's fabric without igniting the hydrogen gas. At

100 yards the great mass, swaying like a jelly-fish caught in a gentle current, towered above them, growing huge. He was aware somehow of a great commotion on the ground, grey figures springing to action. He heard the first crack of Archie, bursting somewhere far above their heads; a good effort by the German gunners but they had not got the range, their barrels probably set for a higher elevation.

At 50 yards he opened fire, the Lewis kicking back hard against his shoulder, the empty cartridge cases streaming from the drum magazine and rolling around under his boots. He could see his bullets tearing through the fabric of the balloon but the flammable gas did not ignite. Instead, the balloon quivered like a bull elephant struck by a ball from a large-bore rifle, its skin wrinkling as it began to deflate. Under his feet Stan felt the Gunbus dive down to bring the observer's basket into his sights. He knew what Guv expected. The observer was watching him come on, his field-glasses hanging on his chest, steadying himself with one hand on the rigging. If he had a parachute he had missed his chance. And so he stood, resigned, not trying to shield himself or crouch behind the basket sides. Stan fired a one-second burst, aiming high to miss the man, but the bullets cut through part of the rigging and the basket gave way like a trap door on a gallows. For a moment the observer clung to a strand of rope but his grip failed and he fell away as Guv took the Gunbus low, hedge-hopping across open country to cover their escape. A few holes showed in the wings and fuselage and a strut had been neatly drilled, but damage was light.

The greater danger was yet to come. At Le Cateau the telephone lines would be humming. Already the nearest fighter squadrons would have been alerted.

They climbed back to 2,000 feet and headed west, hugging the upper surface of the mass of cloud that stretched away below them like an Arctic waste, their eyes on the sky and ready to dive for cover. If they were intercepted now, Stan thought, if death chose them now, they could not complain. He saw again the wicker basket give way and spill out the observer to his death; another death. This one had been more personal. He and his victim had stood face-to-face. He was a boy again in an oaken pew in Alfriston church, a voice intoning: 'Depart from evil and do good. Go from this place, seek peace and pursue it.' He had walked home slowly, turning over the words in his mind. Then he had not been conscious of being evil so he could not depart from it, but he wanted to do good. He would seek peace. He would lead a good life. Yet here he stood in a machine of war, wielding death in the name of King and Country, and God was said to be on his side. The Germans believed the same thing, he had been told: *'Gott mit uns ist.'* That was how they put it. It was all very confusing. It seemed to him that God should make up His mind. It seemed to him now that he was guilty of evil, whatever God might decide. It seemed to him very likely that he would be punished for it. It seemed to him that it might be too late to do good.

For a moment he paused from scanning the sky above and behind them, where the hunters would appear, and lowered his gaze. Guv was hunched at the controls, his eyes bulging, his face black with oil and dirt. He did not seem to see Stan but stared beyond him as though transfixed by the distant horizon, driving towards an unknown goal; as though what had gone before was already forgotten and he was eager for what was to come. Beside him, from the outer wing strut, twisted and snapped his flight commander's streamers that singled him out as a man to follow or, to the Hun, as a man with an extra reason to kill.

They were halfway towards the Allied lines when Stan caught a flash of sunlight on a small object 5,000 or 6,000 feet above them. Soon its shape became more distinct – a monoplane, its markings still unknown at such a distance. But Allied monoplanes were few. No Blériot ever achieved such height. The Morane-Saulnier might, but not at this time and place. He stamped his foot on the cockpit floor and jabbed his finger upwards. Guv started, then banked a little to get a better view. The monoplane was slipping down towards them, dull green with black crosses on its wings and fuselage and tail. The pilot was in no hurry, now he had found his prey.

Guv pushed forward on the control column and they sank into a grey cold world, quickly soaked in moisture and flying blind thirty minutes from home, as vulnerable as a goldfish in a bowl eyed by a hungry cat. Then the cloud began to thin, at first occasional gaps pierced by sunlight that shot through to the brown land below, then giving way to drifts and swirls of mist until, as abruptly as someone opening their eyes, they swept into clear air still deep behind the German lines, their wing surfaces flashing gold. They were quickly picked out from the ground and the air around them was peppered black with anti-aircraft fire, the Gunbus rocking to the detonations. Tears opened up in the lower wings and a nut-sized piece of spinning shrapnel struck the barrel of the Lewis gun and cracked its butt hard against Stan's jaw. For a moment he was dazed, tasting blood, teeth loose in his gums.

Unsteady on his feet, he looked around for the monoplane he knew to be a Fokker. It was coming in on them from above and behind. On the ground the gunners had ceased fire, watching their man as he came in for the kill. Stan waved for Guv to turn towards it but the Gunbus was too slow to respond. In seconds he would be falling as the balloon observer had fallen; falling as he had done in his nightmare, discovering for himself a man's thoughts in the brief moments left to him before he hit the ground a sack of broken bones.

The left wings of the Gunbus suddenly rose, and the machine rolled violently to the right in a bank so extreme that it left him standing upright on the cockpit sides, secured only by his grip on the Lewis gun's butt. Bullets from the Fokker began to whip around him, striking wood and metal and plunking through taut fabric. He waited to be hit himself, for the airframe to be shredded to the point of collapse, for the engine to be pierced and start to burn. The Gunbus was coming level, as though its pilot had been drained of ideas. Clinging to his weapon for support, he looked across at Guv. His mouth was open, his eyes vacant. He was, like him, waiting to die. But no more bullets came.

Stan heard the howl of the Fokker's engine, saw it dive down behind their tail. The only explanation: its gun had jammed. He steadied himself, placed his feet firmly apart, his cheek to the butt, slippery with blood. The Fokker was a few hundred feet below and moving fast. He could see the pilot struggling to free the jam. If he was sensible he would continue the dive and turn for home, not trust his life to a suspect weapon. But there was a quick burst of fire. The German had cleared the jam and was testing his gun on thin air, ready to resume his attack. He pulled up into a steep climb. Stan read his mind. It was the usual ploy of Fokker pilots used to having it all their own way; an Immelmann turn, the old half-loop with a roll off the top and a final dive down to finish the job. Except this joker was doing it literally under his nose. Unlike a Hun to get carried away, not think it through, not allow for the chance that his first pass had not left them both dead. Either he was cocky, impatient, putting on a show for his countrymen below, or all three. He came vertically through Stan's sights, as snug in his cockpit as a baby in a pram, and as unaware. Stan compressed the trigger, holding it hard against its guard, allowing his bullets to rake the length of the Fokker from its metal cowl to its tail-plane. The Fokker stalled and fell into a flat spin, its engine alight, the pilot trying to push himself upright as though he preferred to jump than be burned, but the flames swept over him and he fell back in his seat, clawing the air.

They climbed back to 7,000 feet in a cloudless sky tracked by the gunners on the ground who had seen the Fokker brought down; the unkillable killed. They began to get the range and Guv hung for a moment with the shells starting to burst close around them, then swooped down as though trying to escape and, as the gunners adjusted their trajectory, zoomed up again, his teeth showing white with satisfaction as the barrage appeared again but several hundred feet below, growing more erratic as the Gunbus continued to fly west.

The green landing ground of Chézy-au-Bois opened up before them. As they floated over the perimeter, a small figure was waving from her usual place on the raised bank near the farm where the white lane ran crossways from the north–south course of the Route Nationale to twist and turn through wind-swept plains to occasional knots of dwellings where peasants lived and worked and died bound in by their narrow world. Guv raised his hand as they swept above her; Little Sister who brought the squadron luck and softened men's thoughts, who followed their fortunes with bright eyes and wept when a favourite did not return, who prayed for them in the little church, whose small hands were roughened from work on the farm. Then, with war, the flatlands had become useful for another purpose, not just for raising crops and beasts. The Government paid her father handsomely to use his land, money for which he did not have to work. War created as well as took away. And so she stood on the bank above the white lane and waved to the heroes who had descended from far-off skies. And for Captain Sutro, who saluted her now, she always had a special smile because, they said, he was *un aviateur célèbre* and he looked at her in special way, more like she imagined a man looks at a woman, and she always sought to pick him out by his flight commander's streamers.

By the hangars, before the ground crew reached them, Guv stood up on his seat, stretched and pulled off his helmet. 'You'll keep mum about this trip until you're told otherwise, d'you hear? Shoot your mouth off now, and we'll end up with a bugger's muddle. It's down to me to report this trip. By the way,' he added, half out of the cockpit, 'how did you miss that bloody observer in the balloon? I gave him to you on a plate.' He paused before climbing on down. 'You did better with the Eindecker, though, I'll give you that.'

Thirty minutes passed. Stan was still going over the machine, noting the damage with the rigger and fitter, ignoring their questions about the flight (which made them more curious still), when a corporal cycled over from the squadron commander's office. 'The Old Man wants to see you sharpish.'

'Now what?'

'Search me, Sarge, he don't confide in me. But from what I heard he's jerked Mr Sutro's chain. You'd better take my pedals.'

Outside Sutton's office the duty sergeant raised his eyebrows. Stan could hear voices, low but angry. Not every word was distinct but he could make out enough. 'To hell with the damned Fokker!' the major was saying. 'Set that aside for the moment. I'm talking about your duties as a flight commander. It's more than just flying for yourself, it's looking out for the pilots in your charge, training them to shoot straight and fly crooked, it's handling all the tedious stuff, the returns, the records, the reports. Setting an example as the leader of the team.'

Stan heard Guv say: 'Confound it Sutton, I should have thought destroying a Fokker was example enough, not to mention the gas bag.'

Sutton gave a short laugh. 'That's where we differ. What the devil were you thinking of, taking it on yourself to embark on this escapade without a word to anyone and neglecting your duties here?'

Guv's reply was muffled, something about checking with the Met boys before going up.

'Good God, man,' Sutton said more loudly, 'you know how quickly conditions can change. Didn't it cross your mind that your flight might be called up for an op? While you were gallivanting about in Hunland the weather cleared and young Dixon had to step into your shoes. You'd better pray all your chaps get back or I'll push this up the line.'

There was the scrape of a chair being pushed back and the office door swung open. Stan came to attention.

'Relax, Sergeant,' Sutton said. 'I've sent for you because I want to commend you on an exceptional show.'

Guv was standing by the window with his hands clasped behind his back. He did not turn, or acknowledge Stan in any way. Sutton waved for Stan to take a seat.

'A balloon and an Eindecker on one trip, eh? That's sharp shooting by any standards. If I have my way you'll hear more of this.' He glanced across at Guv who still had not moved and pushed a form across his desk. It was a combat report filled out in Guv's rounded, schoolboyish hand. 'I want you to read this carefully. The recording officer has just handed me Captain Sutro's account of your recent actions. It's certain that Wing will want to make much of it, particularly knocking down a Fokker. It's just the sort of shot in the arm the service needs. Shows it can be done. For that reason, as your commanding officer, I need to be absolutely certain of the facts before I sign it off. That's why, as the key witness you might say, the fellow with his finger on the trigger, I must know whether you concur with

Captain Sutro's version of events. You must understand, no doubts can be raised at a later stage.'

'Not quite sure I'm with you, sir.'

'Read it, man. Just tell me if this is how it was.'

The account was clear enough, although Stan noticed that he was not mentioned by name. Guv had also described the two combats in what seemed to Stan an odd way: *Evading considerable enemy anti-aircraft fire I placed my machine in such a position that my observer had a clear shot at the observation balloon which enabled him to dispatch it without difficulty. Although a burst of fire intended for the observer went wide, the bullets, very fortuitously, cut the supporting cables of the basket and the man was killed.*

Of the attack by the Fokker, Guv had written: *Having lost the advantage of cloud-cover and still behind enemy lines I was bracketed by shells from ground batteries but took the necessary evasive action to keep any damage to the minimum. At this point I became aware of a hostile aircraft approaching and clearly preparing to attack. I quickly identified the HA as a Fokker and realised it had the advantage of speed and height, quite apart from its superior armament. I therefore decided to wait until he commenced his dive before putting my machine into a series of violent manoeuvres that had the effect of surprising him so that most of his bullets flew wide although he continued to direct bursts of fire at me throughout his descent. I then resumed straight and level flight as he passed below me, providing my observer with a stable gun platform because, as I had anticipated, the HA pulled up into a steep climb ahead of me with the intention of executing an Immelmann turn in the habitual manner of its type. Thus my observer was presented with a perfect target on which to open fire. In this he was successful and the HA was seen to dive away in flames and strike the ground in the region of Roisel.*

Stan pushed the form back across the desk. At the window Guv had turned round and was staring at him with folded arms.

'Well?' said Sutton.

'I don't know, sir.'

'What do you mean, you don't know? You must know. Otherwise I can't put my name to this report.'

'I had an idea the Jerry's gun jammed on the way down. He had us cold, despite what Mr Sutro tried to do.'

Guv stepped forward. 'What makes you think his gun jammed, Sergeant?'

'There was no other reason for him to cease firing at that point. That and sixth sense, I suppose, as a gunner myself. You just know.'

Guv laughed. 'I don't agree. He was a fumble-fisted Hun who paid the price. Anyway, the veracity of my report can hardly be questioned on the basis of an NCO's sixth sense.'

'What do you say to that, Sergeant?' said Sutton.

'I have nothing to add, sir.'

'Nothing?'

'Nothing.'

'Well, I must take you at your word.' Sutton took up the form and read it through slowly. He reached for a fountain pen and unscrewed the top. Spread the form flat on the desk. Signed his name carefully and placed the form in a wire out-tray. Looked steadily at Guv. 'Very well, Captain. What I will say is this. You have given your observer remarkably little credit for his obvious pluck and skill. I will make it my business to put that right through different channels. I commend you, Sergeant, for a job well done. Dismissed.'

As the door closed behind him Stan heard Sutton say: 'As to the other matter, Sutro, if there's a repeat I'll have you court-martialled.'

'Really?' Guv said. 'Do you think Wing would approve?'

C Flight returned from patrol intact. They had engaged three German two-seaters with inconclusive results. One had been seen to be damaged but Harry Dixon, Guv's stand-in flight commander, had called off the attack when a superior force of hostile aircraft appeared from the east at 10,000 feet. It was an unfortunate contrast to Guv's success with a single machine, marked that night with a drunk in the Officers Mess, the usual binge in which grown or near-grown men transformed themselves into rowdy sots. These celebrations Stan could never understand. They seemed at odds with the CO's call for officers to set an example. But on this occasion the hullabaloo was more restrained and ended earlier than expected. At first it was assumed by the ranks that this was because in the past, Mr Sutro had shown himself disinclined to celebrate the victories of others and so the others were disinclined to celebrate his. But then it was learned that late in the proceedings Mr Sutro had jumped up on a table and recited some sort of doggerel aimed apparently at Major Sutton and to which Major Sutton had taken exception. Words had been exchanged in a quiet corner and the squadron commander had absented himself soon afterwards.

The scrap of paper on which the verse had been written, screwed up and thrown in a corner, had been retrieved by a Mess orderly. Soon it was passing from hand to hand. It meant little to Stan:

When the sands are all dry he is gay as a lark,
And will talk in contemptuous tones of the Shark
But, when the tide rises and sharks are around,
His voice has a timid and tremulous sound.

He shook his head. 'What's it got to do with the Old Man?'

'Come off it, Stan. It's as plain as bleeding day. It accuses him of being yellow.'

'Pull the other one.'

'There's no denying he's done his bit, but they say he's lost his nerve.'

'Who says?'

'Well, it's Mr Sutro's poem, ain't it? I reckon he should know.'

'Who else?'

'I don't know. The word's gone round.'

'If I were you, I'd be ruddy careful who I listened to. You might end up in trouble.'

'Meaning?'

'Meaning Major Sutton's all right. You'd soon find out if he's yellow or not, if he catches you spreading gossip.'

'You going to tell him?'

'Not if you button your lip.'

'You going to make me?'

'I might.'

'Regular bloody hero, ain't we? Bit of Mr Sutro's guts rubbed off, that it?'

What few facts Stan had disclosed of the Le Cateau trip supported the details in Guv's combat report. He found it easier that way. He did not want any fuss. So it was quickly accepted that he had played a useful but minor role. He was beginning to think so himself. It was becoming hazy. Perhaps Guv *had* been first to spot the Fokker. It was hard to be sure, and if you weren't sure, how you could claim anything for yourself? Neither could he quite recall what manoeuvres the Gunbus had been put through to counter the attack. For certain Guv had thrown the bus about a bit, like he said. And what of the Hun's machine-gun jamming? Well, that was just his theory, with nothing to back it up. It was impossible to be certain of anything in a fight like that, when everything happened in a blur. His part in the whole affair seemed to have been thrown into doubt. Perhaps it was correct: perhaps he had done no more than fire on targets presented to him by his pilot. The more he thought about it, the more Guv's report seemed broadly right. Who was he to quibble about the details? He told himself he was content to let the matter lie. He was pleased he had come to this conclusion because it made the next few days far easier to deal with.

In the morning, a Vauxhall staff car arrived to take Captain Sutro and Sergeant Kemp to Wing headquarters. On the way Guv said: 'You accept that my report was accurate in all respects? We must have no inconsistencies when talking to top brass.'

Stan did not look at him but stared out of the window as they jolted along the bad roads. 'I'll leave the talking to you.'

'Good,' Guv said. 'It's better that way.'

Guv was treated by the senior officers like a favourite but scampish nephew by indulgent uncles. They were not interested in the destruction of the balloon, only the battle with the Fokker. Stan did not think it had been much of a battle, just a brief pass in which the Hun had come unstuck, but Guv gave an account that was more colourful than his combat report, involving more evasive action than Stan remembered, and was required to repeat it several times while the uncles nodded approvingly, laughed a good deal and, at the end of it, slapped Guv's back and pumped his hand enthusiastically. They did not slap Stan's back but shook his hand more briefly and told him he had done jolly well to support his pilot so effectively. No mention was made of Lieutenant Dixon having to lead C Flight in Guv's absence and Stan wondered whether they were even aware of it. If they were, perhaps they had set it aside as it might spoil the story.

The Vauxhall did not return them to Chézy-au-Bois but instead took them on to Brigade where the process was repeated to a slightly larger audience and they were treated to lunch, Guv escorted by a jovial group to the Officers Mess, Stan taken in hand by an admin sergeant who found him some beer and sandwiches.

'It must be something to fly with Captain Sutro. What's he really like?' Other men were crowding round.

'He's a good pilot,' Stan said. It seemed safe enough. He tried to let it go at that but they wanted more.

'Good pilot be buggered,' said the sergeant. 'It's got to be more than that. Special qualities, like.'

Stan gave them what they asked for. 'He's the bravest man I know. He'll never back down from a fight. He'll employ any tactics to win. God help anyone who gets in his way.'

'You mean the Hun?'

'Anyone.'

'There's a word the Frenchies have dreamed up for blokes like him: an ace. According to the grapevine, he's even being talked about in Berlin.'

Stan thought this was probably true. The Germans would not like the idea that any old pilot could bring down one of their Eindeckers. It had to be at the hands of someone special. 'What else does the grapevine say?'

'According to reports in the Yankee press, Fritz is trying to prove it was just bad luck you got their Fokker.'

'What sort of bad luck?'

'Oh, the usual bollocks. They claim they went over the wreckage and found the machine-gun had malfunctioned. Naturally our lords and masters won't have any of it.'

When the Vauxhall collected them, some of the men gathered by the car as Guv climbed in. They were beaming at him, excited and respectful, drinking him in with eager eyes so they could tell their families about meeting the famous flier on their next leaves. Their seniors were standing on a terrace, smiling also; one gave a dignified twirl of a gloved hand and Guv saluted back. In front of him a corporal called: 'Three cheers for Captain Sutro.' Guv let the cheers die away. 'Well, thank you, boys. I'm sure I don't deserve it. But count on me to bag another Fuck . . . excuse my German . . . *Fokker* as soon as one dares to show his nose.' This time the joke was well received, and Guv sat down to a burst of laughter.

'Banging the drum,' he said, searching for his pipe and tobacco pouch. 'That's what the Whitehall wallahs call it. Banging the bloody drum. Very well, driver. Back to Chézy.'

'You're not going to Chézy, sir. My orders are to deliver you to HQ First Army.'

It was almost dark when they approached Montreuil. To Stan it appeared much like Rye, a walled town clustered on a hill above low-lying ground that had once been sea. In front of a stone gateway set into the antique ramparts, a white post stretched across the road manned by red-capped military police. They showed their papers and were waved through, bouncing along the cobbled streets towards the château that First Army had chosen for its headquarters. Light spilled out from the tall windows, and inside there was the glint of chandeliers; no risk of enemy attack so far from the front line.

The entrance hall was a confusion of white moustaches, red collar tabs, breeches and boots. A young subaltern with the blue-and-red armband of GHQ took them through folding doors into an opulent salon. On the walls hung portraits of bewigged French aristocrats and on a table was arranged a bouquet of flowers that filled the room with a sweet and sickly scent. The subaltern told them they might have to wait for some time. They sat on upright, uncomfortable seats and looked at the portraits.

'Bored-looking bunch of bastards, aren't they?' Guv said. 'No doubt the Revolution gingered them up.'

'What are we doing here?' Stan asked.

'I've told you, banging the bloody drum. We shoot down a Fokker so the squadron bangs the drum to Wing. Wing bangs the drum to Brigade. Brigade bangs the drum to GHQ. GHQ bangs the drum to the great unwashed. That's how it works. Christ knows there's enough bad news from the Front. A bit of good is gold dust, particularly for the RFC.'

After thirty minutes the subaltern returned with a general who told them he was the Chief of Intelligence. Stan noticed he was wearing spurs. He congratulated them on their gallant deed and began to pace the salon, his spurs jingling. 'This is manna from heaven for young Rawlinson here,' he said. 'We've just about had enough of the Boche crowing about their dratted Fokkers. It's only a pity the chap you did for wasn't one of their top men.'

'Oh?' said Guv. 'Who was it?'

'Rawlinson, remind me of the fellow's outlandish handle.'

'Schulzenberg, sir, Otto.'

'Never mind his blasted Christian name. Turns out it was his first patrol. I suppose you've heard Berlin's claiming his machine-gun jammed?'

'That's plain rot,' Guv said quickly.

'Of course it is. They're wriggling like mad to minimise the loss. Our official line is this Schulzen-thingummy was one of their particular heroes and that you did for him fair and square. Which of course you did.' The General looked suddenly vague. 'Do you want to come in here, Rawlinson? I'm more broad brush and this sort of thing's your baby.'

'Thank you, sir,' said Rawlinson. 'You see, gentlemen,' he glanced at Stan, aware that he was not a gentleman but lumping him in, 'my job is to pick up on stories of heroism and so forth and get the press johnnies to write them up so they make good reading for the man and woman in the street, to keep their peckers up, so to speak. Naturally I've been appraised of the details in your combat report but I prefer to get things from the horse's mouth. It won't take long. You'll be on your way in the morning. This evening, Captain Sutro, I know the General would like you to join him as his guest for dinner. And we'll make arrangements for your sergeant here to see something of the town.' He looked at Stan doubtfully. 'It's a quaint old place with much historical interest, but no doubt our chaps will find something to amuse you.'

They were taken down a corridor to what used to be servants' quarters, where Rawlinson shared an office with three others. The others were off duty so they arranged themselves at the empty desks and Guv gave a detailed explanation of how to shoot down a Fokker Eindecker as though it was an everyday occurrence. These tips were noted down by Rawlinson who thought it might be worth circulating them to other squadrons, to help them achieve similar success against Fokkers (here even Guv drew in a breath), although, as classified information of use to the enemy, obviously they could receive no mention in the British press. 'But the rest of the yarn we can use,' he said, 'particularly the bit about the Boche saluting you as his machine folded up.'

Stan was taken to a small bistro by two other NCOs who wanted to hear about Guv Sutro. He told them he was the bravest man he knew, that he'd never back down from a fight, would employ any tactics to win and God help anyone who got in his way. He also explained Guv's tactics for outwitting a Fokker Eindecker (how to present your gunner with a perfect target) and how the German pilot had saluted as his machine had folded up in flames. By this time they were regarding him blearily and suggested going on to a place they knew where they could find a proper drink and mamzelles. Stan told them he had a touch of altitude-sickness and walked back to the château. On the way he was passed by a soldier, hunched and unsteady on his feet, escorted by two MPs. His hands were manacled behind his back. 'What's he done?'

The policeman dropped back a little. 'Bloody fool. Got blotto and tried to shag a local girl. Picked a decent one, the silly sod. He admits it, all right.'

'What'll happen to him?'

'Firing squad.'

'Christ.'

'Yes, you watch your step, my lad.'

At the château, as Stan was taken to his quarters, he heard music floating into the fresh night air, a band playing ragtime while the Headquarters staff enjoyed their dinner.

They left Montreuil mid-morning, bumping back down the cobbled streets and descending the hill to the route leading south. At Chézy-au-Bois they learned that Major Sutton had led C Flight on a contact patrol and was missing, and that the family of the girl they knew as Little Sister had raised some sort of complaint against Captain Sutro.

Seven

1

Sabine Pettit

In that first year of war, those scattered communities in possession of the land along the Route Nationale somewhat north of Amiens learned that the large meadows on either side of the Chézy-au-Bois crossroads were to be used as an aerodrome, but whether for French or British airmen was not known; only that the family Pettit who owned them would be rewarded generously by the Government for their use. For Claude Pettit it was great good fortune, the prospect of making a portion of his land pay without having to work it. But Pettit, a patriot, also saw it as his contribution towards the war that gripped his nation like a fever, for France was eager to avenge past humiliations at the hands of the Boche.

At first the news had been bad, the Germans advancing to within 30 miles of Paris and threatening the capital with siege. But the Allies quickly regained the ground the invaders had won, pushing them back to the Aisne where the impetus was lost and both armies dug in, striking at each other from a trench-line that would stretch for 800 kilometres, from the Channel coast to the Swiss border. It was an impasse that did not apply to a new breed of hero, the aviators who were to fly from Pettit's fields. He felt pride that he was to play host to such men, but admitted to anxiety about the impact they might have on his farming of the remainder of his 200 hectares. He was concerned too about his daughter, who was excited by the prospect of encountering *les pilotes* of whatever nationality, likely to be so different from the rustic lads she had grown up with.

Sabine was a light-headed girl not long out of school, her mind full of childish notions, caught up in day-dreams instead of assisting her mother with her chores or lending him and the few labourers he employed a hand with the various tasks about the farm. She was slight for the heavier work and sometimes he wished his wife had borne him a son or a sturdier female, but he would not have been without Sabine and her delicate ways that made him feel protective towards her and also guilty that he had brought one of his own into a life of hardship and discomfort.

Sabine had a particular friend, Violette, who worked in her parents' auberge a mile distant on the route to Doullen. They had known each other from school and shared many secrets. They did not meet as often now, but when they did, it was as it had always been. In the dying summer of that first year, when the guns began to sound, they would lie on the flat grassland picking at the sown clover, visualising what these quiet meadows, deserted now except for a few grazing beasts, might soon become. They imagined the pilots they might meet; fair haired or dark, slim or well built, French or English? Always young, of course, little more than boys, in age so close to them but doing a grown man's job. At this time, imagining the skies over Chézy-au-Bois echoing to the roar of flying machines still seemed a thrill and an excitement, and they were roused by Danton's exhortation to the defenders of Verdun in 1792: *Il nous faut de l'audace, encore de l'audace, toujours de l'audace!* And by words from the French anthem, *Mourir pour la Patrie est le sort le plus beau.*

In the face of such fervour, only the older women remained silent. But the men of fighting age were eager to avenge past humiliations at the hands of the Boche; those like Violette's brother Guillaume, keen to enlist before he missed the chance to serve his country. Sabine, who had known the boy from childhood and was fond of him in a sisterly way, was proud of his patriotism but pleased she did not have a brother; pleased too that her father was too old to be conscripted because, underneath the elation, she sensed that something dark and malignant was approaching, that might even involve her. But she did not talk of this to Violette, stretched out beside her, breathing in the heady scent of crushed grass and clover, and gazing up at the empty sky.

At night she dreamed of her pilot – tall, yes, very tall, and dark, not blond like Violette's fancy but dark with a moustache, a thin moustache, a moustache not too tickly over a broad mouth that was quick to smile. Somehow he was not a Frenchman and stumbled with the language – an Englishman then and an officer, yes, certainly an officer, with a medal, no, two medals, a gallant officer, a gallant English officer. Perhaps he would notice her watching near the landing ground, come over and talk to her in a sweet and faltering way, even take her for a spin in his machine, high over Chézy-au-Bois so that, looking down, dizzy and deliciously frightened, she would see the farm and her father in the yard staring up, his hand shielding his eyes from the sun. Yes, this was how it would be. How it must be. She knew it would happen just like this.

The war took its course. Amiens and the towns and villages around it echoed to the dull peal of church bells, and families wept as fathers, brothers, sons vanished as though they had never been, enduring only in the memory of those who grieved. The reality bit deep. But spirits rose a little when, in the summer of the second year of war, the Englishmen arrived at Chézy-au-Bois. At first the activity was puzzling, with many men marching backwards and forwards across the area chosen for the landing ground, trampling flat the clover that had cloaked Sabine and Violette with its summer scent, to make it suitable for the taking off and landing of aeroplanes. On the far side of the fields, lines of ancient trees were felled for the same reason. Only then did the skeletal aeroplanes begin to fly in, as insubstantial and fragile as moths. She could not conceive of them as war machines capable of fighting the enemy. This only increased her admiration for the men who flew them, who moved around the aerodrome unearthly in their close-fitting flying helmets, with goggles on their foreheads like an extra pair of eyes, their long leather coats almost brushing the ground. But there was no doubting they were human; always mingled with the roar of aero-engines were boisterous shouts and much laughter.

For the airmen, it seemed, there was no shortage of spirit – of *élan vital.*

As the aerodrome became established she took an almost boyish interest in what went on there. But now she was alone. The locals had grown used to the presence of the English squadron and Violette was inconsolable and did not visit any more because Guillaume had been lost in the French attack at Artois-Loos and she could not bear to think or hear of war.

The members of the squadron grew accustomed to seeing the young girl watching them from the farm and grinned and waved to her, sometimes shouting out things she did not understand as they busied themselves with their work on the aeroplanes lined up outside the canvas hangars, or prepared to take to the air. Often pilots would look for her as they returned from a flight and raised their gloved hands in a salute, as though thankful to see her once more, showing they were safely home. She did not know this, but if they looked for her and she was not there they felt that part of the routine that brought them luck and kept them safe was missing, a bad omen. Nor did she know that they called her Little Sister.

Some of the officers lived in rooms that had been found for them in the farm buildings, others in bell tents close to the great barn that adjoined the lane. It became natural for Sabine to find herself engaged in conversation with these pink-faced young Englishmen, laughing at their bad French but having no English herself. They treated her like a child, which made her vexed, because she did not feel like a child. Had she not done with school? Did she not have seventeen years (just)? Did she not work as an adult on her father's farm? Could they not imagine that she had dreams of a gallant English officer with two medals who would take her aloft in his machine and dance amongst the clouds?

A single officer did not treat her as a child, one of those who had a small room to himself overlooking the cobbled yard where the animals were sometimes kept. She never went there but he always looked at her in a certain way, his eyes speculative and teasing. He talked to her in a certain way as well, in decent French with a careless accent. She was surprised that he spoke her language. He said that before the war he had spent much time in France learning to fly. He did not call her Little Sister but by his own particular nickname: Sabby. He was not tall, little more than her height, and had no moustache over a broad mouth. His mouth was small and had a twist to it when he smiled, which was not often. Mostly it was set in a hard line and his eyes were usually narrowed, as though he was thinking bad things, but when she talked of this he told her that with her he only thought of good things. He told her he flew a Vickers FB5. She could not pronounce it the English way so he translated it for her: *Une ef-bay-cinque. Aussi designé* the Gun Bus, *l'autobus de canon*. He thought it very funny when she shook her head in perplexity.

His name was Captain Sutro but he asked her to call him Guv. She found it difficult to address him so familiarly, because he seemed so old, not young like the pilot of her fancy, or many of his comrades, but she grew used to it as, at dusk, he would join her for a casual *promenade*. He told her she reminded him of someone he used to know a long time ago. When she asked about her, he said she went away. He talked of England and advised her to go there one day because it was the best country on earth. She said that perhaps she could visit him there and he smiled to himself but did not reply. Once she asked him why he liked her and he said she was not like other French girls he had met in France and that she made him feel young again. She told him he was young, which seemed to please him, but she did not think so really. She felt odd with him, as though unspoken words hung in the air like bubbles about to burst. People she encountered and knew well would look at them curiously but they only walked and talked, and never touched, so nothing was said and even her father shrugged and said he thought no harm could come of it because the captain was an English gentleman.

One evening Captain Guv was in a strange mood. He had shot down a German machine that day and although one man had died, the pilot had survived. 'He was not much older than you, Sabby, but his precious Kaiser had got at him. His brain was warped with poisonous nonsense. I should have finished the *salaud* with my pistol. Instead he will be well cared for in England.'

'I do not think you could have done it,' she said. 'Perhaps in England he will realise his error. He is only young.'

'His mind is set. One day he will cause more mischief. It would have been better to end it there.'

'You say his mind is set. It seems to me that when there is a war, everyone's mind is set, the French, the English, the Boche. Perhaps the same might be said of you.'

He laughed but there was no humour in it. 'War calls for firm opinions, Sabby. You must believe that right is on our side. Doubt that and we will lose.'

'It breeds hatred too, doesn't it. Do you have hatred in you?'

'For the Boche, certainly.'

'All of them?'

'All who oppose us, yes.'

'Perhaps you feel hatred for anyone who opposes you.' She did not know why she made this observation. It seemed to come from nowhere, as if from another, older brain.

He laughed again. 'You might be right, at that.' He stared at her for a long moment; she noticed his eyes were bloodshot, from flying perhaps. 'Why? Are you thinking of opposing me, Sabby?'

She could not think how she might, but answered: 'If I did, would you hate me?'

'Enough games,' he said. They had stopped walking and he was leaning on a gate looking across the open fields. He turned and produced a flat silver flask from his tunic pocket, unscrewed the cap and held it out to her, jerking it under her nose so she could hear the contents sloshing about inside. It smelled very strong, like the *marc* she had seen her father drink, and she shook her head, so he drank some on his own before slipping the flask back in his pocket. His face had become crimson and his mouth had that odd twist to it, but this time it was not the beginning of a smile, more a contortion. In another man Sabine thought it might be because he was always in danger in the air, but he never remarked on such things or seemed apprehensive or afraid. It was as if he was ready to do something but could not bring himself to do it; not this time.

Then, when alone and unseen on their *promenades*, he began to take her hand. He would place it against his body in places that made her blush and look away. Again he produced the flask and this time made her sip. It burned her mouth and she coughed and choked. He smacked her quite hard on her slender back and told her, his voice rough and impatient, that she was all right, said in English not to 'make a fuss', that she would get accustomed to it. He raised the flask to his lips and tipped his head back, draining it to the last drop. They were near a small copse and he took her arm and half pushed her into the dappled shadow of the trees. She understood what he wanted to do and began to cry, to pull away from him. A motor car was passing in the lane and he let her go. He turned and walked away. When she joined him he said: 'I thought you liked me.'

'I do,' she said.

He said something else in English, bad words, and began to continue down the lane towards the farm. She caught him up and walked beside him, staring up at his face that was turned away. 'I'm sorry,' she said.

'It doesn't matter. Forget it.' He looked down at her. 'You must not tell your father of this. You must not tell anyone. It is between us. Do you understand?'

She was miserable and confused. 'Yes, I understand.'

'Shall we see each other again?'

'Yes.'

'Very well,' he said and strode ahead.

Something compelled her to go with him again. She knew the risk. He produced the flask and they drank as they walked. This time when they reached the copse she followed him. He held on to her, his grip painful on her thin arms, speaking urgently in English, not bothering with French, fumbling at her clothes and dragging her down to the ground, the floor of the copse thick with dry leaves spread about the pungent earth. She cried out but his bristled face was pressed against hers, his mouth wet on her mouth and cheeks, his breath rank from the alcohol he had drunk from the flask. Afterwards, he said she was a special girl, not like the kind that hung about the bars and dance halls. She asked how many girls he had been with. He said that like all pilots he was experienced in these matters but that she could trust him (for what he did not explain). He told her that one day he would arrange for her to go England where she would wear fine clothes and learn how to be an English lady. For this to come true she must not talk of what had happened to anyone because it would spoil what they had together. He made her promise and she did.

After this, he did not stay in his small room overlooking the cobbled yard, but found somewhere he said was more suitable. He would not look at her if he went past with the other men and they did not meet together openly as before but met occasionally at the copse. She understood that he did not love her and that she did not love him but there had been an understanding that one day he would help her to leave the farm for a different life, as long as she did not speak of him to others. In the copse they did what they did again, and drank from the flask. She did not cough and choke as much and the other thing did not hurt as much, but she had not come to enjoy it. It was not what she had dreamed of; her tall, dark English chevalier with his trim moustache and generous mouth, quick to smile, and two medals on his tunic. The Captain did not resemble him in any way and had only a single small ribbon on his tunic. He told her it was a medal but she was not convinced.

She ceased to ask him about the life she might expect in England because he did not listen properly and became angry. 'All in good time,' he said in English. 'It's not as easy as you seem to think.' He used other words that she did not understand and did not want to.

Soon after this she realised she was with child. As someone raised on a farm she understood these things. She did not know what to do. She did not think Violette would be sympathetic, still consumed with grief, and she feared her father and mother would disown her because of the shame she had brought to the family. She watched out for the Captain to tell him, but he did not come. It was as if he knew. She went to the bureau of the commander of the squadron and asked for the Captain there. She knew it was reckless but she did not know what else to do. The men in the bureau seemed to find it amusing and asked her if Captain Sutro was her beau.

'He's spoken for, you know,' one said, but she did not understand what that meant until much later. They wanted to know why she was looking for him but of course she would not say. They promised they would tell him she had been there but still he did not come looking for her. She could not understand how his feelings could change, as though he felt indifference or even hatred towards her. She had not opposed him and he had said he only hated those who opposed him. But perhaps in this, as in other things, he was not sincere.

In time she could no longer conceal her condition and she forced herself to tell her parents what had passed. They were greatly shocked and full of anger. Her father said she had betrayed them, that she was an imbecile to trust an Englishman. He said it was lucky that Sutro did not still occupy the quarters overlooking the cobbled yard because he would very likely have gone to visit him now with violence in mind and retribution in his heart. He said he would pray for the Boche to shoot him down, hoped that he would fall in flames and that his machine would take a long time to reach the ground.

Sabine did not wish this. Although she did not feel love, she was tender towards him as the father of her child. She recognised him for the man he was, had always been and was hard with herself (as she could see now) for being a dreamer and a fool. But she still half hoped that he might return and, even now, honour his promise to take her away and make her into a fine English lady. Her father did not know of this promise and she did not tell him of it because it would hurt him to think she desired another life.

At first, Claude Pettit found it difficult to look at her or speak, but soon enough this changed because he loved her and felt compassion for her, his only daughter. He said the English captain must honour his responsibility, that a marriage must be arranged. He went to the bureau at the aerodrome and asked to see Major Sutton, with whom he dealt on matters of administration connected to the farm, but he was not at his desk. At first the other airmen there were not interested because they could not understand what he was trying to say. His few English words were not adequate. Those he had came out of his mouth as vulgar and without subtlety. The airmen seemed excited about an important victory Captain Sutro had achieved over a particular Boche and told him he had been summoned away to be feted by the British generals. Then Major Sutton returned and directed him to his office and closed the door.

The Major had excellent French and Pettit explained how it was. The Major listened very carefully looking grave, and told him he would come to the farm to talk with his wife and daughter. Meanwhile, nothing more was to be said.

That evening, Sabine opened the door to Major Sutton at the farm. He stood before her on the steps, tall and dark with a trim moustache and a generous mouth. Her heart pounded as she stepped back. 'The English commander, Papa,' she said.

The Major smiled. 'I'm not English, *mademoiselle*, I'm Australian. What they call Down Under.' He pointed at the floor and they both laughed a little but it seemed out of place given the reason for his visit, and she took him through to the best room where her parents were waiting. He heard how it had been with great attention and without comment. At the end, when she sat with her hands clasped on her lap and wept and her mother put her arm around her shoulder, he told them the captain was still absent from the aerodrome on special duties, but when he returned he would put the allegations before him.

'Allegations, Monsieur?' Pettit said.

'He stands accused,' said Sutton. 'He has the right to put his side of the matter.'

Pettit pointed at his daughter. 'Is this not proof enough?' He leaned forward, his hands on his knees, staring at the pattern on the worn carpet. 'I have a solution, as I explained. This Sutro is not the man I would wish for my daughter, but I am prepared to accept him into the family if a marriage can be arranged without delay.'

The Major studied his fingernails. 'I regret that is not possible.'

'*Nom de Dieu*,' said Pettit, understanding.

'That being so, Monsieur, the course open to us is limited. Perhaps you don't realise how serious a matter this is. If it was proved that this officer forced his attentions upon your daughter, he would without doubt pay the ultimate price. Military law does not differentiate between rank or service record. In this case it would appear – if proved, I say – that she was at least compliant, but even so the penalty for such a transgression is severe.'

'He did not force himself,' Sabine said quietly.

'That at least would save him from the worst of outcomes.' The Major stood up and put on his baggy service cap. That afternoon, he told them, he was to lead Captain Sutro's flight on patrol, but he promised to undertake an official investigation as soon as he returned. Meanwhile, as before, the matter was to remain confidential.

Monsieur Pettit went with him to the front door. '*Ce Sutro, j'espère qu'il va brûler en l'enfer.*'

'Burn in hell, *monsieur*?' said Sutton. 'Well, that remains to be seen.'

Pettit watched him cross the yard. When he went back to the best room he said, 'There is one true Englishman, at least.'

'He is not English, Papa,' said Sabine.

A week passed and nothing more was heard from Major Sutton. They began to suspect that he had spoken falsely to them. But when, finally, Monsieur Pettit visited the aerodrome, he learned that he was dead. A successor was to be confirmed, but until that time the Acting Squadron Commander was Captain Sutro. He was in Amiens on important business. Perhaps Monsieur Pettit wished to make an appointment?

Monsieur Pettit thought he might but did not say so; he thought he might go to the farm and take his shotgun from its cupboard and return at an appointed time and do what the Boche had failed to do.

Eight

1

Fraser Sutro

Guv had not been surprised to learn that he was tipped to take command of the squadron on an acting basis. He expected it to be announced quite soon. His stock was high with those who counted. In those quarters, doubts had been expressed about the judgement of the late Major Sutton. It had even been suggested (no one knew from what source) that he had been suffering from some form of nerves, that his foolhardy decision to lead C Flight on patrol had been a misguided attempt to scotch these rumours.

Whatever his motivation, it was clearly understood that squadron commanders should only go up in exceptional circumstances, and this had not been the case at Chézy-au-Bois. The squadron was not short handed and C Flight's number two, Lieutenant Dixon, was a perfectly capable pilot if lacking somewhat in aggression. But not everyone could be expected to be a firebrand like Captain Sutro; after all, that was the quality that singled him out. As for Sutton, well, he had demonstrated a certain conscientiousness, and a final flash of guts, but given his recent lack of combat experience it might be said that he had hazarded the safety of the young men in his charge, a number of whom had been newly posted in from training school and were short on flying time.

Of course, if Sutro was confirmed in the command it could not be expected that he would adhere to any rules about flying a desk (rueful smiles) but that was quite a different matter. The fellow was a positive inspiration. Already, during the short period it took for the decision to be approved, he had rather assumed control despite some murmurings of dissent from his fellow officers, piqued no doubt by being passed over. What other reason could they have? They could not dispute the fact that since Sutton's death the squadron had noticeably raised its game, achieving much success by strafing and bombing ground targets at extreme low levels (risky, by God, but don't it just work?) and showing admirable pluck by engaging Hun machines whatever the odds, with the indomitable Sutro always leading from the front.

Certainly it had cost men, admittedly rather more than before, but that was a price worth paying, quite different to squandering lives on hit-and-miss results. With Sutro it was always hit-and-hit. The only question was: how long could he survive? Already he had lost a third observer, that fellow Kemp who'd shown up at Montreuil – not dead, apparently, but shipped off with a Blighty wound. How soon before Captain Sutro went the same way? Still, there was not much they could do about that. He had the luck of the devil. Perhaps it would see him through for a good while yet. And as long as it did, he stood as a wonderful example of RFC steadfastness and pluck – that is, until wild allegations were made that turned out, when looked into, to be not so wild after all, and the service found itself in a ticklish situation.

For a time it seemed that, for the sake of one feather-brained girl and a lamentable lapse by a no doubt susceptible and over-stressed officer, one of the finest pilots in the service might be locked away in a military prison when he should be serving his country. Worse, if the girl, for vengeance sake or to lessen her shame, chose to claim that Sutro had forced himself on her against her will, he might even be stood up against a wall and shot. You never knew with these damned Frogs. The main thing was to keep the matter under wraps and see if a solution could be found. Of course, young Sutro had been a bloody fool, but everyone did things they regretted at some time or other. When it came down to it, it was all the fault of these flighty mamzelles making themselves available. Pilots were only human, after all.

The first intimation of what was to come was the delivery to the squadron office (by an anonymous peasant) of a sealed envelope addressed to Captain Sutro and containing a brief note, unsigned. In the usual spidery French script it begged him to go to the usual place at this time and on this date because the writer was in a desperate situation and did not know which way to turn. If he did not keep the appointment it would, it was feared, be the worse for him.

Guv read the note several times, then used it to light his pipe. He turned over in his mind the various courses of action open to him. None seemed suitable. He was compelled to present himself and hear what this damned Sabby had to say. He kicked himself now for bothering with her. What had started as an amusing challenge, a diversion, a pleasant change from the worldly tarts of the bordellos and *palais-de-danse* in Amiens, this little affair reminiscent of his early conquests as a lad had become tiresome. She had changed from a fresh-faced little flirt to an anxious and possessive woman who thought she could make claims on him, trying to hold him to whatever promises he might have made in the thrill of the chase. Finally, her only merit had been that she was conveniently on hand and he didn't have to fork out a dozen francs for every fuck. And after all, she'd asked for it, hadn't she? If it hadn't been him it would have been someone else, with her hanging about the airfield like that. Still, it was a downright bloody nuisance. He thought he had seen the back of her, but now he had to make her realise it was over, not that it had ever amounted to very much.

It was dusk when he walked to the copse, and to the south the sky was dark with approaching rain. He took the usual winding path, disturbing a crowd of pigeons that rose up with a clatter of wings. 'Sabby,' he called. 'Sabby? Where the deuce are you?' He heard a click. A man stepped out from the cover of the trees. He saw it was the farmer Pettit pointing a shotgun at his chest, his thumb on the just-cocked hammer, his finger on the trigger. 'And what the bloody hell do you want?' Guv said in English.

Pettit jerked the shotgun at him. *'Donnez-moi vos derniers mots en français s'il vous plait.'*

'Last words? What the blazes are you on about, you damned fool?'

351

'*En français!*'

'I'm damned if I will. Put down that bloody popgun and talk to me like a man.'

Pettit had only a few words of English but comprehended enough to make him waver. The single barrel of the weapon lowered a little. '*En français, s'il vous plait,*' he said, trying to control a voice that trembled with emotion.

Guv switched to French. 'I see I've been brought here falsely.'

'You talk to me of falseness?'

'You mean your daughter, I suppose.'

'We know everything.'

'Well, that's more than I do. May I suggest we dispense with the melodrama? If you have something to say, for God's sake say it and lay aside that damned antique you're brandishing before it goes off.'

The barrel rose again. 'Antique, you say? I assure you it is well looked after. It kills as well as it ever did.'

'I don't know what your daughter's been saying to you. Nothing that happened between us took place without her consent.'

'Her consent? She still a child, you a grown man? You insult me. I should finish you now.'

'Please proceed. You or the Boche, what's the difference? But your daughter will suffer most, losing the man she cared for at the hands of her father and losing her father to the blade of the guillotine, for it will come to that.'

Pettit uncocked the shotgun and lowered it to his side. 'She carries your child,' he said flatly.

'Are you sure it's mine?'

Pettit stepped forward and struck Guv on the temple with the butt of the gun. Kneeling on the trodden mud, Guv felt the man's steel-tipped boot strike his ribs. He rolled onto his side, blood running into his eyes from the wound on his head. Pettit was standing over him. 'You are not worth a cartridge. *Je chie sur vous, salaud.*'

'*À vous aussi,*' Guv croaked, and Pettit kicked him again, harder this time.

Guv heard him move away. He sat up and watched him go, putting his hand to his temple and feeling the deep gash that ran from his eyebrow to his ear. 'It's a capital offence, assaulting an English officer,' he called after him. 'I'll see you face the guillotine yet.'

Pettit stopped and turned and raised the shotgun to his shoulder. Again Guv heard the click. He refused to close his eyes but stared back at the man who was to kill him. The report was deafening in the heavy silence, reverberating through the close-packed trees. Pettit had aimed high into the canopy and shredded twigs and leaves came pattering down.

'You will never get a better chance,' Guv said.

Pettit broke the shotgun but did not reload. 'It is too easy. There are other ways.' He turned and walked away and was lost to view.

It was raining now, everything wet and smelling fresh. Guv pushed himself to his feet, sore and slightly dizzy from the blows. He undid his breeches and urinated on the woodland floor. He held his penis in his hand. It lay there like a slug. He worked it gently and it came alive, quickly hard and extending inch by inch. He dealt with the urge and put himself away. How simple life would be if the Hun did for him what they had done for Stan Kemp. Less trouble but not so amusing. He began to laugh.

A week later, in the squadron commander's office he had adopted as his own, he was visited by an army captain who introduced himself as a member of the provost marshal's detachment. 'Police by any other name,' he added, his manner oddly deferential. He took in the dressing on Guv's head. 'I say, Sutro, you look a bit done up. Catch it in an aerial scrap?'

'Enemy action, certainly,' Guv said. He went to the outer office and sent the clerks away. He closed the door. 'Let me guess. Some Frog yokel's been kicking up a fuss.'

'A complaint has been received. I advise you to treat it seriously.'

'Do you really think I've got time for this? I'm due on patrol in thirty minutes.'

'I'm afraid you won't be going anywhere until this interview is completed.'

'So the war must wait, eh? How long will this take?'

'That's up to you.'

'You know who you're addressing, of course.'

'Oh yes, I've been fully briefed. In normal circumstances it would be a privilege to shake your hand. It's only a pity—'

'Yes, yes, enough of that.'

'At this point we have not gone as far as levelling a formal charge. At the moment the case—'

'The case?' The words sounded oddly familiar.

'Oh, certainly it must be treated as a case although at present it's being batted back and forth between the various levels of command. This is by way of a preliminary investigation to establish the circumstances as seen by both parties. There is a certain reluctance to proceed while there's still a possibility that some sort of compromise might be reached. Once the official wheels start rolling, they can't be stopped. There are far-reaching implications, as you'll understand.'

'I'm not sure I do. Perhaps you'd be kind enough to explain them to me.'

'The French Government, for one, who are for the moment unaware. It would go down very badly, an English officer, an English officer already with a wife and child, an English officer in a position of privilege and influence taking advantage of a young and naive local girl. And the British Government for another. There at least you have the advantage of what are generally referred to as friends in high places. Put bluntly, a considerable effort has been made to build you up. It would be a confounded nuisance to knock you down again.'

'I see. What do you suggest?'

The captain studied Guv through narrowed eyes, holding his lower lip between his teeth, as though the man he saw did not quite match his expectations. 'The options are somewhat limited. You're hardly in a position to make an honest woman of the victim . . .'

'Victim? You seem intent on making me out to be some sort of criminal type.'

'You don't deny that you had unlawful carnal knowledge of her, and that now she is expecting a child?'

'How do we know it's mine?'

'Oh, come now.'

'Anyway, she didn't complain at the time.'

'That's as may be,' said the captain, moving uncomfortably on his chair. 'But she's complaining now.'

'She or that dumb ox of a father of hers?' Guv laid his fingers on his wound. 'He gave me this. Threatened me at gunpoint and then set about me. Surely that would count against him?'

'He doesn't happen to be the one accused. And no doubt a competent lawyer would argue that it all took place in the heat of the moment, the aggrieved father exacting revenge for the dishonour done to his daughter, not to be condoned, of course, but understandable – that sort of thing. I can't imagine there'd be much sympathy for your position.'

'This is extraordinary to me,' said Guv. 'Around us at this moment a million men are fighting each other to the death. Every day I go up in my machine facing the possibility of not coming back. My pilots die in a dozen ways, all of them ghastly, before their time. Yet here we sit debating a trivial matter involving some bit of a girl who knew damned well what she was getting into, whatever her age and whatever she might claim now.'

'There is a difference. This concerns a civilian, a citizen of an Allied country. It cannot be brushed lightly aside as of no importance. After all, it concerns a number of lives.'

'A number?'

'The girl's, her child's, her family's.' The captain paused. 'You must understand that, if it came to the worst, this could cost you your own life as surely as any dogfight with the Hun, or failing that, many years in a military prison.'

'A pretty prospect, I must say. You mentioned a compromise?'

'It's a possibility, but no more than that. This Pettit fellow has the bit between his teeth. However, money talks in any language. I've no idea how much these peasant farmers make, but it can't be much.'

'Buy his silence, you mean?'

'You're a man of considerable wealth. If Pettit pursues the matter, the only satisfaction he will derive is seeing you suffer; that is all. And apparently the girl retains some fondness for you, which helps. It may be that if Pettit was offered a significant sum he might be inclined to be more pragmatic.'

'How significant?'

'I don't know, but it's a solution that might be explored.'

'By whom?'

'There are ways and means, assuming you'd be prepared to put up the cash.'

'That might be difficult.'

'More difficult than finding yourself before a court-martial board, facing disgrace and at risk of your life?'

'No, not as difficult as that.' Guv placed his hands behind his head, puffed out his cheeks and released a long and reflective breath. 'It's a bugger's muddle all right, but I suppose I must agree.'

'There is one more thing,' the captain said. 'I understand you expected to assume command of this squadron – officially, that is.'

'That's correct.'

'Quite impossible now, I'm afraid. You'll be posted away in double-quick time while we endeavour to bring this mess to a satisfactory conclusion. You've put up a black, there's no denying. The brass hats won't forget.'

'You mean they'd discount my service record thanks to some piddling little misdemeanour?'

'Not discount necessarily, but add a note in the margin for future reference. And hardly piddling if you look at it from the Pettit point of view.' The captain stood up but did not offer his hand. 'Yes, well, it's all most regrettable. Next time may I suggest you trot along to the whorehouse with the rest of them?'

'Thanks for your advice.'

'Not at all, old man. Meanwhile I'll take steps to see whether our French friend is amenable to some good old-fashioned English black-mail. Strictly infra dig, of course, but he may well do. I'm told he has quite a hefty mortgage.'

Within days Guv received notice that he had been posted to a single-seater scout squadron based near Poperinge in the Ypres sector.

To the aircrews at Chézy-au-Bois it came as a surprise, but they were by no means downcast and all agreed that now they might live a little longer.

Nothing special was organised to mark Guv's departure, only a perfunctory gathering in the Mess at which he had very little to say to them and they had even less to say to him. Some recalled his sermon from the pulpit of the FB5. 'Remember how he had us screw up our courage to the sticking place? Perhaps we can jolly well screw it down again.'

Usually the slightest excuse was used for a drunk: a notable victory, a lucky escape, a promotion, a birthday, a particular date in the calendar (St George's Day, the King's Birthday, November the Fifth). These started as a solemn rite and ended with people leaving footprints on the ceiling. This time the proceedings were as restrained as a tea party at the Manse, conducted in a general air of embarrassment and something unexplained. Only when the guest of honour retired early, testy and out of humour, did the serious business begin of cultivating sore heads.

For Guv, granted a week's leave before joining his new squadron, there was an extra twist of irritation: he discovered it was equipped with Martinsyde S1 scouts, built by the firm that turned him down as Hamel's replacement for the trans-Atlantic flight. Worse, though good in their day that day had gone and they were little better than BE2s. Also, although of senior rank, his duties had not been specified. He only knew that the squadron commander was held in high regard and that good flight leaders were already in place. It seemed he had taken a step back. He left for England and instead of going to High And Over went direct to a particular office in Whitehall, where he had requested an interview. The same anonymous captain was there but now he was a major, and the same civilian. They knew all about him.

'So you've been poking your stick in the hornets' nest,' the major said.

'Poking,' said the civilian. 'Apt word.'

The major pointed at the dressing on Guv's temple. 'Is there

357

anything under that, or is it just for effect? I know we've helped to build you up as a great British hero, but you mustn't take it too far.'

'Is that some sort of joke?'

'I assume you're here to make your excuses. You should, you know. We've kept our side of the bargain: your promotion, your gong, nearly a squadron at your disposal before you blotted your copy book. You've let us down.'

'I'm deuced if I have. Why—'

The major raised a hand. 'Please, spare us an account of your gallant victory over the Fokker Eindecker. Berlin's made it crystal clear the chap had the rottenest sort of luck. And as for the rest of your exploits, you've probably cost us more casualties than the benighted Hun, from men we can ill afford.'

'That's rich, coming from someone squatting on his backside in the War House.'

'Careful, Sutro. You already stand accused of a serious offence that could see you serving time in Dartmoor.'

'You've got the infernal cheek to talk to me of casualties? What would you know about it? I've had no complaints from the powers-that-be. Quite the reverse.'

'Hmm,' said the major. 'Well, in those quarters they employ a different kind of arithmetic. They deal in thousands.' He opened a cigarette box on the desk and offered them round. 'Let's start again, shall we? I rather thought you'd come to plead your case for causing no end of bother, not least to yourself.'

'That matter's in hand.'

'Really?'

The civilian leaned forward. 'We understand so, sir.' He murmured something in the major's ear.

'Dear me,' said the major. 'A whitewash. How very unsavoury – and expensive. It may well turn out to be one of the most costly fornications in history. I hope it was worth it. So,' he blew out a stream of white smoke, 'why are you here?'

'Frankly, I want some strings pulled and they're somewhat tangled at the moment.'

'Yes, a real cat's cradle.'

'The fact is, I'm being shunted off to a Martinsyde outfit near Poperinge and I don't think it's a proper use of my experience.'

'Where's Poperinge?' asked the major.

The civilian leaned forward again. 'Near Ypres.'

'Oh yes, I've heard of Ypres.' The major took a draw on his half-finished cigarette and stubbed it out. 'Please, continue.'

'Well, I don't know what you know about Martinsydes . . .'

'Nothing. Enlighten me.'

'They're hopeless machines and I'll be damned if I'll fly one.'

'You'll be damned if you don't,' said the major mildly. 'You mustn't believe everything that you read about yourself in the newspapers. You'll go where you're told and you'll fly what you're given.' He reached towards the cigarette box but changed his mind. 'No, bad for me.' He stared at Guv like a headmaster debating whether to use the cane or let off the pupil with a warning. 'Have you tried registering your objections through the usual channels?'

'Didn't get anywhere.'

'No, you won't. The RFC's in a bit of a flummox about what to do with you at the moment. Candidly, so are we. We chose you to help us with our activities on the home front and it looks as though we've picked a wrong 'un. You're beginning to be more trouble than you're worth. So far, luckily, we've been able to keep things under wraps.'

'Christ, all this fuss about some bloody girl who led me on?'

'Who did the leading, I wonder? But it's not just that. Doubts have been expressed at operational level about a number of claims made in your combat reports. Even allowing for – what shall we say? – the natural optimism of the fighter-pilot, there have been rather too many discrepancies with other accounts.'

'Who says?'

'Major Sutton.'

'Oh, Sutton . . .'

'It may surprise you to know that the late major's reputation remains high, despite attempts to render it otherwise. Something else, I believe, that might be laid at your door. However, I'm not just talking about poor Sutton. Before him there was Selby at St Omer, who was equally dubious about some of your statements. You see, there seems to be a certain pattern.'

'I heard none of this when I was wined and dined by the brass at GHQ, or anywhere else for that matter.'

'No, you wouldn't have. We'd just about had enough of this alarmist Fokker Scourge ballyhoo and needed a success. You were in luck, the timing was perfect. It was convenient to give you the benefit of the doubt and treat you as a regular blue-eyed boy – that is, until you deflowered a daughter of France in sordid circumstances.'

'A daughter of France? You'd think we were talking about Marianne herself.'

'If the French authorities hear of this, that's pretty well what it will come down to. You're a liability, Sutro, and life is difficult enough.'

Guv pushed back his chair and stood up. 'Obviously I'm wasting my time, but it seems a damnably shabby way to treat a chap who's just trying to do his duty.'

'If this chap you speak of did only his duty,' said the major, 'we wouldn't be having this conversation. But he does too many other things as well.'

'So I take it this interview is over.'

'You asked to see us, old boy, not t'other way round. That's for you to decide.'

Guv sat down again. 'Look, I'll admit I've rocked the boat but you've invested too much time and trouble to chuck me over now.'

'There's something in that, dammit.'

'In which case, why not see if you can fix things up?'

'What things? You're in no position to make demands. You talk easily of doing your duty. That includes doing your duty on the ground. That includes doing your duty to us.'

'Look,' said Guv, 'I'll go along with any morale-boosting wheezes you dream up, act the hero up to the hilt. Interviews, lectures, factory tours, the whole shebang. All I want in return is a decent machine, not some bloody clapped-out deathtrap like a Martinsyde, so I can get back to the business of killing Hun.'

'That's all?'

'That's all. Meanwhile, I'll pay off this Gallic bumpkin if that's what's concerning you. Obviously I have the means, whatever he tries to screw out of me.'

'What concerns me,' said the major, 'is that you're a disgrace to the uniform, Sutro, and the pity of it is, we can't admit it.' He crossed to the door, opened it and stood back. 'How long are you here?'

'Four days.'

'Where? At your club or will you be reminding your family what you look like?'

'I'll be in Rye. The town's putting on some sort of shindig for me. I haven't been back since the Fokker show.'

'Set a day aside for us. We require you to meet some press johnnies. On the matter of your posting we'll see what might be done.'

'I suppose I must thank you.'

'Don't thank me,' said the major coldly. 'It's a case of saving our own skins, not yours. By the way,' he added, 'how do you view the prospect of a tadpole?'

'Tadpole?'

'A little frog, or hadn't it crossed your mind?'

'Oh, I see. She'll probably get rid of it.'

'Did she say so?'

'No, but these people know how to handle such matters. They'll probably come out of it quite well.'

With the door closed, the major said: 'Do you think he'll do the decent thing?'

'What decent thing?' asked the civilian. 'You mean, the child?'

'No,' said the major. 'I mean get himself killed.'

2

Lydia Sutro had the baby Alice on her lap. She sat in the picture window of the drawing room at High And Over (she had now learned to call it naturally by this name). Outside, beyond the garden, the parkland fell away to the broad valley divided into many fields where animals moved slowly in the late-summer heat. The land had been cleared of woodland two centuries ago to improve the prospect but a few solitary oaks remained, the earth beneath their branches bare and brown where beasts gathered to rub their haunches on the trunks and take the shade.

The baby's fingers were tight around the ivory ring of a silver rattle with little acorn-shaped bells and a whistle at one end. Lydia prised it carefully from her grasp and blew the whistle. Alice gazed at her solemnly but did not smile. Lydia shook the rattle several times with the same result. The small hand reached out and took back the rattle.

'This is such a good thing you are doing,' Lydia said to Guv. He was sprawled sideways on a green armchair, the only comfortable place to sit, the rest of the furniture in Oriental style, black lacquer pieces inlaid with mother of pearl or gilt, not intended for everyday use but designed to be admired like exhibits in a museum. It was a room Guv hated and had plans for.

'What thing is that?' he said.

'Going into business with Stanley Kemp.'

'Oh, that. Well, it seems a reasonable proposition.'

'I thought of going to see him at the hospital.'

'And why should you want to do that?'

'We shared some pleasant conversations here. I thought he was such a worthy soul. So sad that his time in France with you should end so badly. I'd like to lend him my support, tell him how pleased I am about your venture together.'

'It's just a business arrangement.'

'Oh, more than that, surely? After all, he has no family now. You are his lifeline.'

'What nonsense you talk.'

'You always shrug such things aside, my dear, but it is not unmanly to admit to fellow feelings.' The baby threw the rattle on the floor. Lydia sighed and picked it up. 'I suppose I'd be bound to mention his engagement also. Of that I'm not so sure. I must say it came as a surprise. I had no idea he knew our Rose so well.'

'Our Rose? She was hardly here long enough to call her that.'

'Perhaps not, but I always felt there was something between us, a familiarity, something . . . shared. I suppose he must have met her here but he visited so briefly.'

'Oh no,' Guv said, too quickly to catch himself. 'They met at Brooklands.'

'Brooklands?'

'She worked in the tea rooms there.'

Lydia looked puzzled. 'I did not realise she was known to you before. I thought she came here on her cousin's recommendation.'

'She did. But Paget also fixed her up with the Brooklands job, just before the war.' He did not say it was the other way round. 'She was not there long, but long enough for Stan. He was smitten from the first, the loon. It used to be a joke around the Flying Village.'

'How odd,' said Lydia. 'I'm positive you did not tell me this.'

Guv recovered himself. 'I'm positive I did, but it's hardly important. Our acquaintance was no more than her serving me a pot of tea.'

Lydia ran a hand over Alice's velvety scalp. 'I have no doubt she was frightfully popular with all those dashing pilots. Perhaps that explains why she has such a very high opinion of herself.'

'I thought you liked her well enough.'

The baby made to throw the rattle down again but Lydia caught it. 'Oh, she made herself agreeable certainly, but like most extremely pretty young women she is very conscious of the fact and I fear she uses it to her advantage. Men are such gullible creatures.' She moved her position so Alice could look out of the window, and pointed at distant horses. 'I'm surprised she should take up with poor Kemp. I'm not entirely sure it's the right thing for him. I do so hope I'm wrong. He's had such awful luck.'

'Why poor Kemp? A lot of fellows would envy him. He's going to survive the war, he's due to wed a likely girl and he's about to be set up in business at somebody else's expense. Damned good luck, I'd say – the best.'

'Perhaps you're right. His luck, my dear, is knowing you. True friends are hard to find.' Lydia stood up, carrying the baby on her arm, bent and kissed Guv on the top of his cheek and moved towards the door. 'It is wonderful to see you home again. One day it will be like this all the time, to spend as we like together.'

The prospect chilled Guv's blood. He thought he would shoot some crows. In the woodland (his woodland) the wind stirred the tops of the trees. Somewhere pigeons landed with a whistle of wings, reminding him of that copse in France. He took up the shotgun resting in the crook of his arm, placed two cartridges in the chambers, snapped the barrels closed and thumbed back the hammers; the double click took him to another place. He imagined what he might have done, instead of waiting to be struck down like some dumb beast in an abattoir. He imagined how it would be to have that damned Pettit in front of him now, the positions reversed; what he would do. He moved to the edge of the wood and stood knee-deep in bracken scanning the open fields where the crows liked to feed, but they were not to be seen. High up and to his right, two pigeons were moving along a branch, the male puffed up with lust. He shot them both and walked back to the house as their feathers came drifting down.

He saw Paget moving by the hangars. It was days since they had spoken; the first day of his leave. It was then, while Guv was going over his machines, that Paget had said, 'By the bye, Cuz would like to see you.'

'Why?'

'I don't know.'

'Of course you do.'

Guv had treated himself to a fast two-seater Hispano-Suiza. In this he drove down to meet Rose at a small bridge that spanned the Military Canal near Appledore. Sheep grazed the salt-grass of the marsh, calling to each other across the flat expanse, and sky larks sang their silver songs against a clear blue sky. Rose was already there. They stood like lovers, looking at the weed-choked water, each waiting for the other to speak.

'So,' said Guv at last. 'Perhaps you'd be good enough to tell me why I'm here.'

She smiled at him. 'I should have thought you'd guess.'

'You want more money for your rent. Isn't the place in Hastings good enough for you any more?'

'Oh, it'll do for the time being. It's the future that concerns me now. Thanks to you, I'm in a particular fix. Of course, you can deny it all you like but there's plenty I can tell that would win folk round. Mud sticks once it's flung and I've got a whopping handful. So here's a proposition for you.' She had it all worked out – to marry Stan and give the child a father. For that, and for their silence, Guv would pay; perhaps a nice little business somewhere handy.

'You think he'd be fool enough to go along with that?'

'He'd take me at any price.'

'How much does he know?'

'Not much. I've been to see him at Folkestone once, poor devil. I wonder you haven't been yourself.'

'I have no reason, unlike you.' Suddenly Guv laughed. 'Tell me, do you know the nature of his injuries?'

'Not in any detail, no.'

'Oh, I should ask. It might have some bearing on the matter.' His smile faded. He kicked the towpath mud. 'There's still no proof the brat's mine. I'm inclined to suggest you can go to hell.'

'Inclined, are you?' said Rose. She took a piece of paper from her small embroidered drawbag. She held it up. 'This is a copy,' she said. 'Harry has the original safe, the one you threw away.' She began to unfold it. 'What does the name Mary Grey mean to you?'

'Nothing.'

'Perhaps this will remind you.' She began to read aloud: '*Dear Mr Sutro, thanks ever so much for your card and kind thoughts.*' Guv's expression changed. She broke off. 'I see you remember her now. That was nice of you, wasn't it, sending the girl a card with kind thoughts?'

'Not me,' Guv said. 'Stan took it on himself—'

'Come off it,' said Rose. 'Who'd believe that, do you think?' She held up her hand and went back to the letter, tracing the lines with her finger, smiling. '*You must be ever so busy with your flying machines,*' she read, '*and now getting wed to your grand lady. Things are much the same with me. Matters must take their course, I suppose. I have not told anyone about my situation.*' She looked at him. 'What do you think she meant?'

'How should I know?'

Rose read on: '*I'm feared I do not know which way to turn. But as you say, I must keep my pecker up. I understand how this places you but I am your friend and would do nothing to harm you.*' She paused for emphasis. '*That is not to say that any help would not be most gratefully accepted.*'

She folded the letter and returned it to her bag. 'All sounds a bit familiar, don't it? So what do you say to that?'

'I've never seen it before.'

'No, that's true. What you saw was the original Harry stuck back together after you chucked it out. Makes interesting reading, don't you think?'

'Not to me.'

'Oh, it should. It affects you most of all. You see, we looked into the business of Mary Grey. Went right through the newspapers and found the Coroner's report. She died in the most peculiar circumstances. She wasn't at all the kind to take her own life. By all accounts she went off happy to meet someone she trusted and knew well, but somehow wound up drowned. And after, they found she had a kid inside her. They never did find that person she went to meet, though it seems likely he was the one what done her in, so the only verdict they could come in with was accidental death, not having a name. But this note's the connection, you see. It gives a name – your name, and what I think they call a motive in penny dreadfuls – and who knows what steps the law might choose to take?'

Guv took a pace forward. Rose did not move. 'Be convenient, wouldn't it? Another little splash?' She replaced the copy letter in her drawbag. 'This ain't my only insurance.' She pointed across the canal. Paget was sitting astride a bicycle, smoking a cigarette.

The next day Rose went to the hospital in Folkestone and saw Stan Kemp for the second time. Through Paget she got a note to Guv saying it was all agreed, that as soon as he felt able, Stan would stand by her; that she knew what had happened to him but it didn't make no difference. Guv doubted that it would. She added that she had seen a derelict smithy on the Military Road and suggested he took a look, 'as a future partner, like.' It was at this point that he told Lydia of his intention and had to suffer her admiration for such a selfless act.

He had two days of his leave left. On the first a luncheon was held in his honour in Rye Town Hall, not an official civic function but a heartfelt gesture to a local hero by the townsfolk who had got together a subscription to pay for the spread. Market Street was hung about with patriotic bunting and children had been let out of school to see the guests arrive. Captain Sutro, splendid in his uniform at the wheel of the Hispano-Suiza, his wife and baby by his side, raised ringing cheers. The town band, only old men left in this third year of war, puffed and banged its way through its repertoire: 'There'll Always Be An England', 'It's A Long Way To Tipperary', 'Sussex By the Sea'. From the top table Guv gave a short and becomingly modest response to a long and rambling address by a councillor who reminisced about other wars, jingling his campaign medals on his morning coat, and said how heartening it was to see the honour of this Scepter'd Isle passing from one generation's hands (his own, it was implied) to another's (polite applause from the ladies, much banging on tables by the men). Outside, photographs were taken and the church bells began to ring. Alice bawled and Guv took her in his arms, the picture of a devoted and loving father.

At High And Over, with the baby put to bed, Guv and Lydia found themselves alone in the library. 'I can't bear to let you go,' she told him.

Guv poured himself another whisky. 'I'm off to Town tomorrow. More propaganda nonsense.'

'Must you?'

'Duty calls.'

'How conscientious you are.'

'My leave's almost up. I'll stay at the club and go back from there.'

'Do you know what they have in store for you?'

'My posting, you mean? No, haven't a clue. Doubtless they'll have me flying some dreadful old bus they shouldn't use for training.'

'It's a poor reward,' said Lydia. 'I simply can't understand how they can use you like this, when you seemed so certain of your command.'

'It's the way of things in the service. Ours not to reason why.'

'Oh, don't say that. I know how the rest of it goes.'

'Yes, well,' said Guv, rolling the whisky round his cheeks. 'There it is.'

The usual ringing silence fell between them until Lydia said: 'I really can't say too often, my dear, how much I respect you for what you're doing for Stanley Kemp. Poppa would have been so pleased with his son-in-law. It is the kind of thing he would have done himself. What a pity you were not able to see Kemp yourself. He could have thanked you face to face.'

'Rose Pringle conveyed the happy tidings. It's early days. Much detail to be worked out.' He refilled his glass. 'There is one other matter.' He took a gulp. 'There's a rather wonderful chap at Chézy-au-Bois, a Frenchman, rather up against it I'm afraid, farming a pretty hopeless parcel of land. The squadron flies from a couple of his fields. Despite all the upheaval he couldn't have been more helpful. He's become something of a chum. I'd like to help him out – financially, I mean. Strictly on a business basis, you understand, not charity. He'd be too proud for that.'

Lydia came towards him. There were tears on her cheeks. She laid her face on his chest, snuffling gently. 'Oh,' she murmured. 'Oh.' She raised her head and kissed him on his nearest part, his chin. 'Why ask, my dear, why ask?'

'I'm not asking exactly. Just making you aware. It's likely to be a significant sum.'

Lydia shook her head. 'No sum can be too much. With all that you have to cope with, and you spare time to think of this.' She stepped back, her hands clasping his, and gazed at him with wet, shining eyes. 'How fortunate I am, my dear. How fortunate in my husband.'

In the morning he ordered Paget to bring a car round to the front door to take him to Rye station. 'The Hispano?' Paget said.

'No, the Rolls. I don't like the idea of you having fun.'

They turned onto the Military Road, heading towards the town.

Paget slid back the glass partition. 'Still got that ticket for me?' he said over his shoulder.

'What ticket?'

'That one-way ticket to the Somme. If so, I reckon you might have wasted your money, at least if what Cuz says is true. Mind you, I've stuck to my part of the bargain as your devious little worm. Kept my eyes and ears open, but I ain't come up with anything yet. Apart, that is, from keeping myself informed on other matters.'

'One day, Paget, you'll hear something behind you. You'll turn round and you'll see me. It'll be the last thing you do.'

'Oh, I doubt it, Captain. I've got insurance, see, just like Cousin Rose. You should be a bit more careful about what you chuck out. You never know who's about.'

They were approaching a ramshackle building that lay back from the road, its brick walls green with damp. Under a pitched roof its entrance doors stood open, like a yawning mouth, framed by oak timbers in the shape of a giant horseshoe. Behind it, surrounded by a chicken-wire fence, crouched a bungalow of the coastal style that dotted the dunes and beaches from Winchelsea to Dungeness, thrown up with any materials that came to hand, as insubstantial as a tent. Paget pulled in without being told. Guv had closed the glass partition. Paget slid it open again. 'The old forge,' he said unnecessarily. 'This place has possibilities, don't you think?'

'Yes, for firewood. Got a match?'

'What you need is vision, Captain. When this bloody war's done and dusted it won't be just the nobs swanning about in motors. Even worms like me will have one. There's a good little business to be had and this is the right location.' The Rolls began to move. 'I reckon I'll get the details from the agent. It's been on the market for a good time now. We'd probably get it for a song.'

'We?'

'You'd better get used to the idea, old fruit. We're partners, ain't we, in a manner of speaking?'

At Charing Cross, Guv came out of the station and went down the Strand to Whitehall, cutting through the arched entrance to Horse

Guards parade, returning salutes from various ranks who, after France, resembled toy soldiers. At the War Office he was met by the civilian who summoned an official car and accompanied him to the Savoy where a journalist was waiting. On the way Guv said: 'Any news for me about my posting?'

'Oh yes, we've sorted something out.' The civilian handed him a form. He was still to report to the base near Poperinge, but would not be flying Martinsydes. Nor would he be more than loosely attached to the squadron there. He was to be provided with a new Bristol Scout single-seater that had been delivered from the factory to Brooklands where he was to collect it and fly it on to Poperinge. There he would operate as a free-hunt singleton engaged on aggressive contact patrol. 'I gather these Scouts are new types, scarcer than feathers on a fish. Only a few of our best men are to get them. You are still in that category, just. You see what we can do for you as long as you behave as we expect you to behave?'

In the Mall a troop of Blues and Royals clattered past on their black mounts, the sunlight brilliant on their brass helmets and cuirasses. 'A beautiful sight, is it not?' said the civilian.

'An illusion,' Guv said. 'As much to do with war as Peter Rabbit.'

'You are incorrigible, Sutro. A hopeless case. I fear we are wasting our time with you. *Cuisuis hominis est errare, nullius nisi insipientis in errore perseverare.* Do you know Cicero?'

'Didn't he swim the Channel in 1912?'

The civilian sighed. '"Anyone can err but only the fool persists in his fault." As true today as it was in 40BC. You seem to go out of your way to be perverse. Surely you were taught the rudiments of the Classics? You went to Harrow, did you not?'

'Occasionally.' Guv was lighting his pipe. The civilian smothered a cough and fanned away the smoke. 'The truth is, I'm less concerned with Ancient Romans than this scribbler you want me to butter up. Just what is he expecting, apart from a free tipple or two?'

'He is expecting a simple, stout-hearted British hero, modest and unaffected, a true patriot who, like the knights of yore, engages the enemy in single combat because it is his duty, an inspiration to every

man and boy who has not yet answered his country's call, a model
to every woman so that she may shame sluggards and cowards to do
the decent thing.'

'That's a mouthful,' Guv said. 'Perhaps you'd better write it
down.'

The civilian compressed his lips until they showed white. His voice
was suddenly sharp. 'Get as close to it as you can. You can act the
part, when you have a mind – I've seen you do it. If you let us down
again you'll find yourself in the basket of an observation balloon, not
flying a Bristol Scout.'

Guv said nothing to that but watched the women passing along
the baking pavements on the Strand, their parasols shielding their pale
faces from the sun. '*Qui tacet consentire videtur*,' said the civilian.
'"He who is silent is taken to agree."'

The tobacco in Guv's pipe had not caught. He struck a vesta and
held it to the bowl between thumb and forefinger. The flame grew
and died, grew and died as he sucked on the mouthpiece. He glanced
across at the civilian. 'Enough damned Latin. If you don't hold your
breath, I'll set fire to your bloody toga.' He allowed the flame to
burn down the stem of the vesta and sear his flesh. He made no
attempt to blow it out. 'That's what this is about,' he said as the
civilian winced. 'Denial of fear, denial of pain. It doesn't matter.
Nothing matters. Understand that and you're free.' The flame sput-
tered and died in a twist of grey smoke.

'Free to do what?' said the civilian.

'Whatever you like. Nothing can touch you. Whatever you like.'

'There,' said the civilian. 'There lies our difficulty.'

The journalist was waiting in the lobby of the Savoy. When Guv
came through the revolving doors he was recognised but people did
not approach him; they only looked at him in a shy or curious way
and murmured to each other. Some of the women smiled and blushed.
Two or three were passable.

The civilian told him the journalist's name. Guv shook his hand.
It was like a just-washed empty glove. They went through to a private
room where a waiter had alcohol ready. The journalist had a centre

parting, spectacles with one darkened lens, a celluloid collar and a bow tie. The fingers holding the pad and pencil were stained yellow from cheap cigarettes. He did fast shorthand, a talent that struck Guv as girlish. 'Why aren't you fighting?' he said.

'Blind in one eye.'

'You should have been a general.'

'May I quote you on that?'

'You may not,' cut in the civilian. 'And if there's any doubt, this interview ends now.'

Guv gave the journalist the usual serving from the same old menu and saw it gobbled down, to be sicked up in the morning edition that was brought to his attention by the waiter in the Royal Aero Club at breakfast next day. The front page was occupied with photographs of politicians, well-fed men with reassuring moustaches. The headline said they had reorganised themselves to win the war. The waiter opened the paper to page two:

CAPTAIN SUTRO'S THRILLING ACCOUNT
Gallant airman who brought down a deadly Fokker

'That's the stuff to give 'em, sir.'

Guv glanced at the story and put the paper aside. 'Thanks, I'll take more coffee.'

A pilot he knew by sight at a nearby table said; 'Do you pay these Grubb Street hacks out of your own pocket, Sutro, or do they run this blood and thunder of their own accord?'

'It's out of my hands, Packenham,' Guv said. 'All cooked up by the ministry wallahs.'

'But you provide the ingredients, old man. Somewhat vulgar, don't you think? Out of kilter with the spirit of the service. Not the thing at all.'

Guv poured himself more coffee. 'I hear you're doing a sterling job at Upavon, Packenham, teaching schoolboys how to fly. Must be hell.' He went over to Packenham's table and dropped the newspaper beside his plate of eggs and bacon. 'Take a squint, why don't you? You might pick up some tips.' He went back to his room, removed his uniform and lay on the bed in his underwear smoking his pipe.

He had changed into civilian clothes the previous evening and strolled along to the New Gaiety hoping to spot the little brunette in the chorus but was told she had been dismissed. He went on to a low music hall in Shoreditch where the women performers dressed as men and sang crude songs badly to an audience composed largely of women dressed as men and men dressed as women. There was a bar dispensing double whiskies at fourpence a glass and he lolled there befuddled by the scene around him until he was approached by a creature he could not identify and went out into the night to find a taxi to deliver him back to Piccadilly. On the way he thought Percy Fritchley was with him singing his infernal song:

If by some delightful chance, when you're flying out in France
Some old Boche machine you meet, very slow and obsolete . . .

Then he realised he was the singer and the cabbie was looking back at him, wondering whether to put him down where they were. He let the tune die. Odd, to think of old Percy like that. It had not been all that long ago, that evening they spent at the Gaiety where he came across that little tart; and after, at Simpsons when he and Fritchley concocted new verses to Grossmith's ditty until a joint of beef arrived and Critchley had to totter off because the smell of roast flesh reminded him of the Morane-Saulnier crash at Farnborough that crisped his chum. And now he'd gone the same way, his family unable to stop him going back to test flying before his burns had properly healed and he made a cack-handed approach and hit a pylon and the flames had got him after all. That was the thing: no one thought it could happen to you again, and then it did.

At the Club he told the night porter to bring a bottle of Glenfiddich to his room. He poured himself shots in the bedside glass, diluting it with tap water from the wash-hand basin. He was not sure why he drank. The question was: why not? He had not eaten and he felt the spirit swill around his empty stomach like chemical in a flask. He was back in the lab at Harrow school, with the teacher's drone. 'Chemical changes (are you listening, Sutro?) are simply reactions; they are transformations. Clear?' The beak had been bang on. The old Glenfiddich was transforming him all right, as surely as Jekyll's potion changed him into Hyde. But Sutro wasn't changing into Hyde. He was still Sutro, but more so. That was the way it felt to him.

He did not sleep but dozed. He saw Sabine Pettit falling away from him screaming, twisting her head as he came down on her; the journalist who now had no eyes at all, just black holes, saying over and over, 'May I quote you on that?'; Lydia coming towards him with her heavy arms held out and tears in her eyes; an infant in a cot, Alice perhaps, but when he looked closer and peered in, it had a tiny French moustache; Percy Critchley singing, prancing, dressed as a woman, his face melted, his hands charred claws; Rose Pringle and Harry Paget together in the Hispano-Suiza coming at him out of the sun at 10,000 feet and opening fire.

At four in the morning he put on his tweeds and went out into Green Park. A policeman went by on his beat and nodded but did not speak. Everything was heavy with dew. It smelled like country. A dull silence hung over the city, as if its people lay dead in their homes, extinguished by some sort of plague. He walked to the Victoria Memorial and stood on the steps looking across at Buckingham Palace. The royal standard hung limp, a rag on a pole. He imagined the King snoring inside: George, by the Grace of God, of the United Kingdom, of Great Britain and Ireland, and of the British Dominions beyond the Seas, King, Defender of the Faith, Emperor of India who had appointed his trusty and well-beloved Fraser Sutro an officer in the RFC and commanded him to carefully and diligently discharge his duty. George, asleep now, snoring, an old man with a beard.

Guv went back through the park, not taking the paths, leaving a silver trail across the grass. A flight of ducks passed overhead in v-formation bound for the lakes in St James's. They flew well, fast and close, intuitive to each change of height and course. He would fly again, and soon.

Now, after breakfast, stretched out on the bed in his room, his pipe had gone out. His head throbbed and he looked for the

Glenfiddich for an answer, but it lay on the floor empty. He stood up, went to the sink, knocked out the ash and turned on the tap. A stench rose up, the smell of a bonfire damped down by rain. He was briefly sick, but there was no substance to it, only liquid. He brushed his teeth, shaved and stared at himself in the small wall mirror. It was the only time he looked at himself, when he shaved. He hardly recognised the man who looked back.

He checked his Omega watch, Lydia's gift. 'When you look at this, my darling, think of me.' Confound it, he always did. In forty minutes the car would arrive to deliver him to Brooklands. He was curious to take up the Bristol Scout. He had got used to the company of an observer, had not flown alone since before the war. He knew the Scout was manoeuvrable and quick, good for 100 miles an hour with a ceiling of 16,000 feet. His would come unarmed, its single Lewis gun to be fitted to his specifications at Poperinge. The options were limited – mounted to the side of the cockpit or above his head on the centre section of the upper wing; limited because British boffins had so far failed to match Anthony Fokker and devise their own interrupter gear so a machine-gun could shoot through a spinning propeller. But 6 Squadron's Lanoe Hawker had done well enough with the old arrangement, his weapon clamped to the port fuselage, angled at forty-five degrees to miss the wings and prop. It was far from ideal, restricting an attack to the enemy's right rear quarter. If a two-seater, the Hun observer was gifted his best field of fire. Even so, Hawker had attacked three Hun on his own. Guv read the account in the *London Gazette*, how one had spun down and escaped, one (damaged) forced down, a third shot to bits in the air. For this the Captain had won his VC. Guv envied him that. He intended to do the same thing himself.

3

At Brooklands the airfield was overlaid by low cloud, down to 200 feet. A turbulent sky echoed to the thunder of an approaching storm. There were more buildings than before. Outside the Vickers hangar, someone was running up the engine of a BE2. More BE2s were parked nearby; elsewhere some Avro 504s and a Martinsyde Scout. But no one was in the air.

An RFC lieutenant took Guv to see his Bristol, still smelling new, with the lines of a fashionable pre-war racer. 'There she is, sir. Lovely little bus. But you won't get off to France today.'

'Really? Why's that?' Guv pulled himself onto the lower wing and studied the controls; they fell nicely to hand.

The lieutenant waved at the darkening sky. 'Well, it's pretty beastly already and likely to get worse.'

'Oh, I think I can find France all right. It's that big place opposite Dover.'

'All the same,' said the lieutenant, 'I think you should chew it over with the Old Man. He'll have an opinion on the matter.'

'Will he?' said Guv. He jumped down. 'Lead on.' It was a one-sided exchange. In thirty minutes he was on his way.

The Bristol was a delight, lively and responsive. It seemed to fit him as snugly as his flying suit. But he was unable to put it to the test until he climbed to 4,000 feet through still-unbroken cloud, leaving the stormfront behind him to the west, emerging at last into the dazzling world that only fliers know. The cloudscape below was white as fresh-fallen snow and stretched as far as he could see, its phantom mountains and dizzying canyons all washed by a brilliant sun suspended in a pale blue sky. It looked as tangible and unchanging as the Alps, but it would not be here tomorrow.

He threw the Bristol through his repertoire of stunts, a tiny moving speck in the vast arena, unheard, unseen. Then, with the sun over his right shoulder, he set a south-easterly course on his compass and dropped down to the surface of the cloud-mass, skimming across its surface as if it was solid land. The Bristol's Le Rhone engine sounded strong and reassuring, but its unbroken bellow did not help his head. His initial euphoric mood, induced by much Glenfiddich, had passed. He needed another dram or two to restore his joie de vivre.

He was flying a similar course to the one he took before the war, chasing the 5,000 francs put up by *La Tribune du Nord*; Weybridge to Dover, the starting-point, with a stop at Headcorn to refuel except he never found Headcorn and had been forced to put down at High And Over – he thought of it as that, Saxonshore quite forgotten – where everything began.

Below, by now, lay Kent. He planned to refuel at the Flying Corps landing ground on the cliffs above Dover harbour. It was no more than insurance. The Bristol's fuel tank held thirty gallons. With a cruising speed of 100 miles per hour it was enough for a two-hour flight. The calculation was neat: Weybridge to Dover, eighty miles; Dover to Calais, thirty; Calais to Poperinge, fifty. Forty miles left and time to spare, but wiser to top up at Swingate than deplete the stock of fuel in France. Besides, his little display to amuse the gods had guzzled an extra gallon or two.

It was time to pinpoint his position. He would go down and identify a landmark or two; perhaps High And Over itself. He pushed forward on the control column, his senses alert. He knew the penalty for losing concentration. Immersed in cloud, a pilot could become disorientated, confused. It was a hard-learned skill, this business of senses, this feel for the buoyancy of your machine. They called it 'flying instinct', although no training school paid that much attention; it was too vague. It only came with flying hours – if you survived: the gauging of lift and angle and speed, the approach of a stall, the line between flying and falling, all conducted in an element that could be felt but not seen; felt by its howl through your wires and struts, by the stiffness or softness of ailerons and rudder, by the shake and the rattle of a particular machine at a particular point, by the pressure or lack of it coming up through the stick, by countless small ways of testing your buoyancy, all coming together to put yourself down in a perfect three-pointer, so close to a stall that it could only be sensed.

It was an art, flying well, and your situation was never the same. In that huge void above the earth there was no space for complacency, even for the most skilled. How many men, descending through dense cloud as Guv was now, had broken clear to find they had 100 feet to play with, not the expected 1,000; had been granted just enough time to watch the ground come up with nothing to be done apart from pull the stick back into the lap and feel the stall (those senses in play but far too late), the nose shudder and drop, to experience the final plunge, the impact, if lucky nothing more, if not the flames, to leave their blackened remains in a ring of fire that people ran to see and would never forget. All for a careless moment, ignoring the messages sent by brain and body, not reading the myriad signs, not seeing those precious 100 feet unwinding on the altimeter, so easy to miss like not checking a watch. Except the sky is not the Strand, where men may stroll without concern, aware they are late for the start of a show because they forgot to check a watch. Nothing is trivial in the air, where the slightest lapse, the merest complacency, may be punished by death.

Guv was not complacent. He knew the penalties for mistakes; had seen them paid. His senses were fine tuned. He was as close as a man could be to a creature of the air. But even he was vulnerable if the cards fell badly for him; like this damned, impenetrable cloud that seemed to reach down to the tree-tops. But he could not blame the weather. He had dealt his own hand, brushing aside the concerns of the officer commanding back at Brooklands.

'I cannot order you not to take off, Captain, but I must warn you that if you insist on doing so, we can bear no responsibility. Naturally I have to respect your record, but it seems to me that you are displaying a high degree of recklessness, given the conditions.'

'A high degree of recklessness is not unknown in France, Major. Perhaps it is less common here.'

'I see you are determined. On your own head be it. Good luck.'

He had expected the cloud to thin as he progressed east, but he was wrong. He had squandered fuel by stunting in a new-built, unproven machine that might fold up under stress; this was also wrong. Most of all, he had to concede, he had been wrong to go up at all. He put it down to Glenfiddich and would not fly drunk again.

The cloud, cold and full of moisture that fogged his goggles and soaked his flying suit, whipped backed in strands across his wings, giving an impression of great speed, of rushing downwards, suggesting the ground might be rushing up. The altimeter showed 1,500 feet, the airspeed indicator 110; too fast but not to be relied on, no more than a pressure gauge reacting to the impact of the air, its reading varying with conditions – if cold like now, always optimistic. Guv's senses told him the descent speed was right, not too fast, not too slow; not 110. He had good control but the seconds were passing. He eased back on the control column, came out of the dive and put the Bristol straight and level, the lateral floating bubble of the horizon indicator telling him his wings were straight.

He began to reduce height foot by foot, expecting at any moment to see the wraiths of cloud disperse and see below the green fields of Kent. Then, mixed with the engine roar, he heard a hissing sound. At first he thought it was wind in the bracing wires. How did that black joke go? 'When you're about to go west your bracing wires start humming "Nearer My God To Thee".' There was a surge of something huge below, like a great beast stirring. And then he was out and clear and 50 feet above the sea, where white-topped waves of emerald green raced in ranks along the Channel, their spray sharp on his tongue. Ahead he saw broad empty beaches with, behind, great banks of sand stretching far inland; no sign of habitation. The coast was wrong for Calais, his usual crossing-point; more like Gravelines, just west of Dunkirk. The Bristol's engine missed a beat. It was like a meaningful clearing of the throat, a discreet reminder that fuel was running low; the tank not dry, not yet, but likely to be quite soon, in fifteen minutes say.

Guv extended his arm and twisted his wrist to look at his watch. It confirmed that he had been in the air for ninety minutes. He had been aware of the passage of time but ignored it, intent on finding his way out of the infernal cloud in one piece. But this was no bloody good. He had managed to miss the English coast entirely. He was lucky to make land at all. He might have drowned in mid-Channel. He had perhaps fifteen minutes of flying time left.

He tracked the beach east, so low the wash from his propeller raised small storms of sand. If the engine cut now he could land on the strand, but though temptingly flat it could conceal soft mud, and then there were tides. Better to go on to Dunkirk. He knew of the

RFC airfield there, where the squadrons chased Taube bombers that raided the town and intercepted the occasional Zeppelin on its way to bomb England. He would land and report in. Egg-on-face all right but it could happen to anyone (the cards had fallen badly for him, that was all). He had already dismissed any earlier misgivings about dealing his own hand, being wrong to go up at all, wasting fuel on pointless stunting in a untested machine, resolving that he would not, in future, accept Dr Glenfiddich's prescription for well-being in the air. He was going to come through it all right.

Ahead and to the right he saw the twin spires of a large church facing a substantial sea port busy with shipping. He did not remember a church so close to the port of Dunkirk. He turned towards it. He passed low over the town and in the narrow streets people stopped and looked up. He circled looking for the airfield, pivoting on a wing above the church. Its design was old but the fabric looked new; the spires ornate and distinctive. He remembered seeing a photograph of them in some magazine before the war, some grand occasion, a royal event, an inauguration. He recalled the magazine: the *Illustrated London News*. He now recalled the town: Ostend.

At the same moment he heard machine-gun fire and the deep thump-thump of anti-aircraft guns. Bullets were flicking through the canvas of his wings and shells began to burst around him. He dived to rooftop level, counting on the gunners to hold their fire, unwilling to risk damaging houses and killing civilians. One of his wheels took off a chimney-pot. He turned for open country, lower still, flashing across a straight white road. Two military trucks slid to a halt and men spilled out, unslinging their rifles. Their uniforms were grey. He banked to the west, his starboard wing-tip almost grazing the ground, and levelled out with throttle wide, dipping and rising over the hedges and woodland, the Bristol unstable so close to the ground, jinking and twisting, hard to control. A shadow passed over him. He looked up. An Albatros two-seater was manoeuvring above him at 800 feet, wary of coming down on a high-speed scout, unaware he was unarmed. He pulled up to meet them and they turned away. He whooped and pounded the cockpit side but then, as he turned back on his westerly course, the engine coughed and died. His ears were left ringing in the sudden silence; a silence broken by the moan of air across the Bristol's wings and the distant, rising note of the Albatros turning back.

He had good speed to prevent a stall, as long as he was quick. He chose a field close by a sprawl of buildings; too late he realised it was a barracks with men drilling on a square. The ground came up, the wheels and tail skid touched: the engine smell of fuel and oil mixed with furrowed grass.

He turned his head. The Albatros was coming down, the observer swivelling his gun. The Bristol was still rolling fast. Ahead he saw a dark expanse of earth spread across the light green of the turf, a scatter of mole hills. He kicked the rudder and the machine started to come round, lurching and skidding, the port wing digging in and throwing up mud, but the landing wheels drove into the mounds of earth. The Bristol bounced, its nose came up, sank down, the wind-milling propeller dug in and stopped and it flipped neatly onto its back. In a moment Guv was hanging on his harness, the ground above his head. At least there was no fire; not enough fuel for that. He released his harness, careful not to drop out and break his neck, and scrambled clear.

The Albatros was landing 100 yards away. The crew jumped down and ran towards him, one with a pistol in his hand. He found a rag in a pocket of his flying suit and twisted it into a narrow strip. The fuel tank had split and he soaked the rag with the dregs of petrol spreading across the torn fabric of the inverted upper wing. The Germans were very close now, shouting at him to raise his hands. He fumbled in his suit and found his lighter, snapped it alight, put the flame to the rag and tossed it onto the hot engine. It ignited with a satisfying *womp* that burned off his eyebrows.

The German airmen were on him now, pushing him away from the burning wreckage. One said unnecessarily, in excellent English: 'You're our prisoner. Please, raise your hands. It's useless to think of escape.' The speaker waved his pistol in the direction of the barracks where a line of troops was advancing towards them across the open ground. 'I regret you've burned your machine,' he said, 'but of course your action was correct. Tell me, what type is it? It's new to me.'

'It's a Hun-knockerdowner. Mark Two.'

'I see,' said the German. 'Well, may I suggest we move far off? Your ammunition might explode.'

'There is no ammunition. I was unarmed.'

The German began to laugh. 'Priceless! You land forty kilometres behind our lines in an unarmed machine and destroy it yourself.'

'I was out of fuel. Otherwise . . .'

'Oh, better and better,' the German said. 'I really must thank you. Perhaps this is a new plan, the Royal Flying Corps doing our job for us.'

'You weren't laughing when I came for you just now. You buggered off smartish.'

The German nodded genially. 'Yes, that is true. I exercise prudence, my friend. That is why Claus and I have lived so long. *Nicht wahr, Claus?*'

The observer had been trying to follow the conversation. '*Ich verstehe nicht, Herr Leutnant.*'

'Claus does not understand. No matter. Soon, my friend, you will have plenty of time to learn how to speak good German. It is the *Kriegsgefangenenlager*, I am afraid, until we win the war.'

'What's that mouthful when it's at home?'

'Prison camp, my friend. You will be well cared for. You should not believe all the lies that your government spreads. We are a civilised people.'

'That's odd. Didn't you start a war?'

The Albatros pilot grinned. 'I see we might enjoy some interesting discussions. Perhaps I will visit you when you are established in your new accommodation. What is your name?'

'Sutro, Captain Sutro.'

The man raised an eyebrow. 'I believe I have heard of you. I am Leutnant Lothar Schoenfelder.' He bowed slightly. 'Until we meet again.' He handed his pistol to the observer and went to meet the infantrymen as they came panting up. The observer had the wavering barrel pointed at Guv's head. He almost hoped the man might squeeze the trigger. His brand-new Bristol was a smouldering heap and he was about to be marched off to the clink for the duration. It would certainly take some explaining.

4

In *Offizierslager Nr. 35*, a purpose-built camp at Custren on the River Oder, far to the east of Germany and close to the Polish border, Captain Fraser Sutro received a visitor. He had last seen him in a wooden hut at the airfield near Ostend where he flew Albatros two-seaters. There he had been the guest for dinner of Leutnant Schoenfelder and his fellow pilots. They had extracted him, temporarily, from the custody of his guards at the army camp after the crash in the Bristol and welcomed him with several glasses of punch – a powerful blend of brandy, schnapps, wine, champagne and crushed fruit, filled from a silver bowl. The Jasta commander, Rittmeister von Brauneck, toasted him as their 'valiant enemy' without a hint of irony. His name was known – *'eine Englischse Überkanone'*, which Schoenfelder translated as 'big gun'. Everything was familiar, the long wooden table laid formally for dinner with candles and winking silverware, the trophies cut from shattered aeroplanes hanging on the walls (odd to see the shot-up rudder of a BE2), the posters of provocative French mamzelles with scrawled, no doubt obscene remarks. There was music: an orderly placing scratched records of a Pigalle *chanteuse* on the gramophone.

The meal of pork chops, sauerkraut and apples was accompanied by many bottles of Rhine and Mosel wine. Guv quickly felt at ease as the alcohol took effect. This was a German drunk, quite the same as an English drunk. The banter flowed along with the wine. He could not understand it all but got the gist, much shop talk and swooping hands to illustrate recent actions, the usual gallows humour and bursts of laughter that rang a little thin, yarns of exploits in the town with Claudette, Frou-Frou, Hortense.

Von Brauneck rose in another toast. 'To our gallant foe, the Royal Flying Corps.'

Schoenfelder signalled to the orderly for a pencil, wrote something on the tablecloth and pointed it out to Guv. Guv pushed himself up. 'To *die Fliegertruppen des deutschen Kaiserreiches* (laughter at his pronunciation), ditto.'

More brandy was being passed round when an elderly corporal, too old for the Front, appeared at the door. Outside, another man was waiting in a car. The corporal seemed disconcerted by the jollity. He murmured something in von Brauneck's ear.

'I regret,' said the Rittmeister, 'that this fellow has orders to take our prisoner into custody.' He looked down the table at Guv almost apologetically: 'For prisoner, *Kapitan*, you are.'

That was the last time Guv had seen Leutnant Schoenfelder, as he walked with him to the waiting car, passing from the warm conviviality of the Mess to the cold night air and the stony faces and nervous trigger-fingers of his escort. Now, at Custren, Schoenfelder had called to see him. He was not told why.

In the commandant's office Schoenfelder was alone, leaning against the desk and smoking. He stood up, stubbing out his cigarette in an ash-tray. He touched his temple in a fleeting salute that was not returned. 'How are they treating you in this hotel, Sutro? Is the service satisfactory?'

'They're reluctant to say goodbye to their guests.'

'Yes, I understand the regime is more rigorous here than in your previous accommodation.' Schoenfelder leaned back against the desk. 'Please, sit down. It is good to see you again.'

'Really? Why?'

Schoenfelder grinned. 'Let me see, how long have you been a prisoner?'

'Eight months. Here, two weeks.'

'You have led your jailers a merry dance. Tell me, I am curious. Heidelberg, what happened at Heidelberg?'

'Is this an interrogation? I've been through all this before.'

'Not at all, my friend. I like to hear from the horse's mouth. That is the phrase, is it not? My English is a little rusty.'

'Why this particular horse?'

'I am a student of form.'

'What's this about? Where's the confounded commandant?'

'He is a cousin of mine. He has given me leave to renew our acquaintance, one pilot to another.'

'The first occasion was enough for me.'

Schoenfelder sat down behind the desk, stretched out his legs and rested the heels of his boots on the commandant's blotter. 'My family has factories in Berlin. I am on leave and Custren is not too far. What is the harm? Surely you do not object?'

'Well,' said Guv grudgingly, 'I can hardly say I'm not receiving visitors.'

'Yes, for the moment at least we have you detained.'

'Stabled, you might say,' Guv said. It seemed that Schoenfelder imagined a bond. It occurred to him that it might prove useful. Besides, he had no pressing engagements.

'So, Heidelberg,' prompted Schoenfelder.

'Very well,' said Guv. 'Little to tell. I buried myself under a truck full of rubbish and got as far as Baden-Baden. Unfortunately, the civvy get-up the escape committee ran up for me fell short of the sartorial standards of a spa town. As well as that, I smelled. I was picked up before I had a chance to take the waters. They took me back, then moved me east to Torgan on the Elbe.'

'Ah, Torgan. Yes, the German officer's uniform made from blankets. You have a poor opinion of our regimental standards.'

'It was midnight when I walked through the gate. The outfit served its purpose, good enough at least to receive a smart salute from the idiot of a sentry.'

'Your plan?'

'To find the Elbe, stow away on a likely vessel to take me north to Hamburg, then steal a boat. I laid up during the day and moved by night. Laid my hands on some togs hung out to dry at a farm. Got to the river all right and found my way onto a barge, one of a string being pulled by a steam tug. They'd been delivering munitions to the Balkans and were coming back stuffed with supplies from the Turks. I boarded when they put in at a small village. At the next big town there was some sort of hoo-ha. I heard later that en route the skipper had been doing deals of his own with the cargo. Half the German army came on board and they winkled me out.'

'Custren you will find a more difficult proposition,' said Schoenfelder. 'My cousin was Chief of Police in Eisenwald and knows his business. Also, you are far from any friendly borders. It may be, my friend, that you must resign yourself to a life of leisure. Although I imagine you have a plan.'

'Of course,' said Guv. 'Right now I'm thinking of knocking you cold, borrowing your uniform, finding my way to Berlin and getting to know some of the whores on the Unter den Linden.'

Schoenfelder laughed but removed his feet from the commandant's desk. 'Yes, for a man of your tastes, incarceration must be hard to bear.'

'What do you know of my tastes?'

Schoenfelder said nothing to that. 'Your escapades show imagination, Sutro. That I would expect. You have an excellent imagination. I have read, for example, the reports of our encounter at Ostend. The British press made much of it. To my surprise you emerged with credit from what, to most pilots, would be an embarrassment, choosing to fly in bad conditions, getting lost, running out of fuel, landing in enemy territory, destroying a new machine. A disaster, one might say. And yet it seems it was only the weather closing in without warning and malfunctioning instruments that led you so far from your course. Also, that you put up a gallant show unarmed, evading all attempts to bring you down with skilful flying, until a lucky shot from Claus, obviously a fluke, pierced your tank and you were forced to land. No mention that Claus did not open fire. No mention that you had run out of fuel. No mention, incidentally, of those little velvet gentlemen working for the Fatherland whose molehill tipped you up.'

'You seem easy enough with my version of events.'

'Of course. There is glory in it. Otherwise it was simply a matter of us witnessing a pilot make a series of stupid mistakes. As it is, Claus and I have come well out of the situation.'

Guv wondered where this was leading. 'How is Claus?'

'He is in fine fettle, most popular with those ladies you mentioned on the Unter den Linden, proud of his medal for bringing down the famous English *Überkanonen.*'

'What medal is that?'

'The Military Merit Cross, first class.'

'Good for Claus. And how about you?'

'The Iron Cross.'

'First-class or second?'

'An Iron Cross is an Iron Cross, my friend.'

'Ah, second.'

Schoenfelder stood up but did not turn his back. 'This war will not last for ever.'

'How is the war? The newspaper boys are very lazy here.'

'We fought the French at Verdun.'

'Who won?'

'Who can tell? Who can be believed? The Russians have been making a nuisance of themselves in the Baltic. Your countrymen have been active on the Somme. So it goes.'

'The French, the Russians, the British. The Kaiser must be sorry he picked a fight.'

'The effects of war are not entirely bad. Our factory, for example. Business has never been better.'

'What business is that?'

'Components for aeroplanes. Soon, entire machines.'

'I can understand you'd be busy,' Guv said, 'trying to replace the stuff we're shooting down.'

'Before the war,' said Schoenfelder, unruffled, 'I too was a sporting aviator. Not in your class, of course, but in Germany I had a certain reputation. I followed your career with interest.'

'Would you like my autograph?'

'It was not just your prowess in a machine that impressed me. I am also well connected. I understand how you have made your way. As with the incident at Ostend you have a knack for managing the truth, still close enough to be believed but no longer what might be called the truth.'

'Can we get to the point? I have a tunnel to dig.'

'I assume you are joking.'

'Oh no, we're about to break through. But don't tell your cousin. It's taken the chaps months to reach the wire.'

Schoenfelder smiled doubtfully. 'I will put that down to the English sense of humour. Wire has been buried around the perimeter to a depth of twenty feet. No tunnel could be successful.'

'That's useful information. We suspected something of the sort. I'm glad we didn't bother.'

Schoenfelder glanced at the clock on the office wall. 'I have no time for games. As I say, this war will not last for ever. Whoever wins, the world will not be the same. It will grow smaller, because of aviation. People will wish to fly. That is the opportunity, for our company to meet the need with suitable machines, to make them the natural choice for the commercial sector. For that, of course, they must be excellent designs, but that is not enough. It is necessary to prove that *Schoenfelder Aeronplau* not only manufactures products of the highest quality but is pledged to overcome national prejudices and heal the wounds of war.'

'You have a way with words, Schoenfelder. You should go into politics.'

'So I am told.'

'But you think ahead. That might count against you.'

'You also have a reputation, Sutro, that could be most useful to us. You are a fine pilot, of course, despite the mishap at Ostend. You are seen as a great hero, not just in your own country but in many others too. You are of interest to the press, whatever you choose to do. You mix with those who count, through your exploits and your place in society as a wealthy man with a great estate. And you are not constrained by the usual English reluctance to deviate from normal patterns of behaviour; the manipulation of facts, for example, to secure your objectives. With all this we are familiar.'

'So you've done your homework. What are you working round to, Schoenfelder?'

'You're an impatient fellow, Sutro, but you are correct. Perhaps

I am getting ahead of myself, but it is never too soon to consider the future. In a few years, if I survive, I will succeed my father as the principal of the business. Then I will have need of a man such as you, to put our name on the front pages of newspapers all over the world, to open doors where doors must be opened. You understand very well that your achievements in the air are a source of inspiration, that people are eager to be in your presence, to shake your hand, hoping that a little of the hero rubs off on them. In return we would put in your hands world-beating machines. Think of the records you might set.'

'There are plenty of your countrymen to choose from: Boelcke, Udet, von Richtofen himself.'

'A German pilot flying for a German firm? No, that does not accord with my strategy. Besides, Boelcke is dead. Have you not heard?'

'As I say, the newspaper boys are very lazy here . . .'

'Forty victories, but he did not fall to the enemy. He was killed in a collision with one of his own *Jasta*.'

'Do you expect me to say I'm sorry?'

'That was not the reaction of your comrades. A wreath was dropped, to the memory of a brave and chivalrous opponent.'

'What ruddy nonsense. The chap he collided with did my lot a favour. Stopped Boelcke chalking up number forty-one.'

To Guv's surprise, Schoenfelder openly smiled. 'You're a character, Sutro. It is a pity we did not meet before the war, in more favourable circumstances.'

'Can we cut the waffle? If I've got this right, you're offering me a job.'

'It is tentative at this stage. But partnership would be a better word.'

'So, an Englishman flying for the Hun.'

'In time, such xenophobia will count for nothing. Germany, England – are we really so very different? I think not. I was educated partly at Marlborough.'

'Partly?'

'A certain difficulty arose with a waitress in the tea rooms there.'

'I'm shocked.'

'But I was there long enough to gain an insight into your culture.'

'Yes,' said Guv. 'You might pass for an Englishman at midnight in a woollen uniform. But what if you lose the war? How much will your plans be worth then?'

'We will not lose. Victory is assured.'

'You sound like a politician again,' Guv said. They heard footsteps in the corridor outside. 'I'd like to know what the commandant would make of this,' he added slyly.

'Oh, he approves,' said Schoenfelder. 'He has a substantial shareholding in *Schoenfelder Aeronplau*.'

After Schoenfelder had gone and Guv had been returned to his hut the commandant summoned him back to his office. He was not a Schoenfelder but related to the Albatros pilot on his mother's side. His name was Thomson, descended from an English mercenary who had fought for the King of Prussia against Napoleon. 'At that time,' he explained in a friendly manner, 'we were allies against the French, the proper state of things. I take pride in my English connection.'

'The Kaiser's got English connections. It hasn't counted for much with him.'

Thomson shrugged. 'Now, your interview with Leutnant Schoenfelder . . .'

'I don't expect preferential treatment,' Guv said, 'if that's what's on your mind.'

'That is precisely what I wished to make clear. You will understand that such considerations must be, as you say, put on the shelf. I do not look so far ahead. I apply myself to the task in hand, keeping my gentlemen under lock and key.'

'Did Schoenfelder tell you about the tunnel?'

'What tunnel?'

'Nothing,' said Guv. 'May I go now?'

The commandant frowned. 'I am required to respect your rank. But I would remind you that you are subject to German law and must obey the rules of German discipline. Respect applies in two directions.'

'Have there been complaints?'

'I would remind you that if a German soldier gives you orders they must be obeyed without question. And you must salute officers. In these matters you have been neglectful. It is also forbidden to speak to the sentries. I received a report.'

'Yes, some insolent dolt shouted at me to get back from the wire. I simply replied.'

'What did you say?'

'It was along the lines of being a sausage-eating pointy-headed oaf whose mother—'

The commandant help up his hand. 'Please, Captain, enough. I am aware of your reputation for insolence and insubordination. I believe it was not much different in the Royal Flying Corps. Also, you are a slippery fish, hard to keep in the bowl. So far you have been fortunate with your captors. At Custren we are not so lenient. No one has escaped and we have no wish to see that record spoiled. It is of course your duty as an officer to attempt escape. My duty is to prevent it. My orders are that any prisoner apprehended outside the camp is to be shot. Also, any civilians he may speak to will suffer the same punishment. The townsfolk know this. You would find them . . . unsympathetic. May I urge you to exercise restraint and sit out the war? It is not so hard here, after all, if you observe the rules. You will find the time can be used constructively.'

'That's true. I've learned a good deal about escapology. You know, like Harry Houdini.'

The commandant sighed. 'That is quite enough. Leutnant Schoenfelder is a good judge of men. He must see in you what I fail to. May I hope that if there comes to be an association between you and *Schoenfelder Aeronplau* there is an improvement in your attitude.'

Guv looked non-committal. 'You can certainly hope.'

The commandant held out a bundle of letters tied up with string. 'Here is some post for you. It has been chasing you across Europe.'

Guv turned the bundle in his hands. 'I say, these envelopes have been opened.'

'Simply routine,' said the commandant. 'In case you are taking a correspondence course in escapology.' He shouted for the guard outside the door. 'Don't bother to salute on your way out. I will grant you that free of charge. Next time, solitary confinement.'

Guv shared his hut with officers of various nationalities, English, French, Belgian and a solitary Russian. All were at Custren because they were hard to hold. The hut was thick with tobacco smoke and the babble of foreign tongues. He lay on his bed and began to read his post. It had been forwarded to him from the squadron office at Poperinge, the airfield he never reached. The first advised him that his annual subscription to the Royal Aero Club was overdue; another, from his tailor, that a new uniform was ready for collection and that they respectfully awaited payment. A letter from Lydia, eight months out of date, wished him happy landings with his new squadron, told him that Alice was bonnier than ever (had uttered her first word, 'horse') and sent her fondest love.

She wrote again weeks later, distraught:

My dearest husband,

What a horrible time. At first I feared the worst. But of course how could I doubt that you would come out of it all right despite the beastly enemy taking advantage of your defencelessness? You did wonderfully well by all accounts. I am so proud of you. I show Alice your picture every day and she always smiles and kisses your dear face. You must not try to escape. I know it will be in your nature to do so, and that it is your duty. But we hear such awful tales. Please, for our sake, think of the future. This war will not last for ever and then we will be together again.

There was more, about people he did not know or care about. He looked at the postmarks and arranged the envelopes in order. The Royal Aero Club advised him of the renewal of his subscription by Mrs Sutro, acting on his behalf, regretting the news about his circumstances but looking forward to welcoming him back soon. The tailor confirmed that their bill had been settled and the uniform was in storage, awaiting his return. A letter from the Mayor of Rye urged him to keep his spirits up and promised a grand reception in the Town Hall when he was restored 'to England's shores'. One envelope contained a card showing anemones in a jug on a sunlit windowsill. Dorothy Sleightholme, née Weaver, was so sorry to hear of his plight from dearest Liddy. She and Geoffrey were married now, despite his misgivings, and he was somewhere on the Somme. She hoped they would all meet again in Rye in happier times. She thought of him, she added, but doubted he thought of her. It was an odd remark, Guv thought, and well worth following up. Next, another letter from Lydia:

My dearest husband,

I have wonderful but sad tidings. Wonderful because Dr Hollingsworth tells me we can expect a child in seven months' time, but sad because you cannot be here to share my happiness. You must not be anxious for me. I come from sturdy stock and I am sure the birth will be as free from complications as that of Alice, but it would have been so lovely if you could have been with me at this time because as you know so well I have come to depend on you in so many, many ways.

He remembered now when his need had been urgent and he had gone up from the study on his last leave at two or three in the morning, unsteady on the great staircase, and found her heavily asleep. He did not put on the light but stripped and slid in beside her and imagined she was someone else. Christ, he thought, by now the sprog could have been born. He shuffled the envelopes to check the dates but the last from her was five months ago. It opened with the usual sentimental gush but then:

You will be pleased to hear that Stanley Kemp has been discharged from hospital, and although he is much changed and finds it difficult to get about, he and Rose Pringle were married in a simple ceremony at St Mary's in Rye. They were going to set up in her accommodation in Hastings (very respectable, quite genteel, I am not clear how she could afford it) but I offered them the chance to stay here while they continue with their plans for the business you proposed. I am so tempted to boast to everyone about your wonderfully generous gesture but I suppose I must keep my counsel. So much better to come from you.

A survey has been carried out on the old smithy, and the deeds and all that sort of thing are being gone through by Mr Keegan, the solicitor. I hope you will trust me to carry this matter along. However, before we can proceed much further Mr Keegan advises me that I must have your agreement to granting me Power of Attorney, so I can deal with the day-to-day business of the estate. Please despatch a suitable statement as a matter of urgency. To have our finances tied up in this way makes life so awfully difficult, as I know you will understand. I will, of course, keep you informed at every stage.

By the way, it seems that the new Mrs Kemp may be expecting a happy event, which rather gives the lie to the silly rumours about the nature of poor Stanley's injuries. Aren't people wicked? As for me, I am beginning to show. It seems the Kemp child and ours will arrive not so very far apart. Alice sends you a kiss.

Inside the letter was folded a note that seemed to have been written in haste:

My dear,

Since writing this I have had a communication from a gentleman in Whitehall who is aware of your situation and wishes to visit me to discuss the matter of your friend, the farmer in France. I do not understand the rush but he says it cannot wait. I will let you have further news as soon as I can. It seems to do with money. I do hope this Frenchman is not taking advantage of your benevolent nature. I still await your instructions, my dear, about the Power of Attorney. Mr Keegan stresses that this is most vitally important as it is impossible to deal with any larger sums to do with the running of the estate, although everyone is very accommodating and seem proud to assist. I do not like to bother you with such things but I know you would not wish me to suffer anxiety over such matters.

To be presented with a good reason not to establish Stan Kemp in business was immediately appealing. Who could criticise a prisoner of war for an understandable reluctance to yield up Power of Attorney to his wife? It was a complex matter and not to be conducted over so great a distance and with such unreliable lines of communication. Besides, what aptitude had she for business and what was the quality of her advisers? Could they be trusted in his absence? It would be very easy to ignore Lydia's appeal, to sit it out and let the Kemps go hang. Except . . . except for the gentleman from Whitehall (Guv believed he knew the gentleman, quite well) who wished to discuss that damned Frog farmer and his price for not kicking up a fuss; a hefty price no doubt, not to be found in petty cash or, worse, borrowed from Lloyds Bank in Rye, a process that would call for some ticklish explanations that might disclose too much. He had no choice.

He wrote out an immediate agreement granting Lydia Power of Attorney, as well as a brief note expressing pleasure (as any husband would) at the news that he was to become a father again, and with instructions to proceed with the purchase of the old smithy; also authorising an investment in Monsieur Pettit's agricultural business (agricultural business, what a joke) at Chézy-au-Bois. This last was to be negotiated by his contacts in Whitehall whose discretion he relied on (this paragraph was underlined, although to Lydia it remained a puzzle), and he would accept whatever sum they recommended. In time, he wrote, he expected it to return a useful profit. He had to smile at that; more likely that swine Pettit would seek him out, despite the bribe, and try to finish the job he had started on that woodland path at Chézy. Well, next time he would be ready for him.

He took the envelope to the commandant's office, leaving it open for the censor, and asked for it to be added to the camp's mail bag for the next collection. He did not see the commandant, only a clerk, but walking back to his hut he was intercepted by Rutherford, the senior British officer. 'You seem to be getting hugger-mugger with the Boche,' the colonel said. 'You haven't been here long, Sutro. Perhaps you don't know the score. At Custren we don't hold with heel-clickers.'

'I've just had a visit from the Albatros pilot who won an Iron Cross for knocking me down. He called to see if I was comfortable. You know, the *camaraderie* of the air. I was going to put you in the picture. Could be a useful lever.'

'Don't see how. I'm dead against fraternisation of any kind. And I advise you to adopt the same policy. I've been behind the wire from the outset on the Marne so I'm out of touch. But I'm told you're hailed as some sort of blue-eyed boy back home. Just the kind of meat the Berlin propagandists like to get their teeth into. The trouble with you Flying Corps johnnies is you don't grasp the fundamentals of military life. Your heads are in the sky.'

As if to emphasise the point an RFC lieutenant came running past with his arms stretched out, vibrating his lips to simulate the noise of a zooming aero-engine. He banked towards them, then veered away.

'Circuits and bumps, you fellows!' he shouted. 'Circuits and bumps! Got to keep my hand in.'

'It won't work,' said Guv to the colonel. 'Wilkie will never convince the Hun he's barking.'

Rutherford looked sour. 'In my book, Wilkinson-Clark is certifiable. If it was up to me I'd have him repatriated tomorrow.'

Wilkinson-Clark was not repatriated. He grew bored with his sorties, performed his last flight under the noses of the blank-faced guards, landed neatly, crouching to simulate the moment of touchdown, removed with great deliberation his invisible flying helmet, goggles and gauntlets, and took up studying French with a sous-lieutenant of artillery captured at Fort Douamont.

Nobody was repatriated and nobody escaped. Commandant Thomson knew his business. Only one attempt was made, by Colonel Rutherford himself. Disguised as the camp doctor and approaching the main gate he was waylaid and taken to the sick quarters where a *Feldwebel* was suffering from an attack of appendicitis. He was moved elsewhere, and succeeded by a more phlegmatic senior officer, recently captured, who told them the German army was wavering on the Marne, that there were even rumours of a collapse. 'My advice to you, gentlemen, is to sit it out. It would be a pity to get yourselves shot at this stage.'

Time inched by. Unlike other ranks, penned in their own compound, who were marched to a munitions factory five kilometres away, officers were not required to work although their food was not much better: bread, boiled barley and potatoes, sometimes meat, not mutton or beef but more likely, it was suggested not entirely in jest, a creature that finished last in a Brandenburg steeplechase. But their diet was improved by food parcels from home, more frequent now, though news remained sparse, with incoming mail as infrequent as before (the prisoners themselves restricted to a writing a postcard a week, a letter two Saturdays in every month).

These mailings never crossed, and it was six months before Lydia confirmed that Guv's concession of Power of Attorney had been acted upon. He also learned that the smithy on the Military Road had been duly acquired, and that a substantial sum had been settled on Monsieur Pettit in France:

I will not write here how much, but it seems to me a huge amount, representing five years' income. You must think a great deal of his prospects, my dear. We have not received a word of thanks.

Lydia added that nor had she been paid the courtesy of learning the name of her visitor from Whitehall, who had arranged matters. He had, she said, conducted himself throughout in a most mysterious manner and for the duration of his visit to High And Over seemed to be enjoying some kind of private joke. She did not take to him at all.

When she wrote again, it was to tell him that a son had been delivered, a little early and rather small, five pounds six ounces only. There was the question of a name. She thought perhaps of Alfred, after Poppa, but it seemed such a mouthful for a tiny scrap. She had settled on Timothy, after a favourite uncle who died with his men at Spion Kop. So Tim it was, unless he said otherwise, though she had grown used to it by now. And Baby Kemp was in the nursery alongside little Tim, born a month before, a beefier article altogether with apple cheeks quite like his lovely mother who, Lydia was sorry to observe, had developed considerable airs and graces and acted quite the lady, indulged by her husband who regarded her (she should not say this) with the mien of a faithful dog. They still occupied the rooms she had made available to them in the east wing but soon, she hoped, with the smithy transformed into a garage and the bungalow nearly fit for habitation, she would have High And Over to herself once more.

Meanwhile, with a Custren guard, Guv had traded items from a Fortnums food parcel for an atlas of the world. With this he plotted peacetime flights: England to the United States, to the Middle East, to South Africa, to Australia, clear round the world. He did not know what aeroplane he would choose. Most likely something big, like the Handley-Page twin-engined type they were using to bomb the Boche, with 300 gallons in the tank, enough for nine hours' flight. Wilkinson-Clark would sit with him planning the routes, promised the role of co-pilot if he put some money in. His family owned cotton mills in Lancashire so he seemed a likely prospect. Guv knew nothing of his flying skills. It hardly mattered. A co-pilot was little more than a sack of turnips. Of course, if Leutnant Schoenfelder was to be believed, his company might provide a machine free of charge and even add a retainer, but Schoenfelder's word was probably as reliable as his own.

By now, the war had entered its final year but the men behind the wire at Custren did not know it yet. They followed an irksome routine. Guv played gin rummy for IOUs and won substantial properties the length and breadth of Britain. He said he would hold his fellow gamblers to their obligations and only claimed he was joking if they won them back. They played sports in season: soccer, rugby, cricket, and classes were held in many subjects: Latin, architecture, law, and woodwork at which Wilkinson-Clark proved proficient, constructing from scrounged materials a fair replica of a Blériot cockpit with working controls on which he taught pupils the rudiments of flight. It was only when he told an inquisitive guard that he had just completed a catapult made from bedsprings and intended to launch himself over the perimeter wire and fly home that the device was confiscated. 'Not so much for your nonsensical claim,' the commandant told him, 'as your wish to make a member of the Imperial German Army look foolish.'

·'I'm frightfully sorry,' said Wilkinson-Clark, 'but I suggest his mother already did that.' The remark was worth a week on solitary.

As winter once more tightened its grip it became known that Germany was seeking terms for peace. The Kaiser abdicated and fled to Holland, and, in the personal railway carriage of Marshal Foch, in a siding deep in the Forest of Compiègne in the *département* of the Oise, an armistice was signed.

Within a month a gaunt officer of the Royal Flying Corps was delivered by rail to Calais. Was Mamzelle Fifteen Francs still plying her trade? Guv wondered. Even she would turn up her not-unattractive nose at this filthy skeleton of an Englishman. He did not warn Lydia of his arrival. He did not care to be met by Paget at Rye; he thought he might very well punch him down. He took a taxi, and on the Military Road they passed a new-built garage. In a window of the nearby bungalow a dim light shone. As they turned into the familiar drive of High And Over he leaned forward a little from his comfortable seat to see the great house come into view. It was dusk and here too lights were showing, spilling across the close-cut lawns. Inside were Lydia and two children he had never seen. He told the driver to take him back to Rye. There, ignoring all who recognised him, he took a room at the George, drank a great deal of Scotch and sank into a luxurious bed for the first time in almost two years.

5

When the Hispano-Suiza pulled off the road with a final blip of throttle and stopped by the pumps, the boy ran out of the office door and pulled himself onto the running board, one hand on the lowered hood, the other on the strut of the big spotlight next to the raked-back windscreen.

'What ho, Will,' said the man behind the wheel.

'What ho, Captain Sutro.'

Guv vaulted out; there were no doors. He took off his tweed cap, felt in the pocket of his leather coat for a cloth and wiped his face, grimed with oil and road dust. 'Try it for size,' he said, pointing at the empty driver's seat. The boy was quickly in place, gripping the string-covered wheel, craning his head to see above the scuttle where the long bonnet ran down to the bronze stork mascot mounted on the radiator cap, leaning from side to side as he sped round an imaginary race track, his legs dangling from the seat squab, pushing at pedals he could not reach. He hummed an engine noise to himself, the note rising as he pressed down on a phantom throttle. Guv looked for himself in the child, in the face brown from much time outdoors, the set of the small jaw, the liveliness in the eye, the sturdy limbs.

Stan Kemp came out of the old smithy. Only the horseshoe door remained. The interior was a motor workshop now. A battered single-cylinder De Dion-Bouton was up on a ramp. Further back were several other cars ready to be worked on. Guv jerked his head at the boy in the Hispano. 'A regular little Count Zborowski.'

'Yes,' Stan said. 'Fill her up?' The pump began to churn.

'Business good?'

'Not bad.'

Guv looked for Rose. He never asked after her and Stan rarely spoke of her. Sometimes he saw her moving by the bungalow, a distant figure who gave no sign of recognition. Occasionally in Rye he had seen her approaching him in the high street but she had crossed quickly to the other side or got into a hurried conversation with someone she knew or entered the nearest shop. Now Stan saw the direction of his gaze. 'She's not here,' he said. 'She's hardly ever here.'

'The sprog's back from school in a few days,' Guv said. 'Perhaps Will would like to pop up.' He called to the boy: 'Tim's term ends next week. Fancy coming to play at High And Over?'

'Can I have a look at your aeroplanes, Captain Sutro?'

'Rather.'

'Tank's full.' Stan rattled the nozzle of the pump back in place.

'Put it on the account,' Guv said.

'All right. But it's mounting up. It's your profit as well as mine.'

'You don't have to concern yourself with money, do you, Stan? Not with a wealthy backer.'

'It's a business arrangement. You put the cash in, I do the work.'

'Let's not fool ourselves. We both know what kind of arrangement this is.'

'Anything else? If not, I'll get back to the De Dion.'

Guv pointed at Will, still in the Hispano's cockpit. 'Look at the little shaver. It's in the blood, wouldn't you say?' He walked over. 'Here, boy, let me heave you out.' He put his hands under Will's armpits, took the weight of the small body, swung him high in the air and set him down. The boy laughed with pleasure, looking up at him, his mouth open. Guv settled himself in the Hispano but when he turned his head Stan had already gone back into the workshop. Only the boy remained by the pumps, giving him a jaunty wave as the engine roared and the car began to move.

At High And Over Alice ran out of the house and embraced him. 'A man has come to see you, Dadda, from London.'

He untangled himself. 'Really? What kind of man?'

'A scruffy man with dirty shoes. He has a funny tie.'

Guv allowed himself to be led through to his study. Lydia was talking to a visitor sipping tea, not holding the cup by its handle. His shoes lacked polish, as Alice had noticed, and he wore a bow tie. The cuffs of his shirt, protruding from the sleeves of his jacket, were frayed. He stood up, put down his tea cup on the bare veneer of a Regency card-table (to be snatched up by Lydia with an apologetic smile) and held out his hand.

'Burney, Lexters News Agency. An honour to meet you, sir.'

'Well,' said Lydia, 'I'll leave you gentlemen to it. Come, Alice.' She went out, resting her hands on Alice's thin shoulders and closed the study door.

'You're early,' Guv said. 'Your ETA was three-thirty.'

'ETA?'

'That's a good start. Estimated time of arrival, man. Well, you'd better fire away. What do you want to know?'

'There's talk of you flying round the world.'

'A lot of chaps are considering that. Natural progression. Britain was first to South Africa and Australia, first across the Atlantic. Circling the globe is the next challenge.'

'Do you have an aeroplane prepared?'

'A Handley-Page, like the one I used on the trip to Darwin in 1920, chasing the ten thousand pounds put up by the Australian Government. Not that I got that far. A cracked cylinder-head forced me down in Souda Bay in Crete and that particular machine was wrecked. We sold the bits for scrap. The locals built boats out of it.'

'Four other men died trying to win that prize.'

'At least you've done your homework. We didn't escape unscathed. My co-pilot Wilkinson-Clark cracked his head, and one of our mechanics bust a leg.'

'Would you say such casualties are too high a price to pay?'

'Not at all. The possibilities of air transport are enormous, as a military resource and spreading our influence throughout the world.' By now Guv had been interviewed many times; he had the phrases off.

'It's not just Britain though, is it?'

'We're ahead in every way. It's a matter of pioneering the routes and then securing them on a commercial basis. The French are well advanced of course, the Dutch also. The Americans are an unknown. There's no controlling authority for civil aviation over there, and no Federal legislation, so it's something of a free-for-all; a lot of private joy-riding and stunting displays. But they're flying mail between New York and San Francisco so someone's spotted the potential. In Australia they're following our lead and carrying passengers and post on various long-distance routes. And there are other applications. The Canadian Government's using aircraft for forest surveys and fire patrols.'

'And Germany?'

'They're still up against it, thanks to the Treaty of Versailles. Winter flying is out because they've got so little equipment, although they're coming on, with fifteen routes this year against seven last. But they're facing restrictions on aeronautical design and organisation for obvious reasons.'

'Are they allowed to build machines at all?'

'Some, but there are limitations of speed and climb and load which makes it impossible for them to produce really efficient commercial designs.'

'Or manufacture war planes.'

'There is that. But I doubt we'll hear the rattling of sabres from that quarter again. They've learned their lesson.'

'What are your immediate plans, Captain, while you're preparing for the round-the-world bid?'

'To have a crack at the King's Cup air race in September, Croydon to Glasgow and back. I reckon it can be done in under seven hours. I've bought an Army surplus Martinsyde Buzzard that might just do the trick. If you're up for a stroll I'll show you the little bus.'

At the hangar a man was perched high on a set of wheeled steps, working on the engine of the silver biplane. Guv did not introduce him. The man looked down, grinning. 'Harry Paget, grease monkey.'

'Burney, press.'

'Ah, come to get the low-down eh? You've come to the right place. What do you want to know?'

'Nothing you can tell him,' Guv said. 'Make yourself scarce.'

Paget climbed down. 'I hear your son's back from school soon. Timothy, that is. It's a pity he doesn't show more interest in what his father gets up to. Funny really, when so many other people do.' He went through to the back of the hangar and ran some water into a tin kettle.

'What's your bloke getting at?' said the journalist.

Guv mounted the steps of the ladder and inspected the Rolls-Royce engine. 'Hanged if I know. Don't bother with him.'

Burney was curious, sensing a story. 'Doesn't your son like flying? I'd have thought he'd be a chip off the old block.'

'Do you gents want cuppas?' Paget called out.

'What I want,' Guv shouted back, 'is for you to get on with the task in hand. I've got a bloody race to win.'

Later, in the drawing room, Lydia said: 'Did the little man get what he wanted?' Alice was beside her on the sofa with her feet drawn up, watching her mother sew, comfortably drowsy and ready for bed.

'God knows. We'll find out in due course. If I had my way these hacks would have to run their scribblings past me first, before anything appears in print.'

Alice raised her head. 'Isn't that what they call censorship, Dadda?'

'You're getting too old for this Dadda nonsense,' Guv said. 'Why don't you call me Father?'

Alice sat up, her hand over her mouth, her eyes shining with tears. She stood up and ran out. They heard her quick feet on the great staircase and the door of her bedroom click shut, not banged but firmly closed. Lydia put aside her needlework. 'That was a particularly horrid thing to say.' She went up the stairs after her daughter.

It had been difficult with Lydia lately. The Sleightholme woman had been stupid enough to pass on a chance remark he made to her at a dinner-party in Rye; no more than a sounding-out and unlikely to be followed up so close to home, although she was a tasty little piece and clearly not getting enough from her dry prune of a husband. At the time she had shown no sign of taking offence at his murmured remark about her *décolleté*, out of Sleightholme's hearing. No doubt she was short of compliments from that quarter and felt the need to boast about his interest. But that was not all. He had never learned quite what the ministry man had said to Lydia about the Pettit business. It was obvious she suspected there was more to it than he would like her to believe, and an air of mistrust hung between them. She no longer used endearments when they were together, only in company, and when women were about he often caught her watching him with a doubtful eye.

He crossed to the window of the drawing room. Rooks and jackdaws were twisting and turning over the old castle in the valley. It was like a dogfight glimpsed on a dawn show, before you dived in yourself.

Three days later, Tim was delivered home from St Bede's by taxi, with his cumbersome box of belongings and his school report in an inside pocket of his navy-blue blazer. Paget could have been sent to collect him from Eastbourne in the Rolls, but Guv did not want him exposed to whatever the man might say on the journey. The boy knocked lightly on the study door as soon as he had changed from his school clothes.

Guv looked up from his copy of *Flight*. 'Back on hols then?'

'Yes, sir.'

'Well, don't stand there fidgeting, boy. Hand me your report.'

Tim had the envelope in his hand. He placed it on the desk in front of his father. 'It's a good one, sir.'

'Oh, you've sneaked a peak, have you?'

'Everyone does.'

'I'll read it later. By the way, I'm going up to the Handley-Page factory in Cricklewood tomorrow to check progress on the new machine.'

'You mean you want me to come?'

'I would have thought it was any lad's dream. But if you've got better things to do . . .'

'No, sir. Can I see if Will wants to come too?'

'Oh, he'll want to come all right. Why don't you pop down on your cycle and fix it up?' Guv picked up the envelope and turned it in his hands. 'So you're pretty pleased with yourself, are you?'

'Well,' Tim said, 'it's not bad, I don't think, except Mr Matthews says I'll never make a sportsman.'

'Too much rough and tumble for you, I suppose. Have you seen your mother yet, and Alice?'

'Oh yes, sir, but not for long.'

'I should seek 'em out. No doubt they'll make a great fuss of you, sportsman or not.'

*   *   *

That summer, Guv was among the fastest on the first leg of the King's Cup race, but struck a flock of birds taking off from Renfrew airport on the return flight to Croydon and had to put back. He did not recover the time. He was seen briefly on the British Pathé newsreel watching the winner Captain Barnard carried shoulder-high by excited crowds. A caption read: *No luck again for Great War ace Guv Sutro, his Buzzard laid low by pigeons.* In the Royal Aero Club it was considered a good joke. For a time, when Guv entered the lounge, he was greeted by coos. He derived a certain satisfaction when, having sold the Martinsyde to one of the principal jesters, the man was killed in it attempting a speed record in France.

By now the twin-engined Handley-Page transport had been delivered to Brooklands from the factory and Guv had recruited two flight mechanics (who would join the flight) to help prepare it for the round-the-world marathon. Paget was displeased but there was nothing he could do. He was not designated foreman and his position was not explained. But he did not resign, as Guv had intended.

The machine was largely funded by Wilkinson-Clark's family business, although Guv had refused permission for it to be christened King Cotton. In return it was understood that Wilkinson-Clark would once again occupy the co-pilot's seat, despite his narrow escape in the crash in Crete. He had still not fully recovered from the blow to his head that left him with no memory of the accident and a partly detached retina in his right eye. His father had reluctantly agreed to the new venture. The company had lost money over the London to Darwin bid and had received scant recognition for its contribution to a patriotic endeavour. But in the mill towns of Lancashire, Wilkinson-Clark was held in high regard as an aviation hero and so deserved support; it was as if the public there demanded it although, as the only son, there was the matter of succession. Soon enough the management of the mills would pass to him. Against the odds he had come safely through the war. Within the family the question was asked: why tempt fate?

Soon, he did not have to. A fire broke out in the hangar that housed the Handley-Page at Brooklands. The cause was not identified – a paraffin heater left too close to a petrol drum, a carelessly thrown-down cigarette, an electrical fault in the lighting circuit. Because the blaze began in the early hours it was only detected when the fuel tanks of the Handley-Page exploded. Nothing was left.

The police came out from Weybridge. 'Bit of a mystery, isn't it, sir?' the Detective Inspector said.

'That's your business, isn't it, solving mysteries?'

'Any idea how it started?'

'No, have you?'

'Accident, do you think, or something else?'

'Such as?'

'Arson, perhaps. Have you got any enemies at all?'

'I did have. Lots.'

'Really.' The Inspector licked his pencil. 'Care to give me their names?'

'There are too many of them. But they're easy enough to track down. They all live in Germany.'

The Inspector closed his notebook. 'I see, sir. Very droll. So I'm to take it you don't subscribe to the suggestion that this was a deliberate act?'

'Lacking any evidence that I can see, you may.'

Later, inspecting the blackened remains, Wilkinson-Clark said: 'This leaves me in a frightful fix, old man.'

'You?' said Guv. 'That's rich. What about me?'

'No, I mean a really frightful fix.'

'What are you getting at?'

'I hadn't tied up the insurance cover. Meant to, of course, but the insurers were sticking their heels in over the small print. They coughed up for the prang in Crete and weren't about to get caught again without a lot of caveats. I've been caught with my pants down, Guv, and no mistake. Of course, the old man doesn't know it yet. Relied on me to sort it out. He had such high hopes that first time, helping to put Britain on the map, waving the jolly old flag. This time round he took some persuading, I can tell you. There'll be hell to pay.'

Guv prodded the smouldering embers with his shoe. 'What are you going to do?'

'I rather hoped you might help me out.'

'Me? How, exactly?'

'By chipping in.'

Guv laughed. 'By chipping in? It'll take more than a bit of chipping in to sort out this mess. Way beyond my means. The Australian trip soaked up what capital I could muster.'

'You got paid out though, when the insurance came through.'

'I'm sorry, old boy, but you'll have to look elsewhere. This was a business arrangement, after all. If you didn't cover all the bases you can hardly expect me to bail you out.'

'Then what's the answer?'

'Come clean. Throw yourself on the old man's mercy.'

'He'll never forgive me. He was against this from the start.'

'He'll have to forgive you,' Guv said. 'You're all he's got.'

'It's going to knock our profits.'

'You're rolling in boodle, surely?'

'Things have changed since before the war. Other countries have come on – India, Japan. We're short of cash for reinvestment. Margins are tight.'

'I can do without a lesson in the travails of the cotton industry,' Guv said. 'It's not a game I'm intending to get into. Sorry, Wilkie, but you'll have to go cap in hand elsewhere. I've got to make ends meet.'

This was hardly accurate. The directors of the Bowman department store in Oxford Street had granted the Sutros, as owners of a great number of shares, courtesy positions on the board. The money rolled in without Guv lifting a finger, except for lending his name to a letterhead and attending an occasional function to let people gawp at him, enabling him to defray the costs of his various aviation projects, those not met by sponsorship, and to abandon those brain-fagging ideas for a flying school, a golf club or converting High And Over into a hotel. Funds, then, were by no means short, but for the moment the round-the-world bid was off while he scouted about for another Wilkinson-Clark to take the bulk of the risk.

Quickly, he dismissed the two flight mechanics, and Paget resumed his duties in the hangar at High And Over. A week later, returning to his room over the kitchen block, he opened the door to see Guv stretched out on his bed.

'How did you do it, Paget?'

'What?'

'I'm saying you put a match to the Handley-Page.'

'What bollocks.' Paget was off balance for a moment, working his tongue round his lips.

'Save the language for the cretins you hang out with in the pubs in Rye.'

'What are you on about exactly?'

'You're finished, Paget. I want you off my property.'

'I'll bet you do. Well, no can do and we all know why. Me and Cuz, we're both pretty comfortable with things as they are. We're in cahoots, old sport, you might as well admit it. As for the bleeding fire, well, you want to be careful what you say. They call it slander, don't they?' Paget had his arms folded, confident again and unruffled. 'But I will add this. I reckon you should keep me in the picture more, about what's going on. I don't like being kept in the dark, or passed over when something big's coming up. If you what see I mean?'

'You're damned sure of yourself, you little swine.'

Paget grinned. 'Why not? Wriggle all you like but we've got the goods on you, Captain God Almighty Sutro. And don't you bloody forget it. If anything happens to me or Cuz, anything untoward, you don't need me to tell you the consequences. Now close the fucking door on your way out . . . *sir*.'

At the Royal Aero Club, Guv still occasionally came across Wilkinson-Clark, who never explained how the matter of the insurance (or lack of it) had been resolved or how it had gone with his father. It was as if the loss of the Handley-Page had never happened and, as far as anyone could tell, in Lancashire the family business continued to prosper. On his jaunts to town Wilkinson-Clark drank a good deal. He always had, along with the rest, but there was a determination about it now – an urgency to overcome the dullness of his responsibilities at the mills. 'I tell you, Guv, life in France was bloody hell but by God I miss it so.' So when they went to Hendon to buy their de Havilland DH4s for a fiver apiece he was so drunk he could barely stand. But his instincts took over and with Guv he flew wing-to-wing to High And Over without incident and even took Will Kemp up for a spin.

When, after tea, he prepared to fly back to London, he was in a spirited mood. 'It's all been a tremendous hoot,' he said to Guv from the cockpit.

Later, the skipper of a cross-Channel ferry putting out from Newhaven reported seeing an aeroplane dive straight down into the sea off Beachy Head. The lifeboat crew found the wreckage of a de Havilland DH4 but no trace of the pilot. Soon afterwards, the Wilkinson-Clark mills ceased to operate and the receivers moved in.

To Guv it was a set-back. The round-the-world flight still lay before him, a tantalising prospect just beyond his reach. So when he learned that an Italian aircraft manufacturer was contemplating a bid with a long-range flying boat, he telegraphed their office near Milan. They agreed to an interview and he flew himself out there next day.

The *Società Costruzioni Aeronautiche Milano* had reserved him a suite at the Diana Majestic. Antonicelli, the chief test pilot, joined him for dinner. 'I have been instructed to look after you.'

'Not too much of a hardship, I hope.'

'By no means. An honour, I assure you.'

'Please, I'll blush.'

'You had a good war. Isn't that the phrase?'

'You were no slouch yourself. The Austrian front at Isonzo, wasn't it, flying bombers?'

'Good days, although it sounds odd to say so. Tell me, what do you know of Italy, Captain Sutro?'

'That Mussolini is the coming man.'

'He has come. His *Fascita* marched on the Government in Rome and assumed power without a drop of blood being spilled. He is a man of strength and vision, changing perceptions about our country. You must understand, we are not a race of frivolous and exuberant Latins as our detractors would have you believe, but a serious people.'

'I like to work with serious people.'

'Snap, as you English say. Now what do you know of our Aquila, our eagle?'

'Not much, but that's how you'd like it, no doubt. I do know your company has a record of achieving what it sets out to do and has a good chance of being first round the world. I'd like to be part of that enterprise, although perhaps your leader would prefer sons of Italy on board.'

'Not necessarily. *Il Duce* wishes to spread Italy's influence. He believes the spirit of Fascism is universal, that one day there will be a Fascist Europe united against the Left. For this reason he is by no means opposed to what we might call a European crew, drawn from the very best pilots available. He understands that only a few men have the qualities required to secure success and to him success is more important than blind nationalism. Your name would be high on our list. Like us, *Il Duce* has the greatest respect for your country and he is convinced that in time you British will also come to adopt Fascist doctrine and practice. But for the present, of course, your selection depends on your political views according with our own.'

'I have no political views,' Guv said. 'I'm a pilot.'

Antonicelli leaned forward a little. 'In this world we have fought so hard for, it is not possible for a man like you to have no political views. People look to you. You have influence. If you are serious about putting your name forward you must consider your position. What you do speaks volumes. Your deeds can reflect credit in the right quarter, not just nationally or internationally but politically. They can take you to heights you never dreamed of, even in the finest machine. The question is: how great is your ambition, Captain Sutro?' Antonicelli sat back. 'I would counsel you tomorrow, when you meet the directors, not to advise them that you have no political views. Otherwise your journey here will be wasted.'

A waiter asked if they were ready to order and was sent away. They studied the menus. 'It is always hard to choose,' said Antonicelli. 'It is a question of what appetite you have.'

'I never find it hard to choose,' Guv said. 'I'm always hungry.'

Antonicello closed his menu. 'The Aquila, you must understand, is no more than a draughtsman's blueprint at the moment, a number in our research and development budget. We have a long way to go.'

'I've already come a long way,' Guv said. 'I want to go much further still.'

After dinner, over *grappa*, Antonicelli said: 'So, perhaps we go on somewhere. What is your preference? Girls or boys?'

'Boys? Is this some sort of test?'

'You have a certain reputation. Who knows what tastes come with age?'

'I'll never be that old,' Guv said.

The Italian smiled and finished his *grappa*. 'Well, perhaps a more conventional conclusion to the evening. We have a casino nearby. I assume you gamble, Sutro.'

'Show me a pilot who's averse to risk.'

'Perhaps a little roulette then and a good night's sleep. The wisest choice. Tomorrow you will meet the directors of *Società Aeronautiche*. They will expect your eyes to be clear. As I say, we are a serious people.'

In the morning, a Fiat limousine took him to the factory near Lodi on the Lombardy plains. A racing flying boat was under construction in a hangar, a small biplane with a torpedo-shaped single-seat fuselage and a rear-facing V8 Hispano-Suiza engine fixed between the upper wings. Under the lower wings were two stabilising floats. It looked fast and fragile.

Antonicello patted its flanks. 'This is *Il Lampo*, the Lightning, our entry for next year's Schneider Cup at Cowes.'

'It looks like a winner,' Guv said. 'If it holds together.'

'Lightness is speed,' said Antonicelli. 'It merely needs to last the race.'

In the boardroom, half a dozen men were waiting. A model of the Lampo racer was on the long oak table in front of the company president.

'I am Pietromarchi,' he said. 'So, what do you think of our sea bird, Captain?'

'If it goes as well as it looks, it stands a chance.'

'More than a chance, Captain. We have a fine record in the Schneider competition. In Venezia in twenty and twenty-one, Italy won both times.'

'Only the Italians ran.'

'That helped.' There was easy laughter round the table. 'But not so funny this year when Supermarine took the prize. If we had won again, three times in a row, the trophy would have been for Italy to keep.' Pietromarchi picked up the model and studied it critically. 'Do you have any faults to find with our new design?'

'It strikes me as flimsy,' Guv said. 'I wouldn't fancy taking off or landing it in anything other than a flat calm. If you're planning to race it at Cowes, it needs beefing up. The Solent's not the Gulf of Venice.'

'Make a note of that,' Pietromarchi said to an assistant. 'Tell me, Captain Sutro, why did you not pilot the Supermarine Sea Lion in twenty-two?'

'I was in line. Harry Baird got the seat. The cockpit's only big enough for one.'

Pietromarchi nodded. 'Your visit, Captain Sutro, is not unwelcome but somewhat premature. Antonicelli has explained our position. At present the Aquila is little more than a dream.'

'I'd like to be around when you wake up.'

'So I understand.' Pietromarchi began to turn a fountain pen in his hand. 'As I say, this discussion is premature. However, perhaps you would care to outline to the directors the terms you would require for an association.'

'What terms are you offering?'

'Nothing yet.' Pietromarchi rested his hand on the shoulder of the assistant. 'Go into this further and see our guest has an indication of our thinking, without commitment, before he leaves.' He turned back to Guv. 'I understand from Antonicelli that you have some respect for *Il Duce*.'

'Of course,' Guv said again. 'He is one of the most impressive men of our time.'

'He loves his country and is proud of its flag and history, as you are aware, I am sure. He has helped us to oppose the threat of Leninism, a danger that England has yet to face in such a deadly form.'

'If I was Italian,' Guv said, 'I would be with him.'

'Perhaps you will have a chance to tell him so in person, if you fly the Aquila. Now, we must pass on to the next item on our agenda, for which we must welcome another guest.' The assistant left the room. 'I have a surprise for you. I hope it is a pleasant one.'

When the assistant returned he was accompanied by a familiar figure. 'I believe you gentlemen have already met,' said Pietromarchi.

'Ah,' said the newcomer. 'The *Englishe Überkanone*.'

'Hello, Schoenfelder,' Guv said. 'I thought you people were restricted to making children's kites.'

'We are in talks with *Schoenfelder Aeronplau* that might work to our mutual advantage,' said Pietromarchi. 'No doubt after our meeting you and Herr Schoenfelder will have much to say. Please, Antonicelli, take Captain Sutro to the drawing office to see the progress our designers are making. I suggest we resume our discussion more informally over lunch.'

But all plans by *Società Costruzioni Aeronautiche* for a round-the-world flight ended when, within months, during sea trials off La Spezia for the Schneider Cup, the little Lampo flying boat was lost; the engine struts failed and the Hispano V8 broke away from the wing. With the death of Antonicelli and the embarrassingly public destruction of its racer (*Il Duce* reportedly displeased) the company lost heart, suspended its programme of racing and record-breaking and turned to producing safer, more conventional machines. Much later the Aquila, extensively modified, appeared not as an impressive example of Italian *brio* but as a plodding commercial transport. It meant little to Guv; he barely remembered. By then he was spending much time in Berlin.

6

In 1934, driving his Sunbeam in the Tourist Trophy Race on the Ards circuit east of Belfast, Guv Sutro lost control on a surface wet from a sudden shower of rain. His car mounted a bank, rolled through a hedge and killed three spectators. The driver and his riding mechanic, recruited locally, were thrown clear and only slightly hurt. For Guv it was the end of road-racing, not because of the fatalities but because he did not want to risk injuries that might interfere with his flying programme. As well, behind the wheel he found he lacked the flair and natural touch he took for granted in the cockpit of an aeroplane; and it lacked the dimension of the air. Motor-sport had never been more than a pastime to occupy the intervals between his celebrated flights; circling the world in a Schoenfelder tri-motor, a joint venture with *Società Costruzioni Aeronautiche*, although two years after the men who were first, Kingsford-Smith and Charlie Ulm; solo to Australia and back; from Brazil to the Gambia across the South Atlantic; London to Cape Town in less than five days; all the time in pursuit of records set by that small band of record-breakers (Hinkler, Cobham, Mollison, Amy Johnson) for others to beat.

After the crash at Ards he still toyed with cars, but only where courage, speed and money counted, not skill; lapping the outer circuit at Brooklands in his Bentley at 120 miles per hour, taking his MG streamliner down the Autobahn near Frankurt at 186 miles per hour, snaking off the Pendine Sands in the same MG chasing Eyston's record for small-capacity cars, only to be buried by the incoming tide. 'I like to open the throttle and keep it there,' he told reporters. 'You don't have gears in an aeroplane. All this going up and down the gearbox, sawing at the wheel, I find it a ruddy bore. Am I going to have a crack at the land-speed record? No, not my game. My gods are height, long distance and sustained speed, not covering a measured mile in twelve seconds. I'll leave the LSR to old Campbell, who's got it pretty well stitched up. Each to his own, I say. And there's one place I've got Sir Malcolm beat. He might have been in the RFC but he still can't touch me in the air.'

Since the war he had flown many machines, few of them paid for by himself. His face was familiar not just from accounts of his flights in the press but from advertisements all over the world. His endorsements were sought: motor oils, watches, cigarettes, alcohol, cornflakes (*'Keep your energy sky high,' says King of the Air Captain Sutro*). He

415

was pressed to accept directorships by companies keen to add a famous name to their notepaper, all for a price and with no discernible duties to be performed apart from an appearance or two, to shake a hand and speak a few words, a moment never to be forgotten by those thousands who passed before him, a grey and unremembered multitude who shared that look of struck-dumb awe at being in the presence of a hero.

In all this, Guv sensed a power, a potency, an ability to influence the way others thought and acted. He found he could express strong opinions that flouted convention and remain unchallenged, or met with serious consideration by serious people or even, surprisingly, endorsed. He no longer said he was a simple pilot. He remembered what the dead Antonicelli had told him that time in Milan, that he had a voice that deserved to be heard, that he could exercise influence in the world, that his deeds and words could take him to undreamed-of heights, that it was not possible for a man like him not to have political views. He remembered the Italian's question: 'How great is your ambition, Captain Sutro? How great is your ambition?' It had been asked in Berlin, in the boardroom of *Schoenfelder Aeronplau*. The nature of the machines passing through the factory had undergone change. Military types had begun to appear, experimental single-seaters that looked much like fighters and could exceed 200 miles an hour, but said to be for training; larger designs that looked much like bombers but fitted with twenty seats and given a coat of airline paint.

At first, particular care was taken by the Schoenfelder directors, with other German manufacturers, not to be seen to infringe the terms of the Treaty of Versailles that only permitted the production of civil aircraft. But gradually restrictions fell away. The aircraft grew in size and power, the workforce expanded, production increased (a rate as high as that of any European country) and a new generation of young pilots began to pass through flying clubs, training schools for air and ground crews and commercial airlines. If, touring the Schoenfelder factory, foreign visitors expressed concern about the changing face of German aviation and what they saw and heard, they met with urbane smiles and dismissive shrugs; nothing could be further from the truth. Rumours about a secret air force were mere fantasy, anti-Deutsch paranoia. What better proof of their good intentions could there be, the directors demanded, than the presence of a famous Englishman in their midst – a member of their board, no less. As Max Schoenfelder had remarked at Tempelhof airport after Guv's round-the-world flight in the tri-motor: 'Not least among our gallant crew is an old adversary of mine who I am proud today to call my friend, and who serves shoulder-to-shoulder with his German comrades in a new peace that will last for a thousand years. He is an Englishman, yes, but he is *our* Englishman.'

By now, Guv was known to those who counted in the Reich: Air Minister Goering, his deputy Milch, the pilot of pilots Ernst Udet; the Führer himself.

In the Royal Aero Club the members were divided. 'I've always maintained the man's a damned heel-clicker. It was said when the Hun had him under lock and key in a POW camp and it's being said again now. The chap should hang his head in shame, for all his achievements. Makes you wonder what we fought for.'

'That's a bit hard, old boy. You can't deny he's helped to put Britain on the map.'

'Britain, you say? Sutro, more like. And which map, I'd like to know! The map of the British Empire, or Hitler's map of a greater Reich?'

'You can't deny there's much to respect about the German recovery. Herr Hitler's dragged his country out of the mire and inspired his people. Enrich the state and not themselves, opportunity for all and privilege to none, position a reward for service, poverty abolished, class barriers destroyed.'

'Good grief, Edgerton, you've had a dose of Mosley's poison. You're no more than a confounded Fascist yourself.'

'Better Fascist than Red, if you have to choose.'

'Well, now we know which side you'd come down on, along with your chum Sutro. I don't trust the Boche an inch. They're building up their strength in the air, and it's not just for Lufthansa to whisk its passengers to tropical climes.'

'You're too suspicious, Crawshore. The last conversation I had with Sutro, he assured me that there was absolutely no cause for the slightest anxiety. And he should know. He's right in the thick of things.'

'Up to his neck might be more appropriate.'

Six months later, the foundation of the new German air force, the Luftwaffe, was proclaimed to the world with Goering as Commander in Chief and, soon afterwards, Guv was the guest of honour at the professional aviators club in Paris where, watched by his family and representatives of the world's press, he was presented with the Blériot Medal for setting a new altitude record in the Schoenfelder prototype.

A few weeks after that, he was summoned to an address in London's Square Mile. It was not financial business that took him there. In a musty office overlooking Threadneedle Street, a civilian who had the look of a clerk opened a file. Guv watched him sift through the documents. He knew he had done it before, probably knew every word. The man looked up. 'I believe congratulations are in order, achieving new heights for the German Reich.'

'Have you got me here to tell me that?'

'A pity you couldn't have set the record in a British machine.'

'No one invited me. I'm open to offers.'

'The best offer wins, eh? Regardless.'

'Regardless of what?'

'Hmmm,' said the man. 'They'll know of this visit, of course.'

'Who?'

'Your friends in Berlin.'

'I have business associates in Berlin, not necessarily friends. Look, I suggest you explain—'

'Of course. You may refer to me as Felix. It's not my real name. I think it's rather neat – the cat that walks by night.'

'Why do I need to refer to you at all?'

'Oh, we have business together, Captain Sutro. Look on me as another associate – not necessarily a friend.'

Guv pointed at the open file. 'You seem to have the goods on me. What more can you possibly want to know?'

'In my profession,' said Felix, 'intelligence is always out of date.'

'What *is* your profession?'

'I always find it hard to keep a straight face because it sounds so ridiculously melodramatic, but you're in the bureau of the Secret Service.'

'Ah, so you want me to spy on Germany?'

Felix closed the file. 'You're blunt, Sutro, I'll give you that. But recruiting you as an agent would be a little too obvious. No, it's you we're interested in, not Herr Hitler's crew. We're compiling a dossier on those who might – what shall we say? – wobble if matters took a particular course. I'll be blunt in return. A certain doubt is developing in some quarters about your allegiance to this country. You appear to be getting frightfully cosy with the Fascist element in Europe. Oh, you're by no means alone. Various individuals, many of them influential like yourself, subscribe to the view that they are the bulwark against Bolshevism. They also have some sympathy for the Reich, consider they were harshly dealt with in the peace of 1919, and understand why there might be a desire for retribution at some future time.'

'You mean another war?'

'Why not? Germany was knocked back to being a fifth-rate power, but Hitler has united the whole of the Fatherland behind him and led them to recovery. That could be seen as a great achievement. Would you say that reflects your opinion?'

'You sound as though you respect him yourself.'

'Just putting a point of view, not necessarily my own. It's interesting to come at these things from all sides. Helps you to understand.'

'Well,' Guv said, 'I can see the good that's been done over there. It's hard not to admire it, if you've witnessed it first-hand. Of course, if it turns out Germany's intentions are hostile, you need have no concerns about my patriotism. But why would Hitler put Germany back on its feet only to risk it being knocked down again in a pointless war? It won't happen. He's made it clear he respects the British. Why, he's even spoken of us as potential allies.'

'Allies against Russia, I suppose. Do you subscribe to the idea of Germany dragging Europe into another war? And what if Britain says no, and the Reich turns against us? What then, Captain? Whose side would you come down on then?'

Guv's voice rose. 'Look, when I was a lad and war was in the offing I told some backslider who seemed to harbour doubts about his duty that England was the finest, grandest country in the world. I haven't changed my view a jot. You'll find no one more staunchly patriotic, and if any nation dares to act the aggressor I'll be there again to take them on, just as I did in France.'

'You're not addressing a public meeting now,' said Felix mildly. 'Please, my dear chap, lower the volume. The Secret Service does not conduct its business at full shout.'

'But damn it all,' said Guv, 'it appears to me you're questioning my loyalty to the Crown.' He banged his fist on the desk. 'I'd like to know what the blue blazes you did in the Great War. Some under-cover sideshow, I suppose.'

'Infantry battalion, as a matter of fact. Company commander, Ypres, the Somme, Passchendaele. Lost my mitt at Polygon Wood.' Felix held up a prosthetic hand. 'Stroke of luck, actually. Doubt I'd have come through otherwise. That's how I got into this game, where I could still prove useful. But it's not old battles that interest us, it's the possibility of those to come.'

'Who says they're to come?'

'Well, that's rather the point, isn't it? Determining what Herr Hitler might have in mind, not to mention Signor Mussolini. World domi-nation, if the more lurid leaders in our newspapers are to be believed. Do you hold with world domination, Sutro?'

'I hold with the British Empire.'

'Well, that's what we need to know.' Felix tapped the file. 'From our own sources and reports provided by our colleagues in Whitehall we have assembled a pretty comprehensive picture of your activities. To be candid, you're something of a worry to us.'

'I've had enough of this,' Guv said. He began to stand. 'It's like being hauled before the Harrow beak.'

'Ah, Harrow, yes. One of our senior men remembers you there. You were involved in some fisticuffs in the town and got yourself expelled.'

'I was removed,' said Guv. 'There's a difference. This senior man – he wouldn't go by the name of Latimer, by any chance? He always was a hole-in-the-corner sneak.'

Felix smiled. 'None of us go by our real names, Sutro. And as to Harrow, well, let's just agree that you and the world of academe did not rub along and return to the matter in hand.'

'I wonder you don't clap me in the Tower and have done with it.'

'You should have been a journalist, Captain. You have a talent for the sensational. The fact is, while you may have a decent enough record in the air, you have a sordid and questionable past and a lifetime of meaningless fucking. Well, all men have weaknesses, of course – that we are prepared to acknowledge. But in your case there is a larger gulf than usual between the public and the private man. Denied the full picture, the contents of this file for example, the great unwashed look up to you as a shining example of British manhood, a heroic figure, someone to be emulated, to be followed. A leader, perhaps.'

'Who's being sensational now?'

'We need to establish, Sutro, whether your trumpeted views are honestly held or just superficial posturing so you can get your hands on the best machines, in whatever country they may be made. Oh yes, and possibly power.'

'Meaningless fucking, eh?' Guv toyed with the phrase. 'I wondered why I haven't been granted a knighthood like Segrave and Campbell.'

'From our perspective,' said Felix, 'it seems more likely you're in line for an Iron Cross.'

'What tommy-rot! I fail to see what the fuss is about. Fascism is a valid form of government. It seems to be serving the Germans and the Italians pretty well. Meanwhile, we stumble on, divided and at the mercy of any rabble-rouser who cares to shout his head off at Speakers Corner.'

'I believe it's called democracy.'

'While we're all so busy defending free speech we leave the country weak for the Reds to take over.'

'Or the Fascists. Perhaps you envisage a bloodless coup, like Mussolini in Rome? Perhaps you see yourself in Mosley's ranks, marching down Whitehall to seize power, having failed at the ballot box. Perhaps—'

'You and I have both been through a war. We know what it means. Neither of us would want it again. But peace depends on strength of purpose. On leadership. Germany has it, and so does Italy. What's our answer? Ramsay MacDonald, the bastard son of a servant girl, a bloody pacifist who would have let the Hun walk all over us in the Great War and should have been shot at the outset.'

'Yes,' said Felix, 'that would have been the Fascist way.'

'Weakness is unforgivable. It's punished in the modern world. Frankly, I can't see that what might be called benign dictatorship is so very wrong.'

'*Is* there such a thing – a benign dictatorship, I mean? For example, benign hardly sums up Hitler's attitude towards the Jews. Where do you stand on the Jewish question?'

'I've no particular view. Some of the people I know in Berlin get worked up about it. They say they're a malignant force, that the Hebrews want a Jew war, that they're intent on putting nations at each other's throats so they can spread their influence. They say their God is Mammon. Seems pretty much rubbish to me.'

'So you don't see yourself as an anti-Semite?'

'I'm anti-everybody,' said Guv. 'Surely your dossier tells you that much?'

'Apart from the Fascists.'

Guv checked his watch. 'Look, can we end this little chat? We don't seem to be getting anywhere and I've got a table booked at Simpson's in half an hour.'

'I understand Simpson's remains much the same,' said Felix. 'It's always good to know some things at least remain much the same.' He stood up. 'By the way, your family. How are they?'

'My family?'

422

'Your wife, your children. Your sons.'

'Sons?'

'Oh, come now, Captain. Don't be obtuse. Your dalliance in France.'

Guv was silent for a moment. 'Of course, I should have known your snoopers would be onto that. Yes, it was a boy, I understand. I paid through the nose for that little mistake.'

'Hardly little. The price could have been far higher. If the judgement had gone another way, you could have found yourself taking a short walk at dawn. Numbers of chaps did, you know, for similar offences.' Felix removed a handkerchief from his breast pocket with his sound hand and blew his nose gently. 'Tell me, have you ever shown the slightest interest in the lad's welfare? Or that of his mother, come to that?'

'Not part of the agreement. I forked out as directed, and that was the end of the matter.'

'For you, perhaps.'

'Let's not be naive. Such things happen in times of war. I owned up and paid up.'

'Is your wife aware?'

'She knows about the payment but not why it was paid.'

'It would be a shock to her, wouldn't it, if she were to learn the truth? Although I can't imagine she harbours many illusions about you after all these years.'

'Where's this leading exactly?'

'I should have thought you'd be ahead of me on that point. If there's ever any suggestion of you becoming – what shall we say? – more closely involved with those who have other agendas than our own, the particular avenue you appear to be following may well turn out to be a very rocky road indeed.'

'I see. I'm surprised the British Secret Service is prepared to stoop so low.'

'Oh, we can be positively subterranean if needs be. It's our job, protecting national interests. By the way, I have no doubt that your presence here has been noted and conclusions drawn by our opposite numbers in the Abwehr, who are quite as efficient as we are. Your position, I'm afraid, is hopelessly compromised. You will never be trusted by Berlin again – that is, if you ever were.' Felix placed the file in a drawer of his desk and closed it. 'Nor indeed by us.'

Guv paused by the door. 'I never thought my own people would resort to such un-English dirty tricks. Funnily enough, I find it reassuring. At least somewhere there's a firm hand on the helm.'

'An apt metaphor, Sutro. Do check your soundings, won't you, from time to time, just in case you're in danger of running aground?'

In the cab to the Strand Guv reflected that Felix's agents were perhaps not so sharp after all, missing clues that might have sent them to a certain garage on the Military Road to spot a likeness in the youngster working on the cars there who shared so many of his father's traits, his vigour and resilience, his strength of purpose, his quickness of eye and hand; that other boy who lived to be a pilot, so different from the washout of a son who bore his name. He felt a secret pride in Will because he saw in him himself; and also Rose, whose striking looks were tempered in the boy by disregard for swank or affectation. As to Tim, in him he perceived only Bowman traits, clever enough in his way (he could not argue with school reports) but vapid and without direction, a faint-heart who sweated with funk on the shortest hop and was often sick, always quick to surrender his cockpit seat to the eager Will.

Clearly, flying had no part in Tim's future. The tradition would be lost. Instead he was destined for some management role in Oxford Street, would spend his days in a plush office with the windows closed studying departmental returns, pampered by obsequious female staff and growing fat with his fellow-directors as they discussed ways to part impressionable women from their husbands' cash. He would face no challenge in his life, no call to arms, no war, would not even be gifted a chance to prove he had some lurking grit like his grandfather on a torpedoed ship. There would be no torpedoed ships, no battles on the land. No fighting in the air. And as for Will, if he realised his ambition to become a service pilot in the RAF, he would find his only foe was the air itself, unless some unruly tribe in India or North Africa had to be taught a lesson that called for a bomb or two. Otherwise, stunting a Hawker Hart at the Hendon Air Show to thrill the crowds was about the most he could expect.

Over the years Guv had liked to see Will about the place. He and Tim had struck up some sort of friendship, despite their different temperaments. Well, there was nothing wrong with that, although he never felt entirely at ease with it. And it could hardly be discouraged without prompting awkward questions. Besides, what harm could it possibly do? What more natural, reasoned Guv, given their fathers' partnership in a business down the road and the scarcity of boys of their own age knocking about the neighbourhood, than that they should pal up. And so the rolling acres of High And Over had become their kingdom, and only when Tim was sent away to school did they begin to draw apart a little. By then Will had become an extra pair of hands about the estate, and particularly in the hangar, and came and went pretty well as he wished. For him, Guv suspected, it was the kind of opportunity he would have seized on himself, the key to another world where people had money and did as they pleased; the key to a door that would not be so hard to step through, given guile and luck. And Will remained unaware that his greatest luck was the luck of his birth; that it took only a word from the man he called the Captain to pass through into the brilliant light of that other world. The door stood open and the irony was, he did not know it. Guv could choose that moment when it pleased him; and he knew it would please him a great deal, to pass the baton (as you might say) to another generation, to a man in his mould who would follow him in spirit if not in name. There was no doubt in Guv's mind that the moment would come and he looked forward to it, he anticipated it, not planning for it in detail but waiting for a sign that now was the time, the moment when it all fell into place. But then everything changed.

He was passing through Deadman's Spinney, his shotgun broken on his arm, inspecting the feeders put out for game birds when he heard voices, two people talking softly together. They were a few hundred yards away, silhouetted against the rose-streaked evening sky, leaning back against the trunk of a grey beech, nestled against each other, their heads so close it looked like a single head. He recognised Will and thought, for a moment, the other was Tim. He knew of such things but had never seen it for himself. He was careless with shock and trod heavily on a fallen branch that cracked like a pistol shot.

The figures drew apart quickly and looked towards him, their faces in dark shadow against the brightness of the sunset filtering between the trees. He could not see their expressions but then he heard Alice's voice; Alice calling to him: 'Father . . .' There was fear in the word as it echoed in the still gloom of the spinney but also hopelessness, a desire to explain what could not be explained. Will took a step towards him and Alice fell back against the tree. Guv turned and walked away. For an instant he had known relief that what he had seen had been a natural thing, but then the implications consumed him. He felt a wave of revulsion. Behind him, the voices had started again, Alice's muffled as though held in a close embrace, Will talking to her in that breaking man-boy tone that betrayed his years.

In the house Guv locked the shotgun in its cabinet, rinsed his face and hands slowly in the sink in the boot room and went through to the study.

After fifteen minutes Lydia came in. 'I thought I heard you. Cook was asking what she might prepare for supper. Something light, perhaps?'

Guv was on his second Glenfiddich. 'Is Alice back?' he asked.

'Back? Back from where?'

'Don't you keep track of your daughter's whereabouts?'

'Don't *you*? What on earth's this about? You make it sound as though she's done something wrong, something to offend you.'

'Send her to me the instant she returns.'

'She's only been walking in the grounds with young Will.'

'Only, you say. How long has this been going on? This . . . this liaison?'

Lydia laughed a little. 'Good Lord, are you blind? She's always had a soft spot for the boy. There's nothing to it. You make it sound like a grand passion. It's just a sentimental attachment. They're little more to each other than brother and sister.'

He could not bring himself to answer that, could only grate: 'I saw them together.' Nausea rose in his throat along with the sour tang of whisky.

'What did you see?'

'Enough. It can't go on. I won't permit it.'

Lydia stood over him, her eyes suddenly hard. 'Why are you so insufferably pompous about this? It's her first love, perfectly natural in a girl of her age. She could do much worse. Will is a decent boy and would not take advantage. I don't know how deep his feelings go, but clearly she cares for him a great deal. If you're patient it will probably pass.'

'Probably isn't good enough.'

'If you forbid this now, you risk losing your daughter. She'll never forgive you. If you wait, she'll no doubt meet others who'll match your exacting standards, whatever those standards may be.' She laughed, more harshly this time. 'You surprise me. You've always favoured the boy, brought him on. Where he's concerned at least, I never saw you for a snob.'

'When does Alice start at Cheltenham?'

'In two weeks.'

'She must stay with your cousin in Stroud.'

'If that's your decision, you must tell her so yourself.'

'I will. I told you at the outset, send her to me the moment she returns.'

'Why are you doing this awful thing? Why are you so angry? The girl loves you. You will break her heart.'

Guv reached for the decanter. The cut-glass stopper slipped from his hand and rolled across the floor. Lydia bent to pick it up. He half rose, shaking with fury, pouring the whisky into his tumbler with a trembling hand.

'Leave it, you stupid bloody woman, leave it.'

Lydia said calmly: 'I have forgiven you many things. I will not forgive you for this.'

'What difference could that possibly make to me? An end to the charade we play out in public? Thank Christ for that. The Blériot Medal ceremony in the Avenue Kléber, what did you add? Trotting out platitudes of no interest to anyone, as stylish as an old maid at a country jumble . . .'

'Compared to Renate Preiss, no doubt.'

'Compared to anybody.'

'Are you quite insane?' said Lydia. 'I know you have no feeling for me – I doubt you ever had. But this . . . it's as though you've lost your reason. You've blown this up quite out of proportion. This is a small thing, a passing thing. Set me aside if you must. But if you have any regard for your daughter's happiness, her peace of mind, her confidence in herself as a woman, in her future – you'll not take this further and make it worse; make it into something that could blight her life.'

They heard the front door open and close, Alice's feet on the stairs. 'I'm going to her,' Lydia said.

Guv waved a hand as though brushing her away. 'You haven't a clue, have you, the remotest idea?'

Lydia paused. 'About what?'

'I don't need your forgiveness,' Guv said. 'I don't need anything from you at all. I've taken all I want.'

When, a half-hour later, there was a tentative knock on the study door he called for whoever it was to come in, expecting to see Lydia. He could not conceive what she might say. He had a dangerous impulse to tell her the truth; to see how she would respond, see whether she would still accuse him of blowing up a small and passing matter out of proportion.

But it was not Lydia. It was Tim.

'And where the hell have you been?'

'I cycled into Appledore to take some snaps of the church. There are some floor tiles—'

'Spare me the history lesson. What do you want?'

'I found Will wandering about outside. He seems rather upset.'

'Upset, is he?'

'Something about Alice. He wants to see you.'

'It's not a question of him wanting to see me. It's whether I wish to see him.'

'Well – do you?'

When Will Kemp entered the study he was shaking and chewing his lip, his broad forehead damp with sweat.

'Yes?' Guv said.

'I'm sorry, Captain.'

'Sorry, are you? I suppose you imagine that puts things right?'

'It wasn't much, nothing untoward. We're fond of each other, Alice and me. There was no harm in it, I don't think. I know she's above me, that there's no hope for me in that direction. But my feelings for her are honest, Captain, and we've done nothing to be ashamed of.'

'I'll decide that. How old are you now?'

'Eighteen.'

'It's too old to be mooning about this place, or wasting your time mending old crocks for your father. There are great things doing in the Air Force. They're looking for likely fellows to train up as flight mechanics. I've had it in mind for some while now to put you forward. Play your cards right and you could be a sergeant-pilot a few years from now, particularly with my endorsement. You've worked wonders on my kites and that should count in your favour.' Guv was deep into another whisky. 'Well, Will,' (it was the first time he had used the Christian name), 'what do you say?'

'I don't know, Captain. It would mean leaving Dad in the lurch.'

'We can hire a spanner-man soon enough. You've got to think of yourself in this life.' Guv reached for the decanter. 'There is one proviso. I don't want you to see Alice again, not in that way. There's nothing in it for either of you. If you care for her as you claim, you'll end it now. It's the fairest course.'

Will pushed his hand through his hair. 'That's hard, Captain. That's a big price to pay. We go back so far. She's my greatest friend.'

'A ruddy odd way to behave with a friend,' Guv said. 'But that's the price, nevertheless. You're an intelligent lad. You must see it's a price worth paying. You have an excellent future ahead of you. Why

429

spoil it now? You're both young, too young, and as for you, well, the world's full of women. You'll find that out. You can scarcely know your own mind about such things. Sow those oats. Fill your belly with them. You'll discover the world's a bigger place than High And Over.'

'But Alice—'

'Oh, she'll get over it. She's off to ladies' college soon. No doubt they'll stuff her head with useless nonsense but still, it will give her plenty to think about apart from you.'

'She tells me she doesn't want to go.'

'I've no doubt she does. It suits her perfectly to drift about High And Over like the Lady of Shalott waiting for Sir Lancelot to ride by.' Guv had a vague recollection of the poem from his inattentive Harrow days, something about a curse and the Lady of Shalott setting herself adrift in a boat and expiring prettily downstream; at any rate, he knew it ended badly.

'Look,' he said more brightly, 'consider this a test of your devotion to my daughter. I respect your concern for her well-being' (he did not, and thought it incomprehensible), 'but I must receive your answer in the morning. Prompt, mind. Something like this cannot be delayed.' The boy began to move uncertainly towards the door. 'You have a good future as an airman,' Guv called after him, 'and I'll do everything I can to help you achieve your ambitions. But you have no future, no future at all with Alice. I want that crystal clear. I'm sorry, but there it is. The choice is yours. Defy my wishes as her father, and risk the consequences, or do the decent thing, the right and sensible thing for both of you.'

'Yes,' Will said.

'Meanwhile, you're to make no attempt to communicate with Alice or discuss this in any way. Is that also clear?'

'It's clear, all right, Captain, but I still don't understand. I've always respected you, you realise that, looked up to you, been proud to know you and work for you. And you've done a lot for me, I don't deny it, but you seem to think so little of me, after all.'

'You're wrong, Will. I think a great deal of you. I want to give you every advantage. But that doesn't include making up to my daughter. I have other plans for her.' (He had no plans, had never given it a thought.)

'Making up, Captain?' Will flushed. 'It's rather more than that.'

'Your obvious concern does you credit,' Guv said, the sentiment spoiled by his slurred speech, 'but I must urge you to accept the situation and leave Alice to me.' He had an inexplicable desire to laugh.

When, a few minutes later, he went to the study window and watched the boy push his cycle slowly down the drive, he saw Tim join him for a little way and they talked together, but then he turned back. Guv reeled through to the hallway and reached for the banister of the oak staircase to steady himself. Behind him he heard Tim say: 'What on earth's going on? Will's got a face like thunder.' Lydia was slowly descending the stairs. Caught between them, fogged with drink, Guv felt like a squirrel trapped in one of the steel cages his workers set down in the woods; no matter how much he twisted and turned he could see no escape.

Everything seemed to be compounding against him. He wondered what he had done to deserve it. He was Guv Sutro, the people's idol, the object of veneration, a hero. Heroes were not governed by normal bounds of behaviour. That was the bargain: their deeds earned them immunity from petty considerations that applied to ordinary folk. Those who snapped at his ankles were like curs to be kicked away. He recalled a word he had heard Goering use. *Lebensraum*. Living space. Now the Reich was applying it to territory it required for expansion. And he too deserved *Lebensraum* – not this constant raking over of his past or warnings from shabby bureaucrats about which creed to follow. 'I want *Lebensraum*,' he said thickly.

'What is it you want?' said Lydia, continuing to descend.

Guv attempted dignity and straightened up. 'I want to see my daughter.'

'She's in no fit state to see anyone and neither are you.' Lydia pushed past him as he placed a foot on the lowest stair and he lost his balance and fell, cracking his head on the floor. He heard Lydia say: 'Get out of the house, Tim, your father's ill.'

'Shall I call Doctor Powell?'

'Just get out of the house. Get out this instant. I'll deal with it.'

Guv lay back, the ceiling spinning above him, a kaleidoscope of plasterwork and beams, and began to laugh. He was racked with laughter and began to choke. He rolled onto his side but could not gain his feet. He found himself alone. He crawled on his knees through to his study and kicked the door shut. He used the desk to pull himself up and slumped into his chair. He reached out for the decanter and found it was empty. It slipped from his fingers and smashed on the floor, the shards glinting like jewels. He lay back in the chair and went to sleep. When he woke the house was quiet, no lights showing. He had the impression he was alone. The mantel clock showed two in the morning. It was dark outside and night sounds came in through the half-open window. Something was being hunted out there; from time to time something screamed.

He rose, swaying like a deckhand on a Cape Horn clipper, and set off for the library to find the whisky bottle on the sideboard. His feet, in slippers, felt wet and when he looked down he saw they were bloody from the broken glass scattered round his desk, and that he was leaving smudged bright-red footprints on the polished boards and fine carpets. As he was searching for a tumbler among the glasses, he heard the library door open. He turned to see Lydia staring at him as though she had never seen him before, as though he was a stranger; a stranger in his own house.

'And who the hell are you looking at?' he said.

'I want you to leave this place now.'

'What place?'

'This house. My house.'

'Your house, is it? And why would I want to do that?'

'You seem to want your freedom. I'm giving it to you – legally, if need be.'

'I see.'

'I gather you've forbidden Alice to see Will Kemp.'

'That's right.'

'I've told them both to take no notice. If they wish to continue their friendship, wherever it may lead, they have my permission.'

'Your permission, you say. Is that your last word on the matter?'

'It is. I have a perfect right—'

'Oh yes, a perfect right. Except, you see . . .' Guv hesitated for a moment, searching for the words. The only words that came were brutal; it suited him. 'Except, you see, Will Kemp's my son.'

7

When Amelia Earhart went down in the Pacific in her Lockheed Electra with her navigator Fred Noonan in the summer of 1937, trying to be first to circle the world by the equatorial route, it opened the way for others to take up the challenge, among them Guv Sutro. The new Schoenfelder tri-motor seemed the ideal choice, with its duralumin-skinned fuselage, low cantilever wings and 800 horsepower BMW engines that could take 15 passengers to 11,000 feet and cover 600 miles at 100 miles an hour. It had already proved itself a sturdy and reliable machine with civilian airlines in Europe, Asia and South America. Less comfortably, it had served the Fascist cause in Spain. But this, the bid to be first to circumvent the globe the long way round, a journey of 29,000 miles, met with no controversy, viewed simply as another milestone in the advance of peacetime aviation.

Max Schoenfelder had already announced details of the flight. Equipped with long-range fuel tanks and a crew of three, the tri-motor would take off from Quito in Ecuador, head west over the Pacific to Howland Island (the speck in the ocean Earhart failed to find), and on to Pontianak in Borneo, still precisely on the equator. Another ocean crossing, the Indian now, objective Nayuki, Kenya, before traversing Africa to Gabon. Ahead, the Atlantic's great expanse before land-fall at Belem on Brazil's eastern coast and then the final leg, 2,000 miles across the tropical forests of Amazonia to touchdown back at Quito. Such an endeavour did not call for flying skill; just nerve and good navigation. As the doomed Earhart herself had said: 'Preparation is two-thirds of any venture.' Ironic, then, that her loss was put down to radio-navigation errors.

Max Schoenfelder was resolute: no such failure would be allowed to mar his company's attempt. The planning would be meticulous. The machine would be the best, with nothing overlooked, the crew the same. 'Only three seats are available on this historic quest,' Schoenfelder told a news conference. 'Therefore we intend to select from the finest pilots and navigators in the world. Nationality is immaterial. The Germans are an open-minded people. We are citizens of the world. This will be an achievement, not just for Germany but for the entire human race. The Englishman, Captain Sutro? Yes, he has flown for us successfully many times. Certainly his name is in the hat.'

At Croydon, Guv Sutro, formal in snappy trilby and double-breasted overcoat, was pictured by Pathé newsreel boarding an Imperial Airways flight for Berlin. He waved from the steps of the Handley-Page with that fixed, familiar grin under the usual tired headlines: NEW HEIGHTS FOR BRITISH ACE; EQUATOR FLIGHT HOT PROSPECT FOR OUR GUV; ANOTHER RECORD FOR CAPTAIN SUTRO? He responded curtly to ill-timed questions from reporters about his marriage. 'I'd like to scotch these silly rumours now. My daughter is to complete her education in the United States. This is entirely natural. My wife, who has accompanied her, has family there. I might add that it's a poor reflection on the current state of our country that elements of the British press bother with the trivialities of one's private life when the world's stirring with matters of far greater importance than whether my daughter returns to England with an American accent.' But it was noticed that the grin had grown more fixed, looked more pasted-on.

At Tempelhof he was met by a chauffeur-driven Horch saloon that took him to the Schoenfelder factory at Wassergarten airfield twenty miles outside the city. The driver told him his usual accommodation had been booked at the Kaiserhof Hotel on Wilhelmstrasse, favoured by the Nazi Party and the Führer himself. A dinner had been arranged there, to be attended by two company directors and Fräulein Preiss. 'And Herr Schoenfelder?' Guv asked.

'I do not think so,' the man said carefully, as though he had been primed. 'He has a prior engagement, I understand.'

In the conference room, Max Schoenfelder was alone. 'Ah, my *Englische Überkanone*, you are growing fat. Life is treating you well.'

'Well enough, Max, but I'm eager to get my hands on your tri-motor, to put it through its paces. Is it ready to test? I want to find out how the long-range tanks affect the flying characteristics.'

'That may not be possible on this occasion.'

'But surely work's completed? There were photos and an article in *Flight*.'

'Oh, it's ready enough. But to be candid, my friend, the board of directors is still debating the composition of the crew.'

'The board of directors? Pull the other one, Max. We both know *you* make all the decisions round here.'

Schoenfelder smiled. 'You may think that, but these days no company can be managed by a single man.'

'Your country is.'

'An interesting observation that can be taken in two ways. Admiring or critical. That, Captain, is the nature of our concern.'

Guv noted the sudden formality. 'Look, Max, we've known each other a long time. Drop the Captain business and stop hedging around. What are you getting at exactly?'

Schoenfelder began to pace round the boardroom table. Guv noticed that he had his arms folded in the manner of Adolf Hitler, left over right, clasping the right elbow with splayed fingers. There was a strut to him.

'Things have been reported,' he said slowly. 'You will realise that in a project of this nature we must have the utmost confidence in everyone involved, from the most junior worker on the factory floor to the most senior executive. But particularly the men who will fly the machine, the public face of our venture. This flight represents something far greater than any prestige it might bring to *Schoenfelder Aeronplau*. It is an expression of the spirit of the Fatherland.'

'In that case,' Guv said, 'you'd better select your aircrew from your home-grown pool. Why not Udet or Gerd Achgelis, or give

Renate Preiss a chance? She has the potential to be your Amelia Earhart.'

'These suggestions are not in our minds at the present time,' said Schoenfelder. 'You misunderstand me slightly. I am not saying you are no longer favoured as first pilot. Good relations between England and Germany are of vital importance to the Reich. The Führer has the highest regard for your people and believes that both countries – both empires, if you wish – will go forward together. You are seen as a symbol of that unity, like Richard Seaman at Mercedes, and for that reason we still favour entrusting you with this mission. But certain sources have indicated that your loyalty to our cause might be less strong than it once was.'

'You know, Max, that I'm a great admirer of the Reich and everything that's been achieved.'

'That is good to hear, but it is a view that needs to be put before a broader audience. You take the point, do you not?'

'After all these years I'm surprised you question my commitment.'

'Well, you are a patriot, after all. It would be natural for you to be influenced by those who beat the drum of Little England, who see only a future of discord and conflict. Thus, we require what might be called a clear demonstration of your good faith – some pronouncements in the public arena back in England, for example. The right to free speech is one of the great principles which the English treasure. We simply suggest you exercise that right and put such opinions as you may hold to those who care to listen. We do not tell you what to say, of course. That is entirely your affair. But if it becomes clear, quite soon, that you remain stalwart, that you stand by your beliefs about the Reich despite whatever rumours we may have heard, well, then no doubt we can review the situation. But I urge you, do not wait too long. Next spring is the time we have all agreed for the flight to take place, and the team must be confirmed.'

Schoenfelder moved round the table and gave Guv a comradely pat on the back. 'Personally, I have much confidence in you. It is only a matter of fitting that final piece into the puzzle for those less certain. Otherwise, all is as usual. You have been told, I think, that we have reserved your usual suite at the Kaiserhof and Fräulein Preiss will ensure you have an enjoyable stay; also Frolich and Lotz will be joining you for dinner. Unfortunately, I cannot.'

'Yes, that is unfortunate.'

'Oh, next time certainly.' Schoenfelder pondered for a moment. 'Please understand, we place great value in you as an individual of significance in English society. Your opinions are respected there, as well as your deeds. In time, that reputation will stand you in good stead. If you doubt me, consider Reichsmarschall Goering. From leader of a Jasta in France to Commander-in-Chief of the Luftwaffe. Who knows how high you might rise if England goes the way of Germany and Italy? Perhaps a senior command in your own Royal Air Force.'

Guv grunted. 'Well, that's as may be. Dealing with the present, Max, all I can say is that it's a hell of a long way to come to be told I haven't got the job.'

'Not yet, *mein guter Freund*,' said Schoenfelder. 'But I preferred to explain the situation to you face-to-face for, as you say, old times' sake. It is better that way, I think, so I can be sure you understand.'

He clapped his hands together smartly. 'Now, to the Kaiserhof, I suggest, and Renate Preiss. You will find your journey here is not entirely wasted. There you can talk shop with her, among other things. You will find her an excellent hostess. I regret, however, that Berlin nightlife is not what it was. The Führer's concern with moral decay has led to many of the cabarets being closed down. But novelties are still to be found, if you have a knowledgeable guide.'

At the Kaiserhof on Wilhelmplatz, Guv was greeted by the manager who waived the formalities of registration. 'No such trivialities are necessary, Captain Sutro. I am honoured to welcome you to our hotel once again.'

He collected the key to Guv's suite from the reception clerk and went with him in the lift to the top floor of the hotel. As they rose swiftly between the floors, Guv said: 'This is not necessary, Herr Schroeder. I know the way by now.'

'No, no, Captain Sutro – I insist. I only wish to ensure you are comfortably installed.'

They came out of the lift and moved silently along the thick-carpeted corridor to the suite. Schroeder unlocked the door and stood back to let Guv pass through. Renate Preiss was standing by the window drawing on a cigarette in a stubby amber holder and looking across the broad and busy boulevards of Wilhelmstrasse towards the rococo bulk of the Reich Chancellery where, on its balcony seven years before, President von Hindenburg had watched the torchlight parade of the Nationalsozialistiche Deutsche Arbeiterpartei when they came to power.

Preiss turned, but did not smile. Her quick glance at Schroeder suggested some sort of collusion, that meeting like this had been planned. 'It is too boring to be recognised in the public rooms, Sutro,' she said. 'I preferred to wait for you here.' Her voice was hoarse from smoking, had a mannish timbre. To Guv she seemed man/woman in neat grey slacks, white high-collared shirt (of silk, a feminine conces- sion) and practical laced shoes. Her tailored leather jacket, a flier's jacket, hung on the back of a chair.

'This evening,' she said, 'it is just you and me. Frolich and Lotz are otherwise engaged.'

As Schroeder bowed himself out, murmuring and rubbing his hands, Guv said: 'Frolich and Lotz as well? I'm surprised I haven't been left to my own devices.'

'Why is that?'

'There seems to be some doubt about my commitment to Schoenfelder.'

'Oh, no doubt of that. It is the broader question that requires an answer, your commitment to the Reich.' Preiss pushed a hand through her white-blond hair, cropped brutally short. A thin scar ran from the side of her mouth to below the lobe of her left ear, the result of an engine failure on a speed record attempt that ended in a heavy landing. 'Any hesitancy on your part would be quite understandable,' she continued reasonably. 'After all, you have your own country's interests at heart and, between you and me, the Führer can be seen by some as a comical and posturing fellow with a ridiculous moustache and bellowing speeches. Be honest now. Is it not so?'

'Is this some sort of test?'

'I am not sure I understand you. This is just a conversation between fellow aviators, a candid conversation.'

'That was a dangerous opinion, if honestly held.'

'You doubt my sincerity?'

'I don't know, Renate. I'm just a pilot. I fly where I can, wherever there's the greatest chance of success.'

'Oh come now, Sutro, you're not just a pilot. We both know that. False modesty does not sit easily with you. You may pretend to be a simple fellow but you have ambition, as do we all. A greater purpose.'

'My greater purpose right now,' said Guv, 'is to find myself a drink. Care to join me, or are you intent on questioning my motives?'

Preiss smiled, her facial scar suddenly taut like a scarlet thread. 'Oh, I will certainly join you in a drink. But you must realise that you have been compromised by your own people. They have made sure our eyes and ears in London are well aware of certain meetings that have taken place. That is why, on the matter of your loyalty, it seems we require reassurance.'

'Who's we? Schoenfelder?'

'It would be a great pity if you were denied opportunities because of doubts.'

'You mean the opportunity to get my hands on Schoenfelder machines?'

'That is a beginning.'

'What can I say? Look, I helped to put the damned company back on the map. Nobody can argue with that. My achievements speak for themselves. I don't deny I was dragged into a meeting with some faceless little clerk in a Government office who suggested I might be getting too close to the Reich, but Christ, Renate, it's not as if we're at war, is it, or likely to be?'

Renate Preiss reached for her jacket. 'Of course not. You simply need to make your position plain, as Max I think explained. Clear up any uncertainties in words as well as deeds, and confidence can quickly be restored.' She zipped her jacket. 'This is such a simple matter, really. We should not spend more time on it. Just make your position plain, commit yourself, and all will be well.' She laughed and, for a moment, looked like a young girl. 'Do you remember that time in Paris, when we gathered to see you receive the Blériot medal? That club we went on to in Pigalle, the nigger woman with the German Shepherd dog and the string of Toulouse sausages? And Max climbing onto the stage and saying he had a sausage of his own for her to get her hands on? I cannot promise such diversions tonight. These days, Berlin is dull by comparison with Paris.'

'What I remember of that night,' Guv said, 'is you and Max going off somewhere, leaving me to find my own way back to the hotel. Perhaps tonight will be different. Perhaps we will go off somewhere. It seems Max has better things to do.'

Renate Preiss stood by the door with her hands on her hips. She looked like a child. 'Surely you do not have designs on me, Sutro? I am sure you can do much better than that. I am a dry little stick, not your style at all.'

'But Max's style, it seems.'

She held the door open. People were passing in the corridor, looking in curiously, recognising her. 'I do not recommend we dine here,' she said. 'We will find somewhere more private. But do not misunderstand me. If your appetite is for more than food, you will have to satisfy it elsewhere.'

Guv went over to the window and looked down on the early-evening promenaders moving along Wilhelmstrasse. They progressed slowly, as if wary of encountering some unknown destiny that might be waiting for them round a corner. 'You flatter yourself, Preiss,' he said, without turning his head. 'I'm not *that* hungry.' He laughed to show he was joking but he was not joking and she knew it. It did not offend her.

'We all have our tastes,' she said. 'You would not share mine.'

That caught his interest. 'How do you know?' He looked back

from the window but she had left the suite and was waiting for him in the corridor, lighting another cigarette. She blew out the smoke and set off towards the lift without waiting for him.

A taxi took them to a low-ceilinged restaurant in a narrow street off Nollendorfplatz. She was known there. Behind the bar hung a framed photograph of her saluting the Führer after her victory in the Nuremburg air race of 1934. They were given a cubicle in a candle-lit corner, the table covered with a crisp gingham cloth. The proprietor asked Guv to autograph a menu, for display beside the picture of the Reich heroine Renate Preiss.

'They will take us for lovers,' she said. 'This fellow is not discreet. Tomorrow they will write of our liaison in the society columns of *Der Sturmer*, anticipating a brood of little Aryan pilots.'

'A flight,' Guv said. He paused and stared across the table. 'You forget. I'm married.'

'I've heard that of you also. You forget you are married.' She lit a cigarette from the candle on the table. He felt in his pocket for his pipe and tobacco pouch. 'Your son,' she was saying. 'Is he a pilot yet?'

'No. His head's in the clouds but not in an aeroplane.'

'That is a disappointment to you.'

'Of course.'

'You must not be too hard on him. It is difficult to be the son of a famous father.'

'Difficult? It should be a privilege. The boy's a washout. There's no purpose in him.'

'When I met him at the reception in the Aviators' Club in the Avenue Kléber he seemed a fine young Englishman: modest, courteous, loyal. You should not underrate him. He has admirable qualities.'

'You seem to have formed a strong opinion on short acquaintance.'

'I am quick in my judgements.' Renate smiled. 'And not often wrong.'

Guv thought about that, sucking at his pipe, the match flaring as the tobacco began to burn.

Renate narrowed her eyes. 'And the girl?'

'The girl?' Guv said idly. 'What about the girl?' The implication was clear.

'Ah, so predictable. It has not entered your head that aviation might be in your daughter's blood.'

'I've seen no sign of it.'

'Have you looked?'

'Don't have to. Flying's not for her.'

'You leap to these judgements with such assurance. The Führer is not so prejudiced.'

'What, that comical figure you spoke of with the ridiculous moustache and bellowing voice?'

She reached over and covered his mouth with her free hand. '*Schweige*! That is not amusing.' He put out his tongue and licked her palm and she snatched back her hand. 'You are offensive, Sutro. You should be taught a lesson.'

'Are you the one to teach me?'

'Perhaps.' She signalled to the proprietor that she was ready to order. As the man came forward she said: 'Your wife, Sutro, she is in America, is she not?'

'Yes, with my daughter. She has family there.'

'You *are* her family, surely? But there, I play games, because you are not a family man, are you, Sutro?' The proprietor was at her side, his pencil poised above his pad. She looked at Guv speculatively. 'I am fond of games. Do you like games, I wonder?' She gave her order and sat back, saying, 'Ask for whatever you wish. Perhaps something you have not enjoyed before.'

'I'll have the same as you,' Guv said. 'Who knows? Maybe we share the same tastes.'

They ate pork stew with potatoes and drank strong Pilsner beer. She drank little, but Guv had a thirst on him. He felt the uncertainties of the day, the unanswered questions, the subtleties of conversations he could not fathom start to fade. All that counted now was now; this warming meal in snug surroundings, the crackle of a pinewood fire, low voices drifting across from the other cubicles, the gold and flickering candlelight that played on the mask-like face of Renate Preiss, the thump and slop of another stein of Pilsner, its creamy froth trickling down and creating a dark ring on the chequered cloth. He experienced a sudden sense of well-being, as though he had stepped into a shower and washed away all his concerns. He could hardly remember them now. He imagined them swirling around his feet, vanishing with a gurgle down the wastepipe. Gone, forgotten. Why had they seemed important? What mattered now . . . what mattered now was schnapps . . . he called for schnapps.

Renate's face, Renate's face – it hovered like the bloody Cheshire Cat. He offered it schnapps. It shook its head. No, cats hated schnapps. The cat was smiling. Smiling like the Cheshire Cat. The Cheshire Cat in a tree that someone asked: 'Which road do I take?' And the cat said: 'Where do you want to go?' 'I don't know,' said someone. 'Then it doesn't matter,' said the cat.

Guv finished the schnapps. He stared at the cat's face, the Cheshire Cat in a tree. It was no longer a cat but a woman. He stretched out his hand. The woman leaned back out of his reach. 'Which road do I take?' Guv said.

'Which road?' repeated the woman. 'Just what are you saying?'

'Patron,' Guv shouted. 'More schnapps.'

The man came across with a bottle. He was looking at the woman. She nodded. The man poured more schnapps into Guv's glass. Guv took the bottle from the man and poured the schnapps for himself until the liquid was flush to the brim. It seemed to tremble like mercury, its surface slightly raised. He picked up the glass and moved it towards his mouth. His arm was like a mechanical arm, moving smoothly towards him without spilling a drop. Pissed to the world, still steady as a rock. He banged down the glass. He was on his feet for a moment, then fell back heavily on the bench.

'Which road?' he said. 'Which bloody road?' It seemed that some kind of decision had to be made but he could not remember what it was. He relaxed because a cat had told him it didn't matter. He heard the woman cursing him in German. At least he thought she was. That was how the German language always sounded. She switched to English.

'You damned, drunken Englishman. You embarrass me. You deserve to be punished.'

He rallied for a moment. 'I'd like to see you try.'

'Can you withstand pain?'

'I can withstand anything you care to dream up. It's just a question of will-power.'

'*Recht so, der Triumph des Willens.*' The woman laughed. 'We must put you to the test. Then we will discover how steadfast you really are.'

He was in a car. The woman was next to him. They were sliding on smooth leather as the car went round corners. He watched the back of the driver's head. He was wearing a cap. There was a pinpoint of red light that came and went in front of the driver's face. He was smoking. Guv was pleased with himself for knowing he was smoking; that there was a simple explanation for the pinpoint of red light that came and went. He leaned against the woman, his head against her shoulder. She pushed him away.

The car had stopped. He heard voices, German voices, bloody Boche voices, some laughter, the rustle of money. He caught his name. He was out of the car and stumbling down a twist of steps, some kind of basement, his hand running along a smooth iron hand-rail, cold to the touch. Voices again, women's voices, German women's voices. The clink of glass, something being poured. Strong liquor on his lips and in his mouth and burning down his throat. It had a kick that opened his eyes like the eyes of a sleeping doll sat upright; suddenly open and open wide, taking in the cellar, focusing on the cellar. A woman was saying, Renate was saying, Renate Preiss was saying: 'You say you like games.' He turned his head to stare at her with his wide-open doll eyes. She looked different. He could not see her face. It was covered with a mask. Her eyes glittered behind the slantwise holes in the black leather. Behind her he caught another movement; another woman almost naked, in straps and belts and buckles. His vision blurred.

He was facing a wall of bare brick. He was naked too. He felt his arms being raised, metal bands closing shut around his wrists. Someone pulled back on his ankles. His knees gave way, his body sagged, his wrists took the weight of his body, his forehead grazed the wall. He heard a crack like a pistol shot, a noise he knew, a circus noise. His buttocks were struck with a searing pain. A voice in his ear, Renate's voice: 'Do you like my game, you damned Englishman, do you like my game?' The pistol crack and another blow. A flash of light. A long, thin scream. The scream was his. Another blow and another blow. Urine spattering on the floor. Warm urine sticky on his thighs. Another blow, more flashes of light. He ceased to scream and took the pain. And took the pain. And seemed to float and took the pain and closed his eyes and took the pain.

The voice in his ear: 'Do you like my game, *Arschloch*? Do you like my game?' He groaned as the lash cut into him again. 'Yes, yes, I like your game. I take the pain. I take the pain.'

He was back in the suite at the Kaiserhof. He did not know how he got there. He was lying face down on the bed and could not breathe. He rolled over and could not prevent himself from crying out in agony as the raw flesh on his back and buttocks was compressed. He went through to the bathroom and looked at himself in the full-length mirror. The weals and bruises were bilious blue and yellow and ran the length of his body from the nape of his neck to his ankles. He ran a cold bath and lay in it on his side for an hour. He dried himself gingerly. Scabs were beginning to form on broken sores. When he dressed, the slightest touch of cloth made him wince. Images came to him from the cellar, distorted, ugly; arousing. He did not understand arousing. He felt he had survived, come through a test, passed through a portal to somewhere new, an unsuspected world of cruelty and darkness that challenged normal values; where anything was possible, no bounds observed.

He walked in the Wilhelmstrasse, taking small uncertain steps like an old man, each one tightening the lesions on his back and making him gasp. Hidden by the jacket that rested loose across his shoulders he felt his shirt becoming sticky and damp with seeping blood. Passers-by were staring at him. He did not know if they were trying to place his face or curious about his hesitant gait. He forced himself to lengthen his stride, defying the pain, deriving a certain pleasure.

At the Kaiserhof, Max Shoenfelder was waiting in the lobby. 'So, you have been taking a constitutional. May I offer you breakfast?'

'No.'

Schoenfelder grinned. He knew everything. 'Those ladies, they lay it on with finesse, do they not?'

'Well, Max,' Guv said, 'did I pass?'

'Pass? Pass what?'

'Your little trial to size me up.'

'Perhaps the devilish Preiss misunderstood,' said Schoenfelder. 'She imagined you were curious about such practices. Possibly she was wrong. Perhaps you would have preferred to wield the lash yourself.'

'I'd like to get my own back, that's for sure.'

'Such tastes appear bizarre at first, but they have a fascination. Of course, you are an Englishman so naturally you resist such aberrations. You should not take it too seriously. It is merely an amusement, to be experienced and then adopted or abandoned as you wish. Next time, you must try it sober. Your senses were somewhat dulled by drink. Sober, you will find it tests your will to the limit.'

'Ah, the triumph of the will again.'

Schoenfelder's expression changed. 'We do not encourage jokes about such things.'

'Confound it, Max,' said Guv, 'you're as sensitive as my arse. If it's jokes you want, you should know your damned aviatrix described the Führer as a comic figure with a ridiculous moustache.'

Schoenfelder looked around the busy lobby. 'No, that is not quite accurate. She remarked that he could be seen so by some. Not at all the same thing. We wondered whether you might be tempted to agree.'

'Ah, so you were in on this.'

'Come now, you can hardly be surprised. But don't be too concerned. Your response was acceptable. However, if you are confirmed for the trans-world flight you must understand that we require better behaviour. Less tipping of the bottle.'

'We all have weaknesses. Goering's was morphine, wasn't it?'

'The *Reichsmarschall* cured himself. Willpower, you see. The will, a strength. Nothing to joke about.'

'I only drink on occasions. When flying, never.'

'Was last night an occasion?'

'I was led astray.'

'A fair point. But where women are concerned, you are also susceptible. Better behaviour in that respect is also required.'

'I'm going to take another bath. A cold one.'

'Think of our conversations while you soak. I wish you a safe journey home. We will monitor the English scene with interest.'

'You haven't always been so stiff and starchy, Max,' Guv said. 'Do you recall that night in Pigalle?'

'Ah yes, I have not touched a sausage since. A merry time, but not on German soil. Paris is made for frivolity. Perhaps we will meet there again one day.' Schoenfelder's eyes widened and he raised his head, as though looking towards a distant horizon. 'Perhaps one day when France is part of the greater Europe.'

'In that case,' Guv said, 'don't bother looking for that dive in Pigalle. The Führer will have closed it down.'

8

It was at a public meeting in Rye six months later that a voice from the back of the Town Hall shouted: 'Traitor!'

Guv, on the stage, waved the pages of his speech above his head. 'I'd like to challenge the man who said that to step into the aisle, where I can see him, instead of skulking anonymously in the dark.' He saw a figure rise to its feet, move slowly between the seats and advance towards the stage. To his surprise there was something close to a murmur of approval. 'I know you, don't I?'

'Geoffrey Sleightholme – and you're talking tommy rot. We didn't fight a war to stand meekly aside and watch some tin-pot dictator do as he pleases in the name of German unity and expansion. First Austria, then the Sudetenland, now the Czechs. Who's next? If we listen to you and Chamberlain and Halifax and the rest of the appeasers, we'll soon hear the sound of jackboots on the cobblestones of Rye.' Sleightholme turned to scan the audience; people were nodding. 'You supported Quintin Hogg in the Oxford by-election, did you not?'

'Certainly I spoke in his favour.'

'Of whom it was said "A vote for Hogg is a vote for Hitler"?'

'Simplistic nonsense. As I recall, Hogg won a handsome victory. It is called democracy, sir. I commend it to you.' Guv expected approving laughter but there was only silence. He said quickly: 'I give you the floor because we are all aware of your distinguished record in the war. But if Herr Hitler . . .'

'*Herr* Hitler, is it?'

'If it was Germany's intention to attack and overthrow this country, why did it miss its opportunity last September? From what I know of . . . of Germany's leader, he is not a man to miss chances.'

'It seems you're very soft in your attitude towards this so-called Führer. Would that have anything to do with flying his aeroplanes?'

'I'm an airman, not a politician.'

'Well, well, if that's so, why aren't you in the air now instead of addressing this meeting? As soon as you sat in the cockpit of a machine with a swastika on its tail, a machine produced by a former enemy with clear and aggressive objectives, you entered the world of politics.'

'I simply fly the best machines available to keep Britain's reputation to the forefront in the aviation business.'

'*Your* reputation, more likely.'

'Unfair, Sleightholme. If this country was producing the best machines capable of breaking records, believe me I would fly them. It is the same for Dick Seaman. He wants to win races, and the only cars capable of victory are Mercedes and Auto Union. The choice is clear: win with those teams or lose with ours. Perhaps you favour the role of gallant loser. It is not my way. As in motor-racing the British aviation industry has some catching up to do.'

'And whose fault's that? If the Nazis have the lead in aircraft design and production as you say, then you've helped to put them there.'

'You imply, Sleightholme, that everything achieved in Germany over the past two decades has been done with warlike intent, as if you believe in the inevitability of war.'

'Don't you?'

'By no means. And if you would be kind enough to allow me to conclude my address, I will explain why. Then the good people of Rye can make up their own minds.'

At this there was a pit-patter of applause, from somewhere a solitary muttered, 'Hear hear.' Sleightholme went back to his seat. Guv stood for a moment in silence, then threw down his manuscript. 'I burned the midnight oil concocting this. Putting pen to paper is not my strong point, as I learned at school. That is about all I learned.' (Grudging laughter.) 'Let me speak to you direct, from the heart if you like. In my book, and I'm sure this applies to every one of us here, Britain comes first. We've had enough of foreign wars. We will not allow millions of Englishmen to be dragged to their doom, for someone else's quarrel. Our friend Sleightholme, for whom I have the greatest respect, suggests that I was wrong to endorse the none-theless successful candidate in the Oxford by-election, a candidate who was elected by the people of that constituency, who voiced their approval for the platform on which that candidate stood.' Heads were turning in the audience to see Sleightholme's reactions, but he had left. 'I regret,' said Guv, 'that my adversary, if that is what he was, has not remained to hear the rest of what I have to say. He is missing some jolly good stuff.' (Laughter, warmer.)

'Let there be no doubt about where my loyalty lies. Let me repeat: for me it is Britain first. What interest have we in Eastern Europe? We've had enough of Balkan wars. Our focus must be on the British Empire, advancing the policy of peace. This is within our grasp. Some people, and no doubt our absent friend is among them, claim that Hitler has ambitions to dominate the entire world, even that he is insane. What evidence is there for that supposition? No one can deny that he has restored pride to his nation, has brought it to prosperity and, yes, power from being on its knees. Even the most jaundiced eye can see that this is an extraordinary achievement. Now, can you suppose this is to be gambled on the outcome of an all-out war on many fronts against formidable opposition? If so, then Hitler is truly mad. On the contrary, I tell you it is my belief that we are entering a new age of enlightenment. As the Prime Minister described it, "peace for our time". However, and I will leave you with this thought, if such a circumstance came about that propelled us into another great war, if any other country in the world attacked Great Britain or threatened to . . . then I know that everyone here tonight would join with me in throwing those invaders back in the sea so the British Channel, Rye Bay indeed, would be black with their corpses.'

Guv sensed he had regained ground. 'And now, as Prime Minister Chamberlain also said, "go home and sleep quietly in your beds". Excellent advice and I only regret our friend Sleightholme is not here to hear it. But nonetheless, I wish him and every one of you, every man and woman here, a very good night. And take a tip from me, don't worry about bogeymen under your beds. They don't exist.'

There was polite applause, no more. Chairs began to scrape back, people to bend their heads in conversation as they shuffled towards the exit. Only a few approached Guv and commended him. One, elderly, fiercely moustached and wearing heavy tweeds despite the early summer heat, tapped the side of his nose.

'I got the picture, my boy, I got the picture.'

Guv recognised him, a relic of distant wars who lived alone in a small house in Watchbell Street and marched about the town berating tradesmen for insolence. 'What picture's that, Colonel?'

'I can read between the lines as well as the next man. Better! All this hoo-hah about the intentions of the Hun. This country has no reason to fear them. There's not a shred of evidence that they mean to attack the British Empire. This fellow Hitler has given his assurance over and over again and yet our yellow press brand the man a liar. But you're onto that, of course.'

'I certainly said something to that effect.'

'This whole confounded mess could be cleared up with an open and frank discussion, which is apparently beyond the wit of our politicians. We simply say to the Hun, "Look, we won't interfere with your eastern borders and you leave us alone in the west".'

'That's pretty much Chamberlain's position, isn't it?'

The Colonel didn't hear. 'Of course, a lot of our current difficulties were caused by the damned Frenchies. The Germans are a great people, much akin to ourselves. They got a raw deal at Versailles, thanks to the French and that bounder Lloyd George. Now I'm not saying this Hitler fellow is exactly top drawer, by no means, but you have to admit that many of his claims are entirely justified.'

Guv realised that other people were listening, and beginning to move away. 'Well, Colonel . . .'

'Regrettably, views such as ours are likely to fall on deaf ears,' continued the Colonel. 'People won't wake up. Certainly the whole fabric of this country is under threat – but not by Herr Hitler; instead it's thanks to this huge influx of refugees streaming across our borders from God knows where. It's not that they all come here penniless. Many of them, the Jews, come with full coffers and wield huge financial clout in all sorts of fields. Their influence is insidious, changing our values, sapping our moral fibre, brushing aside everything that men like you and me have fought for, our heritage as Englishmen. People don't understand. The Jews are not like us. They're industrious, no one can deny them that, but they're industrious with a purpose. They're part of a mobile nation, always Jewish first, sticking together, working against the national culture of wherever they may be, a race apart, siding with the Left and stirring up dissent.'

'Well, Colonel . . .'

'Nothing would suit them better, my boy, than to instigate a Jew war, set nation against nation and help them to claw in still more profit for their spider's web of enterprises. Well, we're wise to their little game, thank God, and won't permit it.'

'Good night, Colonel.'

'I enjoyed your speech, my boy. Sound sense. Said what has to be said. Why aren't fellows like you in Parliament, I'd like to know? Get to it, my dear Sutro, get to it. You can certainly count on my support and there are plenty of others like me.'

Guv looked around. He and the Colonel were alone, apart from an uncertain youth with lank hair and a reporter's notebook and the caretaker waiting to lock up. The youth chewed his pencil until the Colonel had gone. Then he came over. 'I'm Armitage, *Sussex Recorder.*'

'What, Armitage like the lavatory pan?' Guv said, adding: 'I suppose you get that all the time.'

The reporter shook his head. 'No, you're the first. I was just wondering, Captain, now your supporter's gone, if it's true you'll be standing as our next MP.'

'I don't care for eavesdroppers, and for your information that gentleman is *not* my supporter. If you want my opinion, he's off his rocker.'

'It's your opinions I'm after.' The reporter flipped the pages of his notebook. 'I've got masses of copy here already. But there's room for more. How did you feel about being called a traitor?'

'How long have you been in this job, Armitage?'

'Not very long, six months.'

'It won't be for much longer. I'll be talking to your editor.'

'Have you actually met Hitler, Captain? Would you say he's a great man? Do we need someone like him here? What about the Jews? Are they like your friend said, intent on a Jewish war?'

'Here's an answer for you. Bugger off.'

Next day at High And Over, Griggs told Guv a Fleet Street journalist had phoned. The butler handed him the number on a scrap of paper.

'Urgent, was it?'

'Sounded like it. But of course these reporters always sound that way.'

It was a noisy line. The racket of the newsroom made the journalist's voice difficult to hear. 'Hello, Captain Sutro? We've had some meaty stuff filed by a local stringer about a speech you gave. Folk branding you a traitor. Just wondering how true it is.'

'I gave a perfectly straightforward talk about avoiding the need for a pointless war. A single unhinged heckler can in no way be described as "folk". I advise you to be extremely careful about what you write. Your source is hardly reliable.'

'Well, I wasn't there so I can't judge, can I? It's also said you've got ambitions to be in Number Ten.'

'What's that? Some new kind of kite?'

'No, Downing Street. This bloke says you'll be standing in the next election.'

'Hogwash. Now if that's all . . .'

'There is one other matter. What's this we hear about the round-the-world flight? Not being selected for the crew?'

'What's that you say?'

'We assumed you'd know all about it, Captain. I just wanted your reaction to not being selected. Bit of a let-down, I imagine.'

'Who told you this?'

'Came through on the wire thirty minutes ago. Press conference in Berlin. Goering was there and all the Nazi bigwigs.' A quick drawing-in of breath. 'I say, weren't you in the picture?'

'Yes, of course. But I wasn't aware of it being broken to the press so soon.'

'So what's your comment on losing out to Renate Preiss?'

Guv's grip on the telephone tightened. 'It wasn't a question of losing out. Good luck to her. She's a fine pilot and deserves the chance. I wasn't available, simple as that.'

'So, nothing to do with the international situation then?'

'How do you mean?'

'Just wondered if you'd been warned off by the Foreign Office. I know we're trying to be nice to the Germans, but it's not just people in Rye who reckon you might have got a bit too cosy with Hitler's lot. It seems to be getting about. Care to set the record straight?'

Guv replaced the phone. He went into the hall. 'Griggs, you must answer the telephone for the time being. If it's the press, tell them I'm abroad.'

'Where would that be, sir? These reporters are so persistent.'

'It doesn't matter. Anywhere but Germany.'

Next morning, taking breakfast in his study, Guv found his usual selection of newspapers arranged on the sideboard. At the bottom of the pile, probably tucked away by Griggs, was the tabloid daily he had spoken to. His eye was caught by the second lead on the front page:

'NO WAR IF BRITAIN IS PUT FIRST,' SAYS FAMOUS FLYER

'Traitor' Taunts As Captain Sutro Praises Hitler

Germany will not attack Britain, fighter ace and aviation record breaker Captain Fraser 'Guv' Sutro told a public meeting in Rye, Sussex yesterday. Sutro, who tests aeroplanes for the Schoenfelder factory in Berlin, praised the German leader for his 'extraordinary achievement' in restoring pride to his nation. There was no evidence, he said, that the Reich would risk these advances by embarking on total war. Germany's ambitions to expand to the east were understandable, given the 'raw deal' they received at Versailles, but he urged that in return for Britain's non-intervention there must be no interference by Germany in the west.

'It is my belief,' he stated, 'that we are entering a new age of enlightenment.'

A member of the audience, Captain G. Sleightholme, who served in the Great War, accused the speaker of being a traitor for expressing such views and cited his support for the Conservative candidate in the recent Oxford by-election, quoting the accusation: '"A vote for Hogg is a vote for Hitler." If we listen to you,' stated Captain Sleightholme from the floor, 'soon we'll hear the sound of jackboots on the cobblestones of Rye.' These remarks were later dismissed by Captain Sutro as 'simplistic nonsense from an unhinged heckler', adding that Hogg's victory was evidence of democracy in action.

The air ace also dismissed suggestions of anti-Semitism. He dissociated himself from a supporter who accused Britain of admitting 'an exodus of wealthy Jews' whose influence was insidious and threatened the English heritage. Colonel H.B. Drinkwater DSO, MC, who served with distinction in the Sudan and Boer Wars, was described by Captain Sutro as 'off his rocker'. Later, Captain Sutro denied that he had political ambitions but reinforced his belief in the British Empire and doing what he could, as a public figure, to advance the policy of peace.

In a separate development, Schoenfelder Aeronplau announced in Berlin that they have selected Renate Preiss, the famous aviatrix who tests fighter aircraft for the German air force, to pilot their new Tri-Motor airliner in a bid to be first round the world by the equatorial route, a record still to be achieved after Amelia Earhart's fateful attempt in 1937. Captain Sutro was widely tipped to be named Chief Pilot but is rumoured to have withdrawn due to pressure from the Foreign Office.

Guv screwed up the newspaper with both hands, threw it down, took up his leather flying helmet and goggles from their lucky hook in the cloakroom and went out of the house. At the foot of the porch steps the stripped-down Norton was propped up on its side-stand leaking oil onto the gravel. He kicked the motor alive and raced up to the hangar, the rear wheel sliding and kicking, the racket of the unsilenced exhaust shattering the tranquillity of the estate to its further reaches as it lay, as it had lain for centuries, under a boundless sky where great banks of broken cloud drifted across the sun, throwing the landscape into deep blue shadow until the sun burst clear, bathing with hard and brilliant light the fields and woodland, the lakes and ponds and streams, the tumbled moated castle in its secret valley, the gardens around the house, neglected now and slipping into muddle, and the house itself, the glassy play of light reflected in its windows suggesting that nothing lay within, like a corpse's eyes before the lids are closed. Guv saw nothing of this, only the rutted track that led to the airfield streaming beneath the Norton's wheels.

At the hangar, Paget was outside in the sun, balanced on the rear legs of a kitchen chair. He heard Guv coming from a long way off but only when he appeared did he let himself rock forward, throw down his cigarette and stand waiting with his hands on his hips.

Guv killed the Norton's engine and pulled it onto its stand. 'I'm going up in the DH4.'

'What brought this on?'

'That's no bloody business of yours. I'll give you a hand to push her out.'

Paget slid back the hangar doors and together they wheeled the biplane onto the concrete apron. It still had its Air Force markings. With the doped fabric of the fuselage and wings creaking and pulling tight in the heat, the long nose and mahogany propeller angled towards the sky, the machine's distinctive shadow spread out sharp across the fierce whiteness of the concrete, it could have been France two decades before. Paget went into the darkness of the hangar and came back with two jerrycans of petrol.

'These should give you enough for a flip.'

'Well, get to it, man.'

'I see you've been spouting off. The newspapers are full of it.'

'Full of rubbish. They've distorted what I said.'

'Oh, it was enough to get the gist. I don't care what anybody says. You and me, we've not exactly seen eye-to-eye over the years, but on this business with the Nazis I can't say I disagree with you. I went up to Earls Court on Sunday, to hear old Mosley speak. He's got it right. This country's got its own problems. We don't want no more imported by bloody foreigners, by the Yids who expect us to fight their wars for them. I go along with you. There'd be worse things than Britain going Fascist. No bloody war for a start, and a good kick up the arse for the money-men, the press lords, the milk-sop liberals, the Jews, the Reds. If it happens, I reckon you're going to find yourself in line for something juicy, being who you are and saying the things you've said. But then, you've already got this in mind, ain't you? The newspapers say you'll be standing for election.'

'The newspapers say a lot of things, mostly tosh.'

'I should consider it, if I were you. There's plenty I know who'd put a cross against your name.'

'That's all I'd need, the endorsement of your kind.'

'Well, there's no call to be so bleeding stuck-up about it. You're on a loose rein at the moment, remember. But me and Cuz, we can always give it a little tug, by way of a reminder. Be a pity, wouldn't it, given how you might be placed?' Paget, perched on a ladder, rattled a funnel against the neck of the DH4's fuel tank and began to pour in the first can of petrol. How simple it would be, Guv thought, to toss a match. Paget was saying: 'Actually, I'm thinking of joining up.'

'Good God. Which service?'

Paget glanced down. 'Don't get me wrong. You're not going to catch me in uniform, not that kind anyway. I mean the biff boys, Mosley's Blackshirts. They've got the right idea.' He came back down the ladder. 'What was it Mosley said? The BUF's the party to put this country back in the hands of all true Englishmen.'

'Of which you'd count yourself a prime example.'

'All right, you and me, we'll never rub along. But you could do a lot worse than side with Sir Oswald. He's a chap who's going places. High places.'

'I'm damned if I'd take seriously anyone called Sir Oswald.'

'That's the kind of remark that could get you into trouble with the blokes at Earls Court. You want to make your mind up, the way the wind's blowing.' Paget poured the second can of fuel into the tank while Guv thrust his foot into the step below the long exhaust stack, pulled himself up and dropped down into the cockpit, buckling his helmet under his chin, positioning his goggles on his forehead. He did not look at Paget on the wing as he leaned in to secure his harness. It was unpleasant to have him so close in such an intimate action.

The control column fell naturally to his hand, the instruments, white on black, gleamed on their panel of varnished wood. Years dropped away as he breathed in the trade-mark smell of wood and fabric and fuel and oil. Paget was at the propeller, reaching for the blade. The engine took first time, Guv caught in a wash of dust and air, the Rolls-Royce ticking over smoothly, 400 revs showing on the dial. He pulled down his goggles and waved Paget clear, his ears ringing to the bark of the exhaust, and taxied onto the grass runway where the yellow windsock stirred a little in a gentle easterly breeze. He climbed to 1,500 feet and passed over Rye, this town he knew so well, so close to the sea, so exposed behind its flat, invader-friendly beaches and estuary that led directly to its heart; its church sacked by the French 600 years ago; the bastions of nearby Camber Castle, marooned on a shingle spit once lapped by tides, ordered by Henry the Eighth to guard Rye's port and anchorage against the French (again, the French); the scatter of Martello towers to repel attack by Napoleon's Grande Armée (once more, the French). The prospect had not changed in twenty years. He was back in the Bristol Scout, before it all went wrong. It was hard to believe that south, across the flatlands of Northern France, the war did not go on; that if he pressed on beyond a certain point, Archie fire would not rise to meet him, that he might not expect dark specks against the sun to swoop down on him for the kill, guns chattering.

Over the Channel now he could see both coasts at once. This expanse of sea was nothing in the air, no more than a short hop. The new front-line, if it came to another war.

That useful marker, the tower of Calais's Town Hall, quivered in a silvery haze of rising heat. If, that day in 1917, the weather had been like this, he would have landed safely at Poperinge; would never have wrecked the Bristol; would never have ended up in the bag. Would never have met Max Schoenfelder. Would have missed out on many records and much fame. Would never, though, have been branded a heel-clicker, accused to his face of being a traitor. He saw, far beyond the Pas-de-Calais and deep into Flanders, a mighty tower of cumulonimbus extending to perhaps 30,000 feet. Curtains of rain were spilling from its base pierced by lightning, a storm advancing slowly from the east. He was half inclined to head towards it, fly through it, prove he could come through untouched as he always came through untouched. It existed to be beaten, like any threat, like any time he went up in the war.

He remembered Wilkinson-Clark, what Wilkie said before he died:

'I tell you, Guv, life in France was bloody hell but by God I miss it so.' He also remembered he was low on fuel. He turned for home.

At High And Over, Tim's suitcases, dusty from the rail journey from Oxford, were standing in the hall. He had forgotten Tim was returning for the summer at the end of his second term.

In the study before the evening meal Tim told his father: 'I'm not sure I'm going back.'

'That doesn't surprise me. I doubt you've ever been sure about anything.'

'That's not true actually. The point is, I've learned to fly with the University Air Squadron. Predictably, thanks to my name they expected me to be a bit of a whizz. Well, I'm hardly that but I've managed to go solo so I'm considering joining the RAF. With things as they are, I think I could be useful.'

'Things as they are?'

'Oh, come now, Guv'nor. It's just a matter of time surely?'

'Well, you know more than our Prime Minister then. He says Hitler's speeches are not those of a man preparing Europe for another crisis. Lloyds put the odds against war within a year at thirty-two to one. And the *Daily Express* predicts no war this year or next. The word is, Hitler's got the jitters.'

Tim looked sceptical. 'There are some pretty well-connected chaps at Trinity. Their people are in the know. With the BEF being put on alert and conscription on the cards, I'd say it's obvious what's coming.'

'You would, would you? I've got my own sources and I know a damned sight more than your bookworm cronies about what's going on. You'll find you're joining up for no good purpose.'

'Well,' Tim said mildly, 'if you're right I can serve out my commission, use the time to polish up my flying and return to Oxford to finish my degree. University will keep.'

'I hope you don't expect me to put a word in for you with the Air Ministry.'

'To be quite candid, Guv'nor, I'm not entirely sure how helpful that would be. You've kicked up quite a hornets' nest. I've had a pretty ticklish time dealing with some of the comments going round. I realise you've probably been misreported and misunderstood . . .'

'There's no probably about it. I'm taking legal advice.'

'Is that wise? Won't it make things worse?'

'Worse? Dammit, mud sticks and there's been plenty of it flying about. You know, I suppose, that I was called a traitor to my face by a man who should know better? And it's catching on; all sorts of nonsense. In Rye the other day some swine shouted "*Heil*, Manfred von Sutro!" Riff-raff, of course, but plenty stood by and laughed.'

'You'd have thought people had better things to occupy their minds than insulting you.'

'It's the mob instinct. They're alarmed at the state of things so go for the nearest target. I despair of this country. We flail about to no good purpose, blaming everyone but ourselves. We have no strength of purpose. God help us if there *is* another war. The Hun will walk all over us. And it will serve us right.'

'You might be wrong there, Guv'nor. There's some pretty steely resolve among the chaps in the squadron at Kidlington. I reckon they'd give a good account of themselves.'

'Eager to get at 'em, are they? Keen to teach the Hun a lesson? By God, we never bloody well learn.'

Griggs came in and banged about with a tray of tea and biscuits. 'Refreshments, gents?'

'Tell me, Griggs,' said Tim, 'what do you make of the international situation?'

'I don't know, I'm sure, Master Tim. It's not for me to say.'

'Come on, Griggs,' said Guv. 'Out with it. Do you want a war or not?'

'I'd rather not. Not after the last lot.'

Guv bit into a digestive. 'You see? Griggs would rather not. He was in the trenches, weren't you, Griggs? Had a hard time of it.' Guv brushed crumbs from his mouth. 'You might imagine steely resolve in your Oxford chums, but faced with war our Griggses, our millions of Griggses, would rather not. If it comes to it, if they are required to be cannon-fodder like those poor buggers who went over the top at the Somme, no doubt they'd try to do their duty. But of course, they'd rather not. There speaks the ordinary man, not some Trinity egghead with more brains than sense. All right, Griggs, clear off.'

Tim went over to the study window, his hands cradling the hot tea cup. 'I heard from Will Kemp last week,' he said.

'Oh yes?'

'He's doing tremendously well. You're aware he was a flight mechanic with a bomber squadron in Aden. When they posted him back, he put in for a gunnery course. It meant a lot of time in the air and he got selected for flying training on Harvards at Tern Hill. Went in as an erk, emerged as a sergeant with a hundred and fifty hours in his log book. Above average, his instructors say. They're recommending him for fighters.'

'It's no surprise to me,' Guv said. 'Now there you have a natural pilot.'

Tim nodded. 'Yes. Good for Will. His father must be proud.'

Guv's expression did not change. 'How do you know all this?'

'Oh, he's kept in touch with us.'

'Us?'

'Me and Alice.'

'You mean he's been writing to her in the States?'

'Of course. You know he's always been sweet on her. It was entirely mutual. It's always been that way. It was a rotten time for both of them when Mother took her off to Rhode Island. I've never quite understood why, although I never asked. I suppose I should have. Will was pretty cut up about it. Still is, I think.'

'Why should you care?'

'Oh come on, Guv'nor, Will was my best friend.'

'That's what I mean. Was.'

'It still counts for something, surely? There aren't so many chaps in the world you can get along with. But everything changed when I was packed off to school. It shouldn't have, but it did. On hols it was as if we were embarrassed by the differences that had grown up between us; the knowledge I'd had stuffed into my head, a

461

self-consciousness about this class nonsense, even the way we spoke. Barriers grew up. We never mentioned it, but as soon as you avoid talking about things like that it can never be the same again.' Tim took a last mouthful of tea. 'Silly, isn't it? I wish I'd realised sooner.' He replaced the cup on the tray. 'This business with Alice and Will – I should have spoken up. It seemed to me it was done because Will didn't measure up, that he and Alice were getting in too deep, that you and Mother disapproved. I'm afraid I went along with it, complacent little snob that I was. But looking back, I'm surprised you gave in so easily. You're a hard enough nut but I always thought you had a soft spot for Will, even if it didn't run to him being good enough for your daughter.'

'I don't have to justify myself to you,' Guv said. 'I did well enough by the boy. I'll remind you the RAF was my idea. Without me he'd still be under the ramp in Kemp's garage.'

'It was all part of it, wasn't it? It suited you to get him out of the way.'

'It suited *him*. You've just acknowledged that yourself. If he's as good a pilot as I think he is, he could earn himself a commission. Quite a step up from mending old crocks.'

'Perhaps he might earn more than a commission. As an officer he might earn a chance with Alice.'

Guv did not meet Tim's eye. 'Can I expect to see you knocking about the place or do you have other plans?'

'I was thinking of motoring to Paris.'

'On your own?'

'On my own.'

'With what in mind?'

'I'd like to walk round the place before the curtain drops. I suspect we're coming to the end of a particular time. Afterwards, nothing's going be quite the same again. Have you a car I might borrow?'

'A car? Why not take the DH4 since you say you're such a dab-hand in the air? Drop it down at Le Bourget, hop in a cab and bob's your uncle.'

'I prefer to go by road, thanks. I thought I might trundle down by way of Amiens and look out your old airfield at Chézy-au-Bois. Where you flew Gunbuses with Mr Kemp.'

'What the blazes is the point in that? You won't learn anything.'

'Learn anything? I don't expect to. I'm just interested in seeing how it is now, compared to that old photograph of your squadron. That picture meant a lot to me and Will. We desperately wanted to be like you, you know, Will perhaps more than me. Natural, I suppose. All youngsters wonder how they'd measure up in war, measure up to their fathers. Personally, I doubted I had the nerve.'

'There's nothing there but empty fields.'

'Just the same,' Tim said, 'I think I'll stick to my plan.'

'It's up to you. Your mother's old Riley's not too rorty. That should suit your needs. Bring me back some cognac.'

Tim was not gone long. He told Guv he got as far as le Crotoy on the Somme Estuary, not far from Abbeville, when he heard over the radio in a beachside café that Germany had signed a non-aggression pact with Russia. Everywhere people shrugged. 'Now it will come.' Everyone knew what it was that would come. It seemed that they were impatient, that they were tired of waiting. It was rumoured that petrol was to be rationed immediately, that the British would be allowed only enough to drive their cars to the Channel ports. There was a rush. The ferries were low in the water with every space filled. It resembled a retreat, as if a defeat had been suffered already. Tim did not return with cognac.

Before this, Guv had despatched a telegram to *Schoenfelder Aeronplau*:

Mystified Preiss confirmed equator bid no warning. Poor show Max. Have done what can ensure good relations at great personal cost. Vilified in press and public. Request clarification understanding.

He received a swift reply:

Too little, too late. Doubts remained. FYI, equator flight aborted due British/French political intransigence. Services no longer required. Heil Hitler!

A week later, after closing time, Paget was found outside the Queen's Head in Rye unconscious with a broken nose and missing teeth. He gave a mumbled account to the police of a dispute in the public bar during which he told the crew of a local trawler, fresh put in, that if people had listened to Sir Oswald Mosley the country would not be in the fix it was in. He added some observations about Neville Chamberlain ('a mincing sissy'), Communists and Jews. To the police he confirmed his name, address and occupation.

Next morning, the local newspaper reporter with lank hair paid his usual routine visit to the police station in Cinque Ports Street. That evening a headline appeared in the London press: AIR ACE WHO PRAISED HITLER EMPLOYS BLACKSHIRT!

At about this time, the Prime Minister began to shift his ground. A year before, at the time of the Munich crisis, he had remarked how horrible it was – fantastic, incredible – that his countrymen should be digging trenches and trying on gas-masks because of a quarrel in a faraway country between people of which they knew nothing. Now he talked of fighting.

'We shall not be fighting for the political future of a faraway city in a foreign land. We shall be fighting for the preservation of those principles the destruction of which would involve the destruction of peace and liberty for the peoples of the world.'

It was still hoped that Germany might be bluffing, though the cynical and those claiming to be in the know laid wagers on which country would be next on Hitler's list: Poland, Romania, Hungary, Holland.

Tim had returned to Oxford where, with other members of the University Air Squadron, he signed on at the Volunteer Reserve Centre and settled down in his old college room to wait to be called to fight for the peace and liberty of the peoples of the world. It had been an awkward parting. Griggs and Mrs Carr had been there to see him step into the taxi for Rye station. Mrs Carr had held her apron to her mouth. 'That it's come to this, Master Tim, that it's come to this.' Griggs, swallowing hard, had seized Tim's hand in a manly grip to compensate, so tight it crushed his fingers. 'I still reckon it's just a try-on. You'll be back here in two shakes, wondering what all the fuss was about.'

'Well,' said Guv. He shook Tim's hand briefly. He seemed to be trying to think of something more to say but came up with nothing.

'Yes,' Tim said. 'I'm sorry about your kerfuffle. I hope it sorts itself out. If it comes to it – war, I mean – I can't imagine they'd let it count for much.'

'Who?'

'The powers-that-be, I suppose. Anyone can see you've only been acting for the best, speaking up for what you thought was right for the country, doing what you could to prevent another war. It's hardly your fault that what started so hopefully in Germany has turned out so badly. I think we've all been duped.'

'I think that fairly sums it up.'

'If the worst happens, I imagine you'll be wanting to get involved again.'

'That might not be on the cards.'

Tim attempted to be breezy. 'Oh, surely they'd have to take your past record into account. It's not that you've ever done anything wrong.'

When the taxi had been lost to view down the drive, Guv went back into the house. Despite the summer heat it was cold indoors, a creeping coldness that seemed to come up through the floor. It had something of corruption about it, a sweet and offensive taint of damp earth and mould and cankerous wood, a suggestion of many small and unsuspected creatures living down there that gnawed and writhed and waited, the odour not only detectable by the nose but also somehow by the ears, like a distant murmur that this great and solid-seeming house had little substance after all, that it was an insubstantial and transient thing and like the castle in the valley, one day would also fall.

When Guv looked around, the furniture and trappings resembled so much rubbish; chairs he had never sat in, tables he had not noticed, pictures he had only glanced at, books he had never read. Outside, the hundreds of acres he did not know, tended by tenants he had not met. He stood for a moment in the hall, hearing the distant sound of stifled sobs from the kitchen, where Mrs Carr was preparing lunch, and caught the smoke of Griggs's Woodbine, taken furtively in the yard. He stood there in the hall not moving, momentarily uncertain where to go and what to do.

9

As Guv handed his ticket to the collector at the barrier at Charing Cross and passed through onto the concourse of the station, there was a chirruping like a gathering of starlings. He looked up into the vaulted roof but saw only the usual bedraggled pigeons moving uneasily on the white-stained iron girders. The noise rose from queues of children marshalled at platform entrances with labels on their coats and gas masks in cardboard boxes strapped across their small chests. A few adults went briskly from child to child, as if it was just a summer outing to a mystery destination. But the mothers' faces were marked by grief.

Outside the station, the kerbs and lamp-posts were painted white against the blackout. A steel-helmeted policeman directed traffic that moved sluggishly between the Aldwych and Trafalgar Square, compliant and lacking its usual verve, and on street corners men in khaki, freshly mobilised, gathered in groups around the news vendors to read the latest headlines. They nudged each other and laughed, their stiff caps at jaunty angles, their unfired rifles hanging from their shoulders. They looked eagerly at passing women, keen to catch the eye of any who might be warm towards a man who knew his duty, who faced war with a grin like his father before him, who (like the children in the queues) would soon be departing on an outing to an unknown destination; looked eagerly at any passing woman who might be open for a drink and a chat and a quick shag, paid for or not, before the trains took them off to the coast and France.

Along the Strand, most windows were stuck about with bomb-blast tape, criss-crossed like some sinister new flag, the plate-glass of the larger stores entirely boarded up. Double walls of sandbags twelve-feet high showed where the air-raid shelters were. Spain was a spectre that haunted London; the torrents of bombs tumbling from the bellies of Fascist bombers and onto Republican towns, the Stukas diving down with their primal screams. Already London's air-raid warnings had sounded, soon after Chamberlain, speaking from the Cabinet Room in Downing Street a week or so before, told the nation gathered by its wireless sets that the note handed to the German Government by the British Ambassador in Berlin demanding the withdrawal of troops from Poland had received no reply and that Britain was once again at war. Hardly had the broadcast finished than the sirens began to wail – a false alarm. No Luftwaffe fleets appeared from the east, only a single French aircraft recognised too late by nervous coastal defences; too late to call back the fighter squadrons scrambled from Hornchurch and North Weald; too late to prevent two Hurricanes, identified as enemy by ground control, from being shot down by Spitfires; one pilot dead, the first to die – the muddle dubbed with grim irony 'the Battle of Barking Creek'. It seemed an ominous sign of the way things might go, of a country unfit and unprepared.

Guv's appointment was after lunch. He was recognised as he walked towards Simpson's, but not in the normal way. He had not visited London for months. Now, people did not smile or nod. Instead, they saw him and looked away, whispered as they passed and, having passed, glanced back and talked more boldly. One man cursed and gestured, even stopped as though he might come back.

At Simpson's Guv did not receive his usual welcome, only a cool and formal greeting, shown to a corner table close to a service door that banged back and forth and spoiled his meal. He drank little, aware of his appointment, ate quickly and paid the bill without a tip, stepping into the dazzling sunlight of the Strand. The summer dust stirred up by the passing traffic blended with the petrol fumes. After the clean sea air of Rye it caught him on the chest and made him gag. A girl went by, a young girl, very pretty, the kind of girl he would look at with a particular smile and a narrowing of the eyes and she would smile back because they both understood, knowing him as that dauntless hero, that daredevil of the skies, that gallant man of action (or whatever nonsense might fill her head) whose image was in the newsreels, whose picture was in the papers; that smile that might lead to anywhere he cared to go. Now, in the violet eyes of this pretty girl there was distaste, as though she might think him drunk; a hint of resentment at something more.

He crossed the road by Bush House and went north along Kingsway to the Air Ministry. In Ad Astra House he said to the Airwoman in reception: 'I have an appointment in five minutes. My name—'

'I know who you are, sir,' she said sharply. She told him the room number he wanted and the floor it was on. He came out of the lift, rapped on the door and went in. A wing commander with a black eye-patch looked up from his desk.

'Hello, Sutro.'

'Good grief!' Guv said. 'Pew, isn't it? Pew Selby?'

'Nobody's called me that for more than twenty years. Not since St Omer.'

'So the seagull that clonked you one on take-off at Swingate did for your peeper good and proper.'

'Never flew again. Not officially, anyway. But it suited me to stay on in the service despite that. However, we're not here to reminisce about old times. Bloody old times, as I recall – that business with the Albatros you brought down. You managed to emerge smelling of roses at first, but when the facts came out the whole affair stank to high heaven. By then, of course it was too late. You'd left my squadron for Chézy-au-Bois.'

'You said we're not here to reminisce about old times.'

'Correct. So why are you here? You requested this meeting, not I.'

'I should have thought it was obvious.'

'Not to me.'

468

'I want to offer my services.'

'Decent of you, I'm sure.'

'Isn't there someone else I can see? You're hardly likely to give me a fair hearing.'

'Is that what you want? A fair hearing?'

'Of course.'

'I'd say you've had a fair hearing, wouldn't you? The newspapers have been full of your opinions. Not all of them, of course.' Selby took a file out of a wire tray. It looked familiar. 'I gather you've seen this bumph before.'

Guv's jaw was working. 'Yes, a chap with a false mitt showed it to me. Now it's a type with one eye. Is this what they entrust to the disabled, pushing files around?'

'You're hardly helping your case.' Selby flipped open the file. 'I'm assured this dossier's entirely up-to-date.' He tossed across some press cuttings clipped together. Guv saw the first: *'NO WAR IF BRITAIN IS PUT FIRST,' SAYS FAMOUS FLYER.* He left the bundle where it lay. Selby took it back. Several paragraphs had been underlined. He began to read under his breath: *'German leader . . . extraordinary achievement . . . no evidence Reich embarking on total war . . . German ambitions understandable . . . got raw deal at Versailles . . . belief that as public figure should advance policy of peace.'* Selby replaced the cuttings in the file.

'Yes, well, we know how much difference your comments made, apart from offering encouragement to our enemy.'

'It's easy to be wise after the event. My views were sincerely held. I was simply attempting to do what was right.'

Selby snorted. 'Well, that's a first. We also have these.' He passed over copies of the telegrams exchanged between Guv and Max Schoenfelder. 'May I remind you how recently these were sent?'

'How did you get hold of them?' Guv said.

'Oh, come now, credit our Intelligence chaps with a bit of nous.' Selby scanned the text. '"Have done what can to ensure good relations at great personal cost . . . request clarification understanding". What exactly did that mean? What understanding had you reached?'

'That I was to fly the Tri-motor on the Equator trip. What else?'

'Well, that's the question, isn't it? What else? What services were you providing that Schoenfelder says were no longer required? What's he getting at when he says "too little, too late, doubts remained"?'

'I've no idea.'

'You've no idea. No suggestion, I suppose, that you might be of some use to the Reich, a figure of some influence if Britain turned Fascist, if we rolled over and let the Nazis tickle our tummies?'

'That's bloody ridiculous, Selby! I'm as staunch a patriot as you'll find.'

'You can hardly deny you're a Fascist sympathiser,' said Selby, unhurried, enjoying the moment. 'For example, is it mere coincidence that you've employed one of Mosley's thugs for many years?'

Guv felt as he had in the hallway at High And Over, pinned down, uncertain about what course to take. 'He wasn't a Blackshirt when I hired him.'

'But you've kept him on.'

'A man's entitled to his opinions. I thought this was a free country.'

'Oh, it is. People are entirely free to express whatever opinions they may hold. But of course they must be prepared to be judged by them. When a man is reported to have received preferential treatment as a prisoner of war, affirms that the Germans were hard done by at Versailles, is an open admirer of Adolf Hitler, has done more than most to put the Nazi aviation industry back on the map by flying their aeroplanes and employs a Mosley bully boy, you may be forgiven for drawing your own conclusions.'

'Confound it, Selby, I've always said that if this country's ever invaded, I'll be first in line to do my bit.'

'Or first in line to open the door and welcome them in. Not many patriots have received a telegram signed off with a *Heil Hitler*. Do you really suppose that in the light of all this, we'd still regard you as a suitable candidate for the service?'

Guv stood up. 'Obviously this is going nowhere. If the Air Force is prepared to turn down one of the best pilots in the country who served with distinction on the Western Front with an MC to prove it, that's their look-out. You've got an infernal nerve questioning my patriotism. The Sutros stand four-square. You're probably not aware of it, but my son's already enlisted.'

'Oh, we're perfectly aware of that. He's done very well on Lysanders at Old Sarum and more than earned his wings.'

'I see. So my son's acceptable, but I'm not – is that it?'

'That's about the size of it. To be candid, Sutro, you're not trusted by either side, the Huns or us. It's a situation of your own making – the consequence, I suppose, of playing both ends against the middle.' Selby took a brown envelope from the file. It contained half a dozen glossy photographs. He spread them out on the desk like a suit of cards. 'Of course, this sort of thing doesn't help.' A naked man was hanging from manacles against a bare brick wall. A woman, masked and leather clad but with breasts and buttocks exposed, stood by him holding a whip. 'Can't say I share your tastes, old man. Never took to the cane myself, beaten once at school for cutting the cross-country run. Not my idea of fun, but I suppose you have to be broad minded in these matters. What you might call give and take. Obviously you prefer to take.'

Guv stared at the prints. 'Where did these come from?'

Selby shuffled them neatly and put them back in the file. 'Sources, Sutro, sources. They were made available to the Foreign Office for purposes known only to those who made them available. They must have had something in mind, apart from titillation. But I must say they help to give us what you might call a rounded picture, if you'll pardon the expression. Not the most flattering snaps for your family album, of course, but perhaps you'd still like copies. Where would you like them sent – care of Brixton Prison?'

'What do you mean?'

'It's highly likely, under defence regulations, that when they get round to it, the authorities will have you interned or put under house arrest. Your case is under review. Far from reliving past glories fighting the Hun in the air, you're probably going to find yourself securely under lock and key. I should make the most of that fine estate of yours, while you still can.'

* * *

471

It did not seem to Guv that he could stay as usual at the Club in Piccadilly. He did not allow the reasons to form in his brain but simply decided it was not what he wanted to do. But he was not ready to return to Rye. A taxi took him west towards Knightsbridge and along the Cromwell Road. At the corner of Earls Court Road he paid off the driver and walked a few hundred yards to the narrow entrance of the cul de sac that lay back from the jostling traffic. It was quiet there, lined on each side by terraces of white-painted villas with domed windows and tiny front gardens. Halfway along on the right, the wrought-iron gate to the number he wanted moved rustily on its hinges. The cream paint on the single ground-floor window was peeling, the glass dirty. The doorbell did not work. When he rapped the knocker once, twice, the noise brusied the calm. Curtains moved in a bedroom window across the street and a face peered out. He heard someone coming to the door. It opened a little and Rose said: 'Oh, it's you. Whatever are you doing here? I was expecting someone else.'

'Well? Are you going to let me into my own house?'

She looked past him at the window where the curtain had twitched. 'Nosy old bag, I'll show her something that'll make what's left of her hair stand on end one of these days. You're not intending to stay long, are you? It don't fit my arrangements.'

Guv pushed past her into the small front room. He could see she had been sitting in a worn armchair reading a magazine that she had thrown on the floor. A cigarette lay in an ashtray on a side table inlaid with mother of pearl (a discard from High And Over when he set her up), its smoke swirling in the draught from the door. Next to it was a half-filled glass and a bottle of port.

'I could do with a drink,' he said, 'but not that muck.'

She went to a cabinet, brought him a tumbler and a half bottle of Johnnie Walker, went through to the kitchen and came back with a jug of water. She watched in silence as he fixed his drink and took the first gulp.

'This don't suit my plans, Guv. I've got someone calling.'

'Really? More important than your landlord?'

'Is that what you call yourself?'

472

'It's true, isn't it?'

'Hardly. I don't pay no rent.'

'No, you're right. *I* pay, don't I? I pay for every damned thing.'

'Oh dear, feeling sorry for ourselves, are we? I can't say I'm surprised.'

'Why not exactly?'

'Well, you've backed the wrong horse, ain't you? Round these parts, your name's mud. And everywhere else, I shouldn't wonder.'

He sat down in the armchair and poured himself a second Scotch, this time took it neat. She came over and sat on his knee and put an arm round his shoulders. 'Poor old Guv. Are they treating you rotten?' She smelled of port and perfume and tobacco. He looked up at her and saw she was as beautiful as she had ever been. Her lips gleamed red with lipstick, moistened by the tip of her tongue. How the hell old was she? Forty, forty-five? It didn't show. She had the glow of a young girl, as though she had never been touched by years or men or anything at all.

She stood up and went over to the staircase that came down into the room and rested her hand on the banister and waited for him. He swallowed another Scotch and weaved unsteadily towards her and she led the way up the creaking stairs. When he was on her in the same old way, as if it was the first time or any of the many times since, her fingernails dug into his back as she gasped with her head back and thrust and thrust. He wondered if she felt it any more; so many fucks by him and so many others. It didn't matter. He had her now. It always came down to that: he had her now, and that was enough. He rolled over damp with sweat, panting. She was beside him propped on an elbow, her pale breasts brushing his chest. 'What's wrong with your back?'

He went cold. 'What do you mean? Nothing.'

'It feels funny.' She pushed him away from her so she could see. He resisted at first but then rolled on his side. Why should he care? He was curious to see her reaction. He felt her fingers touching the scars, tracing the weals. 'Blimey,' she said. 'Blimey. How'd you get this?' His balls contracted, his cock stiffened. He thought of the cellar in Berlin, Renate in leather, the whip in her hand. He was telling Rose about it and she was lying back, her hand moving between her thighs, her eyes closed. 'Go on,' she was murmuring, 'go on. What then? Go on.' He took her again, better this time, her legs on his shoulders, her arms stretched wide, her eyes still closed. 'Go on, go on, go on.' She squealed like a sow as he finished again.

Downstairs they nursed their drinks, not looking at each other, like strangers in a bar. 'It must have hurt something chronic,' she said. 'Your back, I mean.'

'That's the idea.'

'Can love be reduced to that? Seems to me it's more like hate.'

'Love? That's rich.'

'You know what I mean. Blooming funny, ain't it?'

'Not funny at all.'

'I mean, peculiar, odd. The idea of it.'

'It was somebody else's idea, not mine.'

'Did you like it though?'

'What do you think?'

'I think you might have. I think you might have got a taste for it. Do you want me to give you what-for? Would you like that?'

'Would you?'

'I might. I'd quite like to teach you a lesson, bring you in line.'

'What if I gave you what-for instead?'

'I might like that too. I very well might. You'd better come back if that's what you want.'

'I always come back.' He went over to the French windows and looked out at the small walled garden with geraniums dead in pots, two gnomes fishing by a broken concrete pond and a cat licking its crutch. 'Do you know the nickname the chaps at Brooklands gave you?'

'The chaps?' she said mockingly. 'The chaps?'

'They called you the Angler, because once you'd hooked your fish you never threw it back.'

She laughed. 'I ain't never been fishing in my life.' She shuddered. 'Ugh, fish. Nasty slimy smelly things.'

He turned back to look at her. 'I thought you liked nasty slimy smelly things.'

'Now you're being crude.' She passed him an envelope. 'Got this today. Stan sent it on.'

The letter was written in a round, schoolboy hand, from an RAF station somewhere in England:

Dear Mum and Dad,

Just a line to let you know I am settling in at my new place very well indeed. I am doing lots of flying, patrols every day but no sign of the Jerries yet. We live in hope. I'll shoot one down for you. The Hurricane is a wonderful aeroplane, one of the best. Please tell Captain Sutro that for me. He will be interested. What a pity he can't try one for himself. He would certainly teach the Luftwaffe types a thing or two. The chaps here are a splendid bunch. I am proud to be serving with them. I can't believe I'm so lucky to be here in the front line as you might say. I know we are all going to give a good account of ourselves when the time comes. Hope the business is going along okay, Dad, and that you are managing without me. When we've beaten Hitler's little gang I'll be back and we'll make it the best blooming (excuse my French) garage in the business!!! At the moment though I wouldn't wish to be anywhere else,

Love to you and Mum,

William

'Touching, ain't it?' said Rose. 'You see how he ends it? "Love to you and Mum". He thinks he's writing to his dad.' She laughed. 'Except we both know he ain't, don't we, poor little sod?' She lit a cigarette. 'Talking of poor little sods, have you seen my hubby recently?'

'Only to fill up with petrol,' Guv said.

'I keep away as much as I can. Can't bear him gawping at me in

475

that way he has, like some sick mutt that's been kicked about. Sort of accusing, though he swears he's not. He takes anything I care to give him, though I give him bugger-all.' She laughed again. 'Not quite true. I let him nibble on a treat occasionally, to keep him well trained.'

Someone banged on the door. Rose stubbed out her cigarette and waved away the smoke. 'It's a gentleman friend,' she said. 'He knows about you, and he don't care. He's a bit like you, that way.'

She opened the door and the room darkened as a man came in from the blaze of light, sharply dressed in a trilby hat and blue double-breasted suit. 'Hat off, dear,' said Rose. 'Mind your manners. We've got company.'

'So I see,' said the man sourly.

'This is Captain Sutro,' Rose said like a schoolteacher introducing one child to another on the first day at village school. 'The famous pilot what I told you of. Guv, this is Rex Fitt.'

'Oh yes,' said Rex. 'I've been reading about you.'

'Is that so?'

'Rex is in motor cars, aren't you, Rex?'

'Is he?' Guv said.

'If you're in the market for a good motor,' Rex said, 'you can always find me in Warren Street.'

'I've got plenty of good motors, thanks.'

'Well, if you want to sell one, just let me know. I can't be beaten on price.'

'What can you be beaten on?' Guv said, glancing at Rose.

'Eh?' said Rex. 'Don't get you, old man.'

Guv walked up to Cromwell Road, crossed over and hailed a taxi already heading east. In forty minutes there was a stopper to Ashford, connecting with Rye. They were passing the Natural History Museum with its display of dinosaurs, creatures from another age, beasts that could not adapt. He envied Will. *The Hurricane is a wonderful aeroplane, one of the best. Please tell Captain Sutro that for me. A pity he can't try one for himself. He would certainly teach the Luftwaffe types a thing or two.* He would. He still could. He ached to be somewhere in England waiting to give a good account of himself when the time came.

In the back of the fume-filled taxi, his cock rubbed sore, his balls tender, his head throbbing, he remembered Pew Selby with his talk of Brixton Prison. Was he serious? Was he really serious or just vindictive, getting his own back, the squint-eyed swine? He wished . . . he wished . . . he did not know what he wished. At that moment, bouncing on the cheap leather seat, he wished only that he was somewhere else, anywhere but here, anywhere but at this time when world events were beginning to move like some great juggernaut with a tightening of ropes and a groaning of wheels as thousands, millions bent to the task and he stood aside, condemned to look on.

10

Nobody came for Guv after his visit to Ad Astra House. Nobody came up the drive of High And Over unannounced in an official-looking car or sent a letter requiring him to present himself at a certain time and a certain place for further investigation; nothing melodramatic of that kind. It was as though he was no longer of interest, irrelevant to the serious matter of fighting a war. Not that there was much fighting, unless you were in Poland, Finland, Norway, Denmark where what fighting there had been was almost over now and in the villages and towns people were jostled by troops in unfamiliar uniforms swelled with easy victory, and in the cities military bands played martial music while gallows were erected in public places and men were hanged, men known for years to the silent crowds, men whose lives had been lawful and mundane until a noose was dropped around their necks for being Jews, or having an education (or worse, both) or in reprisal for some defiant act by patriots they did not know; not always hanged, sometimes tied to posts in the stark sunlight of a leafy square where once they had walked with their families, shot by firing squads.

In England war was not like this. The first eight months went by in dull suspense and did not seem like war, as if both sides had settled back like great beasts resting on their haunches, waiting; the Allies watching for the enemy to show itself, to make the opening move, not prepared to make the move themselves. In France they called this time of tension la Drôle de Guerre, in England the Phoney War; strained humour seemed the only weapon. Few complained. Perhaps it would go on, this period of non-action; perhaps even now, so late, the futility of the whole nonsensical business would be realised, the differences settled by pragmatists around a table, the situation fixed. Perhaps one morning things would be as they had been in the sweltering brooding summer of the previous year, before an old man told them over the wireless that it was war because he had not received a reply to some piece of paper. Perhaps time would be wound back as though it had never passed, before too many died, before the deaths became too abundant to report as individual deaths but were gathered together in unimaginable bundles at they had been at the Somme. And all this time, elsewhere, the corpses dangled in the dappled light of a perfect spring or drooped bent-kneed at wooden posts staining the ground around their feet with blood.

Then, in early May, the beast beyond the eastern horizon began to move. Very soon its shadow had fallen across Luxembourg, Holland, Belgium. The old man who had announced war was replaced by another old man, a bolder one, who dismissed lingering hopes for peace and predicted another long and brutal conflict. His message was blunt: without victory, no survival. Ahead, he said, lay struggle and suffering 'against a monstrous tyranny never surpassed in the dark and lamentable catalogue of human crime'. Churchill had a turn of phrase. The spirits of listening millions rose to learn he took up his task with buoyancy and hope. They shared his hope, but it was among the first casualties when the beast set foot on French soil. Air bombers and armoured tanks broke through French defences north of the Maginot Line, the impregnable Maginot Line that could never be breached, that bastion against invasion, that string of concrete fortifications that stretched from the Belgian coast to the Swiss border. Impossible, surely?

Quickly it was reported that the Allies had regrouped, 'striking back at the enemy's intruding wedge', in Churchill's carefully crafted words. But defeat was only weeks away. Soon France would fall and Italy join the Fascist side. It seemed the war might go on for a long time. The last had endured for four years. This time, why not ten? Or thirty? A hundred, even? Such time-scales were not unknown. Fighting for a hundred years, generation by generation, fighting for so long that the original cause was lost in hatred and retribution, fighting because your grandfathers and fathers had fought the war before you and so you must follow their example, salute their memory, honour the sacrifice of those who died in battle; those who died for a cause now barely remembered and hardly understood.

It was shortly before Dunkirk, that final scramble to save the remnants of a broken army, that Guv saw his son for the last time. Tim and the cavalry colonel had taken their final look at France from the cockpit of the Lysander over St Valéry-en-Caux, bound for Northolt. There the colonel had continued to Whitehall by road while Tim flew on to Hawkinge to rejoin his squadron. But Glisy had been overrun, the squadron unaccounted for. For the moment he had no role, particularly when he hurt himself in a whoop-up in the Mess. They gave him two weeks' leave for the injury to mend, so he went by train to High And Over because that was what sons did; when sent on leave sons went back home. He did not stay long, however, confronted by his father's befuddled views.

'Must mind Britain's business for the British . . . must not be dragged into a Jewish war . . . terms will be negotiated . . . prospect of a united Europe.' On it went, like a cracked record, the same phrases he had heard so many times before. But with it was something new – puzzlement and confusion, bitterness that he was not required, grounded as surely as his son. But his son's torn cartilage would mend, not so his own reputation.

Then came the business of the DH4, Guv trundling round the airfield drunk at the controls in some lost world where life was simple, where pilots went up to glory, where the enemy was marked with a big black cross, where it was kill or be killed, where if you came back it was medals and promotion and respect; that look in the eye of the ordinary man. That look that, if you really thought about it, somehow gave a meaning to things, confirmed that you were above others, had been singled out, had purpose – a destiny, if you like – as though you were working towards some objective, always slightly beyond your reach but taking you higher, always higher, always climbing, seeing the humdrum world recede, looking down like some sort of God, alone in the sky and looking down. Looking down like God.

Soon enough Tim had removed himself to the George in Rye and Griggs told Guv he had been seen about the town with the Sleightholme girl. And then he was gone, no one knew where. A month later, as the Germans reached Paris, Tim wrote briefly that he was operational again. It was a long time since he had written. He said he was sorry for it, though Guv had barely noticed. He was an instructor now, teaching students to fly; also, with battle experience, how they might stay alive.

'Get yourself made an instructor,' Guv said to Griggs. 'That's how you stay alive. Smart feller, ain't he?'

By now coastal shipping had come under attack by Stukas, the bombs (when they missed) opening up white flowers of foam around the merchantmen as they pushed along the Channel. The newsreels showed the action as if it was some kind of game, but did not show what happened when the bombs struck home. Daylight raids began, the skies above the southern coast throbbing with enemy battle fleets, pounding the ports and factories, met by outnumbered British fighters.

Guv kept to the estate. There was nowhere to go. The sky was scarred with white contrails showing where men fought and died. In the fields the remains of aeroplanes burned, with the remains of those who flew them, unless they jumped and pulled a ripcord and came down slowly under a white canopy that delivered them safe to go up again on another sortie, or to spend the rest of the war behind barbed wire.

It did not always work like this. Often the figure that touched the ground was charred black, though still alive, making it hard to tell if it was one of ours or one of theirs. Burned men looked and suffered the same. Often, when pulling that ripcord, the white canopy would not spread out as it was meant to or even release from its pack, and there was time to consider the pleasant landscape rushing towards you, a little time to think about home and family and how you did not want to die – and then you made a hole twenty feet deep in a meadow somewhere or a back garden or in obscure woodland where you might not be found for years.

One day in August, standing on the terrace of High And Over, Guv watched a force of 50 Dornier bombers (he counted them) pass overhead at little more than 100 feet. He stood there, glass in hand, and close enough to see the faces of the crews; a front gunner waved. They seemed on course for Hornchurch or North Weald. Then, against the woo-woo beat of the enemy formation there was a different engine noise, an urgent growl. A single Hurricane dived through them with a stutter of machine-gun fire. The formation wavered and one Dornier dropped away, grey smoke streaming from its port engine. The Hurricane pulled round in a steep turn and came in for a beam attack. Tracer from the German gunners curled in its direction as it rushed towards them, but it was not hit. Another Dornier went down with no sign of damage but vertically, giving its crew no chance of escape, lost to sight as it struck the ground somewhere towards the Marsh. The Hurricane turned back to come in again but a Messerschmitt 109 had dropped down from the bombers' fighter escort waiting at 10,000 feet. It was over quickly, the Hurricane erupting in a sheet of flame, breaking up and spinning down, a man in there somewhere immersed in that ball of fire, leaving a trail of oily black smoke that hung in the air until it was caught by the gentle breeze and disappeared.

Griggs had come out on the terrace. He had seen it too. 'Poor little bugger. What a way to go.'

'There's worse,' Guv said. He found himself wondering about the dead pilot. It could have been Will. But no, he was in Spitfires. Another Will then. Or Peter or Douglas or Dick or George or any of the damned names that young Englishmen bore that went with them into a grave that stank of petrol and oil and glycol and shredded metal and burned wood and something roasted that was better not thought of. If Will still survived, soon he would be dead. Tim would be dead as well. As dead as the pilot of the Hurricane who engaged the enemy with so little regard for himself, hopeless though he did not know it, brave though he would not admit it (would make a joke of it), now thoroughly, finally, uselessly dead. It came to him that he could not stand by.

That night, Guv chose not to sleep in the house. Before dusk he went to the hangar. He had a bottle of Glenfiddich with him. He drank from it as he walked. Harry Paget was not there. Guv found him stretched out on his bed in the room above the kitchen. Like Guv he kept to the estate because there was nowhere left to go and nobody to see, and he did not care to work on the aeroplanes because he said he did not see the point. Guv was in the room over the kitchen for some time, longer than he meant to be. When he came out he walked back slowly to the hangar under a blue-black sky in which the stars glittered as if (as the ancients thought) heaven showed through. He drank again from the bottle of Scotch. He experienced a great calm.

In the hangar he climbed into the cockpit of the DH4. He settled himself down, as comfortable as he had ever been anywhere, removed the cork from the bottle of Glenfiddich, tipped his head back and felt the liquid go down his throat and into his stomach with the fierceness of fire, as though he was burning from inside, consumed by a consoling heat that spread through his body and made everything all right, made sense of it all, although he could not express it in any words, not that he tried to but just let the good feeling come over him and he began to drift and he seemed to feel the old biplane shake under him and come alive and he was back and flying at 30,000 feet and below him was Flanders and his eyes were raw from looking for those dots, those tell-tale dots; not the dots of matter in the eyes but dots that meant death to the slow and the clumsy and the hastily trained, to the Peters and Douglases and Dicks and whatever damned names they went under, chipped out on grey stones in some forgotten corner of France.

He finished the Scotch and tried to pull himself up, to fetch another bottle from the house. His arms felt weak and he fell back. He thought about Paget, how he had left him. He thought about Rose, how he had left her; and Sabine Pettit, her face as she had gone down before him on that woodland path in Chézy; and a girl waiting for him by a bridge over a winding river somewhere, turning with something like relief in her eyes, and gladness, and moving lightly towards him, a long time ago but he knew who she was. He thought about men whose faces came to him in a half-dream; faces without expression but with eyes fixed and staring: Evans, Hargreaves, Sutton, Fritchley, Wilkinson-Clark and so many others he could not recall, but all of them dead, a roll-call of the dead.

He seemed to be drifting down. He was back in High And Over and Lydia was coming down the great staircase with Alice, and Alice was a tiny child and it was a happy time. It was before, then; before it all went sour. He looked for Tim. It was not like him. He never looked for Tim. He went outside and crossed the gravel drive and followed the stony path that wound down between ferny banks towards the castle ruins. He heard voices and saw the boys. Will was there and he was glad of it. They were playing by the lake, playing touch along the grassy bank of the moat. It was when they were very young and they were brown from the sun because it was always sunny when they played by the moat and Will would not be caught; he could never be caught unless he chose to be, too quick for the stumbling Tim. Not like Tim at all, young Will, yet both of them his sons. Like, unlike. It didn't make sense. Nothing made sense. Suddenly they had stopped running and were bending over something in the water. They were up to their ankles in the shallows, pulling at something in the water. He went in with them up to his knees, his feet sinking in mud, feeling the tug of the weeds. The object was large and wrapped about with a linen garment green with mould. He moved it with a foot and it rolled over, slowly. The face had gone, the cavities of the eyes and nose and mouth alive with moving, feeding things that seemed to give it life. The rotted linen of the dress had come apart. The torso was grey-blue like the flesh of a decaying fish, now splitting in the fierce light and opening up and something was inside, small and decaying too, caught by the swirl of muddy water stirred up by his feet. He did not want the boys to see but when he turned they were no longer there. And the corpse was no longer there, or the moat or the castle or High And Over.

Abruptly, he was flying again. A shadow was dropping down on him from the sun. He rolled quickly and went into a spin. He let it go on for a long time, until he thought he was clear, eased forward on the stick to regain control and flattened out in a shallow dive but the shadow was still there and he was beaten and there was nothing to do but wait. He was tired of waiting. It seemed he had been waiting all his life.

He woke at about six. It had rained during the night. It was a wet, fresh world that rang with birdsong. He pushed back the hangar doors and tried to move the old biplane into the open. He needed help. He thought of Paget but then remembered. Griggs was on manoeuvres with the Home Guard. He found the Norton, wheeled it out and kicked it alive, the blare of the exhaust sending the rooks and jackdaws screaming into the air, and rode down to the garage on the Military Road. Stan Kemp came to the door of the bungalow. He was dressed, as though he had been up for hours. A kettle was whistling in the kitchen.

'What's this about?'

'You're coming with me.'

'Like blue blazes I am.'

'I want you to swing a prop.'

'You've come at the right moment,' Stan said. 'There's something you should see.' He went back into the bungalow. Guv stood for a moment watching him, then followed him in. He had not been in the bungalow for years, since it had been renovated. As he passed down the hall he looked into the lounge. A single light bulb hung from the ceiling above a threadbare armchair. On one arm an ashtray of butts, several newspapers scattered across the floor. The dial of a wireless set on a side-table glowed orange, tuned to light music. A crooner was singing 'They Didn't Believe Me'.

The place smelled of fried food, tobacco, oil, petrol and human sweat.

In the kitchen, Stan was pouring hot water into a teapot. 'Want a mug?'

'Got anything stronger?'

'At this time of day?' Stan rattled a teaspoon round his mug. 'The answer's no. We don't run to a cocktail cabinet in this business.' He went over to a dresser where a telegram was propped against a plate. He handed it to Guv, who took it impatiently. 'Came last night,' Stan said. 'I was going to send it up.'

'Look,' Guv said, 'we're wasting time. The bastards will be coming over soon.'

Stan sipped his tea, his eyes steady above the rim of the mug. 'You'd better read it. Then tell me if we're wasting time.'

The telegram was from the officer commanding Hornchurch to Mr & Mrs S. Kemp:

Deeply regret to inform you that your son Sergeant William Kemp is missing as a result of an operation on 18 August 1940 Stop Letter follows Stop Any further information will be immediately communicated to you Stop Please accept my profound sympathy

'I've told Rose,' Stan said. 'I phoned her at her place in London.'

'How did she take it?'

'Quiet. I think she had someone with her.'

'Do you know how it happened?'

'Not really. One of the blokes in his flight rang up. They were mixing it with 109s off Dungeness. No one saw him go down. The lifeboat went out but drew a blank. You tell yourself you should be hardened to it, after going through it last time. But when it comes to it, you aren't, are you?'

Guv folded the telegram and replaced it on the dresser. 'He's a goner, that's for sure. You don't last long in those waters, even in August.'

'Is that all you've got to say?'

'What is there to say? Believe me, I'm as cut up about it as you are, but it's hardly unexpected, is it? We both know the score.'

Stan sat down at the kitchen table, turning the mug in his cracked hands.

'You don't see it, do you? Will was just about all I've got.'

'You're forgetting, he was my own flesh and blood.'

'Maybe, but I was a father to that boy.'

'I did what I could.'

'You did what you could to make sure he was like you.'

'That was born in him.'

'You claim everything for yourself, don't you? You leave nothing for anyone else.'

'I still need you to swing that prop.'

'There's that Blackshirt of yours, or Bill Griggs. Why bother me?'

'Unavailable, both of them. Do you think I'd ask otherwise?'

'Search me. I gave up trying to work you out, years ago.'

'You've done all right thanks to me, Stan.'

'All this, you mean? This shack I live in, the half-arsed business, my tart of a wife, my so-called son? The war-wound that made me less of a man?'

'There are plenty worse off than you. Besides, you knew what you were getting into with Rose. Keeping mum so you could get your hands on her, make it legal. You bloody fool, as though making it legal was going to keep her here.' Guv paused. 'I still need you to swing that prop. Do this one thing for me and I won't bother you again. I'll make over this place to you lock, stock and ruddy barrel, so you can do what you like with it. Sell it, burn it down, I couldn't care less. But do this one last thing for me.'

'I think I know what you've got in mind,' Stan said. 'I don't want any part of it.'

'If you hate my guts you'll do it. Don't you see, this is your chance to even the score?'

'I don't want to even the score. Not with you, not with anybody. There are too many people wanting to even the score. That's why we're all in this bloody mess.' Stan went over to the sink and began to rinse the mug under the tap. 'I'm sorry for you, Guv. You were a great man once. You had it in you to do great things. Some people would say you did, until you came unstuck. But it's come down to this, hasn't it? Where nothing counts for anything any more, not your victories in France, your medals, your records, your wealth, your possessions, all those ambitions you had when we were kids. After all that, where's it got you? Where you can't find someone to swing a prop.'

'Sod you, then,' Guv said. 'I'll work out a way. I'll manage it on my own.' He went out of the bungalow and took the Norton away from the garage in a churn of dirt and gravel. Soon, still in the kitchen, Stan heard him down-shifting for the climb to High And Over. He dried the mug with a tea-towel, looking at his reflection in the small cracked mirror on the wall above the draining board where Rose used to puff up her hair and complain that washing up was ruining her hands. His own hands were pitted and crevassed with labour, not fit hands to touch a woman like that. But they could swing a prop.

On his way out of the bungalow, he went past the door of Will's room. He had not the heart to go in. He knew what was in there anyway: the aeroplane models revolving slowly on their lengths of thread, the flying books, Guv's photograph (*To Will, affectionately, Guv*), the tinplate monoplane, the gift from Rose, the throw-out with a single wheel. He seemed to hear Will's voice, that last time at the Ferry Inn. 'I'll be Marshal of the Royal Air Force by the time this lot's over.' He continued into the garage, climbed into the two-stroke Trojan, repaired but not collected yet, and drove out onto the Military Road.

11

With the tow-rope secured between the back axle of the Riley and the undercarriage of the DH4, Guv eased gently down on the throttle pedal and took up the slack. He felt the rope spring tight, the biplane resist the tug and then start to move out of the hangar. This was going to be tricky. If the machine started to roll from its own weight, the momentum could take it into the back of the car and the flight would be over before it had begun. Even if he succeeded, there was still the little matter of getting the engine started.

He had not gone two yards when he saw, down the hill by the house, the Trojan pull up by the porch. Stan Kemp was out and coming up the path to the hangar. In the Riley, Guv braked gently, felt the tow-rope go slack and looked back over his shoulder. The plane trundled a few feet on the concrete and stopped. He jumped out, put wooden chocks under its wheels and unclipped the rope.

Stan was with him now. 'Fuelled up?'

Guv nodded. 'Fuelled up.'

'All right. Get that car out of the way and we'll give it a shot.'

Guv moved the Riley over to the hangar. His flying coat, helmet, goggles and gloves were on the passenger seat. He put them on, opened the boot and took out a shotgun and the Colt .45 automatic he had bought in Aspreys. He went over to the DH4, climbed onto the wing and placed the shotgun in the rear cockpit. The Colt he pushed into a shoulder-holster he strapped over his coat. He looked down at Stan. 'I've got a spare seat.'

Stan said nothing but moved to the front of the DH4 and pulled at the propeller to gauge the resistance. Guv was in the cockpit now. Stan shouted: 'Switches off, petrol on, throttle closed.'

'Switches off, petrol on, throttle closed.'

'Throttle set.'

'Throttle set.'

'Contact.'

Guv had the control column fully back to raise the elevators. He flicked the magneto switch. 'Contact.'

Stan checked the elevators were in position, stood back a little and tugged down on the propeller with one hand. The engine fired, running smoothly. In the cockpit Guv let the oil pressure settle, maintaining a constant 1,000 revs, allowing five minutes to pass, using the time to ensure the trim controls were working properly, the mixture was fully rich, the altimeter set to zero, the oil pressure normal, the fuel gauge showing enough in the tank for the flight. It would not be a long flight so he expected the DH4 to handle light. The heat from the engine was coming back at him now in the wash from the propeller. He confirmed that the aileron and elevator controls were moving freely and correctly, but not the rudder; that could only be tested as he taxied out. He was entirely at ease, feeling that pleasant tension in his stomach that he always experienced before a patrol; anticipation, not fear – and even that would vanish as soon as he was in the air. He opened the throttle and increased the power, feeling the wheels of the undercarriage pushing against the chocks. He waved them away and Stan, stooping under the wings, pulled them clear and came round by the cockpit.

'Thank you,' Guv shouted.

'What for?'

'For swinging the prop.'

Stan was looking up at him, as though he was seeing him for the first time, or the last; as though he was gripped by indecision. Then the uncertainty fell away and his face cleared. Quickly he was on the wing and stepping into the front cockpit. Guv leaned forward, expressionless, and passed him his spare pair of goggles. Stan raised a thumb and positioned them carefully, his eyes blank behind the shatterproof lenses as if he imagined himself in another place – Chézy-au-Bois, any time in 1916, the whole procedure understood, everything accepted, no questions asked because they knew the answers.

Guv banged on the cockpit rim with his gloved hand and passed the shotgun forward. Stan checked both cartridges sat securely in the chambers, snapped the barrels closed and clicked the safety button. He looked back at Guv, who held up the Colt automatic and pointed to himself. Stan raised his thumb again and they taxied slowly towards the airfield. As they bounced and jolted across the grass their heads moved in unison, as if nodding in agreement about what they knew was to come.

At the end of the runway, Guv turned the machine into wind, gusting briskly from the south-west, and cleared the engine with a burst of power. One final test of the flying controls and he applied full throttle and they moved forward, rumbling and rattling like an old wooden cart, the wings flexing, the tail coming up, gathering speed and the grass streaming by, now light in their straps as the ground fell away.

They rose in a climbing turn to 300 feet and, below, the great house grew small, but neither looked back. To their right, the red roofs of Rye, and its church, were bathed in dawn light. They passed over East Guldeford, the expanses of the Marsh unrolling beneath them and the promontory of Dungeness ten miles ahead. Beyond it, the sea where Will went down and was lost; lost with him his hopes and the hopes of some others, carried away by the tides between two coasts.

They made height and levelled out at 10,000 feet. With his right hand steady on the control column, Guv held back the gauntlet of his glove and checked his Longines watch, that gift of Lydia's all those years ago. It showed 8.30 a.m. It was a good watch, he thought. Too good for this trip. He should have left it behind. He was coming through the drink and had not taken more. He felt clear of purpose; knew that here at the controls, feeling the aeroplane move to his will, fixed in a void high and over the world, this was all he wanted, all he had ever wanted. He looked ahead at Stan's bald crown with the strap of the goggles stretched tight above his ears. It was the head of a child, the head of that child he had known on the Alfriston farm. They had started together, they would end that way. In that moment he was sorry for it, but it was too late to tell him so. It was too late to tell each other anything any more.

Stan had the barrel of the shotgun resting on the rim of the cockpit, vibrating to the beat of the engine. Guv doubted it would be fired. Stan probably knew that too. But there was a rightness to it, being armed, however things turned out.

A flight of Hurricanes went over 1,500 feet above them, not picking them out against the sea, patrolling east to west. Beyond Hastings they banked round urgently and came back again. Guv imagined the commands from ground control to the flight leader, that bandits had been sighted in this particular strength, at this particular height, on this particular vector, the whoops of the English pilots as they prepared to engage. But soon enough he knew the enemy's location. Towards France the sky was dark with aircraft. He counted fourteen blocks of bombers advancing across the Channel, six aircraft to a block, flying in tight formation. Above and behind, forty Messerschmitt fighters, twin-engined 110s. Above the engine roar of the DH4 he could hear machine-gun fire as the Hurricanes went in. Two blocks of bombers broke away and turned towards them, Dornier 17s, probably bound for Biggin Hill. They would meet them head-on. That suited him fine, this was no time for stunting.

He glanced down. The sea was moving to a rhythmic swell, the rise and fall like the breathing of some brute creation, impassive and unruffled, ready to swallow whatever might drop from the sky.

Stan had seen the bombers. He had the shotgun to his shoulder, aiming between the wing struts. It was a comical sight that made Guv laugh. He took the control column in his left hand now, careful to hold the machine steady, pulled off his right-hand glove with his teeth, withdrew the Colt automatic from its holster and cocked it with his thumb. It reminded him of that time with the Albatros with its jammed machine-gun and its pilot dying, when he came up alongside as it yawed and crabbed and how the observer with the crimson scarf had looked across at him and raised his arms above his head before he put six bullets from the Colt through the fuselage where the pilot was slumped and the Hun lurched and turned on its back and went down in a spin. It had been simple then, plenty of time to kill; time to see the other man, even look him in the eye, consider whether he should live or die, wield the power of life or death, act God.

The bombers were closing fast, a mile away, half a mile, a quarter now and growing huge, olive-green and grey, engines with yellow spinners throwing out a wave of thunder, sunlight catching their Plexiglas domes. They were pushing the air before them and the DH4 began to rock in the turbulence. For a moment it raised a starboard wing, and in that moment, they were seen.

Tracer curled from the forward turret of the leader. Guv watched

491

it come. It seemed to take an eternity, approaching slowly in a graceful curve. Even now he did not expect to die. How could he? He had done nothing here. He could not be brushed aside so casually, as casually as a moth. That would be futile, as though everything had been meaningless, all for nothing. Everything for nothing. There had to be one last act, something that proved he was still the man he had always been.

He heard the shotgun fired once, twice. The stick was still shaking in his left hand, hard to control. His finger tightened on the trigger of the Colt. He looked ahead. Stan had dropped the shotgun and was gripping the cockpit rim with both hands, watching the tracer come. But the sky was a dark confusion of rushing shapes. He had no target. He squeezed the trigger anyway. The bullet shattered the back of Stan's head. Blood and brain and bone flew back in the slipstream. Guv's face was a red mask. He tasted Stan's blood.

Ninety minutes later, when Oberst Claus Hemmersdorf returned to his Geschwader base at Arras, he had lost five of his Dorniers. Four more had been damaged, two crash-landing near Fruges. In his report he noted that, despite High Command's assurances that the enemy's resources were severely depleted, the Royal Air Force seemed as well equipped and as aggressive as ever. As one of his gunners had said over the intercom: 'Here they come again, the last fifty British fighters.' He added that, from his lead aircraft, he had witnessed a curious incident south of the coast near Dungeness, the appearance of what appeared to be a training aircraft, 'a biplane of obsolete design obstructing our course to the target. It offered no threat apart from the possibility of collision. It was with some regret that I ordered Feldwebel Kupfer in the front turret to open fire and clear the way. I have no explanation for the aircraft being in such a position at such a time, a bizarre occurrence. It was like destroying a ghost.'

Later the same day, over the Sussex coast, a Heinkel 111 developed engine trouble on its way to the target. It turned back north of Rye and jettisoned its bombload near Romney Marsh, a number of the bombs falling on the nearby High And Over estate. Next morning, the press reported a mystery. A wing of the main house, owned by the famous aviator Captain Fraser 'Guv' Sutro, had been hit, as well as his private hangar containing a valuable collection of aeroplanes and racing cars, none of which survived. Two bodies recovered, though dreadfully burned, were identified as those of Mr Harold Paget, the Captain's chief mechanic, and Mrs Doris Carr, housekeeper. No trace of Captain Sutro had been found. In a further twist, a Trojan motor car belonging to local garage-owner Mr Stanley Kemp was parked in the drive, but of Mr Kemp there was no sign. Captain Sutro and Mr Kemp had flown together in the Great War. News was awaited of their whereabouts. The Captain's butler, Mr George Griggs, who escaped the conflagration thanks to being on manoeuvres with the local Home Guard, could offer no explanation.

Epilogue

In the summer of 1980, a year that marked the fortieth anniversary of the Battle of Britain, a Tiger Moth biplane on a pleasure flight from Headcorn aerodrome near Maidstone lost power on take-off, stalled at 50 feet, hit the ground and immediately caught fire. The pilot, who was alone, could not be saved.

It was ironic that Tim Sutro should die in this way because he had come through the war unharmed, serving with the Royal Air Force in many campaigns in Europe, North Africa and the Far East, and flying many types of aircraft from Lysanders to Blenheim bombers. He had retired from the RAF in 1950 with the rank of Group Captain to assume the chairmanship of Bowmans department store in Oxford Street, a business built up by his grandfather who, it was inevitably recalled, died gallantly on the *Lusitania* in 1916. In reports of Tim Sutro's death there was also mention of his father, the Great War ace and record-breaker Captain Fraser 'Guv' Sutro, whose controversial opinions on Fascism and questionable connections with the pre-war German aviation industry and with it the rise of the Luftwaffe, diminished his reputation. The Captain's disappearance in 1940 had never been explained.

The funeral of Tim Sutro took place at St Mary's Church, Rye, attended by a few family and rather more friends. The deceased had not married. Neither had his sister Alice, who crossed the Atlantic from her home in Newport, Connecticut, where she had lived for many years with her mother, who died two years before. After the

494

service the mourners gathered at High And Over, once the family home. Damaged during the war, it was now a hotel and golf course, still owned by the Bowmans Group.

Some months later, a memorial service was held at St Clement Danes in the Strand, the central church of the RAF. Like High And Over it had been bombed to a ruin by enemy action. From the restored gallery where the Queen's Colours and Standards hung, alongside standards of disbanded squadrons, RAF bandsmen played a fanfare. Below, in the front row of the pews, Alice Sutro tried to make her voice strong as the organ and small orchestra led the congregation in familiar, favourite hymns; next to her, the Lucchettis who had come across from Paris. A squadron leader carried her brother's medals to the altar. An air vice-marshal gave an address. A yachtsman from Rye Harbour read a lesson. A pilot from Headcorn read another. A City of London choir sang the 'Agnus Dei' from Fauré's *Requiem*. A solitary RAF bugler played 'The Last Post'.

As everyone moved from sombre reflection in the calm of the church to the tumult of the Strand, Jennifer Lucchetti touched Alice's arm. 'Poor Tim.'

Alice tried a bright smile. 'Oh, not so poor. He had a good life. Except he did not marry you.' She looked at Carlo Lucchetti. 'I always thought . . .'

'That was his mistake, I'm afraid,' said Lucchetti. 'When I got out of France in 1940, he should not have introduced me to the Sleightholme family. He was more generous than he knew.' He put his arm round his wife's waist. Jennifer Lucchetti rested her hand on his.

'It all seems ages ago,' she said. 'I couldn't help thinking of those times, when he and that other boy, the garage man's son, used to play together at High And Over.'

'Will Kemp.'

'Yes. We'd be sitting in the garden, tiny girls with our mothers, having decorous tea, and hear them making a fine old racket down by the ruined castle. You never saw High And Over as it used to be, did you, darling?'

Frank Barnard

Lucchetti shook his head. 'Only later, after the Boche had knocked it about.'

'It was a magical place, but not – please forgive me, Alice – but not, I think, a happy one. Your father was so very hard on Tim because he showed no interest in flying.'

'Ironic,' said Lucchetti. 'I never knew a man who loved flying more – loved it for its own sake, not as a means to an end.'

'A means to an end?' said Alice. 'Oh, I see. You mean my father.'

'Ah.'

'You don't have to spare my feelings, Carlo. We all know the kind of man my father was.'

Refreshments had been organised at the RAF Club after the service. As they waited for the car to take them to Piccadilly, Jennifer said quietly to Alice: 'I'm awfully sorry I forgot Will Kemp's name. I remember now how much he meant to you. Do you forgive me?'

'There's nothing to forgive. Even if he'd lived, there were reasons why it could not have worked out. Mummy explained it all to me, just before she died. I never understood until then.'

'Understood what?'

'I can't possibly tell you, Jenny dear. Not even you.'

'Did you never think of finding someone else? One of those filthy-rich Leffingwells or Delafields or Wycotts? You must have had masses of opportunities, mixing in Rhode Island society.'

Alice smiled: 'There's a Rhode Island saying about old maids like me. "She's worn out a lot of dancing shoes." It perfectly sums me up. Dear Jenny, I can't honestly feel sorry for myself. It happened once, and it was wonderful. A lot of people can't even say that. It's never happened again, that's all.' She hesitated, speaking almost to herself. 'I can't feel bad about it. There was nothing wrong in it. I still think about him, you know. Think about him almost every day.'

Lucchetti caught a little of what she said as the limousine drew up. 'Who are you talking about, Alice? Who do you still think about?'

'Tim's friend,' said Jennifer. 'Will Kemp.'

'Ah yes, the fellow in Spits. A good year, this, to think about the fellows in Spits.'

496

The guests in the function room at the RAF Club shared that special expression of mourners at a wake; sympathy mixed with an alert eye to a champagne flûte or fresh vol au vents passing on a tray, sincere enough but sharing that subtle pleasure of being alive when somebody else was so recently dead; feeling that the guilty pleasure required a modest celebration. The atmosphere was almost jolly.

Then Alice, nodding and smiling to people she did not know but seemed to know her, heard someone say in a normal, unpitying voice: 'I'm terribly sorry to bother you, Miss Sutro, but someone's asking for you at the reception desk.'

Alice followed the girl into the corridor. By the white-clothed table where they had checked off names on the guest-list a woman was waiting – quite striking, with a broad-brimmed black hat and a fur stole round her shoulders. She had on long black gloves and was smoking extravagantly. Alice had never seen someone smoking with gloves on before. Closer to, her perfume was strong. Closer still, she was old. She had been beautiful, still was, but as an old person is beautiful, softer and imperfect so allowances have to be made, so in the imagination the younger person can be discerned, reconstructed from the shadow that remains.

'I do apologise,' the woman said. 'I meant to come to the church but I got delayed. You know how it is.' She spoke like a telephone operator or a hotel receptionist, that attempt at posh that comes down the nose. 'I heard you was having a bit of a do here after so I thought I'd pop in to pay my respects.'

'I don't mean to be rude,' Alice said, 'but this is a private function.'

'You're Alice, aren't you?' The woman pulled off a glove and extended a hand. 'I'm Rose Kemp as was. You know, the garage in Rye that your Pa had a share in.'

'Will's mother.'

'That's it, lovely Will. You and him were such sweet chums, I recall. I live in Town now, you know. Kensington, the nice part. Have done for years.' Rose looked past Alice at the open door where the guests were gathered. 'I can see you've done him proud. Quite a boy, young Tim turned out, whatever his pa thought of him.'

Alice said: 'I don't think we have anything to say to each other, Mrs Kemp.'

Rose held up a hand. 'Oh, it ain't Kemp no more, dear. It's Mrs Fitt now. My hubby sold cars until he dropped dead, the old rascal. It appears I'm wed to the motor trade, don't it? All my fellers smell of petrol.'

'Why are you here?'

'Well, it's natural to want to pay my respects. The boys were such pals . . .'

'Respects?' said Alice. 'You're sure it's not money?'

Rose did not answer directly. 'Life's very hard, dear, when you get to my age. You'll find out for yourself. Nobody's interested any more. They look right through you, as if you don't exist. It's hard to believe now, but once—'

'Don't you think you've had enough from this family?' Alice said. She took Rose roughly by the elbow, pushed her into an empty side-room and closed the door. 'I'm aware of everything. My mother told me everything before she died. About you and my father and Will . . .'

'What about me and your father?'

'You're not denying you married Mr Kemp to give the child a father? You're not denying that, I suppose, when we know very well who the real father was?'

'Stanley was happy to have me on any terms, dear. Anyway, where did you get all this? I should be careful what you say. There's such a thing as slander.'

'I've often wondered what I'd do if I met you again. Do you realise how many lives you've ruined, you and that cousin of yours?'

'I don't know what you're talking about, I'm sure. If you mean Harry Paget, he weren't my cousin. That was just a way we had.' Rose looked thoughtful. 'He was the one, young Harry was. There was no one else like him. There's always just one, ain't there? And as for your father being Will's dad, well, where'd you get that notion?

Not from me, I'm sure. Dead spit of Harry, our Will was. Beat me why folk couldn't see it.'

Alice thought of slapping her face. It seemed such a little thing – but she could not bring herself to touch her. She turned and left her in the empty room, alone, and went outside. She wanted space and air, even the poisoned air that rose from the throbbing traffic.

In Green Park there were many young people, sprawled amorously on the threadbare grass, oblivious to passers-by or walking, kissing, fondling, their smooth faces unblemished by years, their expressions serene and confident of a future that stretched ahead, limitless and full of promise. She envied them their youth, their lives untouched by war; their finding of each other, and pleasure in it, even if a fleeting pleasure, a pleasure she had never known.

She heard a distant thunder and looked up. A vapour trail was passing across the sky, as if the heavens were being torn in two.

Acknowledgements

In most of us there seems to be something that makes us look to leaders, to individuals who exemplify the qualities we suspect we might lack ourselves: brainpower, confidence, a willingness to take responsibility, charisma, a readiness to take risks. There is no shortage of candidates eager to assume this role, for good or ill. They share the public's good opinion of themselves and in many cases prosper, though just as many are found out.

Perhaps this need stems from our early years when adults presented the world to us in a way that made sense, at least to them and for a time to us. There was security in it, reassurance, respect and often admiration; fulfilling the need to look up to someone exceptional; someone with capabilities you did not possess yourself who appeared to know things you did not know and could do things you were unable to contemplate.

Into this category falls the hero, the man of action whose deeds inspire and provoke awe and something close to adulation, as if touched by the gods, someone apart who symbolises the indomitable spirit of Man. But great achievements can obscure the reality that exists behind the public image.

I was also conscious, when writing, of that ambivalence many of us feel when confronted with past wars and past deeds; how would we have measured up faced with the same challenges if we had been part of that generation that moved from the golden summer of 1914 into unimaginable horror and destruction and came through it, some of them, into a bruised world that had changed for ever; where many of the old traditions, and distinctions of class, and certainties of what the future might hold, had been blown away as surely as those ranks of men who fought and died on the battlefields of Europe and beyond? Or only two decades later were required to climb into the cockpit of an aeroplane to engage the enemy (the same enemy) in defence of their own country, spread out and seemingly defenceless, below.

To these wars the people (of whatever nationality they happened to be) were led by those in positions of power and with very different, often questionable and ulterior motives. And this I could understand because, as the story progressed, I came to realise that in part I was drawing on my experience of numbers of characters I had encountered in my working life; personalities invariably described as 'dynamic', 'forceful', 'driven', 'high achievers', and yes, possessing leadership qualities that convinced those around them to follow, because somehow it was assumed they knew what they were doing, that they knew best, that they had a broader grasp of situations and opportunities than those less gifted. I must admit, on occasions I also fell tamely into line, and believed, only to have those beliefs questioned when a career or a company or even a country unravelled. Fortunately for me, by comparison to the choices that faced some of my characters in *A Time for Heroes*, such issues only had commercial implications, rarely political and never military ones. Even so, I was left with a wariness of those we are encouraged look up to. In the case of my novel it is self-appointed professional heroes like Guv Sutro, who seem to know what they are doing and only require us to show faith. I suppose, then, if this story has a purpose it is this: choose your heroes carefully because it is just possible they chose you . . .

In writing this novel I owe a debt to the following:

Letters from an Early Bird, Donal MacCarron; *Sagittarius Rising* (inevitably), Cecil Lewis; *Winged Victory*, V.M. Yeates; *On a Wing and a Prayer*, Joshua Levine; *Aces Falling*, Peter Hart; a whole batch of Osprey publishing titles: *British and Empire Aces of World War I*; *Sopwith Camel vs Fokker Dr I Fokker D VII Aces of World War I*; *Richtofen's Circus*; *Airfields and Airmen of Arras* and *The Somme* by Mike

O'Connor, and *The Royal Flying Corps Handbook* by Peter G. Cooksley; *My Golden Flying Years*, Air Commodore D'Arcy Greig with Norman Franks and Simon Muggleton; *The Story of Brooklands*, W. Boddy; *Rye & Winchelsea*, Alan Dickenson; *The Long Weekend*, Robert Graves and Alan Hodge; *The Fast Set*, Charles Jennings; *Hitler and Appeasement*, Peter Neville; *Germany Calling*, Mary Kenny; *Kent Airfields in the Second World War*, Robin J. Brooks; *Hornchurch Eagles*, Richard C. Smith; and my two bibles for ensuring my characters behave authentically in the air: *Stick and Rudder*, Wolfgang Langewiesche and *Basic Aerobatics*, R.D. Campbell and B. Tempest.

I also covered ground in England and France and would like to thank the Alfriston & Cuckmere Valley Historical Society for their help in confirming the topography of that beautiful part of England, particularly High And Over, the hill that features prominently throughout the book; and John Pulford, Head of Collections & Interpretation at the Brooklands Museum for arranging for me to roam the site in search of ghosts from the old flying days.

Finally I would like to record my appreciation of my two editors: the unofficial one, my wife Jan, always first to read the day's output with an objective eye whilst wondering if that man in the small room is the chap she used to go about with in the real world; and Martin Fletcher, the Headline professional who gave an aspiring old writer his chance to write fiction not so long ago, and still does.

Frank Barnard, Peasmarsh, Rye, September 2011